CHILDREN OF CLAY

Raymond Queneau

CHILDREN OF CLAY

*Translated from the French
and with an Introduction
by Madeleine Velguth*

SUN & MOON PRESS
LOS ANGELES · 1998

Sun & Moon Press
A Program of The Contemporary Arts Educational Project, Inc.
a nonprofit corporation
6026 Wilshire Boulevard, Los Angeles, California 90036

This edition first published in 1998 by Sun & Moon Press
10 9 8 7 6 5 4 3 2 1
FIRST ENGLISH LANGUAGE EDITION 1998

This book was made possible, in part, through a grant from
The National Endowment for the Arts

NATIONAL
ENDOWMENT
FOR THE
A R T S

and through contributions to
The Contemporary Arts Educational Project, Inc., a nonprofit corporation.

Cover: Gustave Caillebotte, *Champ jaune et rose*(1884)
["Landscape—Study in Yellow and Rose"]
Design: Katie Messborn
Typography: Guy Bennett

LIBRARY OF CONGRESS CATALOGING IN PUBLICATION DATA
Queneau, Raymond [1903–1976)
Children of Clay
p. cm — (Sun & Moon Classics: 92)
ISBN: 1-55713-272-0
I. Title. II. Series. III. Translator
811'.54—dc20

Printed in the United States of America on acid-free paper.

Acknowledgements

My thanks to my colleagues in the 19th and 20th century prose workshop at Binghamton University's NEH Translation Institute in the summer of 1993 for getting me off to a good start on chapter I: Elaine Corts, Alita Kelley, Howard Limoli, Lynne Margolies, Monique Nagem, Jonathan Rosenthal, Gus Segade, Susan Treadwell, and Lauren Yoder; to Barbara Wright for her critique of the first ten chapters; to Monique Nagem for her critical reading of Books One and Two; and particularly to my husband, George Velguth, for his reading, advice and support during the entire translation project. Special thanks to the National Endowment for the Humanities for sponsoring Binghamton University's Translation Institute; to Directors Marilyn Gaddis Rose and Joanna Bankier for selecting me as one of the participants; and to the Graduate School of the University of Wisconsin-Milwaukee for the Summer Research Grant which permitted me to consult Queneau's source material at the Bibliothèque Nationale and complete this work.

CONTENTS

INTRODUCTION

Long considered a writer's writer, Raymond Queneau (1903–1976) has gradually come to be recognized as one of the major voices in twentieth-century literature. His publications include fourteen novels, fifteen volumes of poetry and four collections of essays. Although they are known above all for brilliant wordplay, stylistic innovation and the incorporation of spoken French and phonetic spelling into works of literature, Queneau's novels are also rich in historical and philosophical allusions while presenting a lively picture of French society in the first half of our century. Among his better known works are *Exercices de style* (1947; *Exercises in Style*, 1958), *Le Chiendent* (1933; *The Bark Tree*, 1968), *Un Rude Hiver* (1939; *A Hard Winter*, 1948), *Pierrot mon ami* (1942; *Pierrot*, 1950), *Le Dimanche de la vie* (1951; *The Sunday of Life*, 1976), and his best-selling *Zazie dans le métro* (1959; *Zazie*, 1960). Queneau worked for Gallimard Publishing for nearly forty years, first as English reader, then as a member of the powerful editorial committee and finally as editor of the *Encyclopédie de la Pléiade*.

Raymond Queneau's fifth novel, *Les Enfants du limon*, was published in 1938. The author's own description of the book, written for a back ad, reads as follows:

> The plot of this novel involves three teams of characters: one formed by the grocer Gramigni, devoted to Saint Anthony of Padua, the maid Clemence, who

plays the piano [sic], young Bossu, of bitter destiny, and the humble folk of La Ciotat, where the story begins; the second, by the various members of the Limon-Chambernac-Hachamoth family, wealthy industrialists prey to various eccentricities (attacks of asthma, political activities, superstitions); the third, by M. Chambernac and his secretary Purpulan, a "poor devil."

The reader will find in this novel important fragments and a detailed summary of the opus on which M. Chambernac is working throughout the time covered by the story: *The Encyclopedia of The Inexact Sciences*, biography and anthology of the French "literary lunatics" of the xixth Century. Here are brought to light for the first time the lives and works of some fifty unknown people, whose wild imaginings (this expression is used without pejorative intentions) never met with the slightest echo, were never recognized as valid, by even a single *other* individual. And the reader will thus be confronted with the problem of *recognition*, a problem which various initiatives of certain characters of the novel raise as well.

Exchanges take place, harmonies and dissonances are created among the teams, as between the themes dealt with by the "literary lunatics" and the incidents of the story. These give the book its unity, a unity that maintains itself through the differences in tone—from the comic to the tragic, from the burlesque to the noble—the variations in language, the passing from prose to poetry and the alternations of novelistic and "scientific" material.

All of this is spun out against a subtly-drawn allegorical background hinted at by the title. For *limon* means silt or clay or dust—it's the word used in the French Bible to denote the dust of the ground of which God made man—and the offspring of the patriarch Limon live an edenic existence in the days before the economic crash of 1929. This crash brings about the dramatic "fall" of Limon, which, in turn, occasions the fall in fortunes of the rest of the family. Realism and social criticism intermingle with fantasy, while the boundary between lunacy and sanity is increasingly called into question by the irrational activities of the children of Limon. The very serious issues raised concerning the nature of madness and the treatment to which those so adjudged were subjected, usually against their will, prefigure the work of Michel Foucault, while the variations in tone, language and genre to which Queneau alludes in his final sentence make of this novel a precursor of his own *Exercises in Style* published nine years later.

Les Enfants du limon is an extraordinary novel, stretching the boundaries of the genre. Alain Calame, who has written perceptive analyses of several of Queneau's novels, calls it the masterpiece of Queneau's pre-war period, a demonstration that a creation "of medieval totality" is still possible in our century. This is in part an allusion to the large sections of his research on nineteenth-century "literary lunatics" that Queneau incorporated into the novel: theories on squaring the circle; wild cosmogonies in which the sun is either made of ice or, conversely, is the garbage dump of the universe; writings by people inventing new language systems, people who thought they were of royal blood, people who believed themselves divine.

Queneau appears to have written the novel precisely in order to get this research published. After he broke with André Breton in 1929, for reasons he called personal and never divulged, he was very much at loose ends. Surrealism had been for him a way of life; he had to reconstruct his existence. Unable to settle down to work, he spent the better part of three years in the Bibliothèque Nationale, studying the writings of these people he called *hétéroclites,* eccentrics. When, in 1934, he tried to find a publisher for his finished work, no one was interested. His solution was to build a novel around the manuscript—a slow, difficult process, finally completed in 1938. The result, although by no means an "easy read," is undeniably a masterpiece which, while breaking ground stylistically and linguistically, often in ways highly humorous, confronts some of the burning social and political issues of the day and ultimately the eternal, unanswerable questions regarding the origin of misfortune, pain and evil. Readers familiar with Queneau's other writings will recognize some of his deeply-held principles and obsessions, as well as bits of autobiography distributed among the novel's various characters. Those wishing to delve more deeply into these aspects of the novel will find them discussed in the works mentioned at the end of this introduction.

Anyone undertaking to translate Raymond Queneau must be particularly sensitive to wordplay. With *Les Enfants du limon*, this becomes an issue before the book is opened, since the title, as mentioned above, alludes to the human condition. Queneau did something that is impossible to replicate in English, as our rules demand that all nouns in titles be capitalized. In modern French this is the case only with the first noun, and on the title page *limon* has a small *l*. It is not until some ten pages into the novel that mention is made of the Limon family, and the readers' attention is not actually focused on the name for another 25 pages. So we're well into the story before we suddenly realize that the fallible humans of the title are members of a family bearing a name symbolic of their condition. How could I create in the anglophone reader the same pleasurable jolt of discovery, since I was obliged to capitalize Clay in the title? My solution—adding an *e* to the proper noun—satisfies me, as it simultaneously solves another problem: *Clay* is too Anglo-Saxon a name for a French family, whereas *Claye*, which is a French place-name, will do quite nicely.

This matter of onomastics, the meaning of proper nouns, remains important throughout the work. Without going into any detail—lest I spoil readers' pleasure in making their own discoveries—I should like to point out that I was strongly tempted to transpose the *a* and the *o* of Naomi in order to make it more closely resemble the French *Noémi*, the first syllable of which is identical to *Noé*, Noah.

The presence of the allegorical element made it imperative that I be particularly careful with references to dust, soil, mud, and clay as well as with anything relating to a paradise or a fall. An unexpected example of such an allusion is the "word" *sil*, which is repeated as a tiny paragraph unto itself five times in chapter XI and four times in chapter CVIII. The context suggests that it is an ideosyncratic abbreviation of the word silence. But why use such an abbreviation? And why call attention to it by giving it its own paragraph? Further investigation reveals that *sil* is also, both in French and English, a yellow ocher. And ochers are clays.

My French dictionary is even more specific: *sil* is an ocher-ous clay with which the ancients made red and yellow pottery. In this context, even the number of times the mono-syllabic paragraph appears may signify, as numbers often do in Queneau's writing: in chapter XI five young people are having a picnic; in chapter CVIII two of these people are talking about two others.

The reader of *Les Enfants du limon* is bound to be struck by its lack of punctuation. In some chapters—XVIII may well be the most striking example—this is quite clearly deliberate, a stream of consciousness from Astolphe's point of view. But what of all the dependent adverbial clauses which run unpunctuated right into the sentences they introduce? And what of the proliferation of colons that dot the book's pages like so many fly-specks? After giving the matter a great deal of consideration, I decided not to normalize the punctuation in *Children of Clay*, and that for a number of reasons. First of all, the French text could often have been made more comprehensible by the judicious use of commas—and Queneau did not do it. Secondly, a look at the other novels he wrote during the eight-year period he was working on this one reveals a normal use of punctuation, with commas setting off dependent clauses and with relatively few colons. And finally, Queneau worked much too carefully on this book to have been negligent of punctuation. Do not the many quoted passages respect the punctuation of the originals? That said, I have no ready explanation for the novel's punctuation; I simply reproduce it.

The "scientific" material to which Queneau alludes in his plot summary posed additional problems for this translator with a humanities background. When I could not find the definition of a word unknown to me I had to decide whether it was simply a word difficult to locate, or one invented by the nineteenth century writer (creating neologisms and even private languages being a frequent phenomenon among monomaniacs of the sort studied by Queneau) or one invented by Queneau himself. As many of these expressions lend themselves to wordplay, double entendre and the like, I eventually came to strongly suspect the latter—which, of course, would oblige me to attempt equivalent wordplay in English rather than a "straight" translation. It was Chambernac's poem in chapter CIV that made me realize that, in spite of the author's postscript assuring his readers that "the texts quoted by Chambernac in his *Encyclopedia* are *naturally* authentic," I would have to go to the Bibliothèque Nationale and look at them myself. Desdouitz de Saint-Mars' English etymologies were incredible enough, but when, some lines further along, I came to translate Seb.-François Drojat's "Table-ature," I became convinced that Raymond Queneau was making this up. Needless to say, none of the "phonetic" terms are to be found in any French phonetic dictionary. Words like *Tourniquet* and *Loup-gar* (*loup-garou*? = werewolf) are highly suspect when presented as part of a technical language. Additionally, under the headings of *Obnutity* and *Supernal Paraphones* there is a series of "phonemes" whose names are based on the Latin *lupus* or the French *loup*, both of which mean wolf:

L'Obnutité
(Le Lupanar ou la Bande-aurole
Le Loup-gar ◼ Silence absolu
La Bande-Noire ou le Lupercal)

Les Paraphones supernes
        (Le Loup Cervier
        Le Loup gris
        La Louve
        Le Loup plex

Now *lupanar*, from the Latin, is a learned French term for brothel—and at one time was also used in English, as my *Webster's New International Dictionary* of 1913 testifies—and the *Lupercalia* was the annual Roman festival honoring *Lupercus*, the wolf-god of fertility. In such company the two words beginning with *Bande-* become pregnant with unexpected meaning, for the vulgar meaning of the verb *bander* is to have an erection.

At the Bibliothèque Nationale I consulted most of the works cited in *Les Enfants du limon* plus other books and brochures by the same authors—a total of some 120. By dint of paging through them (since Queneau gives no page numbers in what is, after all, a novel), I was able to locate most of the quotations (over 200 of them) which appear in the novel. I can thus assure the readers of this translation that the works do all exist, that all the quotations I succeeded in finding are indeed authentic, and furthermore, that Raymond Queneau was painstakingly accurate. So Saint-Mars' etymologies, Lucas' cotton bonnet (XLVIII), Roux's excremental sun (LXXXVI), Soubira's poetry (CXXX), Gagne's philanthropophagy (CLI), Berton's breathless telegram to Queen Victoria (CLI), Berbiguier's sprites (XXI), and Bousquet's adulterine cake (XCIV) were all genuine "imaginings" on the part of these nineteenth-century "literary lunatics."

Queneau (Chambernac?) made only two errors of any significance: one a matter of miscopying one letter and the other a misreading. Interestingly enough, both passages gave me considerable trouble and would have been somewhat easier to translate if they had been completely accurate, since they make a bit more sense in the original than in Chambernac's version.

The first is in the discussion of "the compatibility of extremes" in chapter LXI, where the first sentence of the second paragraph reads as follows, on page 6 of the 16-page tract from which Chambernac quotes: "Quant à la synthèse *d'avoir* = *avoir*, elle est nécessairement *s'avoir* voix moyenne entre la voix passive *avoir* et la voix active *d'avoir*." Queneau puts what the original italicizes into small capitals and, instead of *s'avoir*, he says D'AVOIR. Now *s'avoir* written without the apostrophe is *savoir*—to know—out of which I could have made a tad more sense than out of whatever elusive distinction there might be between D'AVOIR and d'AVOIR. As you will see, in desperation I invented *to have*, but I wasn't very happy with it.

The misreading occurs in Chambernac's discussion of the writings of Abbé Mayneau in chapter CLI. Mayneau has very little sense of organization and repeats the tales of his antichrists at least ten times in his formless 509-page *Triomphe de la Vérité*. He also has a tendency to speak in allegory and to go on for a great many paragraphs without repeating the antecedent of the pronoun he is using. It should thus surprise no one that Chambernac misidentifies the subject of the first example he gives of the abbé's fulsome prose style, when he parenthetically tells us that the antecedent of the French pronoun *il* is *le fisc*, that is, the tax collecting agency of the national government. Now *il* translates either as *he* or as *it*, depending upon whether its antecedent is a person or not. Chambernac's parenthetical remark was anything but helpful, forcing me as it did to translate *it* and create some very awkward sentences. A careful reading of the context shows that the antecedent is not the tax department, but Louis XVI, to whom Mayneau allegorically refers as "the sixteenth lily" (188; the passage quoted by Chambernac is on Mayneau's p. 190).

But this is quibbling over minor details when, on the whole, Queneau's quotations from the writings of his "literary lunatics" are a model of accuracy, fairness and compassion. I decided to translate the titles of these writings because they too are part of the story. But the interested reader will find in the Appendix a bibliography of the works used and mentioned by Queneau, with the French titles under which they can be found in the Bibliothèque Nationale. (An interesting footnote: the BN is about to move to new quarters on the Seine at the Rue de Tolbiac—the very place where Chambernac rids himself of his demon at the end of the novel!)

Finally, a word on the editions I used in translating *Les Enfants du limon*. The original, Gallimard's Edition Blanche, was published in 1938. Fifty-five years later, in 1993, the novel was reissued in Gallimard's Collection Imaginaire. I used both, crosschecking difficult passages, and found the two editions to be practically identical. The only correction I've been able to find was the righting of the transposition of the initial letters of the last two lines of Chambernac's poem in chapter CIV. (In exchange, the new edition has a new spelling error in this chapter and another in chapter

CLIX.) Probable spelling errors in the Blanche have not been corrected in the Imaginaire. Two lapses with regard to names have not been corrected either: in chapter LXII Chambernac refers to his brother Edmond as Henry, and on the last page of the novel Astolphe is at one point called Adolphe. I've retained Henry, on the hypothesis that, since Chambernac has had quite a bit to drink, he could conceivably call his brother by his own name. But I took the liberty of changing the Adolphe who says they'll do fine work to Astolphe.

Readers wishing additional information on Queneau, his work and *Les Enfants du limon* can consult the following works.

Esslin, Martin. "Raymond Queneau." In *The Novelist as Philosopher*. Ed. John Cruickshank. London, New York, Toronto: Oxford Univ. Pr., 1962.

Hale, Jane. *The Lyric Encyclopedia of Raymond Queneau*. Ann Arbor: Univ. of Michigan Pr., 1989.

Hewitt, Nicholas. "History in *Les Enfants du limon*: Encyclopaedists and 'flâneurs.'" *Prospice* 8 (1978): 22–35.

Shorley, Christopher. *Queneau's Fiction*. Cambridge: Cambridge Univ. Pr., 1985.

Thiher, Allen. *Raymond Queneau*. Boston: Twayne, 1985.

Velguth, Madeleine. *The Representation of Women in the Autobiographical Novels of Raymond Queneau*. New York: Peter Lang, 1990.

——. *Raymond Queneau's* Chêne et Chien. *A Translation with Commentary*. New York: Peter Lang, 1995.

BOOK ONE

I

"Just think, monsieur," she said, "just think, its area is almost ten centimeters. Not as impressive as a tongue, but still more important than the one in Bourges, I think."

After Ceyreste, came the forest.

"People used to hold lilies in their hands, but the custom's died out. Although there still are lilies."

They were gradually making their way to Cuges, wheels grinding the dust.

"Madame Gramigni stayed at the shop," said Gramigni. "I'm going up for myself. When it's for yourself, you better go up yourself, right?"

"Of course."

In Cuges everybody gets off, then climbs toward the chapel half-way up the hill, with the very old village right at the top, deserted: in ten centuries and a bit it's flattened out. They get there for vespers and the panegyric and the adoration of the Blessed Sacrament and the veneration of the relic. Gramigni invokes Saint Anthony of Padua.

If you seek miracles
in the sole name of Saint Anthony
death error calamities
demons and leprosy flee
the sick are healed
the sea obeys
chains are broken
health returns.

"I'll give you five francs, a hundred sous, right here five francs of my money that I earned with my fruit and my vegetables, Saint Anthony of Padua, if this year the Paris people come back as usual, with their cars and their girls and their friends, 'specially with their girls, 'specially with the tall blonde, and that they come back to my place to buy my fruit and olives to have with the aperitif they have at my neighbor Bossu's café. Let them come back, let them come back, please great Saint Anthony. Their maid is next to me, maybe she's praying they won't come back. Great Saint Anthony, make my prayer stronger than hers. If she's asking for that, it's because her intentions are bad. But I don't have bad intentions. It's not even because of what I make on the fruit they buy from me that I want so much for them to come. It's like this: I want you to make them come back on account of it's a pleasure to see them 'cause they're rich and beautiful, the girls naturally. And I'm not saying that either 'cause of the girls, since I'm married, you know that great Saint Anthony, since I'm married and even if my wife isn't very nice to me."

And he added like a true Cugian:

"Dear God, pray to Saint Anthony of Padua for me."

And he finished:

"And besides, great Saint Anthony, I know you can't forget a fellow Paduan. We're from the same city, you and me; I'm sure that for you too that counts for something. Mussolini had my two brothers killed; I crossed the border to sell vegetables, fruit and groceries, married to a fat bag from across the Loire River that I went and picked up, I sure wish I hadn't, in a real sewer, and my brothers died in Regina Coeli or in San Stefano, I'm not sure which. That's the life God gave me, great Saint Anthony, you see, it would put a little butter on my pasta if you'd let a little sunshine into my heart, by making the people I'm talking to you about come back, their cars and their friends, and their girls too of course."

And now all he can do is wait for the results. Gramigni takes the same ramshackle bus back to La Ciotat.

"You've got to be a real sucker," he hears as soon as he gets home, "you've got to be missing some marbles to believe in stuff like that."

He puts his hat on a little shelf under the cash register.

"Did you at least see the relic?"

"No."

"Why bother going? So you didn't even look at the tibia?"

"It's not a tibia: it's a piece of the saint's skull."

"You damn fool."

He doesn't answer.

"Your brothers would be ashamed of you."

"You leave my brothers out of this."

"They didn't suck up to priests like you, they were real men."

He smacks her across the mouth and kicks her butt out the door.

A housewife comes in. She wants coarse salt, really ripe bananas, a can of Portuguese sardines, a box of sulfurized matches and that's all for today. Wait, she was going to forget the tomatoes.

He wasn't all that religious, his childhood faith had, at least apparently, quite worn off, and besides, he'd heard his brothers explain to him often enough what that was all about. But he feared that the flow of months wouldn't bring back the girl he thought was so beautiful. The fruits and vegetables came each in their season and after their kind, but the luck—he believed in it—of life might make her not return. So he went up to Cuges with his fruitseller's faith and, one day in July, the car came and parked in front of his neighbor Bossu's café.

Bossu's falling all over himself in welcome. There'd be something to read again, for these were customers who bought newspapers and magazines. They'd pick up their supply at Mlle. Chabrat's stationery shop and, after their drinks, leave them behind. In the evening when the last belote players had gone, when the chairs were sleeping belly-up on the tables, by the light of the single small lamp, Bossu would read to his heart's content, devouring printed matter and rotogravure until two in the morning. He learned the strangest things, his brain buzzed with the complication and variety of it all. He'd go to sleep his head in a whirl. The next morning, nothing was left. He remained as dumb, dull and doltish as before.

Thus these ladies and gentlemen installed themselves as was customary facing the harbor pleased and happy; ice and siphon were surrounded by glasses sparkling with multiple aperitif colors; a little fishing boat went round in circles; a low sun, cool shade, and these ladies and gentlemen thought that this was the life.

It was a splendid time not only because of exceptional atmospheric conditions causing fine weather undreamed of by former generations, but also because money was easy to come by: all you had to do was put your hand in your pocket to find lettuce, even if you'd imagined there was nothing there. This singular and marvelous phenomenon naturally affected only a certain class of the population, precisely that to which belonged the visitors so awaited by Gramigni and Bossu.

It was a splendid time not only because peace reigned disturbingly from Spain to China, but as well because money was liquid, fluid, volatile even, thus combining the very different qualities of mercury and ammonia.

It was a splendid time when money shone in the sun like crushed glass, watering in abundance this beautiful old dry Provence, where the weather's good all four seasons of the year, where harmony resounds from the violet indigo blue sky to the green, yellow, orangey, red earth.

II

She was near-sighted to the point of blindness but not at all deaf, and misshapen to the point of infirmity but not at all ugly. When her employers weren't living there, ten months of the year, during the long evenings of wind and rain, in the absence of Baron Hachamoth and his wife, their daughters, relatives and friends, this maid played the violin.

III

Damp and naked, Master Chambernac, principal of the high school in Mourmèche, heard a knock at the door of his bathroom where he was giving himself his second good scrubbing of the day, practicing ablutions in considerable number because of the intense sebaceousness of his dermis, an oleaginousness which he attributed to the excessive concentration of his cervical humors, nonvolatile but fixed and pearlifying absolutely everywhere on the surface of his body as a result of research and special studies which were difficult, singular and rare.

Damp and naked, Master Chambernac, principal of the high school in Mourmèche, was, then, stepping out of one of his daily baths, when he perceived through the drops of soapy water that were burbling in his ears, a knock.

"Don't come in," he yelled not sure that he hadn't closed his door.

"Would you be so kind as to repeat the last two words of the sentence you've just uttered?" said the knocker on the other side (he'll soon be on this one).

"What?"

"I was asking you to repeat."

"Egad who are you? the plumber?"

"No."

"Then leave me alone."

"What's that? I can't hear you very well."

"I'm telling you not to come in."

"'Come in,' you *did* say : 'come in'?"

And in he came.

Flowing out the little hole at the bottom, the gray water, before disappearing, left on the sides of the tub a thin layer of mud.

The newcomer closed the door behind him and sized up his man, damp and naked, with a look uncontaminated by any subjective valuation, neither romantically disgusted by the nudity of a paunchy, flabby sexagenarian, nor homosexually appreciative of a novel anatomy.

"Well," went the stranger amiably, "your tummy certainly doesn't have any folds."

The principal, meanwhile, was slipping into the mazes of fright and the labyrinths of indignation. The one was beginning slowly to relax his visceral activity, the other to reduce his pulmonary capacity.

"I," continued the stranger less amiably, "cannot understand telling people to come into one's bathroom naked as a jaybird."

"Wa-waah?" stutstammered Chambernac.

"Well, it's simple," went the other, furious, "you tell me to come in and you're totally naked. Must be some sort of pervert. Morals like that are just plain disgusting."

His victim was wiping his face, now damp not with healthy bathwater but with the sweat of dread.

"Do you think I enjoy looking at your pudenda? Certainly not! I prefer not to look."

And he turned his back; but in the mirror attached to the door, he was able to keep an eye on the behavior of his guinea-pig: for it was the first time he was indulging in this sport and he was not yet too sure of his technique.

The principal, taking advantage of this discretion, was starting to put his clothes back on; so he slips on his undershirt, he slips on his shirt, he slips on his shorts, what won't he slip on? his pants: they're in the next room. He explains the matter to the invader.

"All right, let's go next door."

He opens the door and shows the way.

"All the same," went the stranger dreamily, "what Mourmèchian father would ever dream that the high school principal indulges in nudistic displays in front of—I stress: in front of men."

Suddenly abandoning his impressive calm, he started to strut back and forth shaking a handkerchief and uttering interjections considered faggy by people who know such things only through caricaturists and cabaret singers. The poorincipal, sitting on his bed, watched in dismay.

"Well," went his persecutor, "have you nothing to say?"

"Get out!" caterwauled the persecutee.

"Come in, get out, that's all you can say."

"But I never told you to come in! You simply came in. And besides, how did you get into my apartment? I'm going to call the police."

"I dare you."

"We'll see."

"When you told me to come in, you probably thought it was one of your students."

"Dastardly slander," exclaimed the principal. "I'm going to put on my pants."

"That won't restore your respectability."

"Ah, ah, ah, ah, you think respectability is lost so easily?"

"I don't think it, I know it."

Chambernac puts the top of his body into a jacket, the bottom into a pair of pants.

"Now that I'm properly dressed, you will do me the favor of clearing out."

The other bats not an eye.

"Consider yourself fortunate that I'm not calling the police to cure you of playing jokes of more than doubtful taste."

"Oho, you've changed your mind from just now. Just now,

you wanted to call the police. I see you've thought about it. That's wise. Now we can get down to serious talk."

"It would have been nice if you'd gotten to that a bit sooner."

"So let's sum up what's happened: one: I come in; two: you do dirty things."

"Oh!"

"And three, you owe me reparation."

The intrudee breathed easier. So that was all: with a bit of money he'd see the farce played out. The intruder read his mind:

"Really, what do you expect me to do with a forty-sou piece? Forty sous!"

Scornfully he spat (for real) on the carpet.

"I," he went, "am not asking for charity. I," he went, "don't live on alms. I," he went, "don't beg. I," he went, "am not a neurotic. What I want is work."

"Work?" repeated the principal, "you're saying: work?"

"I said: work, and I want work. Do you understand me, you nasty sex maniac?"

"And what can you do?" groaned the victim.

"It's not a question of what I can do, but of what I want to do."

"And what do you want to do?" roaned the victim.

"I want to be a teacher."

"Rrrrrrraaaaaahhhhhh," roared the victim.

"Pull yourself together."

"A physical education teacher?" jeered the ctim, who mustered sufficient strength to emit several hiccups tinged with somber joy.

"Don't make fun of me."

"So, just like that, you want to be a teacher?"

"Yes, it's a vocation. The only thing I don't have is a degree. But what's so important about a degree?"

"Yes. What's so important about a degree," repeated Chambernac, his voice muddy.

"I'm not spiteful, I'll take whatever class you think best."

"Ye gods, there *is* the senior humanities class. Bouvard just died unexpectedly."

"I like humanities," said Purpulan.

"Ye gods, what trouble this is going to make for me."

"Less than if you didn't want me."

IV

One day while going to Soilac
The principal de Chambernac
Saw a policeman on the train
Whose boots gave his soul quite a turn
He bode his time and waited till
The train was deep in a tunnel
To the policeman
Then spoke his passion
His reputation would be marred
Had not the merciful trooper
Who bore the glorious name Magloire
Said to the principal: "Now sir
I know the vices of mankind
I'm understanding as you see
But you must leave all that behind"

"The first time it's happened to me!"
"Well let it be the last, you hear
Or you'll get my boot in the rear."
Journey over, filled with rue
Chambernac had realized
At his age 'twasn't the thing to do
This one experience quite sufficed.

V

When Purpulan had arrived in Mourmèche, he certainly didn't know this detail of the private secret past life of the principal. For a long time he'd hesitated. On whom would he try out the precepts that in the course of lessons, which had moreover not been cheap, had been taught him by a dwarf, an expert in the art of parasitism who had even created an entirely new technique in this area? He had naturally eliminated the poor, all the poor, whose kind hearts he felt it would be too easy to exploit: and it was not to the kind heart that, according to his master, one should address oneself, but to fear, funk and superstitution. Though he was neither dwarf, nor bearded, Purpulan nevertheless possessed certain qualities of this nature which permitted him to hope for some success in this branch of so vilized contemporary human activity.

He was handsome, and he had fetid breath, rather more like hydrogen sulfide than sulfur, thus realizing in concrete fashion the terrifying and murky image of a fallen angel.

VI

"I'm going to go buy olives at Gramigni's," said Daniel without moving.

"You can take the car if you're tired," said Naomi.

"Who's Gramigni?" asked Pouldu.

"The grocer next door," said Agnes.

"His olives are fantastic," said Daniel. "I've never tasted better. Gramigni makes them himself; he's got his own recipe."

"You always manage to ferret out the good places," said Pouldu.

"Bah," said Daniel.

He gets up.

Gramigni proudly shows him his merchandise. He fishes for the little green drupes. He's happy. It's happened: the girls have come back. He owes Saint Anthony one hundred sous.

They're purebreds; he's never seen anything like them from Padua to Marseille, including his bitch of a wife. He just can't take it in, he can't get over it. Two sisters that are really beautiful, really tall, really curvy, and what really bowled Gramigni over, so clean they're dazzling, and besides also really rich, really luxurious and really muscled, like their car. And then finally really athletic, really noble and really polite. Young Bossu says if he wanted to he'd make it with them and Lardi says all those people, the summer people, are potbellied, bleary-eyed layabouts. All the same, they don't have fleas, or lice, or bedbugs, or crab lice; you can't imagine these young ladies with fleas, lice, bedbugs or crab lice; it's true they'd catch some if they let the Bossu kid mount them. Gramigni sighs. Beauty moves Gramigni.

They live in a brand new villa beyond the Golf Hotel: near Saint-Jean. The Claye family used to own a respectable house built in the days of Alphonse Karr. Then Baron Hachamoth had this one built in the modern style of Paris. All the Ciotadans went to see it, except Gramigni, both because of his business that takes all a man's time and also because of something like timidity. But young Bossu told him what it's like; he worked on it; he's the one who put in the electricity, with his boss and another guy, who helped him a little. Get this, there's glass on all sides and everything's painted white. Next to each bedroom, there's a bathroom (and to think they spend all their time in the ocean) and personal toilets (that's where you can see luxury turn to vice). All the furniture is square and made of strange materials; there are mirror tables, cork armchairs and rope chairs: lots of people didn't want to believe young Bossu when he said that, and when he added that there are paintings you can hang any side up, people thought rubbing elbows with high society was discombobulating his brain.

Gramigni has a hard time picturing all these things; it kind of chokes him up; there's no doubt about it, beauty really moves him. Here they are right now, Agnes and Naomi passing, even more marvelous than last year. They're going to talk to the captain of their boat. Gramigni admires the way they walk and what gorgeous figures they have. He's interrupted by the sudden contact of his occiput with a can of peas, thrown with dexterity by Mme. Gramigni.

"You dirty bum, there you are jerking off again watching

those tarts. That's what you think about, poor moron, instead of paying attention to your wife and children."

They haven't got any children but it was an expression of her mother's; all she'd ever had were miscarriages, because of her illnesses.

Gramigni turned around and charged at the bitch. Before he could reach her, she sent the jar of olives flying; it broke and the olives rolled wildly under the crates.

"See what I'm doing to your special olives, you mucky butt cream, you. Your olives that you make 'specially for those sluts, see what I'm doing to them."

Gramigni, pursuing his course, slipped on some olives as if they were casters, and cartwheeled to the floor. Taking advantage of this, his spouse dumped a whole assortment of canned goods on him. Her triumph didn't last long; the Paduan trapped her near the cookies and flattened her with two strong punches in the mug. Then he started to stomp on her in a businesslike way.

She vociferated with indignation.

Meanwhile, kids collected to see the wop clobber his wife. Various people, more or less idle, joined the group. It was quite a spectacle. The circle thickened. Scallywags stole wares. Finally, generous souls intervened; they pulled Mme. Gramigni out from under Gramigni's feet. She was in no mood for ribbing. She was foaming at the mouth. He, sweating.

"It was the grocer, putting his wife in her place," said Bossu. "She pissed, if you'll pardon the expression, in his special olives."

"The brute," said Daniel.

One by one, he'd eaten them all up.

VII

Saint Anthony they're here I saw them
Saint Anthony Saint Anthony so you're as powerful as that
It's true they come back every year
All the same you never know: one year
                                      suddenly
                                      it can change
Saint Anthony I owe you one hundred sous
You can count on it
One day I'll go up to Cuges just to give them to you
Saint Anthony you're the Saint of my childhood
I learned to pray to you when I was little
You're right not to drop me
You can see that I'm always faithful to you
and yet I know very well that religion is the opium of the people
and that priests and money are like bees and honey
and seems it's the capitalists that invented God
But you great Saint Anthony of Padua nobody invented you
On the contrary you're the one that invented lost and found
and you go to the moon to look there for everything people lost
and you put each thing back in its place
and each year the pretty girls in their house
I thank you great Saint of my Home Town
If I forget that I owe you one hundred sous
Make me remember it toward the end of the week
But I'd really be surprised if I forgot
Amen.

VIII

When Purpulan arrived unknown in Mourmèche, unknown to Mourmèche and not knowing Mourmèche, he had no reason to choose one person rather than another. Why the sub-prefect rather than the jailer, the bailiff rather than the notary, the banker rather than curator of the museum of paleontology; or else, the grocer rather than the butcher, the mason than the mechanic; or why a person of independent means; or why a cabinetmaker? The fact that he was making his career debut left the matter all the more open.

In the evening, he wandered about Mourmèche, looking at the lighted windows, unable to decide on this or that family. Some appeared to be so solid, calm and peaceful that he would only have met with failure had he tried to insinuate himself into them; others seemed to reveal an anxious uncertainty that would be favorable to his plans: but there again, how should he choose? None of them, after all, appeared to offer an appreciable probability of success. Then the lights went out and he fell back into the night.

In this provincial obscurity he eventually discovered a brothel. Suddenly he knew that the first respectable man over fifty years of age to come out would be his man. A few moments later, Chambernac slipped out. All that Purpulan had to do was follow him to the high school where he lived.

IX

"What trouble this is going to make for me."

"Less than if you didn't want me."

"That needs thinking about."

"It's all thought about. Either you put me in the class-room or I'll put you in jail."

"You think, perhaps, that my respectability wouldn't stand up to the testimony of a suspicious character like you? What are you, after all: a thief caught in the act."

Purpulan smiled:

"How dense you are."

Then he began to moan and draw loud gasping breaths:

"No… don't do that… no… I didn't think that was what you wanted me to do… leave me alone… let me go… it's awful… to fall into the hands of such a dirty bastard…"

"Ye gods," muttered Chambernac, "will you be quiet."

"Do I start teaching tomorrow?"

"Tomorrow."

"Now tell me, don't you think that my hair is a little long and dirty, that I need a shave, that my shirt is hardly clean and it's the only one I've got, that my shoes are terribly worn, that my nails are dirty and need a manicure—I know there aren't any manicurists in Mourmèche, but a woman I know at the brothel does nails—to cut a long story short, boss, that I need to look more dignified, and my wallet's empty."

"I'll be right back."

He had just gotten a nasty idea. Before Purpulan could collect his thoughts, Chambernac had rushed into the next room and was already hurrying back with five one-hundred-franc bills in his hand, bills whose numbers the crafty devil had recorded in a notebook, his private little notebook, the one where he jotted down memorable dates, like the day he'd met the policeman on the train and the one, rather recent since it was the last entry, on which he had, for the first time, gone to the brothel of Mourmèche.

Purpulan took them; Chambernac was triumphant. Once his adversary had gone, all he'd have to do was report the theft and give the numbers of the bills. What scandal would there be then? None at all.

Chambernac felt sorry for such ineptness.

"Go deck yourself out now," he said cordially. "Your class is at eight tomorrow morning. We'll see then what you can do."

"No," went Purpulan, "no, that's not how things are going to be," went Purpulan, suddenly inspired by the fiendish powers fermenting within him, "no, take back your twenty-five *louis*," he went softly, "I've changed my mind, I'll stay for dinner and spend the night here. I can't leave without getting to know you better."

Stunned by such inhuman insight, Chambernac bowed before the singular spirit who had taken up residence in his house for dark reasons of his own.

X

Mme. Chambernac was quivering with impatience to see the face, and the body, of the new humanities teacher. The current one, the deceased rather, was bearded and Kantian. Would the new one be Bergsonian and clean-shaven? Mme. de Chambernac remembered her ardor when, at eighteen, she sat on the benches of the Collège de France afire with the passion of creative evolution.

The newcomer was in fact clean-shaven, but Bergsonian? She immediately spotted his worn shoes, his long hair, and what was more worrisome, one of her husband's shirts on the back of the new arrival. Chambernac sat down wearily after the introductions. Invited in turn to take a seat, Purpulan did it with the assurance of a man who's already scored and isn't afraid of losing his advantage.

While, in the uncomfortable silence that followed, Mme. de Chambernac, an educated person who was interested in etymology, was setting up the equation Purpur + purulent = Purpulan, the latter was exhaling in all directions, smiling blissfully, the colorless but odoriferous clouds of his fetid breath. Giving his hierarchical superior a *sou* for his thoughts, he said:

"Cur videris tristis?"

"Huh?" went Chambernac with a start.

"Quin respondes? Num obsurdescis?"

Chambernac said to himself: it's another one of his tricks to get under my skin and make me suffer.

"Dinner is served," said the maid opportunely.

Thus Purpulan finds himself seated between Madame and Monsieur and before an adequately laden table. So it wasn't any harder than that. As far as being able to teach humanities was concerned, that didn't worry him in the least. His two hosts seemed to be eating with difficulty. To frighten them, he acted even more gluttonous, sponging up sauces, swallowing husks, crunching bones, devouring rusks. The others are less and less hungry, it seems.

After dinner, Purpulan drinks a cup of coffee and a little

glass of brandy while smoking a cigar. No one speaks. The silence is awkward. He examines the male once more: a large, skinny, paunchy body and a spacious skull where ideas are undoubtedly simmering; the female: thickset with a pinhead where ambitions are undoubtedly flowering to scale. They might not be all that easy to manipulate.

"How many students will I have?"

"There were three."

"Three suits me fine. They won't wear me out. And what are the names of these young prodigies?"

"Alexander, Caesar and Napoleon," answers the principal with a snicker.

"My predecessor was undoubtedly Aristotle?"

"M. Purpulan is quick at repartee," said the lady.

"But he has not yet caught all the flavor of my jokes."

"Indeed," said Purpulan impassively and he gulped his brandy.

"You should know," said Mme. de Chambernac, "that those weren't actually the names of the three students; but they *were* their first names."

"It was a strange coincidence," said Chambernac.

"Indeed," went Purpulan, whom this bit of news didn't seem to faze. "By the way, why did you say: it was a strange coincidence? It's not one any more?"

"No."

"Why not?"

"Now they're separated."

"Why are they separated?"

"Because the school year's over."

Mme. de Chambernac's laugh rang out like a little drill.

"Monsieur Purpulan, you didn't stop to think that it's July

13th and that the school year is over," she sputtered through her hilarity.

Purpulan's face took on the pretty tinge of cyclamen leaves. It was the color Chambernac was waiting for; he whistled for his courage, crouched down behind his prudence, and sent it to nip the intruder's ankles.

First: a superior snicker, next:

"You see, my poor fellow, you aren't as crafty as you thought. I must admit that you avoided the first trap I set you, but you fell into this one with lamentable facility. Imagine demanding a teaching job, when the school year is finished! How ridiculous! You're not too bright, young man. The best thing you can do is clear out and return to the obscurity that you should never have left."

First Purpulan didn't answer, then he began to sob:

"I'm only a poor devil."

"Poor excuse."

"I was just starting out."

"Bad start."

"You're not going to throw me out, are you?"

"Out and even further."

Purpulan fell to his knees before Mme. de Chambernac.

"Madame, have pity on a poor devil, who made a bad start."

"You certainly have strong breath, my dear fellow," said Madame, drawing back.

"Madame, I have a terrible heredity," he sniveled.

Chambernac's voice boomed:

"Enough mawkishness, young man, my heart is closed to pity."

The young man slumped to the floor, stopped weeping

and started to moan like a whipped dog. The principal gave his wife a triumphant look. She brought her hands together in silent applause. Chambernac went to Purpulan and said to him:

"I'm quite willing to have you stay. I need a secretary. But you won't be paid. You'll have food and shelter. I'm quite willing to have you stay if you sign a pact with me in blood."

Purpulan signed.

XI

The car stopped near Cuges, at the spot where Daniel had noticed a little path on the Geological Survey map. The five of them got out.

"Wait for us in Aubagne," said Daniel to Florent. "We'll come back from the Sainte-Baume Ridge by bus."

The car turned back to dust. Worried, Pouldu looked at the hill.

"We're climbing up there?"

"How about going to see that little chapel," suggested Coltet.

"The chapel of Saint Anthony of Padua? Not the least bit interesting," said Daniel.

They started to walk on level ground, through a village of three houses with an amusing "Town Hall Square,"

"What charming people," said Agnes,

then they climbed following a path painted in arrows on rocks by a chamber of commerce. The sisters and Daniel set a brisk, athletic pace, Coltet was lagging a bit, Pouldu, deliberately bringing up the rear, was grumbling. When the marked rock wasn't too heavy, he'd modify the itinerary behind him.

"That's stupid," said Coltet. "What if somebody else had done it before us, where would we be going?"

"We'd get lost," answered Pouldu.

"That would be delightful," said Agnes. "Let's get lost."

"We decided to go to the Sainte-Baume and we'll go."

Daniel was in command.

Halfway up the hill, they made a rest-stop, like a troop of soldiers. Insects hummed in the heat, ants moved from mother country to colonies, plants smelled each after its kind.

"Isn't the country wonderful," said Agnes. "What calm."

"An awful ruckus," said Pouldu. "Can't you hear all those cicadas? What a racket," said Pouldu.

"What a boor you are," said Agnes.

"You wouldn't last two days in the little hamlet we went through awhile ago."

"I won't let you spoil my fun," said Agnes.

Naomi wasn't saying anything and never did say much. After ten minutes, Daniel decided it was time to go. Pouldu grumbled again; he was only starting to rest. But he had to follow for fear of getting lost.

There was yet another pose before they reached the summit. They admired the view and after that looked for a peaceful spot. Daniel found one. They opened their picnic baskets and backpacks: nicely wrapped sandwiches and thermos bottles appeared. They emptied the one with port to get their strength back. Below them the countryside was drying in the light. Insects hummed in the heat, ants moved from colonies to mother-country, plants smelled each after its kind.

LUNCHEON ON THE GRASS: They've lost the key of the sardine can. Sardines of excellent quality. The salt has spilled all over the bottom of the picnic basket. Tomato sauce spatters onto a dress, someone else sits on the bacon. A big bumblebee is buzzing around the buttery crumbs. Wrappers, peels, garbage and cans are going to embellish nature with manufactured products. This was before the invention of camping.

They'd worked hard to climb that far; as the saying goes, it's the best way to work up an appetite. They grazed until everything was gone. When the sun had planted itself right at the summit of the world, they took possession of a few spots of shade, each man in his spot and the two sisters together.

Sil.

"I bet Ast doesn't come on Sunday," says Agnes.

"Why not?" says Naomi.

"You can never count on him."

"I wish he'd come soon," says Naomi. "These guys are no fun."

"Not much."

Sil.

"Do you think I'll marry Coltet some day," says Agnes.

"Why not?" says Naomi.

"I can count on him."

"He can't on you."

"Not much."

Sil.

"Do you like it here?"

"It's okay."

"I think there's something genuine about this part of the country. Even that nice Italian down at the harbor, it made me feel good to see him again, surrounded by his fruit and vegetables. And besides it reminds me of vacations the way they used to be. Our childhood—don't you think it's nice to remember our childhood?"

"No. I'll think about my childhood when I'm old and gray."

"Oh how gloomy you are. You're going to spoil my day too. Like Pouldu. Pouldu, where are you?"

"Agnes, I'm sleeping."

Sil.

The cicada's stridulous timpani and Coltet's narrow lungs with their audible wheeze etch themselves into the dense heat. Naomi turns inward and would like to sleep. Agnes is leaning on an elbow to look at the plain, but the stone is rough. So she places her head delicately on some dry grasses and stares at the sky until she's dizzy.

Sil.

Daniel who's kept an eye on the passage of time starts to collect abandoned objects. There's some coffee left in a thermos. He drinks it and announces it's time to leave. Coltet happy to come back down from the heights takes the lead alone and moving fast. Pouldu, whom boredom had put into a deep sleep, wakes up with a furry tongue and a fuzzy head. He's far behind. They get down just in time to take the bus to Aubagne where Florent is waiting for them with the car.

Florent is reading the paper and, bareheaded, is letting

the products of the distillation of his cheap lunch wine evaporate via the pores of his forehead. From time to time he mops his brow.

"What the hell are you doing here," exclaims someone.

It's young Bossu. In Florent's opinion, they don't have much in common.

"I'm waiting for the young ladies and their friends. They went on a hike to the Sainte-Baume."

"They walked?"

"Yes, they walked."

"Got to be crazy when you've got wheels. When I get mine, you won't catch me hoofing it. Hey, come have a drink."

"Okay—till I see the bus coming."

"So they're coming back on the bus. They're tired already."

He laughs drinks then says:

"Hey old buddy, your bosses are beautiful kids. Hey you know every time I go to the beach, I stop to look at them especially the tall one. What's her name again the tall one?"

"Mademoiselle Agnes."

"Mlle. Agnes. Agnes de Chambernac. It's the kind of name you only see in the stories in *Le Matin*. Hey it's driving me crazy. Next time I go to the cat house, I'll say to the hooker: 'Tell me your name's Agnes.' Can you picture that?"

It was difficult for him to know whether Florent was picturing anything—which moreover didn't really bother him much—for Florent didn't answer. Following the ingurgitation of his beer, his dome had started to steam again.

"You know, if I was you, I would have had her a long time ago. It's just what girls like that want. Hey old buddy all those nice-looking rich chicks, they blow me away. I'll end up going nuts if this keeps up. When I think that there are guys, just because they're rich they can touch them all they want and bury their faces between their legs, hey, that grabs me there, right under the tie I'm not wearing. Just talking about it I'm lifting the table with my prick."

"Some imagination you've got," said Florent.

"Imagination? You bet I've got imagination and not just imagination. I've got ideas, ideas about terrific deals, ideas about everything, I can revolutionize the industry, I've solved heaps of problems that bother all the manufacturers. I won't explain, you wouldn't understand a thing. Radio, you know, is the future, and me and radio, you know, we're one and the same. Only, they have to give me a chance and there's just one place where they can give me a chance it's in Paris with Claye. Don't you think if my old man talked to the girls it might be a way to get myself hired in their grandpa's plant? and go to Paris?"

"It's possible," said Florent. "The young ladies are very considerate of others. Hey here comes the bus, I'm off."

Young Bossu salvages, then sucks up the remains of Florent's beer and pays, generously.

"You could have had a drink while waiting for us," Daniel said to Florent.

"You think he didn't?" mutters Pouldu.

One day Florent would dump Pouldu in a ditch.

And now the five take their turn dipping their lips into nicely warm heads of beer, thus reestablishing contact with western civilization. Obviously this place doesn't have the best beer in the world. There's better stuff around. They start talking about where you can imbibe this better stuff and who makes this better stuff. Pouldu knows a lot about the subject. He's researched the matter rather more than he's lived it. He speaks of it with authority. He knows that Serge Salvagno of the Sporting Club of Cannes is a pupil of the famous Nut of the Knickerbocker in New York, that the illustrious Harry made his debut, or just about, before the war, at the Piazza, also in New York, that Bob Card was once at the Clift Hotel in San Francisco and the Alexander Hotel in Los Angeles, that Jean, formerly at the Coq-en-Pâte, is originally from the Solazzi in Naples, and that Paul Kraudwig was in 1913 president of the International Club of Bartenders. He knows their itineraries, follows their peregrinations and thinks he can evaluate their style.

So Pouldu's holding forth, but hasn't yet learned to vary his presentation; he's boring. Coltet ventures to contest the presence of Raoul at the Dinard Casino around 1927. Pouldu crushes him.

"Couldn't we talk about less serious things?" suggests Agnes.

"It's every bit as interesting as anything else. As movies for instance."

"Movies," says Agnes, "I can't stand them since they've made them talk."

"You don't like talkies?" asks Coltet.

"They aren't movies anymore, you can't dream with all those people yelling all the time."

"My goodness, dream," goes Pouldu hypocritically.

"Of course, dream. Now, instead of seeing heroes act, we hear actors talk: like at the theater."

"It's all very sad," sighs Pouldu.

"Of course it's sad: silent films, so near and already part of the past."

"Cheer up, Agnes," says Coltet. "It's not the least bit sure that talkies are here to stay. They have to redo the theaters, and then what'll they show? English talkies? There aren't enough customers. French films? They'd cost too much and wouldn't pay because you couldn't show them outside France. There's still a bright future for silent movies."

"Boy, do you make sense," says Pouldu. "I bet that in two years, there won't be one silent movie theater left in Paris."

"Pouldu," says Agnes, "it's impossible to have a discussion with you."

"In that case, let's go see the people from Marseille at the Casino."

Pouldu can't forgive them for coming to spend the summer in a hole like La Ciotat just because they own a house here when it would be so easy for them to go to Hendaye or Juan-les-Pins, to places where you meet nice people who can be useful to you in the future. And then when they do go to such places or to Italy or to England, they don't invite him. Their hospitality toward him is decidedly homeopathic,—and yet isn't he one of the most important engineers of the Claye plants and didn't his grandfather, a Jew it's true, but no more so than the baron, didn't he put money into the business of the other grandfather when he was still hustling orders?

On top of everything else, they drag him on picnics because they love Nature.

The only true contact between man and nature is science, science which transforms and destroys, science which makes deserts or swamps habitable, science which makes iron run on iron across the most diverse geographical terrain and which makes aluminum fly through the most varied meteorological conditions, science which makes attar of rose from coal and sugar from wood shavings. That's the only true contact of man with nature: a dried-up lake, an irrigated desert, a tamed sea, a leveled mountain, that's man's authentic contact with nature, one of action, destruction and transformation.

But to believe in the virtues of waxed paper spread out on the top of a small hill to the summit of which one climbs by a path painted on stones by a chamber of commerce—no, thank you.

This very evening he's going to discuss a nice little p.r. deal with the manager of the Grand Hotel. That'll bring in some shekels. He'll finish out his stay with the Claye-

Chambernacs; then he'll spend the last two weeks of his vacation in a nice place, not snobbish, a place where you go when you can afford to spend a little money on yourself, Paris-Plage for instance, or simply Deauville. That'll be a real vacation.

"Casino," Agnes shouts at him. "My word, Pouldu, you went to sleep. It doesn't take much to wear you out."

If he had wanted to, Pouldu could have come out with something much more unpleasant.

XII

At the Tavern of the Forty Billiards, Chambernac and Purpulan sat down for their aperitif. The principal, after several swigs of mandarin, expressed himself as follows:

"You gave me one hell of a scare when you started your little game. I was petrified. At that point you had the upper hand. Even after my little speech, if you'd held firm instead of blubbering, you would still have terrorized me. And besides, you made a serious mistake right at the outset: you shouldn't have talked about work, much less demanded it. You see where that's led you: to slavery. I don't have to point out the moral of the story. And besides, it's all water over the dam. Let's not dwell on it."

"What are you going to have me do, Monsieur Chambernac?"

"I've already told you; I'm going to start by employing you as secretary."

"And for what sort of work, Monsieur Chambernac? You see, I'm really not very well educated."

"For what sort of work? Copying, chiefly, research at the library perhaps. Do you have any qualifications?"

"Oh no, Monsieur Chambernac. But I know how to read, write and count and I'm not totally unintelligent."

"Humph. Tell me, why did you choose me as your victim?"

"Because I saw you coming out of a house, if you see what I mean, Monsieur Chambernac."

"Really, you saw me?"

"Yes, Monsieur Chambernac."

"Well, this will probably come as a surprise to you, my boy, but it was the first time I'd ever gone there."

"I'm not blaming you, Monsieur Chambernac."

"That would be the last straw."

Purpulan assured the principal of his most abject submission.

"Tell me now," continued Chambernac, "who taught you the unusual craft that you practiced so badly?"

"First my father, Monsieur Chambernac. He was a poor devil like me and belonged to the lowest order of the infernal hierarchy: a proletarian demon."

"Let's not talk politics," said Chambernac.

"All right, Monsieur Chambernac. So my father began my education but I lost him when I was still very young: an ill-digested exorcism carried him off when I was only thirteen. I lived a few months in the Bondy Forest; I ate acorns and the bark of trees. Believe me, Monsieur Chambernac, it was no fun. At that point the war broke out. When the Germans advanced on Paris, I decided to flee and took refuge in Bordeaux where I spent a few good years. Then I was drafted and after a while discharged, as they say. I learned a lot in the army, Monsieur Chambernac, but not enough all the same to look after myself in civilian life. I've been a housebreaker, a procurer, a swindler, a tipster, an informer, an imposter, a solicitor, a receiver, a freeloader, an opiumer, a morphiner, a cocainer, a heroiner, a robber, a stripper, a defaulter, a marauder, a shady dealer, a defrauder, a pilferer, a burglar, a counterfeiter, a deceiver, an adulterator, a traitor, a falsifier, a despoiler, a usurper, a pillager, a cheater, a sneaker, a tattler, a trickster, an agitator: everywhere I met with reverses."

He sighed, then continued:

"One day as I was walking sad solitary and disillusioned in the suburbs of Paris over near Blagny, I saw in front of me a dwarf, staggering drunk, who eventually collapsed into a ditch. I pulled him out and began by relieving him of his coin purse and billfold. Both were very light. I then understood in a flash that I had just met the man who was to guide my footsteps through life. Monsieur Chambernac, you'll excuse me for not spelling out the different phases of his teaching; in spite of the pact that binds me to you, I cannot reveal these secrets. Permit me however to read you a little description I've written of this individual."

He took from his pocket a billfold and from his billfold a sheet of paper.

"It's in verse," he said.

After coughing twice, he read what follows:

XIII

Bébé Toutout has one pair'v pants
He craps in them at every chance
Bébé Toutout has one snot rag
When he spits in it we all gag
Bébé Toutout has one sport coat
In it he smells like an old goat
Bébé Toutout has just one hat
It's so greasy that it's gone flat
Bébé Toutout has just one mitt
He uses it to wipe his shit
Bébé Toutout has just one tie
With it he dries his gummy eye
Bébé Toutout has just one collar
It's filthy stiff and sweaty yeller
Bébé Toutout has one pair'v shorts
They're so crappy that he gets warts
Bébé Toutout has just one shirt
It once was white: it's gray with dirt
Bébé Toutout has just one soul
Madame it's black as coal
                as coal
Bébé Toutout has just one prick
He uses it in ways ludic
With four men and the corporal
he has a ball he has a ball

XIV

"Your Bébé Toutout was a disgusting little swine," said
Chambernac. "I want you to try to stay a little cleaner. For
instance, with that breath of yours, it would be a good idea
to suck mints."

"All right, Monsieur Chambernac," said Purpulan. "I have
something else to read to you, if it doesn't bore you."

"I'm listening."

XV

Bébé Toutout at sev'n months born
was small as a kernel of corn
He never did grow to full height
but dwarfishness his life did blight
While giving birth his mother died
bereft his dad lay down and croaked
They fed him bread in vinegar soaked
with garlic pimento and onion
and savory and yellow saffron
and some copal nuts on the side
Bringing him up gave them all cause
for grief: for such a brat he was
As favorite foods this guttersnipe
chose boogers blood sausage and tripe
Such were the things he used to want
to eat throughout his years of growth
if you can actually call growth
the burgeoning of such a runt

To school they sent him at age six
and there he played some awful tricks
as into inkwells he would plunge
then blotch up papers like a sponge
And when he was a little older
he made himself a mean slingshot
Just see how he had gotten bolder:
himself into kids' peepers shot
He rode astride fat bugs of June
to scribble on the school's blackboard
The ceiling served as his spittoon
He wandered 'round up there when bored
In truth he was an awful bother
Of such an impolite orphan
without a mother or a father
they'd never make a gentleman
At the precise age of thirteen
as an apprentice he was placed
His boss respectable and keen
sold polish varnish and wax paste
Bébé Toutout the errands ran
and every night he swept the store
His wallet was flat as a pan-
cake, all this while he remained poor
The worst was not his salary
though that was surely inhumane
but that his job was unhealthy
and harassment on him did rain
He had to taste the shoe polish
to see that it was colorfast
He'd use it instead of relish

to spread on bread at his repast
They also gave him on a dish
leftover bits of buskin mash
In short he had to eat rubbish
If he became a parasite
nasty and mean from head to toe
it surely wasn't Nature's wish
Misfortune put him in this plight
and nevermore would let him go.

XVI

"Your poem is very interesting," said Chambernac, "but the ending is rather sentimental. Go on."

"That's all. I didn't go any further," answered Purpulan, blushing. "I must confess, monsieur, that I'm pretty lazy."

"Don't worry, I'll make you knuckle down," said the principal.

XVII

Clemence saw a jar on the table, forgotten. She picked up and held near her eyes the young ladies' suntan lotion. They'd miss their sunbath. It was urgent to take it to them immediately. But Florent's roaming around goodness knows where, Alice would refuse to put down her work, Adrian has so much to do and as for the cook it's silly even to think of her. So Clemence puts on a hat, takes her parasol and goes out.

Clemence has never set foot on the neighboring beach. She even has the habit of averting her nearsighted gaze when she goes by. From afar she sees dark forms she knows are offhandedly undressed and among which she couldn't at this distance recognize either Mlle. Naomi or Mlle. Agnes. So she has to venture among these people laid out, asses to the sun with shorts on them. She faltered a few steps onto the sand. Thanks to her severe astigmatism, all these anatomies seemed very fuzzy to her, which spared her having to make out the gentlemen's phalluses and the ladies' pussies, which she didn't know from Adam—or Eve.

> People who roast themselves like animals on a spit have taken leave of their senses. This is a real inferno: red as demons and black as coal. And then they put oil on every possible part of their bodies: why not salt and pepper and a little vinegar while they're at it? And as if that weren't enough they look as if they're making fun of decent people.

The only attired person among nudified ones, Clemence moves forward, saved from intimidation by her nearsightedness. The only thing that terrorizes her are the big beach balls that streak through the air thrown by maniacs. If she got one of those in the face her eyeglasses would be shattered; however would she be able to recognize the young ladies then?

"Why, Clemence," asks Agnes, "what are you doing on the beach?"

"Have you come to go swimming," asks Pouldu who thinks he's very clever.

"Most certainly not," answers Clemence who doesn't like Pouldu. "Mademoiselle, I was just coming to bring you the suntan lotion you forgot."

There's a completely nude gentleman next to Mlle. Agnes. Thanks to her powerful pince-nez, Clemence can make out the arrow of curly hairs rising to the male's navel. It's M. Coltet. Things are even worse than she had imagined. She flees.

"Strange person," says Pouldu. "Why on earth do your parents keep her on?"

"She's very devoted," says Naomi.

"She comes with the house," says Agnes. "She was born there; not in this one, in the one we had before. Her mother was in the service of my grandmother."

"I see," says Pouldu.

"What do you see?" demands Naomi.

"Nothing, nothing. It's a family matter, incomprehensible to outsiders."

"So stay outside," says Naomi.

He's made his choice: Deauville, a beach that's simple and in good taste, nothing like an obscure little port where you meet only people from Lyons or some such place.

Coltet is now working on his crawl halfway between the diving raft and the beach.

"His stroke's too short," comments Agnes, "and it's not very smooth."

"His head's down too far," adds Naomi. "It makes him roll when he takes a breath."

Agnes gets up, to show what she can do. Pouldu, still all sandy, looks up at her standing against the sky and admires her. He remembers the ribaldry of his father old man Pouldu, and the way he used to say "a fine-looking girl." But young Pouldu hasn't a dissolute bone in his body, and besides, he has no desire to sleep with this noble person.

Agnes moves away with strong strokes, her feet churning the water, swift and competent. Coltet stops to study her style. But she's already past, leaving behind only a few clusters of bubbles on the water's surface to enlighten him.

The others join her on the diving raft: Naomi soon, Pouldu more laboriously, Coltet finally whom they haul out of the water. Has he made progress? Agnes explains what he's still not doing right. Then they all stretch out to dry like laundry and the caramelizing begins again. The sky is blue, the sea green, the sun yellow and the earth several colors. Happiness must be wafting about.

Even young Bossu feels cheerful, leaning on the railing along the boulevard, although disappointed at not catching sight of the young ladies. He consoles himself with others and waits hopefully for the day when they'll come back to the bistro and his father can talk to them. That day, he was quite sure, was this very day. At around one Coltet's car came and parked in front of the Café du Port.

"Will you look at that. Now they're coming in the morning too," says Mme. Gramigni.

Gramigni, who's weighing potatoes, continues to weigh potatoes.

"What's with all these chippies anyway wanting to dress like men?" says the customer.

"They're flat as boards," says Mme. Gramigni, of whom that certainly wasn't true.

The customer leaves, her shopping bag full of nicely sprouting spuds, carefully selected by a vindictive Gramigni.

"I'm going out for a drink," says Gramigni.

"Are you going to Bossu's?"

"I told you: I'm going out for a drink."

He takes his hat from under the cash register.

"You're going to look at them close up, right, you bastard."

"Just you come back in here and I'll show you."

"Ha, you don't scare me."

To call his bluff she comes back in. She gets a big kick in the backside.

"I'm going for a drink," went Gramigni.

He heads for the café, pursued by the cuckolds! and the lechers! of his wife.

"Charming household," says Pouldu.

They make a sign of greeting. He orders a drink.

"He probably gives her a good thrashing for each aperitif," says Pouldu, "once before: so he can go, and once after: when he's drunk."

These remarks were pure slander for the fruitseller rarely got drunk, and when he did it was always on wine. But Pouldu's hardly concerned with historical truth when it's a matter of such insignificant people.

Gramigni puts ice into his pernod-grenadine and counts: today there's one missing. But the two women are there. He gapes, as do visitors (unprejudiced ones) at aquariums or zoos before lithe and powerful animals, the tiger, the boa constrictor and the moray eel. But Gramigni's never seen such animals, therefore his wonder is original and he can't begin to sort out his feelings. If he had ever gone to a zoological garden, he might think of comparing himself to a chained monkey, like the one in the port that watches the sailors who've reduced him to servitude sing and drink, provided he thought a monkey would go into ecstasy over man. He doesn't admire the girls: they amaze him. What comet crossed the sky of their conception? And what food were they fed to make them so beautiful?

He was born in the shadow of dusty garlic and dirty laundry and suffered time and time again the swarming of Mediterranean body lice; what a strange thing were these bodies so often washed, these nails so often cared for, these heads of hair so often combed, these lips so often painted, these bodies so often massaged. Here his imagination stops and parts company with young Bossu's. That boy has too much imagination. Doesn't he claim to hear America with his antennas and his tubes? You can't deny that he's a hard worker. He might have a future, that boy. His father comes forward, spine aslant, tongue twisted seventy-seven times around itself. He explains about his boy.

"It would be so nice of you young ladies to say a word to M. Claye about him."

> CLAYE (Jules-Jules), born in Lons-le-Saunier May 17, 1854. Graduate of the Conservatory of Arts and Crafts, soon succeeds his father as director of a very small plant making precision instruments. In

1884, founds the *Electrical Construction Corporation* and in 1902 *Electrical Equipment*. After October 27, 1898 interested in the development of wireless radio in France. Founder of the major radio stations; manufacturer or concessionaire of the brands: *Marbsconi, Sansfilips, Ducruddy, Sonoritas-Sonoritatum,* the *Shortwave Branlyjack* and the *Infernal Machine*; general concessionaire of radio advertising in France. In a struggle with the Lavasse Agency, created a competing news service, the *Opera Terrae.* CEO of the *Industrial Bank for Industry, Electrotechnical Porcelain, J.A.W.A.A.T.I.D.* and approximatively thirty-six other companies. Married March 5, 1883 to Mlle. Dorothy (von) Cramm (deceased December 2, 1901). By whom he had two children: Sophie, born December 5, 1883, and Astolphe, born December 1, 1901, a little afterthought.

Mlle. Sophie Claye married, on July 25, 1902, M. Edmond de Chambernac (born July 10, 1878, killed in Verdun February 21, 1916) by whom she had three children: Daniel, born April 25, 1903, Agnes, born May 16, 1905 and Naomi, born December 13, 1908.

The widowed Mme. Chambernac remarried July 26, 1924 Baron Solomon Hachamoth, CEO of companies and Officer of the Legion of Honor, veteran.

XVIII

Astolphe who claimed he'd inherited a title from his mother and who called himself de Cramm because it sounded aristocratic, stark naked, was strolling back and forth in his mistress' bedroom, and preoccupied. She, his mistress, after trying out numerous names and surnames, called herself Maud, which is very distinguished. It was around ten thirty eleven o'clock. Maud was sleeping: because sleep was very important to her, not because she'd indulged in too much love making. Ast spent only two nights a month with her, and didn't wear her out. If he was strolling back and forth in this way, stark naked and preoccupied, it was not that he was thinking about his sexual inadequacy; he was quite pleased with himself the way he was, as far as the functioning of his cavernous nerve was concerned, and Maud, since we must call her that, didn't venture to comment on the subject. She was too nice to hurt him and sufficiently unfaithful to find satisfaction elsewhere.

The object of Ast's concerns, therefore, as he was strolling back and forth like this, stark naked, stark naked because first of all it was hot, secondly because the woman was sleeping, thirdly because it was late enough that the cleaning woman might enter unannounced, fourthly because he knew he was well-built, anatomical and physiological qualities not necessarily going hand in hand, this because of psychological uncertainties, fifthly because he was really truly deeply preoccupied, was not situated in the vicinity of his genital glands but near the top of his skull, where Ast like all modern Occidentals even after Bergson, localized his thought, which, if the term to think doesn't seem too ambitious and Ast moreover in no way claimed to be a thinker, was principally, almost solely, concerned with anticipating fashions, intellectual as well as others, with the proud enterprise of launching them and finally, with discrediting the old ones. He'd been the first to go hear Bach played without knowing music, the first to collect glass balls, globes and miniature model boats, the first to wear hand-knit ties, mocassins and plus-fours, the first to discover the second-hand dealers of the Flea Market and the fortune-tellers of the Rue de Rivoli, the first to go to the South of France in the summer, the first to tire of great European express trains and sordid adventures in great ports, equally European, the first to go to the little movie theaters of the outer boulevards of Paris to see non-artistic American films, the first to read Freud, Einstein and Thomas, the first to make cocktails with urodonal and the abbé Souris' rejuvenating waters, the first to paint, without knowing how in which he was not the first, on butcher's paper with A-one sauce and tomato juice, the first to commission a table made from coconuts and chairs made from barbed wire, the first to take paintings by amateurs, bought at very high prices from very rich dealers, and have them framed with automobile runningboards and eggshells, but for two weeks now nothing has brought him to the attention of the select public except the fact that he's stayed in Paris until the end of July. It's true that he let it be understood that nothing is more charming than Paris at 49° Réaumur, but he senses the time's not yet ripe for that fashion.

He also had to telephone this morning regarding a little speculation undertaken entirely on his own initiative; he disregarded the advice of his father as well as of his brother-in-law. For he was lucky at gambling. At the phone he hesitates, is afraid he'll wake up Maud, gets bored, leafs through the directory. Around page 700, he sees this name: Catherine Lescure, and the address: 4A Desnouettes Square, with no further information. Then, like a sheep carried off by an eagle or Ganymede by a god, he's seized by this idea: "I'm in love with Catherine Lescure." But before even beginning to find out what it might be like to love a woman whose name is all he knows, he first wanted to assess what such an innovation might mean to his intimates and admirers; eccentricity had impact. Uncertain, Ast resolved to try it out on a friend, a man whose opinion he could trust, well acquainted with all the subtleties of things novel, a man named Arnolphe whom he'd met during the war.

Ast gets dressed, is quiet, goes to make a phone call at the neighboring bar, buys fifty liters of gas, makes tracks, wonders if you pronounce the s of Lescure: Catherine Lécure or Catherine Lesscure, makes tracks, makes tracks. In Deauville he meets Arnolphe, who's just had lunch. They chat a bit.

"I thought you were in La Ciotat."

"That's right. I promised to be there tomorrow. I'm supposed to take Sophie."

"What? You haven't left yet?"

"I really like Paris at this time of the year: tourists with their kodaks and guidebooks, office workers with their straw hats and lager beer, melting asphalt that your heels sink into, the disappearance of all the snobs, it's splendid. As for Sophie, she was staying with the baron whom business is keeping in the capital, but now she's changed her mind and wants to go South. None of this is very interesting, you know."

"So what's new?"

"I'm in love

　　　　　　　　"Well, well, will love be in this winter?"
with a woman I don't know."

　　　　　　　　　　"I might have known that was too simple.
　　　　　　　　　　That

　　　　　　you

　　　　met
Where?"

"Nowhere. I've never seen her. I don't know a thing about her: just her name, only her name. Her address and phone number too, actually, but I'm not going to try to see her or talk to her."

　　　　　　　　　　　　"It doesn't make sense.

What's he up to? When I was
a kid I read stories about that
sort of thing: knights and kings
who loved women they'd
never seen. But then they'd
try to see them. I don't get it."

"What are you thinking about? What I just told you?"

"I was thinking about the knights of the Middle Ages. In
the stories, they loved like that: without knowing, I mean
without knowing the women."

"Yes, but you see, old man, with me it's not at all the
same thing; they tried to see their princesses, but not me.
I'll love her without anything to justify my love or to tarnish
its purity."

"What balderdash he's
gone and dreamed up now.
Ast is certainly not himself
these days.

In that case,

in your place,

I would have fallen in love with a woman without knowing
even her name, surname, address and phone number."

Mounted on their powerful steeds, the knights of the
Middle Ages have unseated Astolphe astride his hobby-
horse. He gets up, for he sees young Pouldu coming stealthily
toward him. With this good excuse for leaving, he shakes
Arnolphe's hand and, deeply chagrined, returns to Paris.

XIX

Since that hopeless fellow was late again, Mme. Hachamoth had decided to leave alone, in her old Picard-Pictet that she'd bought six months before the mobilization and learned to drive in. It was the thing that most reminded her of Edmond. While Adrian II, thus called to distinguish him from his colleague temporarily transferred to La Ciotat, was loading trunks and suitcases, Mme. Hachamoth was unsuccessfully turning the crank.

"Would Madame permit me?"

"Mind your own business, Adrian II, and not other people's. You're not a chauffeur, as far as I know? So you won't touch my car. Whatever are you thinking of! You're getting ambitious. My car. Touch it. Is the luggage stowed?"

"Yes, madame."

"You do have some merit, Adrian II."

She got back to turning the crank. Bertha III, thus called by the baroness because she was the third maid by this name in her service, had wedged herself in among the packages and wasn't saying a word. The Pic.-Pic. still wasn't purring.

"My God, my God," exclaimed Mme. Hachamoth, "why don't you want me to leave? Did you decide from all eternity that I was to make this trip with my brother and that, although he leaves me cooling my heels, I should wait patiently for him?"

A surprised passerby stopped.

"Adrian II," yelled Mme. Hachamoth, "go ask that fellow to curb his curiosity and, if he won't, throw him into the ditch."

The passerby prudently passed by.

"My God," exclaimed Mme. Hachamoth again, "help me to make this machine work."

Then she had an idea.

"Bertha III."

"Yes, madame."

"Adrian II."

"Yes, madame."

"You're going to say a little prayer with me to ask Heaven to permit my departure presto."

All three crossed themselves and meditated for a few moments, which was by the way pure hypocrisy on the part of Bertha who was a free-thinkress. The passerby at the far end of the street looked back; then he shook his head; finally, turning the corner, disappeared.

One last time, Mme. Hachamoth turned the crank. The motor still didn't respond.

"God's will be done," she sighed. "Adrian II, unload the car."

"Madame might phone a garage mechanic?"

"Very funny. Why not a boilermaker?"

When the luggage had been set back on the sidewalk, Mme. Hachamoth got behind the wheel, Adrian and Bertha pushed and the car went back to sleep for good in its shed.

That's when Astolphe gets there.

XX

Night slumbered in Mourmèche. Even the brothel, where Chambernac had dabbled in debauchery, was closed. Closed the bar, closed the bistros. Clumsily, an old cat hobbled along. Henry was getting some shut-eye, his wife Agatha was dozing, Purpulan: who knew? At two o'clock, they were awakened.

"Hello, Sophie, what a surprise, hello, Astolphe old boy, you certainly couldn't say this isn't a surprise. But what a time to arrive, what a time."

"I'm thirsty," said Mme. Hachamoth.

"I'll make you some lime tea," said Mme. Chambernac.

"Would there be any brandy?" asked Mme. Hachamoth.

Mme. Chambernac reddened. The brandy came. Mme. Hachamoth knocked back a big mouthful.

"Queen Victoria was often sloshed," she said, "That didn't keep her from being a great queen. I haven't gotten to that point yet. My God, who did not want me to be a queen, don't let me sink into drunkenness either."

"Come, come," went Chambernac, while his wife crimsoned.

"What are you up to these days, my dear Henry," asked Mme. Hachamoth. "Modern customs have destroyed the gentle art of letter-writing; one never hears from anyone anymore. That's probably why there are so many people trying so hard to communicate with the dead, to receive messages from them when it's so contrary to the spirit of our times. Paradox! Paradox! I've never wanted to disturb Edmond. Enough is enough."

"How is your husband?" asked Mme. Chambernac tactfully.

"He's sweating," said Mme. Hachamoth. "But what about you, Henry, you haven't answered my question: what are you up to these days? Why bother waking you up at two in the morning and insisting Astolphe make a detour on bad roads if this is all I get for it?"

"Are you on your way to La Ciotat?" asked Chambernac.

"I see you're trying to hide something from me," said Mme. Hachamoth. "Feel free. You don't owe me an explanantion. Certainly not."

"Are my nieces still as fresh and as beautiful?" asked Chambernac.

"Beautiful I think, fresh is starting to be not quite accurate anymore," said Mme. Hachamoth. "Not married in case that interests you, probably lovers though."

Mme. Chambernac purpled.

"Anyway," said Mme. Hachamoth, "I'm happy, my dear brother-in-law, to see you, in spite of the fact that you're holding out on me. I'll say it again: it's your right; seldom as we see each other, I'm not going to force you to tell me the story of your life."

Mme. Hachamoth emptied another glass of brandy.

"One for the road," she said

and got up. Among the varied hues at her disposal, Mme. Chambernac settled on scarlet.

"You see," said Mme. Hachamoth to Astolphe, as they were again speeding south, "there's something fishy going on in that house."

"You're intuitive," said Astolphe.

"You mean I'm not an idiot. Well, there's a gigolo living with them. I saw his clothes hanging on a coat-rack."

"I couldn't care less," said Astolphe.

"I don't care if you don't care," said Mme. Hachamoth. "We're going back."

"No."

"We'll catch them unawares."

"No."

They went back.

"You forgot something?" asked Chambernac.

"You forgot something," said Mme. Hachamoth.

"I'm not following you."

"You forgot to answer my question: what are you up to these days?"

"Please excuse my wife; she's very tired; she stayed in bed this time. But here's the whole story: I'm writing a book."

"Is that all?" asked Mme. Hachamoth.

"It will be a big book," continued Chambernac.

"Might we know on what subject," asked Astolphe.

"On lunatics."

"I didn't know you were a doctor," said Astolphe.

"Oh, but it won't be about medicine," said Chambernac, "at least not very much. It will be mostly a bibliography."

"So that's what you were hiding from me," said Mme. Hachamoth. "At least part of it."

"My dear Sophie," said Chambernac, "would it interest you to know that I have a secretary to help me with my work?"

"Could I see him?"

"But he's sleeping!"

"Dear boy. That is, I suppose he must be very young. One of your former students?"

"No, no, he's an old fellow, a study hall supervisor. He has beautiful penmanship: to copy texts."

"What texts?" asked Astolphe.

"The lunatics' texts I intend to publish."

"Lunatics' texts!" exclaimed Astolphe. "Why, that must be very interesting. Fascinating, even."

Since words are cheap, he added:

"There aren't enough lunatics in the world."

Then, with studied courtesy:

"Couldn't you read us a few of them?"

"No," said Mme. Hachamoth. "That's enough now. We'll let him sleep. Just think, gentlemen, it's already three-twenty A.M. Dawn and matins will soon be here."

"You see," she said to Astolphe, as they were again speeding south, "you see, he lied. An old fellow! A study hall supervisor! Likely story. Either he's sleeping with the boy, or Agatha is. If it's neither, then it's even worse. I can't begin to imagine the abomination that may have insinuated itself into his life. In any event, he's now become a liar. Lying is nasty. My God! help me to never become a liar. And those lunatics, Astolphe, what do you think of those lunatics? Wait, leave me alone, I'm going to say my prayer for the new day."

When the sun had completely detached itself from the ground, over there on the left, Mme. Hachamoth stopped being quiet and repeated:

"And those lunatics, Astolphe, what do you think of those lunatics?"

"I'd have been happy to stay and hear him talk some more about them," said Astolphe.

XXI

"After you, monsieur," said Purpulan.

"Go ahead, go ahead, my young friend," said Chambernac.

"Monsieur, I am your humble servant," said Purpulan.

Chambernac went into his study, followed by Purpulan. And, showing him a glass-fronted bookcase, said:

"Here you see, my young friend, what will be the object of our work. This collection was put together by one of my great-uncles and expanded by his son; I've recently inherited it. It's made up solely of books written and published by what are generally called 'literary lunatics'; I'll try to explain later just what this term means; for that matter, you'll see that I won't be able to do it. Originally I merely intended to publish a catalog of this collection, then I became ambitious and now I'd like to write a comprehensive work on the matter, a work that would be at once a biography, a bibliography and an anthology of all the French literary lunatics of the xixth century. I say French because I know only this language, and I say xixth century because one must know where to stop."

Since there was no reaction from Purpulan, Chambernac continued:

"There have already been works on this subject, but they are few and incomplete—or too complete: by which I mean that they classify as literary lunatics people who have no right to this title. They are: Charles Nodier, *On Several Eccentric Books*, 1835; Delepierre, *Literary History of Lunatics*, London, 1860; Philomneste junior (pseudonym of G. Brunet), *Literary Lunatics*, Paris, 1880; Iv. Tcherpakoff (pseudonym of Auguste Ladrague), *Literary Lunatics* (these are corrections of and additions to the preceding book), Moscow, 1883. Your first job, my young friend, will therefore be to read these four books and to make an index card for each author mentioned."

"An index card," exclaimed Purpulan, "you want me to make index cards, monsieur?"

"It's absolutely necessary."

"Please monsieur, don't make me make index cards. It's too dreary."

"Purpulan, are you not my humble servant?"

"Monsieur, I didn't think it would be so awful."

"Purpulan, you will put on index cards the four above-mentioned works."

"Yes, monsieur."

"That's not all."

Purpulan groaned.

"You will do the same thing for the articles by Delepierre published in the *Miscellanèse Off Zé Philobiblion Sociétie* from 1856 to 1866; for *The Eccentrics* by Champfleury and for *Singular People* by Lorédan Larchey; for the *Stultitiana or Little Biography Of The Lunatics Of The City of Valenciennes, by a demented man*, published in 1823 and which is by Hécart, for *Literary Lunatics Of Quercy* by L. Greil and for *Literary Eccentrics and Grotesques Of Agenais* by J. Andrieu. You will also go through this collection of the *Anecdotal Review* and the *Little Review* from 1855 to 1870 and you will copy from the *Bibliographical Manual of Psychic Or Occult Sciences* by Caillet the names mentioned under the headings: 'Philosophical Oddities, Paradoxes and Singularities' and 'Singularities, Satires, Pamphlets.' Later,

I think we'll have to do research in psychiatric literature. As for the catalog of my library, it's finished."

Purpulan was wiping his brow.

"Once this work is done," continued Chambernac, "we'll undo it."

"Monsieur, couldn't we undo it first," went Purpulan, smiling timidly.

"This is no time for jokes. First try to understand what I mean. Indeed, when we've gathered three or four hundred index cards, we'll see that three-quarters of them don't interest us because they're about authors incorrectly classified as literary lunatics. What is a literary lunatic? Nodier restricted his list 'to recognized lunatics who did not have the distinction of gathering a following.' This last point is indeed an excellent criterion; whoever had disciples couldn't be considered a literary lunatic; the latter must—by definition—remain unknown. But how do you judge the recognized lunacy of an author—eh? How? Where is the borderline between madness and eccentricity, simple eccentricity? After all, true lunatics are locked up; and one would be right in saying that our authors have their freedom since they publish their creations, since they're in print. And look, a psychiatrist said, wait, I'll find the quotation, it was Leuret, it's in his *Psychological Fragments On Madness*, published octavo in 1836, never forget when you find a book to write down its date of publication, its format, the number of pages, the name of the publisher or, if you don't have it, that of the printer, the city where it was published, there it is, page 41, well this Leuret, who was a physician and a psychiatrist, writes: 'I was unable, try as I might, to distinguish by its nature alone'—by its nature alone: that's the very situation we find ourselves in—'a mad idea from a reasonable one. I searched in the Charenton, Bicêtre and Salpétrière Hospitals for the idea which would seem to me the most mad; then, when I compared it to those that are circulating in society, I was most surprised, almost ashamed, not to see a difference.' So?"

"Science has perhaps made progress since 1836," said Purpulan.

"Well, well, one would think you were beginning to get interested in the matter."

"I'm your humble servant," said Purpulan.

"All right all right my young friend," said Chambernac. "In short, I think we should begin our work without any preconceived ideas; but we'll eliminate from our lists first all those who had disciples or who were recognized as having any sort of value by critics or the public or even a very small part of the public, second all mystics, visionaries, spiritualists, theosophists, et cetera whose wild imaginings can be related to notions that are more or less accepted and which prudence advises us not to rashly label lunacy. Let's take for instance Brunet's enumeration. I'll naturally skip the foreigners and the French before 1800. All right. So we have: D'Aché (we'll see, but his *Historic Tableau Of The Misfortunes Of Substitution* was suppressed by the imperial police and is therefore not in our library), Jules Allix (a simple eccentric), J.-J. Aristippe (ditto), Arson (the banker who was a disciple of Wronsky: no), Aulis (didn't publish), Barreau and A. Colin (no: Saint-Simonians), the Abbé Baston (no: a Catholic mystic). You see that, sifted this way, there aren't many left."

"So much the better," said Purpulan.

"You'll make index cards all the same. Let's go on: ah here's Berbiguier. Very interesting, Berbiguier. Alexis-Vincent-Charles Berbiguier de Terre-Neuve du Thym, native of Carpentras, author of three octavo volumes, published in 1821, illustrated with a portrait and eight superb lithographs and entitled: *Sprites Or All Demons Are Not Of The Other World*. Do you want me to read you a passage?"

Purpulan, very uncomfortable, said: yes.

"Here, I put a bookmark here, in volume III, pages 148 and 149. It's the account of a combat with the Sprites. I'll begin: 'Several days later, I received a second letter from a legion commander of spritism, informing me that on the evening of that very day he would send a deputation of thirty sprites to learn of my decision and have my answer. This letter came from the royal authority of the sprites, for it bore the royal seal.

"'My only answer to this proposal was to get ready by arming myself with two hundred black pins, the longest I was able to find. I also equiped myself with a very pointed little instrument, very sharp, shaped like an awl. I waited for them thus until midnight, and I went to bed, with no intention of sleeping; I was too busy with my plan. I placed my hands between the sheet and the blanket. A quarter of an hour later, I heard the gibberish of their commander; and, at the agreed-upon signal of this infernal band, I saw myself assailed from every side. As soon as I felt their movements, I stabbed with my awl all those who had come near.

"'When they were caught, they tried to get away: I then ensured their captivity with black pins, which I stuck firmly into them;'"

" Ah."

"'which amused me a great deal. To increase my enjoyment, I got the idea of sticking pins from underneath my blankets, so they were caught from above and below.'"

"Monsieur Chambernac, please."

"'The number of my vanquished foes was twenty-five; my blanket was full of them, and so heavy that, in the morning, before getting up, I felt crushed under the weight of these wretches, who, all stabbed in various ways, were grimacing frightfully.

"'Rising, I wished them good day with blows of my awl.'"

At this point Chambernac noticed that Purpulan had passed out. He rushed to revive him according to classical procedure. Purpulan opened one eye.

"Come, come my young friend, how impressionable you are. Come, come, pull yourself together."

"Thank you, monsieur. I'm all right."

"Are you well enough to listen to me?"

"Yes, monsieur."

"In these three volumes by Berbiguier I marked a certain number of passages that seemed interesting to me. You will copy them."

Purpulan bowed his head.

"Later we'll do bibliographical research on this author. I think he's mentioned often in psychiatric literature. For that, we'll have to go to libraries: perhaps even to Paris. You'll come with me."

"Feliciter exit parum sapienter institutum."

"Egad," exclaimed the principal, "that's right, you know Latin. I remember, the first time, you spoke to me in that language. But didn't you tell me the other day that you weren't very well educated? Would you lie to me, Purpulan?"

"Oh no, monsieur. I regard myself as not very well educated. I know that in this day and age it's considered a great thing to know Latin, but in my opinion it's a bare minimum."

"Don't become conceited, Purpulan. And where did you learn this language?"

"I taught myself; I wanted to pass for a seminarian. It's a rather unusual story that I may tell you one day, Monsieur Chambernac."

"Now you're going to get to work, Monsieur Purpulan, and see to it that your index cards are written legibly."

"I am your humble servant, Monsieur de Chambernac."

BOOK TWO

XXII

Agnes had, once, slept with Denis, but that wasn't why she was going to marry him, in the month of November supposedly. Mme. Hachamoth had made the decision and, on this point, Agnes didn't mind obeying her mother. She didn't dislike Denis, inferior to her in all sports, even a bit too much so; he was a nice boy, but she'd have to see to his training. The company of this little male would not in the least disturb the course of her life, she'd pull him along behind her without dislike or regret. Marriage would change neither her tastes nor her occupations, since it would be only another form of idleness.

Agnes was convinced she lived a natural and healthy life, and even this union, coldly considered, seemed to her one of the most certain signs of her perfect stability. She believed that life on the beach was analogous to that of prehistoric man or at least of savages, more politely called primitive peoples, life on the beach with its suntan lotions, its waterslides, its two-piece swim suits and its lifeguards. She'd acquired, by dint of methodical application and thanks to good stock, a lithe and muscular body, resistant to all illness, skilled at all exercise, tanned, with small breasts and firm buttocks, and this body was her reference point in orienting her life and stabilizing her age, in creating an ever youthful identity. Proud and sure of herself, she calmly went her own sweet way, like a cow, browsing happiness in every moment with unvarying success.

The number of her worries was greatly limited: her grandfather's companies, her stepfather's business ventures, her mother's extravagances, her uncle's distinguished eccentricities were for her merely subjects of conversation, not preoccupation. In all this family agitation she saw only cause for tranquility. As for the behavior of her sister and brother she considered them such nonentities, that is so little bother, that they, her brother and sister, were for her only well-trained humans rounding off a pleasant decor. So Agnes was interested only in her muscles and her reflexes, her dresses and her beauty.

Naomi had stopped confiding in her years ago and made up for her sister's lack of curiosity with a ceaselessly active investigative mind, which had only one object: Astolphe. She did not content herself with collecting every story concerning him, she went so far as to follow him and bribe his valet. Astolphe was aware of all this and Naomi doggedly held out toward him every day a mirror in which, in spite of the secret collusion of the object, no coherent image was reflected. For she managed to collect only scattered acts, dissociated deeds, gossip and grimaces of her uncle's life, whether because this life actually was like that, or because its essentials escaped her. Enigma or disorder were for her one and the same misfortune.

Those little holes that Naomi had succeeded in piercing into the partition behind which Astolphe liked to busy himself, he'd caught sight of them at times when his life having clouded over to the point of darkness the light she moved from place to place in her efforts to see him better made them look like stars, but such dim ones that he could think they belonged to his night. So indifferent was he to these investigations that he'd sometimes let her glimpse all sorts of things about himself that she couldn't have begun to suspect; he'd talk away like that, not so she could complete her documentation, but because he thought he'd found in her a receptacle so fragile that it would invariably shatter when it received such strong drink and that thus even the reflection of his life would finally dissipate.

Agnes wasn't sure of the meaning of her sister's curiosities, and didn't know them all. She never thought of clarifying them. And if, on the other hand, she didn't hide an impassioned interest in all the new fashions her uncle would put into circulation, she had none at all in his person. Always ready to set off after him into some new fad she didn't suspect that he could be anything but a guide to novelty and had she understood it she wouldn't have let: that, distract her.

But the third Chambernac was completely indifferent both to the person and the deeds of his uncle and had no more curiosity for the former than infatuation with the latter. He was absolutely uninterested in what anyone, and particularly Astolphe, might do; not one of the others was concerned with him: neither with his deeds which were unobtrusive, nor with his thoughts, which in general they considered nonexistent, nor with his feelings, which they couldn't even begin to make out. The care and apparent detachment with which he applied himself to work and to pleasure put off the embryonic curiosity of his fellow beings. No one could get a handle on him. People finally didn't even notice him anymore. While Astolphe was like a schoolboy hiding his test paper with his arm, Daniel left his out in plain view: it was blank.

XXIII

Clemence, when they'd go out to eat in Toulon or follow Astolphe to gamble all night in Monte Carlo, Clemence would send Alice, Adrian and the cook dancing or to the movies, would wash their dishes, put everything away, drink a little glass of Fernet-Branca for her digestion, inspect the premises, click off all the switches behind her, go up to her room, position her music stand, set on it the chosen piece, pick up her violin, tune it and play the overture of the *Dame Blanche,* her favorite melody.

XXIV

After some days, not many, Astolphe dropped out of sight. He'd gone to Juan-les-Pins to meet friends who in turn soon noticed he'd disappeared. He stayed in Monte Carlo two nights, expecting to lose as he did when he was there with his family. He won. He left again for Genoa with a woman he'd picked up in Nice. Abandoning her on Italian soil, he set out once more in the opposite direction and stopped first in Villefranche. Then he deposited in his bank the money he'd saved, the eccentric.

XXV

Baron Hachamoth likes to be with people. He lunches with his friends, he dines with his relatives, he sups with his acquaintances. On these August days, he no longer has in Paris either acquaintances, or relatives, or friends, and there he is, suddenly feeling very much alone. And yet, he must go to lunch.

Where is he going to go for lunch? He might as well make it a good restaurant. But which one? Difficult to decide in this heat that makes you ooze dampness from your temples to the backs of your knees. The baron would gladly fan his underarms if good manners didn't forbid it. With no less pleasure, he would dehydrate the hair of his thorax, but there you are: good manners again. This tyranny does not on the other hand prevent a person from deciding on this or that place. It's indeed getting to be high time that Baron Hachamoth go to lunch.

In order to facilitate the functioning of his discursive faculties, he considers it a good idea to sit on the terrace of a café and have a drink. Apéritif or beer? The Claye-Chambernac family has only contempt for those who take beer before lunch, but since he's alone, he opts for this drink. He swallows his beer, exhales, wipes his balding pate. Where the devil is he going to have lunch? It would be absolutely ridiculous if in the end Baron Hachamoth did not go to lunch.

He knows more than one restaurant in Paris, more than one bar, more than one grillroom, more than one inn, more than one tavern, more than one club, more than one bistro even, (total ignorance on the subject of dairy bars). He knows what day and where you have to go to eat in Norman or to nosh in Swiss. He knows that here you can order wine in a carafe, a little savings from time to time is not to be sneezed at, and that there only wine with a label is acceptable. He knows that here the caviar is genuine and that there the camembert is not. He knows that here steaks sizzle and that there stews stew. He also knows that it's becoming absolutely urgent that he go to lunch.

His memory bristles with forks, is cluttered with menus. Each commune of France represents for him a (or several) revel, feast or costly satiation. His travels are marked with cookstoves and saucepans, with storerooms and cellars. He distends his itineraries to stuff himself in some inn recommended by professional culinographers. In this Paris of the month of August, which of their counsels is he going to follow, since he must go to lunch?

Moreover, he really can't complain about this Paris of the month of August, for he's taking advantage of certain absences to conclude a few business deals. Who would think of certain speculations at this time of year, if not he who from the Circumcision of Christ to New Year's Eve never rests. All the same, he's going to spend a few days in La Ciotat, not more than a week. He needs to relax. He's not a machine after all. And since he's not a machine, he must go to lunch.

What might he feel like having today? Goose conserve or salt pork with cabbage, duckling or cassoulet, bouillabaisse or country style blood pudding. And once the dish is chosen, where to get the best? He suddenly thinks about the people who have lunch just anywhere, without knowing, or rather on the contrary knowing only too well, some here for the sake of economy, others there there for the sake of snobbery. He envies them all, a bit like he envies tramps who live any which way, without cares, he certainly has cares, or gypsies, or convicts who no longer have to worry about their freedom, or provincials in very small towns, or even pious and devious old farmers whom fluctuations don't distress and who don't know the meaning of oil, sugar, pepper, and materials generally called raw. He compares the sum total of torments he takes upon himself with that of a shepherd, or a rabbi, an old rabbi naturally, or a Hasid, and then feels himself most unfortunate. And besides, he's gotten into this habit: bad lunch, day ruined. May this not be one of them and may he go to lunch.

What a lot of good meals he's had in his life, and how he's appreciated them. He could become ecstatic over each deserving plateful presented to him. It was not in vain that chefs cooked up and simmered, that restauranteurs sniffed melons and cheeses, that wine stewards sprinkled their magnificent bottles with dust: for he does not forget. Not a single day of his life when he didn't delight his palate, except during the war which the baron doesn't talk about in spite of his citations. He remembers only the present, a present rich in sauces and moistened with fine wines, a present which has in every street multiplied good skillets and in every neighborhood rotisseries, a present in which from every chimney waft subtle odors, a present resembling a huge meat pie fresh from the oven and bubbling at each hole pierced into it. All right, now all there's left to do is go to lunch.

He'll take the first street to the left and go at random into the first restaurant of said street. Which he does, and here is: the Duckling. Reading the menu, the baron is suddenly bored: Russian dishes don't tempt him; so he'll ask them to bring him a cold consommé, a slice of ham with spinach cooked in water and without cream and a bottle of Evian. Because for years and years now, Baron Hachamoth has been sentenced to mineral water and fresh vegetables.

After calculating with precision the ten per cent it was appropriate to leave with the check and abandoning about a franc in exchange for his Stetson, he was once more out in the sun. He started to walk toward the Opera, considering the succession of his steps as constituting a digestive walk. It was a subject he often changed his mind about, for he sometimes took a nap. For a moment he considered reopening the question and resolutely opted for a review of the good lunch he'd just had. The savor of the ham came immediately to mind, dominant, with all its variations from the outer layer of fat, which he ate in spite of doctor's orders, to the compact central eye. He tried to find among his memories an equivalent slice and found better only the one he'd eaten in Saulieu at the Côte-d'Or Hotel. Saulieu brought in its wake the terrible bilious attack that had struck him down there. At this awful remembrance, the baron's face lengthened like a rubber mask and his cheeks hung, flabby. In spite of the care he took to repress this image, Hachamoth couldn't help several times a day seeing before his eyes, or rather just behind: his liver, in the form of the leaf of a plane tree shriveled by autumn. When he got to the Café de la Paix

Shalom

, he

sat down, asked them to bring him a quarter-liter bottle of

Vichy water and, while around him foreigners, provincials and tourists thought they were in Paris and watched other tourists, provincials and foreigners walk by, undertook a meticulous and objective examination of the various aspects of his existence.

Wealth and visceral problems certainly appeared to be its two poles, but Hachamoth no more thought that money was happiness than he considered that liver ailments made his life intolerable. More than moolah, honors occupied an eminent place in the hierarchy of his happiness: the Legion of Honor, the presidency of the Association of Jewish Veterans, the friendship of politicians no less Christian than well-known. At the opposite end of the scale, Hachamoth heaped up his problems and worries, all big as mountains and he let contempt for the vanities and ambitions of this world sweep him away to the point of wishing he were a beggar. But at the center of these antitheses is the crown of his possessions: Sophie Hachamoth, the most beautiful and intelligent woman he's ever met.

> House and riches are the inheritance of fathers: and a prudent wife is from the Lord.
> (Proverbs XIX, 14)

Yes, Sophie is intelligent, there's nothing in her father's business affairs she doesn't know and little in those of her husband: moreover the baron is keeping a close eye on old Claye, and deplores what he's discovering. The struggle with the Lavasse agency is foolish, the American speculations dangerous, contempt for his competitors wrong. He has no doubts at all: old Claye's fortune is going to vanish. Not only old Claye's: Hachamoth scents imminent disaster.

Thus one unpleasant thought brings with it another, like a string of sausages. The mutt chooses only one but the others follow and in the end the quadruped gets a taste of sticks and stones. In quick succession, Hachamoth has drawn three unlucky numbers: the foolhardiness of his father-in-law, the deficiencies of capitalism, his children.

For he hasn't any.

Sophie brought him three, it's true, but all trained and who remembered their father, even Naomi who was only seven at the time of his last leave. Chambernac survives himself threefold, but for him there is no hope, for Sophie will bear no more children. He will therefore die without posterity.

> Then I returned, and saw vanity under the sun. There is one alone, and there is not a second; yea, he hath neither child nor brother: yet is there no end of all his labor; neither is his eye satisfied with riches; neither saith he, For whom do I labor, and bereave my soul of good? This is also vanity, yea, it is a sore travail.
>
> (Ecclesiastes IV, 7–8)

For whom *is* he working? For Sophie Claye, the widow Chambernac? For Daniel? For Agnes? For Naomi? There's an immense fortune already lying in wait for them, which it's true he considers jeopardized. He senses that, following some catastrophe which he scarcely dares imagine, it will be up to him to give his step-daughters dowries. The stream that flows into a river near its mouth doesn't widen its estuary and when the sweet water arrives at the sea it bears the name of the river and not that of the stream. Thus will die the name Hachamoth and his posterity will remain in his loins.

Amen.

"Garçon!"

In his office, he's back with truths that honor him, realities he touches, riches to manipulate. There he acts, that is he speaks, sometimes in front of devices that work by electricity, sometimes in front of a young person who very rapidly writes abbreviations with a pencil she can't help licking occasionally. Thus he creates truths that honor him, thus he touches realities, thus he manipulates riches.

> Again, I considered all travail, and every right work, that for this a man is envied of his neighbor. This is also vanity and vexation of spirit.
>
> (Ecclesiastes IV, 4)

Baron Hachamoth will leave this very evening for La Ciotat. There are lots of expresses at night for the South. He'll have dinner at the station buffet in the Gare de Lyon, which isn't a bad restaurant. He'll have a quarter-liter of Vichy in the dining car. And then he'll sleep.

XXVI

Naturally they'd gotten the best seats to watch Alain Gerbault play doubles with Brugnon against Raynaud and

Jean Vlasto. His victory by 8–6, 4–6, 6–1, 6–3 pleased everyone, naturally.

"A very nice young man," said Hachamoth.

"In what way?" asked Astolphe, who'd just reappeared in La Ciotat, a stop on his way to Sologne where he was going hunting.

"In every way. I think he's splendid that young man, to sail around the world all alone in a little boat. During all that time he was rid of all the problems that make your life miserable, tax collectors, competitors, the future."

"Bah," went Ast.

"What I appreciate in that young man is his taste for solitude. I envy him."

"I can't picture you on a eleven-meter cutter," said Astolphe.

"I have no trouble picturing you on one," said the baron mildly.

Ast almost blushed.

"You have a strange opinion of me."

"How can one help having a strange opinion of you." said Mme. Hachamoth. "My God, don't let people have strange opinions about me. I really go for that Alain Gerbault too. Months and months all alone, alone with the ocean and alone with God, what an ideal!"

The baron looked at his wife dazzled.

Astolphe inordinately annoyed left.

"Now you've had another argument with my brother," said Sophie.

"You think so?" asked Solomon.

"You annoyed him inordinately."

"That wasn't my intention."

"God alone knows intentions, my friend. You can't expect Astolphe to know yours. Anyway now he's angry. This touchiness is a bad sign, baron. Ast must be in love or be feeling suicidal bang bang. Something's bothering him. My God, let me discover what's bothering him. And Henry, there's something bothering him too. Ah we're living in a most bothered world; most mysterious. What about me, dear friend, don't you sometimes find me somewhat mysterious?"

"I always find you adorable."

"Hush! only God is adorable."

As for Astolphe he didn't adore anything and at that moment hatred was burbling in his heart so that he almost wished he were antisemitic. For he was angry only at the baron, who'd wanted to make fun of him. He ought to have his ears boxed, and Arnolphe too. The one sees him as a knight, the other a sailor, it was a real pain. Wasn't there anyone left who could appreciate an authentic originality, like his. He did, after all, have to excuse the baron, but Arnolphe was unforgiveable. Most certainly: he loved this Catherine Lescure (Lécure or Lesscure?).

He ran into Naomi.

"I was going for a walk," said Naomi. "I didn't feel like going to Toulon with the others".

She sat down next to him, near Cassis.

"Do you love?" Ast asked her.

"What do you mean?"

"I'm asking you whether you love: a man, a woman, anything."

"Let's not talk about that," said Naomi.

"But I want to talk about it. Listen, Naomi, I love: a woman whose name is the only thing I know."

A little farther along, Astolphe continued:

"Do you understand what I mean? What do you think?"

"You're free to love whomever you want however you want."

"That's an empty phrase, moralizing. Listen: she's a woman whose name I saw in the phone book. That's all. I love her. Why not?"

"Why not."

"That damn fool's trying to pass me with his Peugeot."

He stepped on the gas pedal.

"I get the feeling you're like Arnolphe: you think it sounds phony. I'd like to point out to you that I don't want to see this woman. Platonic, chivalrous love is obviously not a thing of our times. Shit. If only you'd say something. But no. Agnes would maybe at least tell me I'm an idiot. Naomi, when it comes right down to it, you're a strange person. You're even a curiosity, among so many chatterboxes, I mean people nowadays. There's that moron again, driving in my dust."

He stomped: he got more speed.

"What's this woman's name?" asked Naomi.

"Catherine Lécure or Lesscure, I don't know exactly how to pronounce it."

"And," asked Naomi, "what does your love consist of?"

"I think about her."

"How happy she must be, this Catherine, not to know she's loved," said Naomi.

A little farther along, to avoid an careless person, Astolphe flew into the greenery and crashed into a tree. Naomi, flung from the car, was picked up without notable contusions. Astolphe had a slightly sprained wrist. They'd just had what's commonly called an accident. A spectator took them back to La Ciotat, to consult the pharmacist, who was a nice fellow.

A garage man was summoned to bring back the car. Astolphe suggested going to the harbor for a drink. At Bossu's they'd already heard the news; the owner hurried over.

"Yes," his son was explaining to Gramigni, dressed in his Sunday best, "they're going to hire me at Claye, I'm going to go work in Paris. What's there for me to do here? I need room. Around here everybody's so provincial, they don't understand a thing. What I need is space. I've got ideas, inventions you know. They'll see what I'm worth in Paris, won't they though!"

He points to Astolphe:

"You see that guy there with his money, he can't even drive a damn car. I'm the one that ought to have a car, and not just any car, but a beaut."

Lardi who had just watched the last racers of the Byrrh Circuit sign in at the checkpoint sat down at Gramigni's table.

"You know I'm gonna work at Claye? The answer came. They think I'm good. You know, what I need is room, space. I need to fulfill myself and Paris is the only place I can fulfill myself."

"There's some that want to go to Paris and don't know," proverbialized Lardi, "and there's others that know and don't ever want to go back."

"What are you implying?" asked young Bossu testily.

"I'm talking about Alain Gerbault," said Lardi.

"That guy has a screw loose," said young Bossu. You've got to be nuts to live all alone on a boat for years. I'm not like that, I want company, and women, 'specially women. Ah, when I think that I'm gonna be able to do some real work and earn heaps of dough, I feel like I'm streaking into the air like a rocket."

"You think you're a foreman already," said Lardi.

"Engineer you mean. I'll go to night school and get qualified. I'll really pull out all the stops. Ah, old buddy I've got what it takes not to stagnate in a corner. And besides I'll have somebody to pull strings for me: the girls, you know."

A wink and a grimace indicated Naomi.

Gramigni's watching her. In one month maybe even sooner she'll be gone again, then darker days will come back shorter days and then winter. He'll no longer see these beautiful rich girls whose mere existence is enough to make you feel alive.

"You're getting carried away," said Lardi.

"I'm telling you they'll pull strings for me with the big boss."

"If you think in Paris they'll have time to think about you," said Lardi, "they won't even remember your name. That's the way those people are."

"Yes, but I'm not going to let myself be pushed around. I'll remind them what my name is. I want to live, I don't want to be crushed."

"So he went around the world all alone in a little boat," asked Gramigni, coming back to an earlier stage of the conversation.

"What?" asked Bossu junior, who wanted to make further revelations concerning his person.

"Alain Gerbault?" asked Lardi. "Yes. Whim of a guy that doesn't have to work to earn his bread and butter."

"Gotta be cracked to live like that I'll say it again," said young Bossu.

"Maybe it's real nice to live like that," said Gramigni, "you don't have anybody around anymore to bother you."

"Your wife, for instance," said Lardi, laughing.

"When people bother me I break 'em," said Bossu the younger.

"That might be fun," said Lardi, "but you can't have anything else to do," said Lardi.

"What do you mean," asked Gramigni.

"I mean you have to really think just about yourself."

"Everybody thinks just about himself," said young Bossu.

"Not at all," said Lardi.

"You mean to say you don't think just about yourself?" asked Bossu junior.

"Yes."

"What do you think about then?"

"I think about all my buddies that are in jail on the other side of the border, and on this side too."

"You've got depressing thoughts. I think Mussolini's a big joke."

"Ask him," said Lardi, pointing to Gramigni, "if he thinks Mussolini's a big joke, with his two brothers dead because of him."

"Let's not talk about that," said Gramigni, "let's not talk politics."

"He's right," said Bossu junior, "your country's troubles are a pain in the ass."

XXVII

To get to Sologne, where he was going hunting, Astolphe was going to pass through Mourmèche. Agnes asked him to take her there. As soon as the car was in driving condition again, Astolphe, for whom the area had lost all appeal since the accident, left with his niece. Both of them wanted to find out a little more about Monsieur H. de Chambernac's research.

In the eyes of the Claye-Chambernacs, the principal of the high school in Mourmèche was a kind of gentle, academic deviant, without capabilities (how could they assess that?) and without fortune. But he held an important place in each one's memories, as much because of some whimsically comical show of learning as because of an obvious ignorance of worldly things. Since the (heroic) death of his brother, they'd pretty much forgotten him. Sophie's caprice, Astolphe's interest made him an important person again, at least for Agnes.

Agnes had not only studied under the direction of pious minds as her mother wished but had also gone to the Sorbonne and better yet the Collège de France where one can free of charge hear the wild imaginings of the best representatives of French science, those that've really made it, that know how to pompously titillate with their paradoxes the dormant intelligence of the donkeys of the faubourg Saint-Germain and the xvɪth arrondassment. From the Sorbonne you easily progress to an acquaintance with avant-garde publications like the *Revue de Paris*, the *Nouvelle Revue Française* and then the *Revue Européenne*. Thus Agnes was well aware that mental pathology was of primordial importance in shaping the world-view of the cultured people of her day: four dimensions whose solid pillars and firm supports are one multiplied by the square root of negative one, the inferiority complex, primitive mentality and the Kantas. Thus also, since her uncle seemed to be one of those scholars whose work greases the slopes that the snobversations of the people she frequented would troll upon, she hoped, by making a date and going right to the source, to one-up her co-saloners and nesses, her co-tennismen and wimmin and her co-modes.

They arrived in Mourmèche in the afternoon, not many days before the beginning of September. The maid who came to let them in informed them that monsieur was in Paris, but if they wanted to see madame. They were hesitating, for they didn't like her, when there appeared a young man, of modest bearing but nonetheless not without elegance and who introduced himself as M. de Chambernac's secretary.

"I thought his secretary was an old study hall supervisor," said Astolphe in an offhand way. "At least that's what he told me."

"He changed secretaries, sir," said Purpulan. "How can I be of service?"

"I would so much have liked him to tell me about his lunatics," said Agnes.

"M. de Chambernac is indeed admirably conversant with the question," said Purpulan. "His erudition on this subject is phenomenal and the work he's writing will be a sensation. Unfortunately M. de Chambernac is presently in Paris, working in the libraries."

Agnes was sorry.

"M. de Chambernac," continued Purpulan, "is working on what he hopes will be an exhaustive list of all the authors who wrote on the Squaring of the Circle."

The two visitors whom this news had made rather morose, said nothing. Purpulan suggested they take a look at M. de Chambernac's library. Agnes read a few titles that seemed most uninteresting; so she feared that Astolphe had played a trick on her, or even worse: that he himself had gone astray.

"Although it's far from complete," explained Purpulan, "this collection is unique in France and almost all these works are extremely rare. M. de Chambernac would certainly have shown you the most curious of them. Will you permit me to be so bold as to stand in for him? But since I haven't the competence of my esteemed master, I'll merely tell you about the life of a squarer or rather choose for you the most important passages of his autobiography."

Though terrified at the idea that they might be bored, Agnes and Astolphe assented.

"He dictated it to one of his admirers," continued Purpulan, "for he had admirers, and, besides, he didn't know how to read or write."

"The fortunate man," said Astolphe.

"Delightful," said Agnes.

Purpulan took from the bookcase a little booklet that he told them was entitled *Ratio of the Diameter to the Circumference*, published in Paris in 1856. After coughing twice, he began to read the following:

XXVIII

"'Joseph Lacomme was born in Craste, the department of Gers, on March 3, 1792, of a decent family of farmers, but no less ignorant than poor… At the age of twelve, Joseph Lacomme, already strong, entered into the service of a farmer…

"'At sixteen, he was apprenticed to a weaver, and after two months he was more skilled than his master, who then took him on as a journeyman and paid him accordingly.

"'At nineteen, fate called him into military service and he left for Spain… He was discharged at the fall of Napoleon, was married, and went into business as a weaver, continuing to improve his craft… In 1836, having begun to dig a well, he wanted, when it was dug, to know precisely how many freestones he would need to pave its bottom. To this end, he went to see the head mathematics teacher of the high school in Auch, and told him the diameter of the well. The teacher answered that it was impossible to tell him exactly, since no one had yet established the exact ratio of the circumference to the diameter.

"'This answer aroused in Joseph Lacomme a strong curiosity, and an ardent desire to solve this problem. Although they told him that the greatest geometers had given up, and that nowadays anyone who seriously tried to find the answer was considered a lunatic, he nevertheless decided to consecrate to it his life, his faculties and his means. He consequently sold all his looms and all the possessions he had acquired through his work, and there he was, working on his problem from morning till night, almost always at the bottom of his well, lining up and measuring freestones, and trying in every way possible to make this great discovery.

"'Unfortunately, his resources, for obtaining such marvelous results, were quite limited; for not only did he not know how to read or write, but he did not even know numbers. Thus, when he was told that Archimedes had found that the approximate ratio of the circumference to the diameter was as 22 is to 7, Newton, as 3.14 is to 1 and Metius, as 355 to 113, it was all Greek to him. But he did not give up and, in order to teach himself numbers, he invented a very simple method which demonstrated great will power. He went to Auch, and, starting at the first house of the longest street, he examined the numeral 1, which he copied, then turning, he copied the numeral 2, then 3 and 4, and so on, to the other end of the street. In this way he learned not only to form the numerals, but also to write all the consecutive numbers up to the numeral on the last house, which exceeded the number 100. That was all he needed to figure out the law of the formation of numbers in the decimal system, and even more, spoken and written numeration. Then combining the numbers in his own way, he discovered an astonishing method of multiplication and division, which shortens these operations considerably, and he soon became a great calculator.

"'Once in possession of arithmetic, he found, by means of some practical experiments, and by having someone make him hollow solids, such as cubes, cylinders and spheres, by filling them with water and weighing them, he found, I say, that the true ratio of the circumference to the diameter is as 25 is to 8, which is indeed the exact ratio, and does not leave a remainder after the third decimal.

"'When this discovery became known, he was asked to submit it to the Academy of Sciences in Toulouse for assessment, and he went there without delay. It was in 1837, that is one year after the digging of his well.

"'The academicians of this learned city examined his result with much distrust, for they considered Lacomme a lunatic rather than a serious inventor. But the latter, who did not leave a stone unturned to make sure, by means of a thousand verifications, of the accuracy of his report, suggested that he cube, according to his method, the pool of the fountain in the Place des Carmes, which he did at midnight, by moonlight, in order to be alone and at peace. But plainclothes policemen, who had him under surveillance, arrested him and took him to the lockup, since they also considered him a lunatic. He stayed there for a week on bread and water, without anyone paying further attention to him. On the seventh day, a prisoner, who was a trusty, presumed to insult him and call him a lunatic. He was even so mean as to tell him that he was suspected of theft, since they had found whistles on him (which were actually only cubic inches that he used to check his calculations), and that he would soon be put into solitary.

"'Joseph Lacomme, justly indignant, answered that if he wanted to take the trouble to come into the cell, he had other whistles to give him. This trusty, who was something of a giant, accustomed to baiting and even beating the prisoners, entered resolutely to teach him a lesson; but he found himself on the receiving end...

"'Although Lacomme had acted in legitimate self-defense, he was remanded in custody; but two days later they had him taken to Auch, as a lunatic. He made the trip from Toulouse to L'Ile en Jourdain, in a driving rain. It therefore goes without saying that when he arrived he was soaked to the skin, and his feet were lacerated. He was nonetheless upon his arrival at L'Ile en Jourdain, thrown into a damp dungeon...

"'The next morning, he had to put on his frost-stiffened clothing, for it was the month of January and leave barefoot on the ice.

"'Upon his arrival in Gimont they lodged him with a genuine lunatic, and he spent the night in the same room; but there at least they gave him a bed and food, they dried his clothes, in short, they took care of him, and the next day, he was able to set out and get to Auch, hobbling along; for although he had no shoes and his feet were lacerated, he nevertheless had to walk fifteen more leagues on the ice…

"'When he arrived in Auch, he was taken before the prefect… But this worthy magistrate… judging him to be much less crazy than those who had had him arrested, at once ordered his release.

"'So many vexations, fatigues and torments having affected his health, he went, on the advice of his friends, to Bagnères-de-Bigorre, to recover. There, since all he spoke of to everyone was his problem, the other people taking the waters also considered him a maniac and made fun of him fairly openly… But when a policeman also ventured to tease him, and he felt he could answer him in the same tone, the policeman boxed his ears. Then Lacomme, who is uncommonly strong, seized him and threw him to the ground as he would a child. The entire brigade soon arrived to put him in prison, but he declared that he would permit them to put him there only after he had spoken to the king's prosecutor. They then wanted to use force, but to no avail, for he knocked over all who laid a hand on him, beginning with the brigadier, whom he was holding suspended in the air, at arm's length, when the king's prosecutor arrived. He found it very easy to justify himself to this magistrate, who, upon seeing that he had merely acted in self-defense, ordered him released at once, and sharply rebuked the policemen, who had exceeded the bounds of their authority.

"'Still concerned with his problem, Joseph Lacomme

went to Bordeaux in 1839, to submit the results of his work to the Philomathic Society, which did not act upon his request. In order to make a living, he was obliged to give lessons in arithmetic, according to his method, which offered him but meager resources…

"'Plunged into a sort of despair, and having moreover exhausted his resources, he found no better expedient, to arouse interest and publicize his discovery, than to pick a quarrel with a policeman over nothing at all, and thus put himself into a state of revolt against the police force. He was consequently thrown into prison and charged in criminal court. There, before his judges, in the presence of a large audience, he confessed his stratagem and obtained the permission of the presiding judge to prove that he was not crazy, by explaining his discoveries in arithmetic and geometry. The tribunal, spellbound, acquitted him unanimously, and, knowing that he had no money, forthwith started a fund in his aid, which enabled him to return to his country, after having achieved in Bordeaux a triumph of sorts, which earned him a certain celebrity…

"'Lacomme then went to live in Guitre, near Libourne, making no mention of his precious discovery, devoting himself exclusively to agriculture… But Joseph Lacomme, who could not forget his problem, left Guitre in 1854, to come to Paris and submit his discovery to the Academy of Sciences and to the other learned societies. But he met only with unbelief, and had to return to Guitre.

"'Hoping to be more successful in 1855 than the preceding year, he returned to Paris, but with no better results, and returned a second time to his point of departure, much annoyed, but not at all discouraged.

"'Finally, toward the end of the same year, he burned all his bridges behind him, by selling all that he possessed in Guitre, and left a third time for Paris, convinced that justice would finally be done.

"'At first all the steps he took were of no avail, and his cause seemed hopelessly lost, when Providence appeared to lead him by the hand to the honorable M. Vinter, police commissioner of the Place-Royale district… It was under this patronage that he was able to contact the president of the Society of Sciences and Arts of Paris…'"

XXIX

"…which awarded him a medal of honor," continued Purpulan. "What is more, a certain M. Husson, a city building inspector in Paris, issued him a certificate which ends as follows: 'his experiments on the problem of the Squaring of the Circle seem to me to be conclusive, and… what is more they reveal, in this capable professor, who can neither read nor write, a great genius turned wholly toward the exact sciences.'"

"Why not?" said Astolphe.

"What you've read us is rather boring," said Agnes.

"In any case," continued Astolphe, "I don't see how this Lacomme was crazy. Maybe he'd discovered how to square the circle after all?"

"Squaring the circle is a geometry problem," answered Purpulan, "and Lacomme thought he could solve it through experimentation."

"Well, he was wrong: which happens to lots of people who aren't called crazy," said Astolphe.

"And besides," said Agnes, "I have a feeling a true lunatic would write more interesting things."

"That's what I was thinking too," said Astolphe.

"Very disappointing," said Agnes.

They got up and, without further delay, left. Astolphe drove Agnes to a train station from which she could return South.

The last put-put of Astolphe's car had just faded out on the horizon when Mme. de Chambernac came into the study.

"Wasn't someone here?"

"A man named Cramm and a young lady Chambernac," answered Purpulan, "of your husband's family."

"Didn't you tell them I was here?"

"That's not my job. Carotte must have."

"They knew I was here and they left just like that? What boors!"

"They're even worse," said Purpulan. "They're stupid."

"Purpulan!"

"There's no way around it: they're stupid, and pretentious on top of everything else. If you'd seen that Cramm, what a show-off. I would like to have crapped on his schnoz, the shit."

"Purpulan, in my presence, you're going too far."

"He's made me so damn mad. He didn't think my Lacomme was loony enough! A conceited jerk, madame, that's what he is, a conceited jerk, and what's more, as you said it so well yourself, a boor. Just imagine, madame, he makes me read the life of a lunatic, and then he calls it boring. That's impolite. Don't you think so, madame? And naturally the young woman who was with him always had to go him one better."

"And that young lady is my niece! And she left just like that! It's inconceivable! My niece!"

"Which one?"

"The older one, Agnes. I'm outraged," continued Mme. de Chambernac.

Purpulan exasperated, shrugged his shoulders.

"Right, well now, madame, I'd like to work."

Mme. de Chambernac went out repeating her I'm outraged. In a traditional gesture, Purpulan held his head in his hands. The froth of rage was swamping his cerebellum. He couldn't dismiss Astolphe and Agnes' insulting behavior. He was thinking of vengeance. Unfortunately, since he'd signed that pact with Chambernac, he couldn't use as he pleased the fiendish powers with which he was afflicted. So the expressions of his hatred were reduced to human limits, all too human: murder, the anonymous letter, and slander. But even then in order to be able to use them with any sort of facility, he needed to know a bit more than he did about the habits of his two visitors and the company they kept. So he decided pronto to get some inside dope from his employer.

XXX

Mme. Chamb. stretched out on a love seat was reading. Before her blazed a little wood fire. It was very pretty.

Mme. Chamber. was not reading; she was trying to. Quivers of anger were sapping all her attempts at it. The blazing fire was dying. It looked sad.

Mme. Chambernac saw Purpulan sit down near her. He teased the fire and a few flames started up again.

"This Astolphe, what does he do?" he asked.

"Why nothing at all. He has private means."

"Married?"

"Oh no."

"Mistresses? A mistress?"

"I have no idea."

"You're naive, madame. Do you really think he's celibate?"

Mme. Chambernac blushed.

"Let's say then," continued Purpulans: "mistresses. By the way, could he be a homosexual?"

"What's that?"

"Delightful naiveté!" simpered Purpulan. "A homosexual is a genlman that paws another genlman; and all the rest."

"That's not possible," exclaimed Mme. Chambernac. "But I don't know if I'm following you very well."

"Well yes, they make love to each other, you know."

"How awful! That's horrible!"

"Bah!"

"Besides, I don't see how they would do that."

Purpulan shook his head sadly.

"I'd have to use gestures to explain it to you."

Mme. Chambernac frowned, less offended than intrigued. But Purpulan side-stepped suddenly:

"Let's get back to the subject, to our jackasses, to our ninnies, to this little miniature farmyard formed by your goose of a niece and that beast of a Cramm."

"Funny farmyard," went Mme. Chambernac: a beast…"

"Where does this Astolphe live?" asked Purpulan, annoyed.

"Why I haven't the slightest idea," protested Mme. Chambernac. "I hardly know him."

Purpulan sighed.

"And your niece, you must after all be slightly acquainted with your niece."

"Not well either. Since our marriage, my husband has not seen much of his sister-in-law's family, and I either, as a result."

"You *have* heard about them."

"But, Monsieur Purpulan, what are you driving at with this third degree? You're acting like a public prosecutor."

"I want to get even. Those people insulted me: I want to get even."

"They've certainly insulted me a lot worse than they've insulted you. And yet I don't want to get even. If you'd had a Christian upbringing…"

"Let's not talk about that," went Purpulan.

"Oh I didn't mean to give offense," said Mme. Chambernac, taking his hand. "But tell me, what did those people do to you?"

"Well they came to see your husband, to get him to talk. They're interested in what he's doing. I tried to take his place. I read them the life of a squarer."

"What's that again?"

"I'll explain that with gestures too."

Mme. Chambernac abruptly dropped his hand.

"So I read that to them. And they didn't like it. They wanted something nuttier. A lot they know about it. And they left with scornful looks that no decent man could put up with, by all the gods!"

"You can't torment yourself over such unimportant things."

"It's not myself I'm going to torment, it's them."

"I forbid it."

"By what authority?"

"Are you not our most humble servant?"

"Let's get this straight: I signed a pact with M. Chambernac, not with you."

"Ah, ah, you want to act independent, my little Purpu. You don't know me, I see. I may be naive, but I'm not weak. You will obey me. I forbid you to think any longer about your stupid plans of vengeance."

"Very well madame."

"Do you understand: not even the slightest thought."

"Very well madame."

"And now let me read. Go on, I'm the only one who's been insulted in this matter. You'll give me the explanations with the gestures some other time."

Purpulan got up, bowed and went out.

XXXI

On a nasty September night, rainy and fit only for a dog, in the third-class waiting room completely saturated with night, Purpulan was waiting for the midnight seventeen train which was to bring back Chambernac after a two-week stay in Paris.

Hands in his pockets, Purpulan pressed against the pane of glass in the door a forehead heavy with dull worry. He felt very young and the malice of men seemed very great, that of women surpassing it, that of Mme. Chambernac supreme. But he hadn't known how to talk to her either; and his dialectical deficiencies, when he thought about them, made him want to cry. Four years of this slavery lay before him.

Purpulan had been told there was only one way to handle women, when you're reduced to ordinary and purely human means: you have to make love to them. With Carotte, that didn't make sense, and there would have been no point in it. As to Mme. Chambernac, he found her completely impervious; maybe he didn't know how to go about that either. In short, contrary to all the customs of the civilized western world, Purpulan had neither cuckolded his master, nor assaulted the maid.

It was doubtless all these shortcomings that made the heart of the poor devil so melancholy, while he was watching with pale, glazed eyes the gleaming, icy tracks of the Mourmèche station. A worker started to walk about with a lantern that looked like a will-o'-the-wisp in the rain. Purpulan lamented his fate: lighting up swamps with an intermittant glow seemed to him a fate far better than tormenting humankind with only limited means at his disposal.

The train coming into the station cut through his thoughts. A few travelers scurried along the platforms. M. Chambernac and his suitcase came toward the gate.

"Well, hello, Purpulan. It's nice of you to come get me at the station. What's new?"

"Ah, Monsieur, all sorts of unpleasant things, as much for you as for me."

"I'm surprised."

Purpulan, disconcerted by such optimism, continued with feeling:

"Very unpleasant. But I can't tell you about it here."

Since the only taxi of Mourmèche had already found a customer, M. Chambernac and his secretary hurried through the rainy night. Purpulan was carrying the suitcase, heavy with papers.

"I got a lot done," began the principal.

"That's nice," said Purpulan, "but let me tell you."

"You could at least ask me if I've had a good trip."

"Ah, Monsieur," exclaimed Purpulan, setting the luggage down in the mud, "let me tell you, just let me tell you about all the unpleasant things that happened while you were gone, as much to me as to you. To begin with: I committed with Mme. de Chambernac the sin of adultery."

"Find something better next time," said Chambernac. "Your slander's a bit too naive, Monsieur Purpulan. Don't let me catch you at it again. All right, all right. Now tell me what's happened to me that's so unpleasant."

"What's happened to me," corrected Purpulan.

"I was joking," said Chambernac.

Purpulan sighed, then picked up the suitcase and set out again.

"Company came to see you about ten days ago. Mlle. Agnes de Chambernac and M. Astolphe de Cramm."

"That was nice of them," said Chambernac. "I never see them. Oh, wait a minute, Astolphe did come in August, in the middle of the night. What did they want?"

"To get you to talk about your work."

"You see, Purpulan, people are already getting interested. And I know others."

"I didn't want them to leave without getting some idea of it. I took the liberty of reading them the life of Lacomme."

"That was a mistake. For that matter I plan to leave him out of my book, because he's not strictly speaking the author of that booklet. He only dictated it: that's not enough for me. Just like with Berbiguier, I discovered in Reboul's book, *Anonymous and Pseudonymous Authors and Literary Hoaxes of Provence*, that he wasn't the one who put together his *Sprites*, but François-Vincent Raspail and a lawyer named Brunel; the introduction is even entirely by this Raspail. And besides, he's too well-known: he's in all the dictionaries, even in the one on the occult sciences by Migne; Champfleury and Larchey talk about him; Doctor Frachoux, a childhood friend I met in Paris, by chance, in the middle of a crosswalk, we even almost got run over, he's very interested in psychiatry, I talked to him about Berbiguier and he told me that the expression 'demonopath, type Berbiguier' was sometimes used by specialists, you see, he's too well-known for me. And what did Astolphe say about Lacomme?"

"It bored him and the young lady too."

"I can understand that."

Purpulan sighed again and very deeply. The principal shrugged his shoulders:

"What was it you went and told me a little while ago? Adultery! With Mme. de Chambernac! Are you crazy? Crazy! I mean: you're awfully scatterbrained to tell me such twaddle. And Carotte, I hope you didn't try to debauch her? For that matter, I'm sure you wouldn't have gotten anywhere: I've tried myself. She's a decent girl."

In front of the high school door, Chambernac stopped:

"But tell me, Purpulan, you're young, you seem to be well-formed, would you by any chance be celibate? If not, what do you do? Do you go to the brothel or, something I'd really deplore, do you indulge in self-abuse?"

"Formerly, sir, that is before I signed that pact with you, I practiced incuby; not often for that matter, for I'm not very hot-blooded. And now, I'm waiting; I'm waiting for better days."

"In short, you're celibate."

"Yes, monsieur."

"Then you really did lie to me, with your story about my wife."

"Alas yes, monsieur. What do you expect, sir, Larousse says it: a devil is someone who slanders."

"So, you did lie about it?"

"Yes, sir."

"I'm glad to hear you say so, because I wasn't all that sure."

XXXII

The next morning, Chambernac brought Purpulan up to date on the research he'd done during the two weeks he'd spent in Paris.

"We now have sixty-four squarers; some are in my library, others I found in the *Bibliographie De France*: a job you could have done by the way and besides there must be some that have escaped me, and then the others I found them mentioned in books devoted to the matter, look here's my bibliography."

And he handed him the following paper:

J. E. Montucla, *History Of Research On The Squaring Of The Circle*, Paris, 1754. New edition by Lacroix, Paris, 1831.

History Of The Royal Academy Of Science, Paris, 1775, pp. 61–66.

Condorcet, *Letter To The National Assembly Of 28 January 1791, Works*, Paris, 1847– 1849, vol. I, p. 525.

A. de Morgan, *A Budget Of Paradoxes*, London, 1872.

Haton de la Goupillière, in *Review Of Scientific Work For The Year 1884*, pp. 221–224.

Hermann Schubert, "The Squaring Of The Circle In Qualified And Unqualified Minds, A Study In Cultural History," in *Collection Of Scientific Lectures For The Lay Reader*, New Issue, Third Series. No. 67, Hamburg, 1889.

G. Maupin, *Opinions And Curiosities Concerning Mathematics*, Paris, 1898; 2nd series, Paris, 1902.

Rouse-Ball, *Mathematical Recreation*, 2nd ed., Paris, 1908 vol. II, pp. 309–321.

E. W. Hobson, *'Squaring the Circle,' A History Of The Problem*, Cambridge, 1913.

For proof of the impossibility of the squaring of the circle, cf. Félix Klein, *Lessons On Certain Questions Of Elementary Geometry*, Paris, 1896, pp. 10, 67, 73 and 94–96.

Ed. Maillet, *Introduction To The Theory Of Transcendant Numbers And Arithmetical Properties Of Functions*, Paris, 1906, ch. IX, pp. 147–160.

"And now here's the summary list of my squarers," said Chambernac handing to the crushed Purpulan another list, no less weighty.

XXXV

Jules Adde, Algiers, 1863.
A. L. F., Brest, 1843.
Silvestre Agussol, Paris, 1812, 1813.
J. F. d'Attel de Luttange, Metz, 1842.
The anonymous author of the rue du Four, Paris, 1828.
The anonymous author of the rue Copeau, Paris, 1843.
An anonymous Parisian, Paris, 1843.
Beaupied, Paris, 1829 (3).
Bobée-Galli, Paris, 1872, 1875.
L. A. Boillot, Paris, 1817.
Borucki, Dijon, 1847.
J. C. G. Bosquet, Bar-le-Duc, 1873.
Bourdillat, Paris, 1881 (2).
E. Bourgeois, Paris, 1890.
A. Callamel, Avignon, 1843.
C. F. D., Besançon, 1846; Paris, 1847.
J. B. Cheval, Avranches, 1829 (2), Paris, 1829, 1830.
F. Chicouras, Montpellier, 1888, 1891.
Martin de Corteuil, Paris, 1858.
L. Darget, Auch, 1875, 1899.
Delhommeau the elder, Béziers, 1868.
J. B. J. Dessoye, Paris, 1862.

P. E. Dupoux, Paris, 1890.

Félix Dupouy, Auch, 1837; Agen, 1839.

A. Favre, Saint-Maixent, 1837; Paris, 1866.

Fondary, Paris, 1869; Lyon, 1872; Paris, 1873; Dijon, 1876.

Onorato Gianotti, Paris, 1874 and 1875.

P. J. Goubet, Arras, 1882.

B. Graffeilhe, Limoges, 1879.

Grossin-Dubois, Paris, 1814.

L. Guion, Nîmes, 1898.

Hourcastremé, Paris, 1804.

> (cf. L. Barcave, *Pierre Hourcastremé de Navarreux*, Orthez, 1896 and G. Flaubert, "Preface" to the *Works of Bouilhet*, Paris, 1880)

> L. Karcher, Paris, 1867.

> Joseph Klimaszewski, Paris, 1895.

Joseph Lacomme, Bordeaux, 1838, 1847, 1854; Paris, 1854, 1855, 1856 (2), 1857, 1860; Bordeaux 1862 (2), 1867, 1869; Paris, n. d.

Abbé Lagay, Lyon, 1882, 1888.

F. Lagleize, Paris, 1853.

J. V. Lambert, Epinal, 1867.

A. G. Lanzirotti, Paris, 1873.

J. A. Laur, Paris, 1854.

R. P. Le Geay, Lyon, 1833; Paris, 1840.

M. Lhéritier, Bourges, 1873 to 1876 (9).

J. P. Lucas, Paris, 1844.

J. M Magnin, Lyon 1862; Paris, 1869.

J. Maigron, Montpellier, 1866.

Malacarne, Paris, 1824, 1825, 1826, 1827, 1828, 1829, 1833, 1840.

G. A. Mansion, Paris, 1871.

L. P. Matton, ?, 1862,; Lyon, 1875 to 1878 (9); 1888.

A. Mérault, Paris, 1882.

M. Miladowski and A. Izbicki, Paris, 1850, 1851, 1852.

Moat, Bar-le-Duc, 1871, 1874.

E. V. de N., Caen, 1869.

O'Donnelly, Brussels, 1853, 1854; Paris, 1856, 1857.

Pierre Petit (of Dreux), Paris, 1815.

A. L. Poirier, Le Havre, 1893.

Potier-Deslaurières, Paris, 1804.

L. F. Poussard, Paris, 1875, 1876, 1879.

F. Raynot, Périgueux, 1852; Brussels, 1856.

C. J. Recordon, Lausanne, 1865.

Ruthiger, Paris, 1817, 1821.

N. J. Sarrazin, Pont-à-Mousson, 1816, 1817, 1819 (2), 1821,
    1831, n. d. (circa 1835), 1836, 1837, 1838; Metz, 1840.
    Tahy, Toulon, 1835.

    H. Vanleem, Paris, 1892.

    A. E. Vaucher, Lyon, 1895.

XXXVI

"And then there are the trisectors of the angle," added
Chambernac, "and the duplicators of the cube, and those
who wrote on perpetual motion, and that anonymous writer
from Tours (1845) who didn't want all right angles to be
equal, and I have the impression that, among all those who
worked on Fermat's theorem, we could pick up a few sub-
jects. The squarers will do us nicely. One must know how to
choose. Regarding Fermat's theorem, you know, do you
know? of course you don't know, that in 1907 the University

of Göttingen established a prize of 100,000 marks to reward the first rigorous proof of this theorem. Now, many squarers imagine that an equally impressive sum will reward their efforts. You see, it's the love of lucre that pushes people like this into fruitless research. Money, money, always money. Money and stupidity are the two mainsprings of humanity. I can be a philosopher when the fancy takes me."

"Yes, monsieur."

"Good. Well, now, you're going to bring my notes on all these people up to date. Purpulan, I must confess: all these squarers really disappointed me. Reading their works is really dreary and monotonous. They're all ignoramuses who want cheap glory: what attracts them is that you don't seem to need much knowledge of geometry to solve such a simple problem; and most of them don't even understand its terms. Their confessions of ignorance are sometimes amazing. Delhommeau the elder, for example, in his pamphlet entitled *The Mysterious Or Geometric Ball With Two Thousand Five Hundred Facets And Four Different Points Of View*, writes, wait let me find the quotation, ah here it is: 'One day when I did not know what to do with my ideas, I took a Ball and, considering it attentively, I understood that it enclosed something serious, difficult even, for determining its surface area and its volume. It is true, too, that I had never studied geometry.'"

"Neither have I," said Purpulan. "I let you talk, but I don't even know what it's all about, really."

"Don't worry," said Chambernac absent-mindedly, rereading his notes.

Suddenly he expectorated violently due to a powerful guffaw that seized him.

"I'm thinking about what you were telling me awhile ago, as we were coming in. Look, do you know what in-cubi and su-cubi were for N. J. Sarrazin, a man of independent means in Metz, who felt that the Pythagorean theorem was an unspeakable absurdity which could lead one into Manichaeism, hm? Well, for him in-cubi and su-cubi were geometric figures that fit into each other."

Having explained himself, he went off into another sputtering fit of laughter.

"Nihil agis nisi nugas," said Purpulan. "Aufer cavillam."

Chambernac stopped laughing. It always upset him when his secretary spoke Latin.

XXXVII

The baron was the first to leave, then Mme. Hachamoth, then Daniel then the two sisters. Gramigni saw the season fade, collapse then dissolve in the late September rains. In October, the weather turned nice again. Clemence remained the sole inhabitant of the villa, and every day, perched on a velocipede, she came to do her marketing in La Ciotat.

For some years she had patronized a fruit and vegetable store on the Rue des Poilus; they waited on her attentively and gave her full measure. But it so happened that the greengrocer, happy rival of Gramigni, expanded his business and took on a new clerk, one who didn't like the weak and who hung pussy-cats and kitties from bells and tied tin cans to dogs' tails. This customer, quite nearsighted, rather hunchbacked and slightly lame, meticulous as well, and demanding, this cripplish being displeased him and by means of studied snubs he succeeded in removing her from his sight. Clemence, who had dignity, withdrew her patronage from the Rue des Poilus and put it into the hands of the Italian.

When Gramigni saw her enter his souk for the first time, it made him drop a can of Portuguese sardines. And while he was picking up his canned goods, Clemence had at once begun to appraise his merchandise.

"I've seen better melons," she said.

"They're the last of the season," said Gramigni.

"What about your muscat grapes, are they good?"

"I'll give you a sample," said Gramigni.

His manners were good and his merchandise quite acceptable. Clemence fell into the habit of shopping at his store. And so they got to know each other.

"So just like that," said Gramigni, "you spend the whole winter all alone in the villa?"

"I'm the caretaker," said Clemence.

"You're not afraid to be all alone in the villa all winter long like that?"

"Most certainly not, I'm not afraid."

She laughed tetanically, like a frog leg on a dissecting table.

She couldn't explain to him that she wasn't afraid because she wasn't afraid; that fear didn't mean anything to her; that she was plenty busy with the house and the cooking, she took care over her grub, and the violin; that she didn't have time to think about other things and to dream up things to scare herself.

And then, when she was alone in her room, on winter evenings, sawing away on her violin, who on earth would have been afraid, except an intruder with his horrid imagination.

"Your employers seem really nice," said Gramigni, impressed by the laugh and embarrassed by the subsequent silence.

"You know them, do you," asked Clemence.

"The young ladies are my customers," said Gramigni self-importantly. "They're very nice."

"Of course, they're well-mannered," said Clemence.

"It's not just that they're well-mannered," insisted Gramigni, "but they're not proud."

What he meant was that in their eyes he was probably not an indistinct individual but a person.

"That's what you think," retorted Clemence, who understood his pretentions all too well. "Girls for whom a thousand-franc bill has no more value than two sous of your change, girls who have a Hispano like yours…"

"I don't have any," said Gramigni.

"…would have a scooter, girls whose grandfather is something like the king of wireless telegraphy, I may add that it's difficult to understand how one can be the king of something that doesn't exist since there aren't any wires, you expect girls like that not to be proud? They'd be crazy if they weren't."

"You're probably right," said Gramigni, crushed.

"Naturally I'm right. And I'm telling you: what are you to them? I'm saying you just as an example, not to offend you. What are you to them? Nothing at all. They're nice because they're well-mannered, but that doesn't mean a thing. It's just the way rich people act."

"All the same they got young Bossu into M. Claye's factories," said Gramigni.

"What did that cost them?"

"I see," said Gramigni sadly, "of course."

All night long, he thought about this reduction of his personality.

The next day, they talked about the baron, and the day after about Baroness Hachamoth, and the day after the day after about the uncle who'd had an automobile accident, with the result that finally Gramigni suggested to Clemence that she have dinner with them on Sunday, which she accepted. Mme. Gramigni was quite shocked, but a thrashing snuffed out her surprise. And besides, it was rather flattering to have the baron's maid among one's acquaintants.

Clemence didn't leave until after eleven. You could hear the squawking of the little trumpet that adorned the handlebar of her velocipede grow ever fainter in the night. Mme. Gramigni was dozing in her chair, knocked out by the numerous glasses of liqueur she'd drunk to chase the heebiejeebies brought on by the presence of the myopo-gimp.

All that night Gramigni thought again. It was becoming a habit. He decided to offer another hundred sous to Saint Anthony of Padua since in letting him get to know Clemence without his even asking, he was prolonging the benefits of his first intervention; for Gramigni it was as if Agnes and

Naomi were staying on, in spite of the obligatory flow of the seasons.

So one Sunday he left for Cuges to put the five-franc piece into the saint's collection box. As he was leaving and when he returned, he booted Mme. Gramigni, who liked neither priests nor superstition, in the behind. He had to give this rationalist another couple of kicks in the ass to get her to fix dinner, for he'd invited Clemence. That too was becoming a habit.

XXXVIII

The departures had succeeded one another in the following order: Baron Hachamoth then Mme. Hachamoth then Daniel then some time later Agnes and Naomi. Everyone's getting back for the automobile show.

Important decisions were made: Agnes was to marry young Coltet in November, and, increasing her activities, suddenly wanting a social existence that was not too idle, she was working for a fashion designer after thinking for a while about the luxury antique trade.

Daniel in the exercise of his occupation as well as in his recreational activity continued to go unnoticed.

Naomi was watching Astolphe not live.

Astolphe was watching himself not live.

XXXIX

M. Jules-Jules Claye, the famous money man who made
Hertzian waves sweat shekels, took the plane at Le Bourget
for London, a special plane by the way ordered for his im-
mediate use. En route, at some distance from the coast,
above the water, M. Jules-Jules Claye, the famous money
man who made Hertzian waves sweat shekels, opened the
door and fell.

XL

The papers talked a lot about the death of M. J.-J. Claye
and the Ciotadans no less. They talked about it a lot at Bossu's
and at Gramigni's no less. From that moment on, Clemence
came to nosh at the grocer's twice a week. They learned
that M. J.-J. Claye's business affairs weren't holding up and
that now they'd all tumbled down. Bossu worried about his
son, Gramigni about the girls. The papers were adding seven
and eight digit numbers that gave you the shivers. Those
who were curious interviewed Clemence to find out more;
she didn't know anything, but she talked. These events made
her even more feared than popular, for you couldn't always
understand what she was saying, and besides her dull blue-
green, myopic eyes made people uncomfortable.

That's when the Italian's insomnia began: the destiny of
the Chambernac girls haunted his sleep. While next to him
his wife snored, his mind wove endlessly the dark threads
furnished him by Clemence's gossip and the reporters' pes-
simism. He got headaches from it, migraines, didn't want to
go to the doctor and bought aspirin; the druggist advised

barbiturates; such chemistry frightened him; he opted for camomile tea with orange petal water in it. He nonetheless slept little, and when he managed to, nearly at dawn, Clemence passed through his dream, cycling feverishly with her misshapen shanks, soon replaced by Agnes or Naomi more beautiful than ever. Then Gramigni sighed so loudly that his neighbor groaned.

Around that time people stopped talking about the Claye crash because of that of the New York stock market. Lardi was exultant, it's the end of capitalism he claimed.

"The Americans will get over it," said Bossu. "And besides it has nothing to do with us. Didn't Tardieu say the other day in the Chamber of Deputies that we're now heading toward prosperity in France?"

"Eyewash," said Lardi. "This depression is the last one. After this there can't be any more capitalists. There'll be communism all over the world, like in Russia right now."

"Russia's far away," said Bossu.

Gramigni would listen silently and on the pattern of the ruin of the American speculators would imagine that of the two girls, also on the pattern of the Russian émigrés he'd seen defend themselves more or less well all along the coast. They were going to sell their jewels, their cars, and then afterwards they'd sing in night clubs too expensive for somebody like him to go hear them. Finally, what most probably would happen was that Baron Hachamoth would sell off the villa; Clemence supposed as much and repeated it endlessly. Thus the next season would not see the return of Agnes and Naomi, nor the season following, no season ever. Other people would come live there, intruders, perhaps it would fall into ruin, and in any case Clemence would have to get out and leave. So every tie that connected him with the image of luxury would be broken; he would fall back for always into his Southern greengrocers' grime. Clemence hoped the Hachamoths would keep her on; she would therefore have to emigrate and go live in Neuilly; if not, what would become of her? And she wasn't all that happy about returning to the normal forms of flunkeyhood.

By dint of knocking rough, crude, rudiments of thought against one another, Gramigni managed to draw from them teenyweeny sparks, of an occasionally striking color, but so weak that they went out while still in the air. One of them nevertheless fell into some brush and fire began to crackle and teenyweeny flames started to rise. Gramigni was thinking about selling his shop and establishing himself in Neuilly-sur-Seine.

Now Clemence came to dinner three times a week; before she arrived and after she left, Mme. Gramigni got slapped around: on account of she said she was jealous. While Clemence was there, she didn't say a word; their guest impressed her so much that she actually became friendly. But otherwise, she'd say:

"You bastard," she'd say to Gramigni, "you bastard, you're stuck on that gimpyshanks, right you fathead, that spoonbacked old bat. You go look for your sweeties at the hospital, you fat swine, and you bring that to me, your wife, you heartless, shameless, conscienceless bastard. That bag, if you offered a dirty beggar a hundred francs to mount her, he'd refuse. And you think she's wonderful, that slut becomes a madcap mistress, you poor sap, and you dare to sit her down at my table, that runty piece of slime. I have my dignity, you old pig."

Then Gramigni would make a fist and start to hit. Since he was the stronger and he had his idea in his mind that gave him some direction while his wife's jealousy was a bit of an act, Clemence continued to come on Thursdays, Saturdays and Sundays.

Mme. Gramigni sought consolation in red wine: she got plastered to the point of being falling-down drunk and the whole town could see her gesticulate along the waterfront.

Taking a cue from his wife's suggestions, Gramigni began to look closely at Clemence. He found that if her eyes were nearsighted that didn't make them any the less beautiful, that her back was not all that curved nor her leg that twisted, that her face, although made strange by the feelings it expressed, was nonetheless that of a fairly appetizing girl whom youth had not yet abandoned. Next he noticed, after he'd eliminated all the symptoms of her infirmities and of the absurdities she accepted, when he'd stripped away all the manias and tics that had settled on her in her solitude, Gramigni noticed that Clemence looked a little, very little, but still a little, like Agnes and Naomi. She had undoubtedly borrowed a bit of charm from the radiant proximity of the two sisters. For there was no other explanation.

"Don't you think that Clemence shares a sort of family look with the Chambernac girls?" he asked his wife one day, to see whether the most ill-intentioned of minds perhaps also saw what he saw.

"Now what are you trying to say?"

"Don't you think that there's a slight resemblance between Clemence and the Chambernac girls?"

"Off his rocker," screamed Mme. Gramigni. "Why he's completely off his rocker. Now I understand why old bandy-legs excites you, it's because of the two other tarts. Talk about a perverted imagination."

He beat her up that day too.

Toward the end of January, when she was drunk, she fell into the water of the harbor and drowned.

XLI

When Baron Hachamoth took the train in Paris, it was raining; when he got off in La Ciotat, things hadn't changed but it was a little less cold. A taxi took him toward Saint-Jean.

Clemence was waiting for him. He payed the driver, stepped in puddles, shook himself off, caught his breath, made himself comfortable. Clemence was waiting for him to speak.

Now that he knew, Hachamoth looked at her with amazement. Nothing could be more obvious; in the whirlwind that had been shaking him fiercely for two months, this fact was far and away the most astounding. Was he that blind about everything? Old Claye's ruin, their financial difficulties, he had only to note them and then to defend himself. But here, there was nothing against which to defend oneself, save a great, enormously heavy doubt a great anguish undermining all his confidence in the world.

Clemence had no trouble guessing that Hachamoth had come to La Ciotat to sell off the villa; she was waiting with curiosity to see what he was going to propose to her and meant to astonish him whatever his proposal might be. Because of her nearsightedness, Hachamoth's stare didn't bother her, but she would really have liked him to be the first to speak.

Which he finally did.

"Bad news, Clemence. May as well tell you right away: we weren't intending to spend our vacations here anymore. I'm going to sell this villa; the business is already settled."

He stopped talking.

"And what becomes of me in all this," asked Clemence.

"Whatever you want."

"I don't understand what monsieur means."

"Naturally you can no longer remain in our service."

"I'm being kicked out if I understand monsieur correctly."

"Oh no, not at all. Here's how things stand: before leaving on this trip, M. Claye gave me a letter to be opened two days later."

"So it was a suicide if I understand monsieur correctly."

"All this is between the two of us, Clemence. What I'm going to tell you is also a secret that I'm asking you to please keep to yourself."

"Monsieur knows my discretion."

"Not only am I asking you, but you must also swear to it. You're Catholic, aren't you?"

"Roman Catholic, yes monsieur."

"Then swear before God not to reveal this secret."

"I swear before God."

"Clemence, according to what we must call the testament of M. Claye, you are now in possession of I won't say a little fortune but at least of a rather respectable sum; that is: two hundred thousand francs."

"That's what monsieur calls bad news."

"The bad news is only for us, Clemence. We must part with this house where my wife and my daughters will leave so many memories. It's hard, Clemence: it's a piece of the family that's going. And you, Clemence, a house where you were born, leaving it doesn't bother you?"

"Not at all, monsieur."

"What'll become of you? Whatever will become of you?"

"I'm going to get married, monsieur."

"Happiness on all fronts, eh Clemence? Congratulations. My most sincere wishes. That's very good. By the way, Mlle. Agnes' wedding has been postponed; the events; it won't be till January. And whom are you marrying, if it's not indiscreet to ask?"

"Monsieur Gramigni, the grocer down in the harbor."

"I see. That's very good. Well, Clemence, you're going to have a nice dowry."

"I'm delighted, monsieur."

"Mme. Hachamoth is to know nothing of it, nor my children, nor anyone; please."

"Monsieur can be sure I won't talk. I've sworn."

"It's curious, you don't seem to find it extraordinary, this luck of yours."

"I find it natural, monsieur."

"Really? natural? two hundred thousand francs?"

"Am I not M. Claye's daughter?"

"What makes you think that?"

"Numerous clues, monsieur. And now would monsieur permit me no longer to say monsieur, but you; from a sister-in-law to a brother-in-law, it's natural."

"Naturally it's natural. Everything seems natural to you, Clemence."

"I've prayed so hard to God and his saints, monsieur, that I don't find it astonishing to have my prayer answered."

"You think God is like that, Clemence? That he concerns himself with your dowry?"

"Why not? After all, he takes care of the little birds. But monsieur is Jewish, monsieur hasn't read the Gospel."

There was a pause. Outside the rain had stopped. A car passed, spraying up muck.

"Clemence, if I may say so, you don't seem, you don't appear much affected by the death of your father."

"No one has the right to reproach me," said Clemence.

Again there was a pause.

"I have," resumed Hachamoth, "come to liquidate everything. My wife didn't want to do it; this task would have been too painful for her. I'm going to sort it all out as quickly as possible, for I have many other things to do. I'll give you instructions, etc., etc."

They continued to talk far into the night.

XLII

And you oh great Saint Anthony
I find I have to thank you once again
for if all is finished
(they won't come any more
La Ciotat's deserted
future seasons will be empty
and the sands abandoned)
And you oh great Saint Anthony
I find I have to thank you once again
for if all is finished

all's starting over too
my house will be near theirs
I'll live in the same city
I'll live on the same street
not very far from them
one day they'll happen to pass in front of my place
I'll see them once again
one day something better will happen
Clemence has told me so
we will supply them with
oil, mustard, vinegar
nutmeg, pepper and salt
there was no reason at all for it to happen this way
and yet it will happen this way
again I owe you five francs one hundred sous
Saint Anthony of Padua
my faithful fellow Paduan

BOOK THREE

XLIII

When Purpulan saw the new students come into the court-
yard he had a feeling of nostalgia, not that he regretted the
time when he hadn't been in high school, but he remem-
bered with bitterness the day when, trying out his feeble
powers, he had demanded a job as a teacher. At present he
didn't know exactly what to think of this remarkable idea,
for after all his duties as secretary didn't give him too much
cause for complaint, but they did not afford as great a po-
tential for terrorization as his original plan. And then there
was this pact. He sighed and tried to find a moral in his
failures. Furthermore, he was glad that his educator Bébé
Toutout couldn't see what a nice pickle he'd gotten himself
into, and shuddered to think of the snickering convulsions
into which it would have plunged the illustrious dwarf.

By Christmas, Purpulan had not yet finished the notes
on the various squarers discovered by Chambernac. The
latter, whom the start of the school year had engrossed until
then, worried about such slowness; Purpulan pleaded the
difficulty of the work, which made the principal laugh. All
the same something must be wrong. Purpulan seemed pre-
occupied. His behavior reminded Chambernac of the good
student who suddenly starts to collect stamps and whom
this philatelitis pushes to the bottom of the class.

"This won't do, Purpulan, this won't do. Your mind isn't
on your work. It's not progressing. This won't do, Purpulan,
this won't do."

"I'm doing my best, monsieur Chambernac."

"Your best is a worst, Purpulan. Come tell me what's wrong? Could you be in love?"

"Oh no, monsieur Chambernac."

"You're not? You have all the symptoms of a secret passion."

Purpulan blushed and didn't answer.

"Come, come," said Chambernac, "don't act so mysterious. Get what's bothering you off your chest."

"Honestly, monsieur Chambernac."

"Come, come," said Chambernac, "don't act so mysterious. I'm sure there's something fishy going on."

"Oh, take your fish and shove it up your ass," said Purpulan, "and leave me the hell alone."

"Come, come," said Chambernac, "don't get upset."

"All right, monsieur Chambernac, I'll tell you everything, but later, not now."

"During all that time the work won't progress," said Chambernac.

"I'm not doing all that badly," said Purpulan.

"The work is not progressing very fast," said Chambernac. "This won't do, Purpulan, this won't do."

Purpulan gnashed his teeth.

"Come, come," said Chambernac, "don't act so mysterious."

After miming rage and despair, Purpulan put on an air of innocent sweetness.

"I would have liked to surprise you, monsieur Chambernac, a surprise for the New Year, a happy, joyous, strange surprise, something you're certainly not expecting."

"You worry me, Purpulan."

"You'd be wrong to worry, monsieur Chambernac. Unfortunately I can't promise you that it'll be ready for January first."

"You're definitely pulling my leg, my boy. Well the fun is over. Don't forget what you have become. I command you: speak."

Purpulan bowed his head like a good boy, then leaning in the direction of the Chambernacian ear that was closest to him, whispered into it these words:

"Monsieur Chambernac, I'm on the verge of discovering how to square the circle."

The principal opened his mouth like a fish on a counter at the market, adding to his very human surprise the muteness of this animal.

"I can understand that this might amaze you," resumed Purpulan. "Maybe you think I'm as crazy as the characters you went and dug out of the dust of the libraries, but let me tell you, monsieur, how it happened. By dint of summarizing all their attempts, I became obsessed with this problem and as one of your subjects, L. Karcher, said, 'once on this path, it was not possible for me to resist the fever of learning; the combinations I tried number thousands; ream after ream of paper was filled with numerals and figures. Oh the ephemeral joys, the dashed expectations, the poignant disappointments following negative or discouraging results! But also what satisfaction the day when like Archimedes, I cried out: I have found it!'"

"My poor friend," said Chambernac, "you're really in a bad way. And just what have you found?"

"It would take rather long to explain."

"I can well imagine."

"All the same, I can try to give you some sort of idea."

"I'm listening."

"Well it's like this, given a circle, I define a certain curve which determines a certain straight line which is equal to the quotient of the square of the radius of this circle by the square of its circumference. All that remains is to construct the straight line equal to the quotient of the square of the radius by the aforesaid to obtain the quarter of the circumference. That's all."

"And your curve, can you construct it with a straightedge and a compass?"

"What the hell does that matter?"

"Why that's the whole problem, you stupid idiot. Your curve's been known since antiquity, my poor boy. You're just reinventing the wheel. But one cannot construct this curve with a straightedge and a compass. That's the whole problem. Haven't you understood that yet? That the squaring of the circle is a problem of geometric construction, with a straightedge and a compass? No? Haven't you understood that yet? And that that's the way in which it's impossible, that's all. And that with your curve you won't succeed any better than the others?"

The poor devil sighed heavily.

"After all, monsieur Chambernac, you must admit it wasn't all that stupid."

"I'm not saying it was, I'm not saying it was."

"And on the other hand I think it's ridiculous to get all worked up over a matter of a straightedge and a compass."

"That's mathematics for you, monsieur: one doesn't take details lightly, one doesn't play games with precision and one soars above ridicule. In short, you're not a mathematician, Purpulan, no more than my squarers."

"The more I think about it, the more I think you're over-doing it with them. Look at me, am I crazy? And you must admit one more thing, monsieur Chambernac, you must admit that I'm the first squarer that you've met in real life, not in books. You can see that it's nothing to make a fuss about."

"So you'd like me not to have the squarers in my book?"

"Yes. Mlle. Claye was right: it's not very interesting. To think that I thought I'd solved a problem that poor guys have been racking their brains over for centuries and here it won't do because of a thingamabob for drawing sticks and a thingamabob for drawing rings; why it's nothing but a surveyers' quarrel."

"Don't start on that again, my friend, you don't understand a thing about it. It's also, at the same time, a matter of algebra; I won't undertake to explain it to you, but it's all been settled since 1882: the squaring of the circle is impossible, the number pi is not algebraic."

"1882? But I thought the Academy of Science has been refusing to consider any paper on this subject since 1775?"

"That's right."

"Some nerve they had, the academicians of those days. What? They couldn't prove it was impossible and they wouldn't hear of listening to others? some arrogance. Are they still as stubborn?"

"Hush! let's not go off in that direction. So tell me, Agnes—say, by the way, I forgot to tell you: I'm going to have to go to her wedding. I'll use the occasion to do a bit of research in Paris; the Mourmèche library is decidedly inadequate."

"Monsieur Chambernac, permit me to remind you that I too was to go to Paris; you were supposed to send me there."

"A bit of patience, my boy. When your squaring fury has blown over, I'm not saying I won't."

"It's blown over, monsieur… What a disappointment…"

"All right, all right, let's not get started on that again. To go back to what I was saying: so you agree with my niece that squarers aren't interesting."

"Yes, monsieur."

"So I delete them?"

"I would."

"So be it. But there's one whom I won't delete."

"Who's that?"

"Jean-Pierre-Aimé Lucas, born in Dieppe on September 15th, 1796, author of a *Treatise On The Application Of Geometric Lines To The Lines And Surfaces Of The First Degree Or Principles On The Relationship Of The First And Second Powers*, a work which was published in 1844, and of *What Is The Institute (Section of the Exact Sciences)? Or What It Has Been, What It Is, What It Would Like To Be, And What It Will Be*, published the following year."

"I don't know him," said Purpulan. "I don't have any notes on him."

"No. I saved him for myself. I'm going to read you a few passages and I want you to tell me what you think."

"I'll be impartial," said Purpulan.

XLIV

Chambernac put on his spectacles and said:

"First of all I must give you an idea of the results he achieved, but perhaps you won't be able to appreciate their tremendous importance, master squarer. By the way, that's pretty good, figuring out Dinostratus' quadrature all by yourself. Did you really discover that all by yourself, Purpulan?"

"I looked a little bit in books," admitted Purpulan, blushing.

"Lets leave it at that. So for Lucas,

"I—The area of the circle is independent of the perimeter.

"II—The number pi has two values according to whether it is used in the calculation of the perimeter or in that of the area of the circle.

"III—In the first case, it is equal to 3 times the radius plus one tenth of the side of the inscribed square, that is to say, 3.141421...

"Notice," said Chambernac, "that it's a very well known approximate construction; for a circle with a radius of one meter, the error is less than one tenth of a millimeter, which is imperceptible; but it is after all only an approximation. To go on,

"IV—In the second case, pi is equal to 3.144727...

"V—The hyperbola does not exist, no more than the dodecahedron; 'as for the icosahedron, the structure attributed to it is so absurd that it really doesn't merit refutation.'

"There are still more assertions of this order," said Chambernac. "I'll skip them."

XLV

Self-portrait of J.-P. Lucas:

"The author of *The Squaring of the Circle* was not only

favored by nature as far as intellectual faculties are concerned, but was also endowed with great physical advantages; he enjoys a robust constitution, despite the fact that his facial features would seem to indicate the contrary; he possesses penetrating vision, he has an exquisite sense of taste, the most impressionable sense of smell, acute hearing and a delicate sense of touch; his physical strength is considerable, if one considers his build, which appears slight, and that is so true, that he can in one day walk twenty-five leagues and start all over again the next day; I may add that he has practiced all athletic games to advantage, to the great disappointment of his adversaries.

"Nature has also endowed him with great dexterity, since he is able to engage successfully in whichever of the manual arts he pleases; for, and you may as well know it here and now, reader, nature loves and protects the arts. At the age of nine, he was a blacksmith; he became a carpenter, a wheelwright, a cabinet-maker, a mechanic, a ship-builder (for he made models), a sculptor, a wood and metal turner; he is a mason, a stone-cutter, a masonry foreman, a coppersmith, a glazier, a decorator, a painter, a draftsman, an architect, a lithographer, a tailor, even a shoemaker, for he has succeeded in making a seamless shoe; and when having his work typeset, he understood that it was possible to place the characters into the composing stick without touching them, a procedure that existed, but of which he was ignorant. All these advantages cannot be disputed, since he has furnished proof of them; nonetheless, he learned nothing; seeing the operation is sufficient for him, he immediately understands the difficulties to be overcome, he gets to work and succeeds.

"He could successfully occupy his time with literature,

history, politics; he would write verse as beautiful and more regular than that coming from the pen of the most celebrated poets, yet without knowing the rules that they established. In a word, the author of *The Squaring of the Circle* can do all that is possible for other men, often to the same degree of perfection, and can also in certain cases surpass them. But the field in which he excels, and to which he is most particularly attached, is that of the exact sciences. The only thing which he finds impossible is the study of foreign languages; consequently his success in Latin was less than mediocre; the cause is to be found in his pronounced aversion to all that is foreign, being by disposition and principle eminently national.

"Independent of these advantages, the author of *The Squaring of the Circle* is, in addition, noble-hearted: he is sensitive without wanting to appear so; he is humane by nature and without ostentation, and finds happiness in service; he is simple in his manners, his dress and his way of life; he loves his family, and particularly his mother, whom he has failed only twice, and for a reason which was above reproach. Intense, exuberant and confident of his superiority, he hates clumsy opponents, and when they attempt to stand up to him, he flares into anger and sometimes even strikes them. A sincere friend of truth, he goes to extremes to combat liars and hypocrites, and even more particularly corruptors and schemers; finally, similar to nature, whose living representative he in a sense is, he brings down his enemies without mercy, and cheerfully pardons them when they admit their wrongs. …You must then, as you are, however reluctantly, admit that the author of *The Squaring of the Circle* is a superior intellectual force, seeing that with the profundity of his thinking he combines keenness, skill, cunning and perseverance, for he has not only solved the problem which ensures his immortality, and all those that derive from it, and then conceived and traced all the figures relative to them, but he has, in addition, succeeded in interpreting all the enigmas which have been proposed to him,"

"I'll explain later what that's about," said Chambernac.

"however specious they may have been, and in deducing from these same enigmas principles of the highest morality, this morality being destined to serve as guide to the truly virtuous man, and that finally he was able to turn against his adversaries the snares that they had set for him; in a word, he possesses, independent of the faculties which are peculiar to man, the advantages which animals enjoy, combining with the strength and courage of the lion the caution and vigilance of the wolf, the acuity and slyness of the fox, and finally the will and perseverance of the tortoise, in this alone that he holds these selfsame advantages from Nature whose principle extends to all that exists.

"…My work will always stand, and will be expanded only by the hand of the new genius whom nature will be pleased to create in the most remote times."

"He observes in a note that the year 4444 'should offer great chances' for the appearance of this new genius; but he cannot affirm this expressly."

XLVI

"Well, you must be happy," said Purpulan, "there's at least one that's first-rate."

"Please don't express yourself like that," said Chambernac, "it's not scientific. Now I must explain to you who his adversaries were and what snares they set for him. His adversaries are naturally the members of the Academy of Science, who, since 1816, also know the solution of the squaring of the circle thanks to a paper sent them by a foreign scientist. They had a work printed which is identical to his, but the existence of which they are keeping secret."

"I'm not following you very well," said Purpulan, "if someone else discovered the squaring of the circle, how can he continue to take himself for the greatest of mathematicians?"

"You're an implacable logician, Purpulan, but that's an idea which must not have bothered him for one instant, no more than when he arrived at identities like $2-\sqrt{3}=3$. The entire second part of his *Treatise* is the historical background of his discovery and, you see, it's printed in two columns. '...I thought it appropriate,' says Lucas, 'in a first column to give an overview of the various phenomena which came to the knowledge of my adversaries in the course of their research, phenomena of which they can be all the less ignorant since they recorded them in the work which they had printed and which they avoided making public; and because, on the other hand, I was in a position to hear, according to the wish of nature, their most secret statements, nonetheless without seeking the occasion to do so, statements which I remembered successively while obtaining my solutions, while in the other column I listed opposite this the details relative to analogous impressions which I experienced in the course of my work.'"

"It's awfully obscure," said Purpulan.

"Look," said Chambernac, "here's an example. First column:

"'It… came to my memory that whilst in Paris pursuing my studies, I had entered an apartment where there were two distinguished-looking individuals; one of these individuals, as far as I am able to remember, was busy drawing at an elevated table set against a wall. Raising his head, he said to the other who was standing (neither the one nor the other could see me, due to the arrangement of the room): This solution is really surprising; when one does research, one repeatedly hears a knock on the door, one goes to open it, one finds no one; one goes out, one looks outside, and one sees nothing. He had gone toward a door, imitating the action that he had just described; nevertheless he did not see me, for there were two doors in the room where we were. Returning to his place, he caught sight of me and urged me to leave.'

"Second column:

"'While I was engaged in this research (on the division of the circumference into 64 equal parts), I heard from time to time a knock on the door; but this knock had a very particular character which of necessity incited me to meditation; as a sort of proof of what I am claiming, I will add that a 10-year-old child, who spent quite a bit of time with me while I was doing my research, heard as I did the knocks and was even frightened by them; several times he suggested that I go open the door; but I refused, for I had already understood what it was. Nature, in short, who likes to play on words, was showing me, by striking the door, that I, for my part, had hit the nail on the head, that is that I had found the right expressions, and it was true.'

"Notice," said Chambernac, "that, more cunning than his adversaries, he did not go to open the door. Another time, present, one could say, incognito, at a meeting of three of them, he heard them say:

"'If the author of *The Squaring of the Circle* comes, he will publish in 1844; if he finds the proof, which is probable, he will have used an octagonal glass inkwell inscribed with the letter B.'

"And:

"'Indeed, the inkwell which I used is octagonal, it is made of glass and has in relief the letter B.'

"Here, in connection with what you were saying before, here's how he knows that the Academy is in possession of the solution of the famous problem and how his adversaries know how he found out. The scene takes place in July, 1816, nearly thirty years before his discovery, during a visit to the Observatory:

"'In spite of the fact that I was placed at a fairly great distance, I was nonetheless able to hear the words addressed by the man who had just entered to the old man whom I've just spoken of, who, upon seeing him, hurried to meet him. These were his words: 'You know, *the squaring of the circle has been discovered.*' 'I know,' answered the old man. Then they both went to the table; the man dressed in black very quickly sketched some plans. Since I was still at my place, I could neither see nor hear. Several moments later, they got up again. The one who had just entered then began once more to speak, expressing himself in the following terms: *The Institute has not yet decided what to do; I cannot tell you if they will make it public, they want to wait;* then he added, bowing his head: *it is indeed the solution.*'

. . . .

"'It may be useful to point out that two or three months

after our visit to the Observatory, I also had the opportunity to find myself in the presence of people, one of whom was saying to the others: it's at the Observatory that *the author of the Squaring of the Circle* will learn that we had the solution. As is evident, he was right.'"

"Well," said Purpulan. "Doesn't that send shivers down your spine?"

"I'm not impressionable," said Chambernac. "You should know that."

"Your memory flatters you with its lapses," said Purpulan. "Remember… the bathroom… your cold sweat…"

"Bah, I was putting on an act."

"You took advantage of my weakness," said Purpulan, "that doesn't mean you're all that strong. If it weren't for Mme. Chambernac, maybe our roles would be reversed right now."

"Come, come, let's not start that again. Don't delude yourself either. And besides, I don't think you have much to complain about."

"All the same, monsieur Chambernac, slavery…"

"That will do. To work. You're going to read the *Treatise* and *What Is The Institute?* from cover to cover, which by the way I haven't done myself, and you will make a selection of the most significant passages, we'll compare it with mine. You will also note all the information which might be useful to me in composing his biography. For instance, in a note on page 315 he tells us that he began to work on the squaring of the circle on December 31, 1841; on page 338, I think, that he was of Protestant origin; et cetera. And you'll also have a look at the Atlas to get an idea of his 'layouts,' some of which call for more than 'one thousand lines drawn from various angles.'"

"Very well, monsieur," said Purpulan.

XLVII

They got up early at the principal's; at seven they had to be ready for breakfast. Purpulan had countless times asked permission to dawdle a bit, Chambernac had always refused. Consequently Purpulan was in a most awful mood every morning: but Mme. Chambernac didn't let him go around making disagreeable remarks: she was teaching him his place; consequently he thought it prudent to put on a happy face. A few times he was the first one there, in the dining room; then he'd say dreadful things to Carotte. Carotte would flee and not reappear unless accompanied by one of their employers.

After the café au lait, Purpulan had also begged them to replace it with the chocolate he preferred, with no better results, after the café au lait, which gave him a stomach ache, after the café au lait, Purpulan would work, or was supposed to, until noon; he'd begin again, or was supposed to, at two, and continue, or was supposed to, until seven. At least once an hour, Chambernac would go have a look at what he was doing. After dinner, they discussed the work of the day and prepared that of the next. When there were guests, Purpulan dined in his room and did not make an appearance. At ten o'clock they went to bed.

Bitterly, Purpulan watched the parade of days pass by. It

was a dreary life for a poor devil; and this work as copy and file clerk made him melancholy. He was awaiting the day when he'd be sent on a mission to Paris; it didn't look as if it were coming quickly and yet Chambernac had promised. All the same, the work was progressing: Brunet, Tcherpakoff and the others reduced to index cards, the squarers nicely squared away; but it was after all only the beginning, a very small beginning. It would take him at least two years, three perhaps, four made him shudder.

As for Chambernac, he thought that in two years at most he would have completed his *Anthology and Bio-Bibliography Of The French 'Literary Lunatics' Of The XIXth Century*. He saw his work as a series of introductory notes and selections, each author appearing in his alphabetical order. But since Berbiguier, Lacomme and the other squarers (certain cases were nevertheless being reconsidered, notably that of Onorato Gianotti) were excluded, there was, at the end of almost seven months, nothing done.

"Have you finished reading the *Treatise*? You've been on it for more than ten days. And *What Is The Institute*, have you read it?"

"Five hundred pages quarto isn't easy to swallow," said Purpulan. "It doesn't go down any better than a cup of café au lait."

"Chocolate is very bad for one's health," said Mme. Chambernac. "I read in *My Doctor* that overindulgence can cause epilepsy."

"I couldn't exactly overindulge here," said Purpulan.

"Look who's complaining about quantity," said Mme. Chambernac. "You eat as much as ten men, you mop up all the platters, by the way you're putting on weight, soon you'll have a double chin, my poor boy. Your café au lait's getting cold."

"I'll show you my selection this evening," said Purpulan to the principal.

"And the biographical details, you did note them all?"

"Yes, monsieur."

"I'd really like to have this note done before Agnes' wedding. This book isn't getting anywhere."

"When are you thinking of leaving?" asked Purpulan.

"Saturday morning. We'll get back Tuesday, early. While Mme. Chambernac does some shopping in the department stores, I'll work a bit in the libraries. I'll also get some information from my old friend Dr. Frachoux. I'm going to have to bone up a bit on psychiatry and mental pathology."

"So I'm going to stay here alone?" said Purpulan.

"You'll be good I hope," said Mme. Chambernac.

"So you're not taking me?" said Purpulan.

He was addressing Chambernac.

"What do you think?" said Chambernac.

He was addressing Mme. Chambernac.

"We already have a great many expenses," said Mme. Chambernac.

Purpulan sighed and swallowed his bowl of poison.

XLVIII

That evening Chambernac and Purpulan agreed on the following passages:

(Structure of the circle)

"I was thus compelled, I repeat, in imitation of the surgeon, to seek in the interior of the circle its organic principles, which I was fortunate enough to discover; its bony framework is to be found in the presence of the four squares of perfect equality; the marrow of its bones, which is its most subtle part, is represented by the sections of quadrature; the nervous and muscular parts are indicated by the tissue of the square of quadrature; the flesh is represented by the area of the circle; the center of this curve joins its heart and its head; finally, the straight lines which determine the angular sections of quadrature, are its arteries which vitalize the flesh and consequently polish the skin, represented, as I have already observed, by the perimeter."

(How he made this discovery).

"The next day, when the hour of dinner had arrived, I placed on the table the few dishes which were to compose its menu; among them was a piece of veal cooked in its juice, where there was a marrowbone. After eating the soup, I took the plate which held the veal in question; I was busy as usual doing it justice, when with a spontaneous movement I fell upon the bone as a famished dog would have done; I began to suck it, the marrow was delicious, and so as not to miss any, I used the point of my knife: I went so far as to suck the cartilage. When I came back to my senses, I thought about this action, and shortly thereafter, the bony structure of the circle came to me; it is, of course, the object of No. 216, the reading of which I cannot recommend enough, for there one can find the entire metaphysical part of the organic system of the circle.

"I maintain that one of my adversaries (it must have been the compiler of the work, that is the lover of Mme. Racine, his concierge) experienced the same impressions; he also fell upon the marrowbone and gnawed it. I shall add that my adversaries deduced from this phenomenon the same consequences as I, having heard them discuss this subject without being seen."

(Symbolism of the cotton bonnet.)

"Let us examine the question from the metaphysical point of view: to that end, I shall begin by inviting the reader to set aside his sensitivity to the reading of a word which it is absolutely impossible for me to be able to avoid; it is, what is more, a question of the sympathetic relationships that exist between the letters which compose the word *cotton* in French, *coton*, a word which when translated into sympathetic language, should be written thus:

CO—TO—N,

given that each of the letters C and T finds itself not only in identical conditions relative to the letter O, which is itself repeated, but also with regard to the letter N, which must in this case be taken in a double relationship; from the sympathetic bringing together one obtains these two words transformed, TON CON, the French for your cunt. Since *cotton*, according to the preceding discussion,"

"Which we will not reproduce," said Chambernac,

"is meant to envelope man all over the world, nature is therefore telling us: Envelope yourself in *cotton*, put on your cotton bonnet, or, according to the sympathetic principle, fill TON CON, a natural idea which, transformed into ordinary language, should be reproduced as follows. Everywhere on earth man should work at the task of generation; by engaging in it he is in accord with nature, for he thus increases his power while at the same time perfecting his own species. Such is the metaphysical interpretation of the *cotton bonnet*, a sublime thought to which nature alone could give birth."

(Reflections inspired by breaking a pipe.)

"In the course of the day, I began to smoke a pipe with a short stem; it slipped from my mouth, the bowl broke, according to the axis of revolution, into four equal parts; the stem remained intact and bounced toward me. I again began to think; here is the idea which came to me: The stem of my pipe was the symbol of man, or of the *first degree*, while on the other hand the bowl by analogy represented woman, or the element of the second degree, an element which is found in the circle, and which itself can be broken into fourths; that is, woman is the symbol of power squared. Such is indeed the situation when she has reached the age of puberty, since she comprises the two elements, namely: 1st *her own element, which is of the second degree*; 2nd *the element of man, which belongs to the first degree*, as it exists for the circle. Thus woman represents *power squared*; that is to say that, as far as the organic system is concerned, she is much more perfect than man. One can, what is more, convince oneself of this truth; all one need do is examine two cadavers belonging to each sex.

"I heard my adversaries say: The author of *The Squaring of the Circle* will be a smoker, and it will happen that when he breaks his pipes at a certain time, he will then make a metaphysical application of the nature of the break; according to him, the bowl will represent woman whom he will call power squared; the stem, man or the element of the first degree."

"That will be enough," said Chambernac.

"We could add the passage where he tells what happened when he discovered the squaring of the circle," suggested Purpulan. "This one:

"'…I could see, when doing the operations in my head, that I had the solution. Then, according to my so-called brother, I began with a look of alarm to utter the words: *Why, I have it, I have it!* At the same time, and by an involuntary movement, I found myself on my feet and was thrown almost instantaneously onto my bed which was placed on the floor very close by, arms outstretched and reduced to a state of immobility; I was also foaming copiously at the mouth; I wanted to move, it was impossible… I was completely exhausted, my chest was tight, I breathed with difficulty.'"

"It's interesting," said Chambernac, "it sounds like the description of an attack of epilepsy. I found another one."

"Overindulgence in chocolate, no doubt," said Purpulan.

"Don't joke about it."

"All right. So are we done with this one?"

"I'm now going to write a little biographical note. Then, we've gone a bit astray with the squarers, then we'll continue in alphabetical order. Of the names I've kept, which one comes first?"

Purpulan looked for the first index card not marked dele.

"Auguste B…, *Discovery Of The Veritable Material Organization Of The Universe To Refute Science And Destroy The False Ideas Invented Concerning This Subject*, Lyon, noted by the *Anecdotal Review* in 1855. But we don't have it here."

"I'll see about that. Next?"

"Next: *The Visions Of Jacques Baudot Surgeon In Frolois Which, From 1777 To 1787 Announced The Desolation Of Christian France And Of All Catholicism.* 1802. We have this work. Next, thanks to the *Anecdotal Review*, Bertron."

"That fellow," said Chambernac, "I really think I'll end up eliminating him, like all of the more or less innocent reformers, eccentric candidates, et cetera. Perhaps I'm wrong. You see: I'm hesitating between something very complete and very broad, in that case I would reintroduce all the squarers, and something more selective and incisive. What do you think, Purpulan?"

"I don't give a damn."

"Still in a bad mood then. What's the matter?"

"Is mamzelle Agnes' wedding going to be a big wedding?"

"You don't really expect me to get you an invitation."

"I could make excellent contacts."

"That's the very reason I don't want you there."

"You're sequestering me. When will I go to Paris to do research?"

"You're not even interested in your work."

"Oh yes I am, monsieur Chambernac, it fascinates me it fascinates me. I was a bit snappish there for a minute, I'm sorry."

"All right. But in any event you're still going to stay put this time. And I'll give you work to distract you during our absence."

"Won't I even have a few days of vacation? Even on Christmas Day I didn't have off."

"Don't tell me you wanted to commemorate Christ's birth?"
Purpulan blushed.

"Ah!" he sighed, "I've fallen into very cruel hands."

"Let's not exaggerate," said Chambernac.

XLIX

As soon as he got to Paris, Chambernac hurried to read Auguste B…'s little brochure which he found in the Bibliothèque Nationale under the call number Vp 10358. That evening he dined with Dr. Frachoux who brought to his attention an observation by Molin de Teyssieu about an epileptic who had, as psychic equivalents, sudden and pro-longed attacks of a feeling of déjà vu, another by Chaslin relative to a case of delirium palingnosticum in an epileptic and finally a remark by Hughlings-Jackson on the transitory existence, in epileptics, of an exceptional neutral state rather similar to the return of a former dream.

Chambernac was delighted and was glad he'd read his note and his selections to his old friend. He regretted that he hadn't studied medicine, but on Monday rushed to Le Soudier's to buy a few learned treatises on psychiatry, some new, others old.

In the meantime, Agnes had gotten married. For Chambernac, it was a chore, all the more chore because quiet, due to the events. A faint atmosphere of ruin drifted gently and knowingly about the Neuilly house. Mme. Hachamoth thought it advisable to look that way; but they remained wealthy the same. Only Astolphe had really hit rock bottom.

The millions had evaporated, but Hachamoth's were left, although diminishing. Once the enormous losses of the suicided ancestor were liquidated, the baron hoped to get the firms the other had founded back on their feet; the future belonged to radio, he was now convinced of it. He was getting rid of some secondary concerns, closing two or three condemned shops and consolidating whatever was viable under Daniel and Coltet's direction. But for the time being it was a complete disaster, at least for the spectators whom it was not necessary to interest.

Agnes had left her fashion house so as not to appear to be working for the money; she denied herself this luxury. The dowry her grandfather had put aside for her was nothing but a fond memory. She and Coltet were now a household that had to keep an eye on expenses; the family lodged them on the third floor of the Neuilly house, which had its own entrance. They'd sold the big cars; Hachamoth and Coltet each had his own; that was quite enough, they now found, Daniel would use one or the other. As for Mme. Hachamoth, she'd taken to public transport. She found it quite charming and prided herself on thus demonstrating her aristocratic simplicity, far superior to the democratic variety.

All these people asked Chambernac how his great undertaking was progressing, simply to be polite, for each one accepted the severe, summary and superficial judgement formulated by Agnes after her visit to her uncle in September. They asked him like that, just to say something; but he, enthusiastic, took advantage of their inquiries to read them a few fragments from the brochure of the anonymous writer from Lyons, Auguste B…

L

"I've copied this little brochure in its entirety," said Chambernac, "but I won't read you everything, only the last pages.

"'In nature, everything leads us to believe that infinite immensity is made of hard, frozen matter.

"'In the interior and within the enclosure of this hard matter, air and water must be contained; the earth itself is anchored in and upheld by it.

"'It is this conception that impels us to bring to light the following ideas. In this document, I shall give the convictive causes which alternatively produce night, day and the different seasons.

"'We shall no longer say that cold is the absence of heat, but we shall say that cold is a natural effect which, like heat, generates different degrees in the air; that it has existed from time immemorial along with darkness; that this selfsame cold is the invisible arm which sustains the infinite immensity of frozen matter.

"'Principle on the beginning of all nature.

"'In the interior of this frozen matter, an excessive frost must have given birth to a principle of void (as, for example, put water into a pitcher, let it freeze, break the ice in the middle, you will find a void); this void having grown larger due to explosions, or other causes unknown to this day, must have produced in the interior of immensity icy debris which, having then melted, increased the amount of liquid.

"'This water became polluted, produced clay and mist, a

mist which after rising, arranged itself in layers or clouds, and formed the different regions of air which exist, which replace each other alternatively, and enter into the composition of this matter or luminous bodies, by whose aid man could acquire great enlightenment, through agriculture, organized and practiced administratively throughout the world.

"'This same water having diminished, as much by evaporation as by the clay which it formed and deposited, and which also piled itself up likewise by layers, in the form of mountains; which can be proven.

"'The earth which we inhabit can be augmented and enlarged to infinity; for the earth must be of the same nature as that which it produces.

"'Subsequently, we shall demonstrate convictively this statement, which man will be able to execute.

"'This clay covers a very large area atop the frozen matter which is part of the interior shores of immensity.

"'In the bowels of this clay fermentation must have caused heat to form, which must have produced a fire similar to that of Mount Vesuvius, which supplies itself with water, nevertheless making due allowances.

"'The bowels of this clay'"

"It hurts me to hear that," says Mme. Hachamoth who leaves the room.

Reader and listeners, uncomfortable, stare stupidly at one another.

"Do go on," says Astolphe.

"'The bowels of this clay must be made of a material or metal of this sort, which has the ability, when it is red, to swell and lengthen, to shrink and become shorter when it cools. That would make me think that when the bowels of the earth are heated sufficiently to swell, they would make the earth rise above the sun; which would give us darkness or night.

"'When these same bowels receive water in a great enough quantity, they cool, they contract, withdraw and make this mountain come down lower than the sun; then, as the latter receives its rays, they provide it with heat, light or day.

"'The sun continually revolves around the universe, and that horizontally.

"'The earth must be attached to the North by matter producing effects of the same nature, that is, capable of shortening and lengthening, which would be the causes which produce the seasons.

"'The earth, from noon to midnight, rises, and, from midnight to noon, comes back down again; it continually repeats these two movements. When it moves away from the sun, the days lengthen; and when it comes near to it, the nights become longer.

"'These various effects produce the seasons.

"'Spring and summer take place when the earth draws away from the sun, and autumn and winter come when the earth nears the sun.

"'The sun is the heart of elemental celestial nature; it must be cold, since the animal heart is hot. It gives heat, light and day to the earth by the perpendicular rays which shine onto it.

"'The air and this heat give to plants the power to grow and produce, as well as to all living beings the power to live and multiply.

"'Salt, which the sun draws to itself at the same time as the salt water which it pumps, must be an important element in the eclipsial process.

"'I believe that the eclipse is the cordial and sympathetic kernel, or general copulation for all of nature, and that at the moment when the sun and the moon meet, they are in reflection opposite one another; and the effect of the reverberation has the power to melt the salt which is spread over the surface of the sun; that is what can darken it. I do not believe that one can attribute this darkening to the fanciful conception that a small object could hide a larger one from our eyes.'"

LI

"That's certainly wrong," said Coltet solemnly.

"And that the sun is cold too," added the baron.

"You can't be sure," said Astolphe. "One day a scientist will maybe manage to prove it, or at least to formulate it as a plausible hypothesis."

"Pardon me, gentlemen," said Chambernac, "it's not a question of truth."

"It's a question of insanity," said Coltet.

"No. No. It's not a question of truth or insanity. I'm looking at things from a completely different point of view. Look: I'm calling 'literary lunatic' an author—a published author, that's essential."

"Why?" they asked.

"Because it proves that he still has enough social adaptability to keep from being institutionalized and to put out a book, which is, I believe, a fairly complex activity. So, as I was saying: a published author whose wild imaginings (I'm not using this term pejoratively) diverge from all those professed by the society in which he lives, either by this society as a whole, or by the different groups, even the minor ones, that compose it, are not related to earlier doctrines and in addition weren't taken up by anyone else. In short, a 'literary lunatic' has neither masters nor disciples. Thus Fourier, in spite of the eccentricity of certain of his affirmations, cannot be regarded as such since he had disciples and had a statue erected in his honor."

"But then a literary lunatic can stop being one," said Astolphe.

"Naturally. All he must do is eventually find admirers, I mean: sincere ones."

"Come on, all unknown authors aren't literary lunatics."

"No, naturally not; in addition they have to write things that an average person, like me, considers inordinately odd. Let me add that I've limited myself to the XIXth century because beyond that judging the genuine oddity of an account becomes very tricky. One must take fad and fashion into account."

"Still, all that doesn't seem very clear to me," said the baron.

"So," said Mme. Hachamoth who had just reappeared after mourning old Claye's death in the next room, "so, you're still talking about your loonies. My God," she exclaimed, "see to it that I never fall into that."

She lit a cigarette and poured herself a glass of brandy.

"And your secretary, Henry," she asked, "are you still happy with him?"

"Very happy."

He would rather they talked about something else.

"And where did you dig him up? It mustn't be easy to find a secretary in Mourmèche, or who wants to bury himself there."

"I'm not at all unhappy with him," said Chambernac. "Anyway I hope to have finished this research in a few months. I hope I didn't bore you too much with all my scholar's tales."

"Oh not at all," they said.

Mme. Hachamoth murmured:

"My God, do make me a little less curious."

LII

Twenty-six and one half hours later Chambernac was getting back onto the train for Mourmèche in the company of his wife and a big bundle of books. Mme. Chambernac settled down to go to sleep. The principal was ruminating: whatever could Sophie be thinking about? What was she imagining? What did she think she knew? As it was impossible that anyone could begin to suspect the truth, she could obviously only be fiddling with falsehoods, just like the Mourmèchians intrigued by Purpulan. What harm could that do him? He was at the close of his career: what difference did malicious gossip make? After thoroughly reassuring himself on this point, he set about considering his great undertaking.

He wasn't as happy with it any more. He was becoming ambitious. Compiling an anthology, drawing up a bibliography, and even composing little biographical notes wasn't something one could be proud of. That sort of thing was unskilled labor, grunt work; that sort of thing didn't ratify a life; that sort of thing didn't merit posterity. He would like to have done better. Glory was now hounding him.

He got up to go and piss. Bumped about, he stumbled between the empty compartments and the windows steamed with condensation. On his way back he lingered in the hall, wiped the glass with his sleeve, saw nothing but night. The train went into a tunnel, evident only by the sound, not by a deeper darkness; the locomotive's smoke stuck to the pane, whitish like sperm. And Chambernac saw the contours of his book taking shape, at first with a certain apprehension as upon meeting an extraordinary, perhaps hostile, stranger. Then he took possession of the idea in its totality; he leaned his forehead against the copper bar and felt joy galloping within him, trampling on his lungs, his heart, his brain. He went back into his compartment and sat down exhausted.

He now envisioned his great undertaking no longer as a string of notes presented in alphabeto-chaotic disorder, but as a well-ordered work which even had a title. He would write an ENCYCLOPEDIA OF THE INEXACT SCIENCES. The subtitle would be: *On The Borders Of Darkness*.

First part: THE CIRCLE. In it he would discuss the squarers.

Second part: THE WORLD. In it he would discuss the various cosmologies, cosmographies, and aberrant systems of physics.

Third part: THE WORD. In it he would discuss linguistics and grammar.

Fourth part: TIME. In it he would recount the history of France in the XIXth century:

He knew what he'd use as an epigraph for this fourth part,

> "I could give the history of our country from 1789 to the present day, by observing a few insane people whose madness acknowledged as its cause or character some remarkable political event in this long period of our history."
>
> (Esquirol, *On Mental Illnesses*, Paris, 1838, vol. II, p. 686.)

He had read this passage the night before and, now that he was thinking things through, he understood that this was where his inspiration was coming from. He considered awakening the snornapping Agatha to tell her of his new, and brilliant, plan, but decided to do nothing of the sort, to consummate his glory and his exaltation in solitude.

It wasn't until evening, after dinner, a good dinner, in the presence of Mme. Chambernac and Purpulan solemnly invited to hear, that he expounded this transformation, which he thought grandiose, of his original book. They congratulated him; Agatha amazed at such intelligence, Purpulan not giving a damn.

Their work was reorganized straight away. While Chambernac was writing the first part in its definitive form and boning up hard on psychiatry, old and new, Purpulan was gathering the material for book two. In the evening, they had long conferences to decide which world systems would appear in the *Encyclopedia*; after countless eliminations, there remained outside of Bousquet and Roux to whom Chambernac wanted to devote special chapters, only:

LIII

Demonville (Antoine-Louis Guénard, born in Paris February 24, 1779, author of *The True System Of The World* and of 35 other works or brochures published between 1812 and 1852).

> There is nothing real but the earth, the sun and the moon. All the rest is a catoptric illusion. Venus and Mercury are only double reflections of the sun and the moon on the polar ice. The sky is not spheric; it forms a horizontal plane on which the stars are placed. The lower, austral sky is only a reflected sky. The sun is fifteen hundred leagues from the earth, et cetera.

LIV

Jules Maigron, of Montpellier, published, in Paris in 1838, under the pseudonym of Nelson: *Universal Movitism, Discovery Of The Solar Revolution: New System Of The World*, and in Montpellier in 1866, *The Illustrated Sics. Astronomic Revolution. New System Of The World, Uranography, Metaphysics, Physics, Chemistry, New Cosmogony; Discoveries Of The Causes Of Winds, Of Rain, Of Snow, Of Hail, Of Storms, Of The Ways To Predict Them. Discoveries Of Hell, Of Paradise, Of The Vital Principle. Followed by The Art Of Living Forever*!

The sun is no larger than the earth since the latter is constantly lighted and shadowed by half. The moon floats on the atmosphere like a bladder full of air on water. The rotation of the earth is produced by an interrestrial motor. The yellow, black and red races descend from lunates fallen from the moon when it bumped into the earth; the shock was so strong that the equator jumped to the poles and only imperfectly resumed its original place. As for the whites, they descend from Adam whom God formed in Ceylon 4,000 years before the Christian era. The damned are crushed by the interrestrial propeller. Paradise is located on Saturn. (It would be a very long and difficult matter to explain how, by imagination, by comparison, by reason, going from the known to the unknown, from the visible to the invisible, I managed to see in my imagination the elect.) Pi equals 3 1/8. (The discovery of the exact relationship of the diameter and the radius to the circumference, is a marvel of human imagination; I am publishing it, not only to be useful to mathematics, but also to prove that the one who was able to perform this sort of miracle, impossible to this day, is truly capable of explaining and discovering the causes of all celestial phenomena.) Et cetera.

LV

Mandy, native of Lyons, author of *Naturism*, published in 1865.

> The earth is hollow and as light as a balloon, since it holds itself in the air. 1502 years and 10 days passed between the moment when the earth cooled and the flood. Paradise is turned straight toward the side where God is, consequently toward Sirius; at the lowest point in paradise, the temperature must be about 25 degrees Réaumur. Et cetera.

LVI

Abbé P. Matalène, author of *The Anti-Copernicus, New Astrometry*, published in 1842.

> The Sun is one meter in diameter; its maximum distance from the earth (at winter solstice naturally) is 7,812 leagues. The star Venus is not as large as an orange (34 millimeters in diameter). The earth is larger than all the celestial bodies put together. Et cetera.

LVII

Renault de Bécourt or Regnault de Bécourt, author of *The Creation Of The World*, Philadelphia, 1813, 2nd ed. Givet, 1816, Eng. trans. London, 1827, and of *The Tomb Of All Philosophies*, Briey, 1834.

The diameter of the moon is 18 or 19 leagues and its distance from the earth about 80. The diameter of the sun is smaller than that of the moon since the latter eclipses it and they are only some 40 leagues apart. The distance from the earth to the firmament, a solid, diaphanous concretion, blue in color, is about 500 leagues. The firmament forms the shell of the Universe, for the world is an egg whose air is the white and the terrestrial globe the yoke. The earth was first a spherical mass of fleshy, living matter from out of which came all the vegetal and animal species. Their detritus, their excrement and their cadavers formed the first layer of sediment. All the celestial bodies come from here below and take their sustenance from here. Following original sin which destroyed the first order, they must now make an effort to procure their sustenance; hence lightning, thunderbolts and tides. Et cetera.

LVIII

Chambernac's enthusiasm for psychiatry made him a bit scornful of all these systematizers. He had eliminated a goodly number who would have seemed extravagant to anyone else, but who in his opinion were not worthy of the honors of the *Encyclopedia*.

"We must be selective," he'd say to Purpulan. "I'll stick all the rejects into an enumerative appendix just to show that I was aware of them. Which leaves us for a special chapter, Vernet, landowner in Saulse, and the anonymous Marseillean, the man of the conciliation of contradictories and the man of the compatibility of extremes. In his *Universal Contemplation, Manual Of Journeys Around The Universe, Poetic Institution, Spiritual Code, Morality, Geography, Universal System, Unique Prophecy Of The World*, Valence 1853, Vernet tells us that having 'continually performed his duties as a faithful servant to the supreme authorities,' 'wisdom came to take (him) by the hand' and entrusted to him 'the passkey of all the dependencies of the divine creator,' permitting him to complete the 'map' of the universe. Now I quote.

LIX

"'One single, unique, absolute spirit, first cause, first character, genius, science, artist, architect, was able to draw the world out of nothingness, was able to form all the parts of the universe, gave bodily eyes to his creatures, to see, contemplate, examine, meditate upon his universal, marvelous display, above our heads, under our feet, to the right, to the left of our ignorant, unbelieving, guilty, mortal bodies, in short of all our faculties in general. Harmoniously organized beneath the celestial vault which preserves the whole, situated between two extreme points where all exists, classified, graduated, placed, spiritualized, admirably characterized, magnetized, here listed comparatively in two sections, one to the right the other to the left, in the middle the center or equator, which forms, indicates easily the two extreme points, reduced to one single, unique, absolute, of conciliation.

"'In such a manner that union, all its universal dependencies be spiritual, be material, exist in this position, situation.

Example:

Pole to the left (equator). Pole to the right.

Basin to the left (pivot). Basin to the right.

1. The lamp	and	light
2. Evil	and	good
3. Darkness	and	brightness
4. Ignorance	and	knowledge
5. The scholar	and	science'"

"Et cetera," said Chambernac, "there are thirty of them. 'Contradictory questions and answers in order to arrive at the great, universal conciliation or golden mean.

Oh! how great is France.

Ah! how small.

Oh! how rich is France.

Ah! how poor.

Oh! how vigorous are the French.

Ah! how lazy.'

"Et cetera," said Chambernac.

"'Example of the principal magnitudes or objects which appear to be single and are double.

'The earth in its dimensions is:

Very hard	and	soft
Very good	and	bad
Very flat	and	hilly
Very fertile	and	very barren

'Man being double, he is at one and the same time:

| Very pure | and | impure |
| Very just | and | unjust'" |

"Et cetera," said Purpulan.

LX

"Naturally," said Chambernac, "I'll tell of his journeys to Paris to take his works to the Elysée or the Tuileries Palaces. He undoubtedly tried to see Napoleon III.

> 'Although I spent six years gathering my discoveries on one item, nevertheless, I am inundated with greatness, with genius, which permit me to say that one hour of very serious consideration would be sufficient to give sufficient means to honor Paris, to spiritualize it, characterize completely by the enormous ensemble of faculties, to be considered capital of the administration of the globe for its new capacity... So that it would be desirable that before reaching my grave I be called to fulfill faithfully, scrupulously my striking mission, moral phenomenon; finally, for my fatherland and for myself, it would be deplorable that such rare news remain unnoticed, unconsidered, in a word not applied, not exercised...'

"Next," said Chambernac, "I'll speak of *The Book Of Reason Or The Original Institution*, published in Marseille, in 1855.

"'The problem of science should (therefore) be formulated as follows:

To Find the Compatibility of extremes.

"'… The thesis and the antithesis of HAVING being identical to the thesis and the antithesis of BEING (essence, *Esse*, from *esse*; *habere*, from *habere, debere*, debt), the two most comprehensive extremes are of necessity HAVING and OWING. Now, by HAVE one can only mean the PASSIVITY of a stated totality; and by HAVE TO (debt, duty, have to) the ACTIVITY which would successively put into place all the parts of this totality. HAVE TO and HAVE must therefore be put into the equational form HAVE TO = HAVE.

"'As for the synthesis HAVE TO = HAVE, it is of necessity to HAVE, intermediate voice between the passive voice HAVE and the active voice HAVE TO. Indeed, to HAVE, in first formulating itself passively in HAVE, then actively in HAVE TO, furnishes the two means I and ME (subject and object) which sustain together the same relationship as the two extremes HAVE TO and HAVE, the relationship, single and double at the same time, of active to passive and of passive to active.

"'It is double equality in unity or REASON represented by the equation HT = H.

"'… Such is the solution of the problem of the COMPATIBILITY (of extremes) or of COUNTABILITY, for these two words, having the same constituent elements, are linguistically identical.

"'…

"'2. The formula SHOULD—HAVE is the satanic mutilation of the formula HT = H.'"

"What do you say to that?" asked Chambernac.

"You learn something new every day," said Purpulan.

"'…

"'4. The formula SHOULD—HAVE is double entry accounting or dualism; the formula HT = H is single and triple entry accounting or Catholicism.

"'…

"'14. The formula HT = H is God's balance scale; the formula SHOULD—HAVE is Satan's seesaw.

"'…

"'28. There is no other CANKERWORM than the current teaching of accounting.

"'…'

LXII

"He closes," said Chambernac, "by advocating the formation of an Order of Reasoners. Well, what do you say to that? Isn't it interesting, curious, this appetite for synthesis? In spite of the extravagances and naivetés, there is in the one and the other something that makes them superior to all the philosophers locked into dualism."

"Don't get carried away," said Purpulan.

"I can easily understand," said Chambernac, "that, error's henchman that you are, you cannot appreciate this effort toward conciliation, in the words of the one, toward compatibility, in those of the other."

"You see," said Purpulan, "between error and truth, there is incompatibility."

"Are you saying that you are," said Chambernac, "pure negation irreconcilable with any thought of good?"

As Purpulan didn't answer, Chambernac sighed:

"We're not going to bring up the problem of evil, are we?"

Purpulan made a gesture that meant he couldn't care less.

"I have chosen," resumed Chambernac heavily, "the domain of error and madness: how can I get out of it now? Come, come," he brightened, "to work to work and let's not think about it any more."

Purpulan acquiesced; but the work wasn't progressing fast. When summer vacation came, they were still on the physical sciences. The day after the close of the school year, there was an intimate little dinner party at the Chambernacs. Purpulan, gluttonous, was amazed neither at the abundance, nor at the delicacy of the dishes. He ate. After the chocolate and cream dessert, when he saw the principal uncork a bottle of champagne, he said:

"Gosh, now there's bubbly too."

"We're celebrating a little anniversary today," said Mme. Chambernac very pleasantly.

"Well," he said letting the rest of his chocolate sauce run to the lower part of his tilted plate, "nobody told me anything about it."

He rose with the other two, his goblet in his hand.

"Here's," said Chambernac, "to my first meeting with our friend Purpulan."

Purpulan, his hand trembling, was sprinkling the tablecloth with vinous little cascades.

"You're really rotten," he said.

Carotte came in. He drank his champagne. They sat down again.

Carotte went out with the dirty plates.

"It's one year over with anyway," murmured Purpulan.

"And I've written only a quarter of my book," remarked Chambernac.

"Monsieur," said Purpulan, "if you're not happy with my services, you can tear up our contract."

"A lot of good that would do you," said Mme. Chambernac. "Where would you go? What would you do? You're not exactly resourceful. What would become of you? You'll see, later, you'll miss the time you spent at our house."

"In any case," said Purpulan irritated, "you promised me I'd go to Paris and all I've done is stagnated here."

"You'll see," resumed Mme. Chambernac, whom the champagne had made emotional, "later, you'll miss the time you've spent at our house, your little room, your peaceful work, the children's cries, the concierge's drum, the tall trees of the schoolyards, the tasty little dishes prepared by Carotte, the soft Mourmèchian dusks, the calm life of our little town, the savory breakfasts."

"Not likely," exclaimed Purpulan indignantly.

"Starting tomorrow," said Agatha emptying her goblet, "you'll be entitled to chocolate every morning."

"That's nice," said Purpulan abstractedly to hide his satisfaction.

"You'll see," resumed Mme. Chambernac, "when you're without lodging and shelter again and can't find anyone to play a dirty trick on, when November's rain drenches you to the skin and December's snow flails your nails, all alone and poverty-stricken in the night, you'll remember the time you spent at our house, chocolate every morning, a glass of brandy every Sunday, the tranquillity of scholarly occupation, the quiet country evenings. But perhaps you can't understand all that."

She started to cry.

"Agatha why don't you go lie down for awhile," said Chambernac.

"I think I will. Good night, monsieur Purpulan. Good night Henry." She went out enteared.

"She's not used to it," said Chambernac.

He rang for Carotte and had her bring another bottle.

"I've made an important decision," he said. "We're leaving Mourmèche for two months and we're going to live in a little house that's part of a farm I own. My dear Purpulan, you have nothing against my being a landowner, do you? Well, we'll go there for two months and we'll get through loads of work."

"I don't like the country much," said Purpulan.

"You won't have the time not to like it," said Chambernac, "you'll be too busy. Come come don't make such a face, we don't treat you all that badly here. Admit it."

"Champagne is good," said Purpulan.

So good he was licking his glass.

"Ah you see," said Chambernac. "Admit, admit that we don't treat you that badly here."

He tapped him amiably on the shoulder. Purpulan admitted nothing, but Chambernac was happy all the same. He told him stories of his service as a volunteer in the cavalry, and taught him the words to the bugle calls.

"Monsieur Chambernac, you're a character," said Purpulan.

"That's what they always used to tell me in my younger days. Later," sighed Chambernac, "I developed a middle-class outlook: not because of my marriage, not because of my profession, no I'm not complaining, but because of my morals; yes, my morals. I'll have to tell you about that, Purpulan."

He went to get the bottle of brandy and poured two little glasses generously filled.

"I'm listening, monsieur Chambernac," said Purpulan.

"Let's go back twenty-five years," began Chambernac, his voice husky with emotion. "My brother was still alive, naturally, it was well before the war—you didn't know those times, my boy, everything was calm, stable, tranquil, everyone had a secure life, with a little investment income you could live a life of leisure, in short we lived like pigs—pigs that they bled in 1914, I'm not talking about my poor brother, poor Henry."

He started to cry.

"Besides," he resumed, "he was killed in 1916, on February 21st, the day of the German attack on Verdun. Well. Anyway. So, twenty-five years ago, I was spending the summer at my brother's in La Ciotat, in a villa he got from his father-in-law M. Jules-Jules Claye, you know the one who fell down from an airplane."

"I don't read the papers," said Purpulan.

"There—I mean in La Ciotat—I met a lady X…—you'll understand my discretion—and I don't know what happened, but I got her pregnant."

"Impossible," exclaimed Purpulan.

"Well I did; but wait I haven't finished my story; this child, I don't know what became of him, I never even wanted to know, and yet I could have found out. Isn't that a boorish, bourgeois way to act?"

"And now you could find out?" asked Purpulan.

"Of course; but what's the use, if he's still alive, he must be some twenty-four twenty-five years old, I don't even know anymore when he was born; at that age he doesn't interest me anymore."

"I can understand that," said Purpulan who, since he had to stay, preferred not to have a rival.

"I wonder whether you understand that," sighed Chambernac. "In any case, the people who used to say about me when I was young: he's a character well, when I've published my *Encyclopedia*, they'll see they weren't mistaken."

"For sure," said Purpulan.

Then they talked away, each for themselves, until late into the night.

LXIII

A few days later, they and Mme. Chambernac left for their house in Cravonne, commune of Sandignac, canton of Pluy, arrondissement of Mourmèche. Two boxes big with books followed them. Massicot the farmer greeted them politely, and his wife. The animals cried out each after their kind. They settled in.

BOOK FOUR

LXIV

At the far end of the garden was the laboratory, a shed next to the pump past the vegetable garden. It was a tiny little laboratory, and quite primitive, although the work done there concerned all the experimental sciences. Here a dichromate battery: physics; there, milk going bad with chalk (lactic acid preparation): chemistry; here, beans sprouting in cotton: natural sciences.

Every day, Daniel would stick the communiqué on the door.

LXV

Agnes despised the laboratory; she considered these occupations dirty smelly vulgar; and besides her poilus, her soldiers, took up a lot of her time: writing to them, knitting them socks, sending them packages. Meanwhile, Daniel with Naomi's fervent help, was trying to discover a new element that was initially called chambernacium or chambernium. Then the two chemists considered that designation too general: as a Chambernac, Agnes could glory in it though despising their work. So Daniel decreed that it would be danielum; but when Naomi cried, the substance to be discovered was definitively baptized: danaomium. The atomic weight of Dn would certainly not be less than that of uranium and would come to something like 250.

LXVI

The preparation of danaomium required constant attention, continuous care and an unquenchable imagination. A first attempt had taken as its point of departure a mixture of equal parts of arable soil, kitchen salt, bicarbonate of soda crystals and ground bone meal; next this mixture had been successively imbibed with ammonia, vinegar, 90% proof alcohol and vitriol ($SO^4 H^2$). After each imbibition, the mixture was dried over a little spirit lamp. Finally Daniel decreed that this was not the right track.

They attempted other attempts: melted some tinfoil, the kind that surrounds chocolate, also melted the chocolate, threw the whole thing into a boric acid and water solution, heated, decanted, filtered. Danaomium was not yet discovered.

"Maman," said Agnes, "Daniel and Naomi peed in a bottle and they snitched some of your cologne to mix it with and they put that filth out in the sun to rot with leaves in it."

"My God," said Mme. Hachamoth, "if you've given them a taste for science, may your will be done."

LXVII

"It smells too bad all your chemistry stuff," Agnes told them.

"You better not tell on us again." said Daniel.

"Playing with pee," said Agnes, "you ought to be ashamed of yourselves."

"You leave us alone, you leave us alone," said Naomi who began to cry.

"Yes," said Agnes, "you're dirty, you play with pee."

"You're stupid," said Daniel. "You're so dumb. You don't understand a thing about science."

"Science," said Agnes, "my oh my."

"First of all," said Daniel, "we're not playing with pee: we're working with uric acid. If you read books like me, you'd know that. Uric acid is just an acid like all the others."

"I can see that," said Agnes.

She backed away a few steps.

"Soon you'll be playing with poop."

She ran away.

"With poop," she shouted.

They threw pebbles at her.

"Is she dumb," said Daniel.

Naomi said softly:

"Say, Daniel, you wouldn't do that, would you?"

Daniel looked very serious.

"What if that was the only place to find Danaomium?"

Naomi sighed.

LXVIII

Clemence, the daughter of Bertha I, was now fifteen; but sickly and almost disabled, although she was of servile station she did not do much work. She was learning to play the violin. She had a taste for the arts, this misbegotten thing. Daniel with his test tubes and litmus paper scared her. And she in turn made Agnes and Naomi uncomfortable. The children as well as the adults avoided talking about her.

A few times she ventured into the vicinity of the laboratory.

"Hello Clemence," Daniel would say.

"You're so smart monsieur Daniel," said Clemence.

"Hello Clemence," said Naomi.

"So you're as smart as your brother mademoiselle Naomi," said Clemence.

She was thinking it's not for little girls, stuff like that.

With dread she'd watch the chalk bubbling under the vitriol ($SO^4 H^2$).

In a corner something smelled bad.

They could see Agnes coming with something up her sleeve.

So Clemence would go away. She'd go back in. She was learning the overture to the *Dame Blanche*, her favorite piece.

LXIX

Once, M. Claye stopped off in La Ciotat for two or three days, on his way to Italy on business. He needed these two days of rest; the government was keeping him busy. His grandchildren looked at him with disgust: he wasn't all that old he could have enlisted; guys who'd been in the war of seventy were in this one again. M. Claye hadn't taken part in any, just like their uncle Chambernac who sometimes came to see them.

"You have no right to talk about your grandfather that way," Agnes would say.

"You're a hypocrite," said Daniel, "you think the same thing I do."

Naomi mourned her father whom she had trouble remembering and who appeared transformed by his decorations.

M. Claye didn't like his grandchildren.

LXX

"So," said Claye, "you like music little girl?"

Clemence blushed mute.

"Are you happy here?" asked Claye.

Clemence nodded.

"Come on, say something," said Claye.

She was too big now for him to take her in his arms, kiss her, caress her. You always have to be careful not to give the wrong impression.

"I'm happy here," said Clemence. "I'll always stay here."

"Don't you want to go to Paris to study with a good teacher?" asked Claye.

"Maman can't afford it," said Clemence.

"I'll pay for it," said Claye.

"No thank you monsieur," said Clemence. "You don't have to."

"I want to make you happy."

"You don't have to," repeated Clemence. "And besides I want to stay here. I'm happy here."

LXXI

Gently, he asks her about his grandchildren. Agnes?

Clemence doesn't play with her. She's too old, Clemence, and Agnes too. Mlle. Agnes is very serious. All she thinks about are those over there, and she writes, and she writes, and she knits, and she knits.

Clemence doesn't play with Mlle. Naomi either. She's too little, Naomi, and besides she's always with Monsieur Daniel. Clemence describes the laboratory. There are bottles full of poison, vials full of filth, stuff that stinks.

Claye muses, smiles, that'll be something anyway: an aptitude for science; a natural engineer.

But all the same, art is far superior; he looks at Clemence, tender, admiring.

LXXII

During that summer, the summer of '18, many visitors came to the villa near Saint-Jean. Henry de Chambernac, for instance, spent more than a month there, supposedly to console his sister-in-law. One day a captain Hachamoth turned up, a soldier on leave. They knew his name. Their father had been killed beside him. They received him; he gave an oral account of the death.

It then appeared obvious to Daniel that in Danaomium they would be making an asphyxiating gas that would eliminate all the Boches in one fell swoop.

Naomi was secretly praying that he would not discover such a horrible thing. But she felt very guilty, especially on days when Daniel would break a jar or burn his hands with an acid.

Danaomium became chambernacium again, to honor their father.

LXXIII

Mme. Chambernac's brother-in-law was a batchelor and he was in teaching. His age entitled him not to go to war. He spoke with reserve about all that was happening in the theater of the vast world and did not comment on newspaper reports. He was said to be working on a great philosophic undertaking; on that subject, he wasn't talkative either. Perhaps this great undertaking did not exist.

M. Chambernac enjoyed talking to the gardner; he was interested in the knowledge of weather and in the dunging of the soil, but as an amateur: only as an amateur. He often went for walks in the town, always alone. Occasionally, he honored the laboratory with his presence. Daniel and Naomi blushing showed him their jars and their test tubes but didn't talk about the chambernacium. He advised them to get litmus paper and phenolphthalein to ferret out acids and bases. It was great fun. He gave them a relatively clean five-franc note from the Chamber of Commerce of Marseille so they could get some as he was advising.

Daniel and Naomi did in fact like the changes of color.

LXXIV

M. Henry went regularly to Bossu's cafe.

There was no Mme. Bossu, because she was deceased. A little boy of about twelve played among the tables. The proprietor would explain the progress of operations and the various clauses of the future peace treaty, when the French would be in Berlin. Chambernac listened while watching the building of a ship.

"You've got a nice little boy," he'd say.

"And intelligent," Bossu would add. "He'll be somebody."

The hammer striking the bright red hull made quite a racket.

LXXV

"Maman I don't understand," said Agnes, "why you let Naomi play like a boy. They spend all their time in the cabin. I saw that they have a bottle of vitriol. Maman vitriol is very dangerous. It burns. The other day Daniel burned himself again. It serves him right. Naomi ought to be helping me. I'm the only one here doing something for our poilus. Naomi'd rather fiddle around with filth. You know Maman what else I saw? Daniel put out slices of bread to get moldy one with jam on it and the other one with cheese and the others with still other things. He says he saw that in a newspaper and that it's going to make beautiful growths. It's disgusting."

"My God," said Mme. Chambernac, "what a tattletale daughter you've given me."

But Agnes never cried.

LXXVI

The beginning of September saw the arrival of Ast. He'd come straight from shelled Paris. Nieces and nephew surrounded him.

"That Bertha's really terrific," he said. "Bang! shells fall methodically. You never know if the next time won't be your turn. That's what I call living."

Bertha hadn't been shelling any more for almost a month, but nieces and nephew were dumbfounded.

"You guys live in a hole," said Ast.

Ast was going on seventeen. He was still too young to enlist and the war seemed quite won. It was infuriating.

LXXVII

Ast was acquainted with aviators and drank in bars.

Nieces and nephew were dumbfounded.

Chambernac too by the way. He'd never had that kind of youth. He was saying that to himself while sadly balancing a chunk of cheese on a piece of bread. Sophie was watching her young brother indulgently.

The father was quite forgotten.

LXXVIII

Ast went and poked his nose into the laboratory. He had ideas on the subject, and some knowledge of chemistry. He turned everything topsy-turvy. The hope of discovering chambernacium disappeared. Daniel hid and sniveled in corners. Naomi in anguish saw her prayers answered. For that matter now that the Germans were beaten, gassing them all became futile. But she too was sad to see her plaything broken. Agnes loudly and thoroughly approved Ast's throwing the molds onto the manure heap and the odd jars and the grubby vials. The litmus paper and phenolphthalein were spared as were a few serious products that happened to be there, manganese dioxide, potassium dichromate, mercury bichloride.

After sweeping, cleaning, putting in order, they had to piece things back together again.

LXXIX

Ast advised taking out a loan from the powers that be to buy retorts, bottles with lateral tubes and assorted glassware; in addition, the substances necessary to do Lespieau's experiments. The philosophic lamp interested Daniel, but generating chlorine left him cold. He persuaded Naomi to devote herself to the natural sciences. They started a herbarium and captured insects.

So Ast and Agnes occupied the laboratory alone. When they saw that the children weren't coming anymore, they abandoned it.

LXXX

In the middle of the night Daniel gradually woke up. He was breathing with difficulty. His lungs were hardening and seemed not to want to work any more. He sat up in bed, inhaling painfully and not understanding what was happening to him. Through the open window he saw the black mass of trees and the stars, nocturnal nature. He turned away and looked at the dark wall opposite him and the washbasin reflecting a vague glow. He was breathing with more and more difficulty. He was sweating. His chest leaning against his raised knees, he tried to find a position that eased the feeling of suffocation. He heard two o'clock strike, then three. Little by little the feeling of oppression eased. There was still something like a sort of sharpness in the breathing itself. He heard four o'clock strike. He murmured: "I'm happy, I'm happy, I'm happy."

LXXXI

Ast had destroyed everything. The cabin was now abandoned, chambernacium forgotten. Ast's prestige had increased in Naomi's eyes by the addition of all this bitterness. She couldn't stop admiring his beauty his strength and his intelligence; and this vitality that swept him along to the point of cruelty. He didn't pay any attention to her but what consoled her was that Agnes meant no more to him.

For that matter Ast made no secret of the fact that he

was bored to death in the midst of all these children. One day he disappeared.

LXXXII

Every other night now Daniel had an asthma attack. He decided it wasn't important and didn't tell anyone about it. Every other night, broken in two by the feeling of oppression, wheezing and sweating, he looked at the dark wall opposite him and, thinking about death, about happiness and about himself, became a philosopher.

LXXXIII

Ast ran away to Marseille. They brought him back black and blue and limping: beaten up by guys who meant business. It was an adventure. He stayed in bed for a week; his initial pride turned sullen. He read (pretended to read) all day long and didn't want to see anyone. Naomi brought up his meals, an initiative that hadn't occurred to Agnes. Naomi watched him eat. He enjoyed holding forth before this touching audience.

But as soon as he was up and about, he disappeared again, this time using the pretext of a baccalaureate exam he had to study for.

LXXXIV

But when he was gone, and even to annoy Agnes, they didn't resume their search for the new element.

BOOK FIVE

LXXXV

After the noon meal, quite copious and quite heavy, all three made themselves comfortable in the chaise longues in the shade of a large mulberry tree. The heat pressed gently on their stomachs, like a poultice; Mme. Chambernac closed her eyes and went to sleep dreaming of her youth. Sweating, Chambernac drank. Purpulan drank without sweating: a sulphurous dust drifted round his recumbent body; he passed from a solid state to a gaseous one without going through the intermediate stage of liquefaction.

"I really don't know how to approach this Roux, nor how to begin," said the principal.

"Pooh," went Purpulan perkily.

He mustered the energy to get up again to pour another glass of red wine.

"Will you give me one too," said Chambernac.

Still stretched out, he slid it deftly down his gullet.

"In my opinion," he resumed, "after a brief biography, the following points should be clearly brought out: dualism, the excremental nature of the sun and thirdly, the use of synonyms. Beginning by clearly bringing out his dualism doesn't seem like such a bad idea; in the preceding chapter, I present the search for conciliation; this one, on the contrary, will feature a radical dualism: that'll flow well. You see, Purpulan, when there's a connection like that between the chapters of a book, it shows you've mastered your subject. And I have. So, in a first part, I put together all that can be known about Pierre Roux's life from what he says about himself in the two works of his that I'm acquainted with, *Pure and New Hygiene*, Paris, 1850 and the *Treatise On The Science Of God*, Paris, 1857; he was a Protestant shop-keeper from Geneva; around 1842–1843, he had revelations, visions, raptures; in 1845, he gave up his business and came to live in Paris. That's all. One can add to that the extremely dangerous experiments, so he says, that he carried out in 1851 and 1853 and that consisted, it seems, of long walks around the refuse dumps of Montfaucon and Bondy. He almost died as a result. His books are based, so he claims, on 'one hundred thousand observations' and 'one hundred thousand experiments;' he boasts of 'thirty years in the prac-tice of medecine,' on himself probably; while still a child he's supposed to have written 'more than 800 pages folio of calculations and thoughts' on infinitesimal calculus. He ap-pears to have read a great deal: the Bible and medical books, principally; he frequently refers to the sacred books of the Orient; he quotes approvingly Ph. A. Aubé, the French Brah-min, and L. M. Salentin, who tried to revive Descartes' theory of tourbillions. Finally he'd traveled widely and was acquainted, in addition to France and Switzerland, with England, Scotland, Ireland, Italy and Istria. It seems to me that these few bits of information already give something of an idea of the man. What do you think, Purpulan?"

But Purpulan was sleeping. Chambernac put his papers down next to his chair on the gravel and joined the others in the amplitude of their naps.

At around four o'clock, they had a game of lawn bowling, sometimes with the farmer. At around seven, they had a leisurely dinner. A few hands of manilla rounded out the day; they thrashed trumps by lamplight while swatting mosquitoes.

They never bit Purpulan.

They didn't get up till around eight thirty nine o'clock; breakfast was enjoyed under the mulberry tree, slowly. Work hardly ever began before ten. It was already oppressively hot. Flies buzzed above the papers; the sun pushed against the closed shutters.

Yawning, Chambernac and Purpulan reread their Rouxian selections. The *Encyclopedia* was not progressing fast.

LXXXVI

Two principles.

"Dryness and dampness, or cold and heat, or rest and harmony and irregular motion, or light and darkness, or purity and impurity, or freedom and slavery, or the celestial and the terrestrial, or good and evil, or lightness and heaviness, or the celestial ether and the terrestrial atmosphere, etc. (which is all one); this division of elements into two or dualism which hydrogen (or base) and oxygen (or acid) represent for us, and which was the foundation of ancient Chinese philosophy and of that of Moses and of the entire Bible, is the most pure and truthful of all philosophies and is the one that we have adopted throughout the S. of G."

Five fundamental laws.

Law 41.111: Impurity puts grace to flight.

Law 72.169: When purity is dominant in a being, it chases away impurity or silences it.

Law 76.20: The more one body is similar to another, or resembles it in matter, the less tendency it has to combine with it; that is the less attraction or affinity it has for it. Contrary law: The less one body is similar to another, the more tendency it has to combine with it.

Law 73.97: There is a purification or a perfectibility and an elevation of impure matter and it comes about by means of the caloric or motion.

Six primordial substances.

"*Ether* is... a synonym very close to the word *sublime agent*; it is the wife of the sublime agent, and it is composed of more or less oxidized carbon. The ether is thus an egg, or a sponge, or a mensis prepared for the flow or the work of electricity. The *sublime agent* is the river of life which proceeds out of the throne of God and the ether is the bed prepared for this river and for its branches. And the *atmosphere* of the worlds is a more or less oxidized ether. And grace is pure electricity. Here are these terms listed in the order of their power. Grace, sublime agent, ether, spirit of Satan, magnetism, atmosphere (the latter three represent the infernal powers, that is which are not capable of anything good in and of themselves)."

Injections and excretions.

"Hydrogen, or pure electricity, represents injections; and magnetism, or oxygen or impure electricity, represents excretions.

"We mean by injections, or absorptions, or endosmosis, all that which touches man, or which enters into his body, either by the senses and by the orifices in the skin, or by the pores and the lymphatic vessels. Thus, in the first place, the inhalation of air, and all the mediums, then the remedies, eating, drinking, the gratification of the flesh or the passions and carnal sins, carnal attraction or worldly friendship, resorption, lasciviousness, the heat of the flesh, contact or any proximity of a being, or thing, or instrument, or material, liquid or gaseous object with our bodies, the view of a being or object which influences our senses or passions, emanations of all sorts or odors, savors, colors, sounds, or speech, or music, touch and thought.

. . . .

"We mean by excretions, or exhalations, or ejections, or exosmosis, all that which comes out of the body of man. Thus in the first place, respiration or expiration, then excrements and vomitings, or fecal matter, gas of the upper and the lower part of the body, saliva, spittle, sweat, snot, invisible emanations and exhalations of all sorts which come out of our bodies, either in a state of life or death, emissions of urine, sperm, tears and others; losses of blood, water, fluxes or flows, pus and humors, and others; perspiration or exhalation, evacuations of all kinds; the sebaceous humor of the skin, and the acids and fats that ooze from it; discharges, purulence, the beard, hair, body hair, corns, nails, dead skin, ulcers, calluses, callosities, hard skin, indurations, fistulas, pimples, abcesses, excrescences, deformities, chancres, cankers, bumps, swellings, wens, rashes, exocrine glands, aphthous ulcers, tuberosities, bubos, pustules, and exudations of all sorts, purulence, fetid fluids or others, the expulsions and emptyings which precede or follow parturition; the placenta, amniotic fluid, abortion, monstrosities, lochia, pusses and venoms, vaccines and viruses of all sorts; transudation, perspiration, mucus; in a word all diaphoresis and all that comes out of all the orifices of the body, pores and lymphatic vessels, and even all the internal secretions produced by the matters above, any serosity whatsoever, phlegm, nodal matter, kidney sediment, gravel and stones

"… Finally error, lies, hypocrisy, and all bad sounds, signs, motions, forms, looks, encounters, views, writings, drawings, figures, emblems, types, colors, magic, bad or impure or indecent phantasmagoria; magnetism, somnambulism, and the whole packet of pythonico-mesmerian inventions, whatever they may be. All useless, deceitful and bad or idle signs, speeches, or words. The bad thoughts and all the bad actions or sins of man.

. . . .

"… all the poisons and impure or dirty matter of the globe are included under the name of excretions: such are mud, earth, garbage, scrapings, scrap, waste, rags, sweepings, dust, dirt, manipulation, impurity, yeasts, filth, vermin, riffraff, old houses, debris, fill, old plaster, beings at the bottom of the scale, rot, fermentation, droppings, dregs, silt, sediment, scum, verdigris, colored matter, and especially that colored by the impurities mentioned above, acids, all loathsome and corrupted matter, manure, bad company, the impious, the impure, hypocrites, deceivers, corrupters, thieves and all those who rally to the banner of Satan, that is the carnal, or sensual, or worldly, and who unfortunately form 99 one hundredths of humanity… woodworm, putrefaction, oxidation, wakefulness, impure air, sluggishness, insufficiency of movement, venereal sins, bad habits, impure clothing, the passions."

Origin of the world.

"… it is the corrupt angels who formed or created the visible material universe with their excretions…

"In the material universe, the central trunk of impurity are the suns; the comets are the roots, the aerolites and infernal spirits are the branches, and the planets are its flowers and magnetism its sap."

The sun.

"The sun is one of the satans of the universe, hence: like a true hypocrite, he wears the mantle of God. He is a whited sepulchre, which inside is full of bones and rot, Satan to lead men astray dresses as an angel of light.

"… The sun is impure… The core is excremental, it is the cesspool of our system, but its crust is formed by the souls of the damned of the different planets, and these souls are made of H. S. and of impure matter. They live in an acrimonious and terrible friction, and are nourished by the exhalations of the core. But this feverish motion similar to the bearings of an electrical machine, attracts the H. S. of interstellar space in virtue of law 76.20, and this same attraction also produces the orbits of the planets and comets. The H. S. which reaches the sun cannot stay there in virtue of our law 41.111; it therefore seizes its spouse, carbon, contained in the souls of the damned, and by radiating in all directions, goes to carry life and being to all the globes of our system.

"... All that man can do on the earth, is to copy nature, and he reaches perfection only when his work resembles that of God; hence: large-scale reservoirs should be made for the excrements of pure animals and very civilized men, and the magnetism emanating from them should be collected; but that is an impossible thing, because there are no pure beings here below. A city like Paris, for example, is a sun, for there are half a million devils disporting themselves above fifty thousand and more cesspools...

"Men are little ambulant suns..."

LXXXVII

"That will be," said Chambernac, "the central point of my exposition; then will come the following propositions:

1

Cooks' cooking is the devil's cooking.

2

Medicos' medicine makes of the body a madrepore, or sun, an impure coal.

3

No civilization is possible as long as there exists a single rag picker.

4

Coitus or masturbation is exactly the same phenomenon as magnetization.

5

Human sperm is materialized spirit or matter so very perfected that it is the last degree between matter and spirit.

6

It is infested by ferocious and voracious animalcules, the spermatozoa.

7

The Song of Songs produces in the Bible the same effect as a large dish of excrement brought in in the middle of a sumptuous and pure meal.

8

Nudity and body hair characterize the brute.

9

If men had the purity of angels, all women would conceive photographically (like Mary—J. C. is the son of the angel Gabriel) and would give birth to perfect hermaphrodites who would be taken up to heaven.

10

Poverty is a punishment from God.

11

Nothing on this earth resembles the kingdom of heaven more than a well-run business or factory or industry.

12

The reign of God is the reign of penitentiaries.

13

It is only by holding in penitentiaries all the poor and the most licentious beings of all classes of society that the friends of God will be able to establish a semblance of peace and joy on earth.

14

Before the end of the world, half of humanity will be locked up in penitentiaries.

15

99/100ths of men will go to hell.

16

The adoration of woman or of the phallus has been the only religion professed for 4,000 years.

17

1790 struck a fatal blow on earth to the age of orgy, which was the ancien regime.

18

Lamennais, Cabanis, Lavater, Gall, Lavoisier, Azaïs, Leroy, Daguerre, Raspail and Foucault rank foremost among the great John the Baptists of the scientific revolution in the xixth century.

19

Pierre Roux, traveling salesman of the Everlasting, comes on his behalf to take the key of science from the hands of the Lamaists and give it to those who labor in pure hygiene.

20

The reign of true science is moral chemistry. Chemistry is half of religion. The Bible is the most perfect treatise on electricity which will ever exist in the world.

21

The reign of God on earth will be made effective by the omnipowerful battery (200-meter tower built on the summit of a mountain on bared rock; its base will be of glass; on its summit a windmill or a steam engine will turn an enormous glass wheel rubbing against amalgam-lined bearings.)

22

This discovery is so immense that there has not been one like it since the flood, and it surpasses that of Newton by as far as the heavens are higher than the earth.

23

Other discoveries: aerial locomotives; ambulant, artificial suns."

LXXXVIII

Ambulant suns, Chambernac and Purpulan were strolling along in the country, one slow and ponderous, the other hissing the air with a thin stick and decapitating flowers. The footpath ran along a slope, between fields, to the highway. There the principal sat down in a little shelter put up by the Mourmèche Regional Bus Company. Purpulan put his foot on a kilometer-marker, leaned his elbow on his knee and watched the cars whizzing by on the beautiful straight line offered them.

"The sun," said Chambernac, "the sun will be the central point. It's the center of the system. Excremental, satanic—now who could ever have conceived of that? What do you think of it, Purpulan?"

Purpulan didn't deign to answer.

"Well," said Chambernac, "you must know something about it, after all."

Purpulan mimed ignorance, as if determined to let the other soliloquize.

"How," resumed Chambernac, suddenly resigned to ignorance on this perhaps supposed subject of demonology, "could this opinion have come into being?"

Purpulan's gesture indicated that he didn't give a damn.

"What," resumed Chambernac, "is curious, is that a similar, one might say, theory is to be found in the writings of a 'seer' whom I'm not using since he found disciples and an audience, I mean Louis Michel de Fignières. Because, for him, if divine sustenance reaches the planets through the intermediary of the suns, reciprocally the latter are the site where celestial garbage collection is done and the place where the residues of this sustenance and the carcasses of the planets accumulate. It's an analogous point of view. No. Actually not. Not at all."

"Make up your mind," said Purpulan without turning around.

The cars were still testing their speed on the hwy.

"It," said Chambernac, "'s different because for Louis Michel the residues are plunged into liquid and thus revivified. While for Roux, the sun is a diabolical thing: a satan. Why don't you say something, Purpulan."

Purpulan left his marker and came to sit next to the principal.

"Why," he said mildly, "worry any more about this than about the abbé Matalène with his sun that's one meter in diameter or any other wild idea?"

"There is here," said Chambernac, "something scandalous. I'd like to understand."

"Understand what?"

"How a man can get to thinking that way."

"Felix qui potuit rerum cognoscere causas," said Purpulan.

"Come come, be serious."

The MRBC bus came along. They waved their right arms.

They went as far as Sandignac. During the ride they didn't talk. Purpulan was looking the people over with a critical eye; Chambernac, hands crossed on his stomach, continued his worrying.

From Sandignac to Cravonne, it was three kilometers broken two thirds of the way along by an old inn which had become a gas station. The two encyclopedists were well-known there; on that day, as on so many others, they stopped to restore their strength. The sun, flat and red, was slowly sliding toward the horizon.

After clinking glasses with Purpulan and the proprietor, a fellow named Chamèche, Chambernac murmured:

"One meter in diameter or shit."

"What was that, monsieur Chambernac," asked the inn-keeper hoping he hadn't heard right.

"M. Chambernac is thinking," said Purpulan with a self-important air. "He works a great deal, and on difficult subjects."

"I can imagine," said the other.

"Of course," said Chambernac, "I did not set out, in this book, to understand nor to explain, let's say, the ravings of our authors. My work is purely enumerative, descriptive, selective. Moreover, who understands madness? No one. Especially not the psychiatrists. All they do themselves is describe, enumerate, classify. Though Doctor Frachoux did say something about a doctrine called psychoanalysis that explains dreams."

"I know about that," interrupted the station man, "I have a key to dreams upstairs, just as a joke of course. I'm not superstitious."

Chambernac was silent. Purpulan was tapping the tip of his shoe with his switch in a very cavalier way.

"I have to go now," said the proprietor. "I have some work to finish."

He'd made a little canal that passing by the johns came out in his field down below. He took his pick to the low wall that was holding back the water and soon a blackish liqueur came to soak the humus. Chamèche, in boots and kneedeep in the pit, was activating this herculean cleansing.

The encyclopedists as they were leaving, stopped to watch him at work, in spite of the bad odor. Chambernac came near the hole; big bubbles rose to burst on the surface of the loathsome liquid. The fermenting fluid was now spreading out over the earth, and the furrows were drinking.

"Some job I'm doing here, eh," said the garage man, "but wait till you see my vegetables next year."

The principal went away encouraging him in his agricultural work.

"You saw that bubbling," he said to his companion. "That's life, like the sun,—the life of the earth, elemental life. There's no escaping it."

"So?" asked Purpulan.

Sadly, Chambernac looked at him.

LXXXIX

When Chambernac once again caught sight of the splendor of the sun, it was already the end of August. Then he shook Purpulan and shook himself, determined to finish before school got under way cosmology in the person of Bousquet as well as the natural sciences and the science of language. Then, with the coming of winter, they'd tackle history and doubtless the next year would see his great undertaking brought to a close.

Purpulan driven hard submitted on August twenty-eighth selections of the book entitled:

"The name of the book entitled the Mystery of the Supreme Being Book of life, immortal perfect undertaking, made in Cessenon, by M. Bousquet Augustinian. Year of

1860. *Year of the beginning of the world, etc. God alone knows: The Beginning and the End.*"

XC

"1.—Science is the spirit and the light of the virtue of the knowledge of the things which come from God.

2.—Prophecy is the truth of things discovered from the beginning to the end.

3.—Philosophy is the knowledge of things present, past and to come.

4.—Astronomy is the reconnaissance and the knowledge of things, of stars and of planets.

5.—Geometry is the measure and the correct calculation of things.

6.—Chemistry is the true knowledge of natural and material things.

7.—Zoology is the discovery of mineral and material things.

8.—Engineering is the work of the invention of things.

9.—Physics is the nature of the things of the world and animals.

10.—Magic is the work of the things of the hand of man and creatures.

11.—Patrea is the work of things, of animals.

12.—The formality of things is the nature and matter of creation.

13.—Natures are the matter of things of all the elements of the entire universes.

14.—Matter is the formality, uniformality and transformality of things.

15.—The planet in forming itself beginning at the gram of the impossible, grows to a year of rotation of approximately 400 days, of 13 times of cataclysm; and in burning and coming to an end, diminishes to the second of the breath of God."

XCI

"You see, monsieur Chambernac," said Purpulan, "he had an encyclopedic mind like you."

XCII

Circles.

"*The impossible*.—the stable sky, alpha, globe, ball, nilis, mind, work of God.

Irresistance.—Paternal and maternal, natural word, masculine and feminine.

Eternity.—Formality, nourishment, food, delicious fruit, cahos.

Infinity.—Space, unity, circles.

Always.—Spiritual and material enlightenment.

Time.—Existence, beginning and end.

The universe.—Distillatory splendors.

Creation.—Perpetual evolution.

Thenus.—Stone, life and death, plural and singular.

Venus.—Beings and ice, cereals, humor.

Mercury.—Water, bones, mountains, coal, volcanos.

The moon.—Matter, firmament, stars.

The sun.—Fire and flames, purification, omega.

The earth.—Material and natural planet, flesh and bone, world and animals.

Politere.—Flowers, sanctification.

The celestial.—Glories and paradise, angels.

The throne of God.—Purity, right, the I justice of the Supreme Being, eternal homage.

The inferior.—Sufferings, hell.

Limbo.—Darkness.

Nothingness.—Nothing more."

XCIII

"Why not?" murmured Chambernac.

XCIV

"Explain to me the four parts of the members of the world on earth?

"The four parts of the members of the world on earth are the domege and the savage, the good and the evil, as much the world of the day as of the night, continuous, the top, the bottom, the right and the left, the front and the back, the inility of the surroundings of the earth, that it is the black, the white, the yellow and the red, those are the four parts of the world on earth with all the animate beings, and so forth.

. . . .

"How are the earth, the firmament, the moon, the sun and the sky formed by naturality itself?

"Yes, the earth is formed by the deposit of the dead body, and the moon by ice, and the sun by fire, and the star by being, and water by blood, and ice by cold, and the earth by flesh, and stone by bones, and the air by breath, and the sky by infinity, and the weather by wind, calm, serenity, humidity, fog, cloud, rain, snow, hail, the infusions of the sky, lightning, thunder, the bolt of the great distillatory.

. . . .

"What do you mean by a time, by times, ages, generations and centuries?

"By ages I mean fifty years, and by generations one hundred years, and by centuries one thousand years, and by times all the existences accomplished or to be accomplished by God himself and by a time one year.

"What do you mean by teeth, beings, winds and cake?

"By teeth I mean the first things, which began to harden in natural existence, and by beings and winds the first things of the globe which began to (a)rise, where nature came into existence, in the infinite space of all the elements, and by cake adultery with all evil of every sort.

. . . .

"Please explain to me how the planets begin and end?

"The planets of the kingdom, in infinite space, begin to form by the humor of the glacial cereal: with time became a large body of ice, which formed the moon; with time this ice, struck by heat, became water; this great mass of water formed a deposit which turned itself into a crust and became mother earth; after awhile the earth heats up and catches fire and becomes a burning sun, which disappears in flaming gas; that is the beginning and the end of all the planets one after the other; it is the veritable and principal calendar of the great glacial body which always calls forth the keel and holds it by its great weight in its equilibrium of natural creation not including the other kingdoms of unknown planets, nor knowing what concerns beyond the limited space of the height-so-long, separate cahosments that God placed without being able to decipher his incomprehensible and inestimable formalities, it is the impossible that the Supreme Being placed to infinity."

XCV

"You see," said Chambernac, "it's like the anonymous writer from Lyon: the origin of things is ice; exactly the opposite of what our astronomy teaches us. For them ice, therefore cold, is very near the first cause. That gets us back to Roux's horror of heat and the sun. I find that rather disturbing. No doubt these two qualities appear to be single, as Vernet puts it, and are in fact double. And perhaps there are reasons why a given individual is struck by one aspect rather than the other. What do you think Purpulan?"

"I think, monsieur, that you're philosophizing. Sutor ne ultra crepidam."

"Henry," remarked Agatha who for some time now had been present at all their sessions, "he spoke Latin again. He hasn't done that in a long time."

"It's a front," said Chambernac.

He studied his secretary, a brief moment, in silence.

"He obviously," he said, "has a dysodipyric and scatothermal nature."

"You can't hurt me with words you went and found in the dictionary," said Purpulan.

"Let's get back to work," said the principal.

XCVI

"The Unity of calculative numbers for learning how to count.

Number, Ten or So, One Hundred or So, One Thousand.

Ten Thousand or So, One Hundred Thousand or So, One Million.

Ten Million or So, One Hundred Million or So, One Billion.

Ten Billion or So, One Hundred Billion or So, Legion.

Ten Legion or So, One Hundred Legion or So, Thenus.

. . . .

10000000000000000 Thenus.

"Ten hundred thenus make a circle of the impossible incalculable remaining fixed to thenus of each planet ball and of the entire contiguous ball of the temporal container of the natural and material globe, occidental, boreal of aurora, to know the cause of traced, formed, transformed things; naturalizes and denaturalizes, some of others; one must study them, go deeper into them with experience to understand them well. The thenus comes and goes, ends and begins while forming, uniforming, transforming and changing itself in nature from the impossible to the breath of God and in the distance of nothingness itself. In dying beings leave the stone of its gaso which passes into the planet from one time to another and each time the planet changes in nature from the beginning to the end, as one dominates the other; and 20 circles of 20 cataclysms of the 20 times of the existences of approximately 2,000,000 years and 100,000 years of burial from one cataclysm to the other, from a time of space without the fixed point with respect that the natures furnish more or less; and in a few thousand years from today the months will consist of 32 days, and the year of 13 months, and the eighth called sabbath. In forming themselves natures grow, and in burning diminish by an accomplished time by distance from one planet to the other. On earth there are five stages of circles, mountains traced from one another, that waste away and come back to the surface and the others swallowed up in the nouho of the ball cape ourgues abe.

"1. The stage of the lands of the mountains of salt, nilis vericler silia limpid, light, stone, ice, copper, kwarss, white galena, diamond, gold, silver, manganese, magnet of the nature of the boreal beings of the impossible and springing from thenus.

"2. The stage of the lands of the black carbonic coal mountains, zinc, lead and mineral iron, warm water of the natural fire of the nature of the glacial beings of venus.

"3. The stage of the lands of the reddish and limey, sinewy and woody mountains; coal, gas and oil, heated by the material fire of the nature of the temperate beings of mercury.

"4. The stage of the lands of the white, chalky mountains, gritrock, frejal, ore, melting gush, lime of the corporal fire of the nature of the animate beings of the moon.

"5. The stage of the lands of the mountains of hardened

gravel, sands and shells, open boil sulfur vulcanized by the burning fire of the natures, of the human and artful beings of the earth.

"— And the nature of the burning beings of flaming fire, will be the soral time, and formal nature comes from the impossible and the material of thenus.

"— The planet bears all the marks of the traces, the passages, the globes, the matters and natures of circles, the turns of the ball, times, centuries, generations, ages and years from the impossible which God created to the majesty of the divinity of his throne.

. . . .

"Heritory natural and formal planets in the glacial globe and in the globe of the burning air of the firmament, suspended, which travel the open space, conspicuous and inconspicuous inhabited by animate beings, beautiful giant genius, with unforeseen and unknown things in its naturality, that live and form themselves in the open space of the infinite globe like all the others, among which the glacial one is one day around and eight leagues across, and the one with the firmament one league and twenty minutes also in the burning air, and the sun twenty-four leagues around and eight leagues across, and the moon one month around and ten leagues across, and the earth one year around and from the circumference to the circumference four months across and one year of time of distance from one planet to the other, the distances are equal with respect that each one goes through at its peak and in turn becomes the same thing, and the comets one meter around and three meters long, and the stars one piece around and three pieces long and smaller ones and larger ones and as for the distances are vulgar as also comets, and the sky embraces all infinite space, reaches the Supreme Being himself infinitely incomprehensible in his infinity; one cannot lift the wheel which God has set in place, nor truth in its infinity, the first of ice, the second of the sun, the celestial planet brings to infinity and the inferior one to nothingness, begins with the day and ends with the hour."

XCVII

"Let us think about the fact that all is but a light mist of a sanguinary slaughterhouse cahos, of a section of age which appears and disappears into nothingness without God."

XCVIII

"Anyone who would go beyond the circle of the impossible will lose his marbles."

XCIX

"Any printer, bookseller, philosopher or poet who shall take away or violate by evil any of the words written in the prophecy or philosophy of this book of life, spiritual and luminous of God in the world, of creation and of the entire Universe, will bear the consequences before the divine justice of the Supreme Being."

C

While Chambernac was drafting a comprehensive commentary of these texts, seeking the meaning of the neologisms, the conciliation of the divergent enumerations and the ultimate cohesion of this cosmology, while Massicot was harvesting his grapes, while Chamèche was shaking down nuts and while Agatha was making jam, Purpulan was nearly bringing to completion the second part by preparing the two separate chapters concerning meteorology and botany, devoted respectively to Le Barbier (Pierre-Louis, 1766–1836), dominatmospherizer, dominaturalizer, dominatrizer, dominhominizer, retemperizer, prolongopinizer of the entire world, temperaturizer, almost omnipotentutilizer omnibus and, in a mild winter and without interruptions in the work, without an increase in fuel, be it wood or coal, donamillionizer, donabillionizer, and when the rain falls at the right time donagoldmineizer and to Hussenot (Louis-Cincinnatus-Severin-Leon, 1808–?) author of *Thistles of Nancy* and of the *System Of Unprecedented Translation With Neither Periods Nor Commas*.

CI

"Dominatmospheria

. . . .

"Instruction for sailors.

. . . .

"I spent seven days in Dieppe, saw fourteen tides, and by means of the air stirred with care, as long as there was in evidence any craft or vessel, not one missed the entrance of the port during the tide.

"In order to obtain the stirring of the air during a long period of time, I used a kitchen bellows, worth three pounds fifteen sous, and a long screw with ring attachment worth two sous six deniers, to steady the flow of air coming from the bellows, and to have something to lean on that gives more strength to the man, who always operates the bellows with his back to the west, because the rain that stills the wind almost always comes from the west.

"One must use this means moderately with circumspection, above all when the winds come from the west northwest. The duration of this work of stirring the air, makes the winds start up again, so that in order to keep them favorable, one must not stir the air by this process too continuously.

"From this procedure, I've gone on to discover a new one, which man possesses in whatever situation he finds himself; it is his BREATH.

"Thus, instead of blowing hard into a wind instrument, he will blow into the free air a drummer's march.

"A third, more economical than the bellows, and costing only fifteen sous, came to mind; it is the feather duster that is used to maintain or increase the heat of the coal that cooks cutlets.

"A fourth, the marine cotillion.

"A fifth, aboard a naval ship, the fire fighting equipment; it can be used in five ways on board.

"… One can, by throwing water with force from buckets onto the deck and with as many buckets at once as there are on board, increase the mass of air, since, according to scien-

tists, water contains eighty-five parts of vital air and fifteen
parts of flammable air…

> Le Barbier."

CII

Hussenot.

REFORM OF BOTANY

"An herbarium as I conceive of it and as I am working to
make mine, is nature itself, complete; I want to have a dried
field of each plant; how can one be sure of the value of a
feature, if one cannot follow it in a hundred specimens? If I
succeed in winning acceptance for my ideas on this subject,
I shall have laid the groundwork for a great revolution in
Science and from today on, my admirers can say to me as to
the Everlasting 'Renovabis faciem terrae.'"

OPIUM

"…Last winter was for me a time of hard labor; here is my
winter routine: I get up at 10 o'clock, I swallow down a cup
of coffee, then I dissect until 5 o'clock, when I have an un-
distinguished meal; from 6–7 black coffee more often twice
than once, newspapers (I'm a dyed-in-the-wool republican)
or some sort of relaxation; I get back to work at 7, 8, 9 o'clock
until 2–7 in the morning. I climb to the temple of Memory
the least of all. As a tranquilizer, I make liberal use of beer;
as a stimulant, of coffee, tea and opium. I contracted the
latter habit during the domestic harassment that I've been
subjected to for two years: without this drug, I would cer-
tainly not have endured life."

THE HUMAN HEART

"I have, in my spare time, scrupulously analyzed all the human hearts that I've been able to lay my hands on. First I rinse the object properly to rid it of all the ointments, unguents, perfumes, aromatic substances that people think they must annoint and grease themselves with in order to mask its natural odor, to disguise its composition and throw the Chemists off track. When I've washed it thoroughly in hot and cold water, ether and alcohol solutions sharpened with acid then with alkali, when I've removed all the foreign matter of every sort which formed a sort of thick shell of varnish, then the object gives off a strong odor of decay *sui generis*, a most nauseating combination of sh… and of carrion, which makes one feel very sick and even provokes vomiting if one is so careless as to expose one's olfactory nerves to these disgusting emanations for too long.

"…there is a certain human Heart which one cannot straightforwardly and rigorously consider as coming under the law of mire, it is the heart of the carrion that loves us. To others, it is not worth a pfennig more than the others, but for us, it would let itself be hung, it would let itself be killed. One should not however feel too obligated to it, for as I have said, to the rest of the world, it is and remains carrion; it loves us by instinct, irresistibly, like our dog, that throws itself into the water to follow us without knowing whether it can swim."

THE PYRAMID OF HIS GLORY

"…I want to raise the pyramid of my glory as Moralist as high as that of my Botanical glory: then I shall be able to die without regret, or go happily to the madhouse in Charenton, I will have lived a full life, for, without money, I will have gotten myself talked about, without help, I will have ruined all my enemies in my disaster.—Meanwhile long live joy and potatoes."

CIII

"You're the one," said Purpulan, "he'll owe his glory to, Monsieur Chambernac. Have you considered, Monsieur Chambernac, that all these lunatics who thought they were geniuses and wanted glory and remain unknown, are going to come out of obscurity when your *Encyclopedia* is published: thanks to you, their names will receive some luster and go down to posterity. They didn't deserve so much honor, but they'll pay you back one hundredfold. These unknown sparks brought together by your breath will light the inextinguishable torch that will shine on your glory forever and ever."

"Be quiet satan monster of pride," said Mme. Chambernac. "Don't listen to him, Henry."

"There's some truth in what he says," said M. Chambernac.

"On the other hand," resumed Purpulan, "from the moment these 'literary lunatics' become—thanks to you—known, by that very fact they'll stop being 'literary lunatics,' since—thanks also to you—they'll acquire that reknown the lack of which permitted them to appear in the *Encyclopedia*. Don't you think, Monsieur Chambernac, that there's a sort of contradiction there?"

"Watch out Henry," said Mme. Chambernac. "He's trying to discourage you. He's backing both horses: pride and despair."

"I know what he's doing," said Chambernac.

"And," resumed Purpulan, "if you lead some to glory you leave so many others in obscurity… Have you thought about that, Monsieur Chambernac? How unfair."

Chambernac told him to be quiet; but his zeal had slackened. When they left Cravonne, Language was still untackled. It was the work of the new year.

CIV

Behold said Chambernac
to the public he was not to know
behold said Chambernac
the five philologists I have chosen
(I have I have seen quite a few others
both those who have found the original language
and those who have found the universal language.
— Some of them are wise and many more mediocre
behold those that I have chosen)
DESDOUITZ DE SAINT-MARS wrote a *Dictionary of Gallic
Etymologies*
of which I'll give a few examples
Fleuve = FL-EV-V-E = Flowing every vast end in English =
   all great end of current in French
Rivière = RI-VI-ER-E = Rise with every end in English =
   an end of source in French

Montagne = M-ON-TAG-NE = Masse one tapering needs
in English = a block, a mass necessarily ending in a point
in French.

Secondly

Joseph BOUZERAN

(born and died in Agen, 1799–1868)

He translated La Fontaine's fables into Greek verse,

To his students explained his ideas on

Systematic Linguistic Unity Or Philosophy Of The Word
In the Catholic Trinity

which got him dismissed

When he protested he was interned

for 31 months in Charenton

Every word, said he, is composed of three consonants or
keys

guttural K, labial P, dental T

Every word, said he, can be reduced to the model word
KPT, caput

The word caput exists alone, said he. It means head, first
principle, father, creator.

and all the others are only its synonyms

Third the Abbé Terence-Joseph O'DONNELLY

to whom God *offered* three discoveries:

the squaring of the circle,

the key of the hieroglyphs

> The obelisk of the Place de la
> Concorde is the work of
> Nimrod. A single hieroglyph
> was refractory to the abbé's
> method, he was in despair; he
> finally discovered that it was

only the diagram of the erection of the monument under Louis-Philippe, diagram engraved on its pedestal.

the original and universal language

"Of all the events that have happened since creation" this discovery "ranks third after the flood and the redemption."

For him there exist only vowels
and the Hebrew alphabet put
"to the test of mathematical equations"
revealed to him 66
In the fourth place
Séb.-François DROJAT who found
The Master-Key Of The Tower Of Babel
in the Vocont language (he lived in Die)
"contubernal language of the whole human race"
The Table-ature is composed:
    of the Irome: formed of full phones:
        44 consonants including 8 sodals,
        11 vowels including 2 sodals and
        4 resumptives;
    of the Parirome, formed of Paraphones:
        The Gytton
        The Infernal Paraphones
            (Prosodic
            The Chabrille
            The Daille
            The Lene

The Tourniquet)

The Obnutity

(The Lupanar or the Golden-Band

The Werwolf ▣ absolute Silence

The Black-Band or the Lupercalia)

The Supernal Paraphones

(The Lynx

The gray Wolf

The She-Wolf

The Wolf plex

The Pausterics)

The Phoenix

and of the total redemptive vowel, the **I** in the ζ,

"the very richest spoils there are"

For each graph has a moral:

that of the closed *é* is infaust

that of the M detestable

that of the *n* quite happy

Finally LE QUEN D'ENTREMEUSE whose

Sirius, New Insights Into The Origin Of Idolatry,

was published in 1852.

CV

"And now can I not say, without fear of being accused of systematic monomania, that this Great *Tho-Th* to whom the earliest Egyptian antiquity attributes the head of a dog, while it represents the constellation of the GREAT-DOG by the sacred signs T-T, pronounced *Thau-Thau*, is none other than the great TOUTOU (*Bow-wow*) of the Heavens?

"… Is there not a manifest identity, *dazzling*, if I may express myself thus, between these names of the *Dog, Taau-T…, Thou-T…, To-T…* in Ethiopian, and *Tou-Tou*, in everyday French.

"… Shall I show CHIENS—dogs—in these QUENS or counts of the old French provinces where the word *chien* was pronounced QUEN, KUEN, a form that de Guignes gives as that of dog, in China, where this word QUENS is a title equivalent to *Governor* of a *Province* or a *City*, while it is to be found, among the Etruscans, in this same form QUEN, with the meaning of *King*.

"… Whatever may happen, I will deserve well of Dogs, in general; Dogs in name and arms, as well as Dogs in fact.

"I would have been happy had I been permitted to put this schoolboy's work under the aegis of an authoritative and highly regarded name; but since this honor is forbidden me, I dedicate it to my humble collaborator, to my faithful and brave DRAGON, FIDELIS ET AUDAX,—and I entrust to him its defense.

"Help me, DRAGON!

"Help me, all the dogs and DOG of the world!"

BOOK SIX

CVI

Toto-the-Pallor-of-living lived on the prostitution of women, two of them, over near the Place de la République. He lived sadly, his lip always stiff and his look always stern. People explained that by saying it was because there'd been a great misfortune in his life, no one knew what, not even the two women responsible for his support and who loved him as he was, his lip stiff and his look stern.

He spoke little but with authority, and read the newspapers carefully. From the way he talked, you could tell he knew many things people in his profession don't usually know. He knew all about mechanics and electricity; he could explain why airplanes are heavier than air and fly all the same, why radio doesn't need wires and why loudspeakers make so much noise. He filled in crossword grids with capital letters, knew his geography and knew how rich people lived. His information on the latter subject proved so complete that some people ended up thinking he was of high birth and calling him the Swell, for a time. But one thing at any rate was sure, his southern origin, although after prolonged efforts he had succeeded in dulling his accent.

Astonishment, more than sadness, more than despair, was the feeling that most usually held sway in his heart, a melancholy and frightened astonishment that a mean look concealed from the eyes of observers. Toto-the-Pallor-of-living was as anxious as the next person to defend his honor and look like a man, but when he thought about it, he was astonished at his fate and couldn't understand what had happened to him. He remembered a time when ambition swelled his veins and when he could start every sentence with I, without being ashamed of his vanity. His father had put into his head the notion that he had a future; he was sure of it. Triumphantly he'd taken the train for Paris. And look at him now, he's pimping pathetically behind the Place de la République.

In the small town he'd taken off from some four years earlier, they considered him a good worker, a future foreman, a probable boss of a small business, and he thought: an engineer, for powerful and rich people had turned their attention to him and were protecting him. He believed in the solidity, in the durability of this support and look at him now, while climbing the ladder, he'd fallen flat on his face, he didn't really know how. He hadn't gotten over it. He thought about it often and his stupefaction just kept growing. Sometimes it was the sight of a tramp, sometimes the sight of a beautiful car that propelled this train of thought always leading to the same dead end of amazement. The fact that after setting out with such high hopes he'd only gotten to the realm of pimpage and nowhere else seemed to him immensely inexplicable and absurd, almost comical, like in the movies when a guy wants to sit down and another guy takes away his chair and he falls down instead.

He didn't see how he could be responsible for his fate; he didn't blame himself; he had to look elsewhere. So he thought that there was in the world a force called Injustice that revealed itself in failed destinies like his. He'd often read articles in the paper where they discussed social injustices; stuff like that didn't interest him. His own personal injustice was a much different matter, it went much further, it was much nastier, in every way. One evening as he was going home, his woman on his arm, he wondered why the sun never illuminated the night whereas the moon was perpetually sentenced to it. That, he thought, was a great misfortune comparable to his. He kept these ideas to himself, exemplary and secret victim that he was, and didn't share them with his buddies, colleagues or friends, whose fate he found natural. At times, when he was playing cards, he'd look up, coldly examine X or Y and see that their destiny fit them like a glove and that there wasn't any injustice in their living like grubs. But as for him, he'd been stupidly cheated and not a single soul could give him an explanation for his misfortune.

Until now he'd never actually led a really wretched life: the women's work was productive and every year he'd go spend a month fishing on the banks of the Marne. While waiting for the animal to make a mistake, he would think. Afterwards he'd play quoits, and that didn't keep him from thinking either. For others, that was having a good time; for him, just more of the same. If nothing had disrupted the expected course of his existence, right now, he'd have his car and a villa on the Riviera, in spite of the depression. And now men were thinking twice before taking their money out of their pockets, because of the depression.

Sometimes people he knew would invite him along on a job; he knew how to refuse so it didn't look like he was chickening out. When the others had left, he'd grow pale with fright; he was sure that if he happened to do something illegal, the injustice that was hounding him was so savage that he'd be caught and sentenced. He was afraid of cops, judges, warrant officers, all those who have the power to strike at random and to commit judicial errors. Therefore his prudence had advised him to be nice to the guys from the vice squad without however taking it as far as professional snitching, with the result that his good relationship with the police gave him security, but no dough.

Industrial activity was withering in the breath of the depression and that too was starting to look like a lousy trick. For what did it matter to him if Flemish wheat or English cotton, Brazilian coffee or Malayan tin weren't selling? In the tumult of a world still trembling with the emotion of a war, he'd seen himself following a splendid trajectory whose landing point would be a death crowned with riches and honor, surrounded by grandchildren and very expensive doctors. He'd crashed into an invisible wall, a clear, hard diamond; he was lying shattered at the root of this iniquity and was dragging himself without enthusiasm toward an end which would certainly have nothing brilliant about it. And now dullness was turning to chaos, because of people you didn't even know and who were overproducing overseas. Like a driver speeding along at night on a highway closed off by an inexplicable mirror and who, after running into a tree to avoid the real image of his own car, continues on foot only to have someone dynamite the peaceful little path thanks to which he was hoping to reach the nearest tomb, thus he whom Injustice struck so stupidly felt anew this absurdity ready to lay waste to the quiet corner where he was living out his resignation.

As a matter of bitter fact, wireless telegraphy was progressing and prospering: the domain he had chosen for himself. He'd foreseen that one day every window would disgorge dark bellowings, and that it would be his work; and now, every day the noise was intensifying, and he'd had no hand in it. Every loudspeaker told him of his disaster; every time he heard one of those machines spew forth, he didn't howl with despair but stupidly astonished let himself drift into the muddiest of melancholies. Then everything would start all over: the ruminations and the perplexities.

Injustice for him did not consist in the various inequalities that classify men; he wasn't asking for an explanation of beauty and ugliness variously apportioned, of money unequally divided; for him Injustice was not that there were the strong and the weak, but rather that the strong, which to him meant the clever, the guys who knew the ropes, among whom he included himself, might conceivably succumb. It seemed quite natural to him that those who didn't go to battle weren't victors, but that those who plunged into the fray might conceivably be vanquished dumbfounded him. All combat meant victory to him: he didn't like taking risks.

One day he found in his pocket an old scrap of dirty paper that had lain there since who knows how long.

CVII

With Gramigni gone and the clerk in the back room, Clemence using a slack period was putting away bills and doing accounts with a sputtering pen on a little piece of paper. In the deserted street, a fellow happened to pass, and the grocer made a note of his appearance in her memory in spite of her sums, a hesitant and timid appearance, obviously suspicious. When he happened to pass again half a minute later, the grocer stopped all arithmetical activity to actively observe the individual. He stopped in front of the door, wiped his right shoe against his left pant leg and his left shoe against his right pant leg, fixed his fedora firmly on his head, spat off to the side, then came in. Clemence catalogued him first of all in the category of novice traveling salesmen, those you chase away without listening to them, and who know it; but his very last bit of behavior precluded placing him in that social category: ultimately he looked much more dangerous. She abruptly closed the cash register and reassured herself by the invisible but potentially effective presence of the clerk.

"Lo," said the entrant.

Clemence didn't answer.

"Lo," repeated the other moving forward with swaying uncertainty.

"What do you want?" asked Clemence.

"I'm here to see Gramigni. Monsieur Gramigni."

"Not in."

"I can see you don't recognize me."

Politely, he took off his hat.

"I worked two or three times for M. Hachamoth, in La Ciotat, for his villa. And I know Gramigni real well."

He looked around him at the beautiful, modern, gleaming shop.

"Monsieur Gramigni," he resumed.

Clemence was eyeing him holding in her talon the keys to the cash register.

"M. Gramigni went out," she answered, "and I don't know when he'll be back."

The Pallor-of-living indiscreetly scratched his head.

"That's awkward," he murmured. "I'm glad I saw you anyway, Mademoiselle Clemence. I should say: Madame Gramigni, but I'm calling you Mademoiselle Clemence to show that I really know you. I'm the son of the owner of the Café du Port, Robert Bossu, you know."

"Oh, of course," said Clemence without enthusiasm.

They were silent.

"This here's a nice shop," said Robert Bossu.

And he finished off his statement with a whistle.

"Yes, but the depression," said Clemence.

She sighed without relaxing her grip, indirect, on her sous.

"So Gramigni went out?" asks Toto. "I can maybe wait for him."

"There's not much chance he'll be back before five six o'clock."

"I'll wait a few minutes anyway."

Clemence was starting to get interested in the visitor. Her temperament led her to ask the most anguishing of possible questions.

"So what have you been doing," she asked, "since Claye Manufacturing closed?"

"They live around here huh my former bosses?" he asanskwered.

"Yes. Not far from here. So," insisted Clemence, "when the baron had to close his father-in-law's factories, what did you do?"

Although she didn't care at all for his sort of elegance, she told him flatteringly:

"You don't look out of work."

"Well," answered the Pallor-of-living, "I went into business for myself. I make radios, terrific ones, with sound you wouldn't believe, and a gadget I invented to eliminate static, terrific."

Then Clemence bitterly regretted having led the conversation in this direction: she thought she'd discovered the reason for this visit.

"As it happens, we've just bought a radio," she hastened rudely to affirm.

Young Bossu nearly blushed.

"Well I can see Gramigni isn't getting back."

He held out his hand, she offered him her left one (not the right because of the keys).

He went out stating he'd be back.

Clemence reopened the cash register. Awful, this depression. She started on her bills and accounts again without letting herself get emotional over the past. When Gramigni came back, she didn't consider it urgent to tell him about the visit. She waited until after dinner and the minute dose of Chartreuse they allowed themselves every evening.

The two little glasses glowed on the table. Gramigni was fiddling with his radio and now the crackling of a machine gun, now the moans of a monster, now the explosion of a shell percussed the tympana of the two delighted listeners. Finally the grocer happened upon a wavelength that served up piping hot the twang of a clevaire announcaire splaining the virtues of a brand of noodles or mustard and the kindness of their manufacturer in offering to each and every person owning a radio set an artistic, musical, popularizing concert. The name of the noodles or the mustard is repeated and wham here's the orchestra going off wildly. It's playing the overture to the *Dame Blanche*. Clemence listens moved.

When it's ovaire the clevaire announcaire reagain recommends the noodles or the mustard patron of the arts and the crashbangboom gets going on another theme.

"You remember young Bossu?" Clemence asks Gramigni.

"What? What did you say?" he shouts.

"You remember young Bossu?" she shouts.

"What? can't hear you," he shouts.

"Turn down the music," she shouts.

He tones it down reluctantly.

"What were you telling me?"

"Young Bossu came to see you."

"Young Bossu? No. I don't believe it. What did he want?"

"Didn't say. I think he wanted to sell you a radio. He's making them now; so he says. Between you and me, I thought he was dressed funny: not very nice-looking."

"I don't believe it," said Gramigni.

He drank a tiny little swig of Chartreuse and smacked his lips as charmed by this ingestion as the evening before, the evening before that and the preceding days and the days to come.

"I don't believe it," resaid Gramigni.

The reduced activity of his radio distressed him. He looked at the machine compassionately, like an old grandfather at his grandson made to sit in the corner. Finally he decided all the same to think about young Bossu.

"I wonder what he wanted," was what he came up with.

He was reswigging Chartreuse when at the door someone rang. As expected on Wednesdays Bertha III was coming to chat for the evening in their company.

"It's pretty what they're playing now," she said.

Gramigni making the most of the chance rushed to the

honky-tonk to give it back its full strength. He started to enjoy life again. When the concert had come to a close with a last reminder of the name of the patron noodles or mustard, a new radiophoning individual started talking biology. Gramigni immediately turned off the program and the marvelous instrument of culture that is radio was granted a brief rest.

"Do *you* remember young Bossu?" Clemence asked Bertha.

"Young Bossu, I'll say I do. He was in love with the young ladies. In love isn't exactly the word. They just plain excited him. He'd go eyeball them on the beach. Did he ever get an eyeful, the sex fiend. And since he couldn't get anywhere with the young ladies of course, then he'd fall back on me. He always wanted to take me into corners and paw me. And when I danced with him what he didn't try. So that eventually I didn't much enjoy going dancing in La Ciotat. A good thing Adrian, the second one, you remember him, Clemence, he didn't stay long, so I was saying it's a good thing Adrian, the second one, gave him a couple of clouts and after that he left me alone. Then he went to work in Paris. Whatever do you suppose happened to him? He must be out of work by now."

"He came to the shop this afternoon," said Clemence. "He wanted to sell us a radio, one of his. He says he makes them. But I think he dresses funny."

"How's that?" asked Gramigni innocently.

"There was a shady look about him," said Clemence.

Bertha understood.

She opined:

"That wouldn't surprise me at all of him. Vice sticks to you, no way to get rid of it."

"Well," said Clemence. "Anyway, we can't trust the fellow."

"Don't worry," said Gramigni, "I'm not going to let myself be pushed around. And how are things going at your place? Everything still the same?"

"Still not good times," answered Bertha: "the depression. And then morale still isn't good. The old lady's getting a little nuttier every day, M. Daniel seems funny, when she's not all worked up about politics madame grouses about her sister, the baron's gloomy, monsieur's the only one who's holding up."

"He's no great shakes, that guy," said Clemence.

"What?" exclaimed Gramigni, "an engineer?"

"Have to admit he won't set the world on fire," said Bertha. "If the baron wasn't there to run the business, he sure couldn't do it. He's just got a very ordinary job, you know."

"I know," said Gramigni. "But it's still more than being a grocer."

"What's the latest on Mme. Hachamoth?" asked Clemence.

"Oh nothing new," answered Bertha. "But I'm telling you, if there's something bugging her, it's since her sister-in-law died, since she came back from her funeral. Have to admit it's a strange story, the way she tells it."

"I can imagine," said Clemence.

"About politics," said Gramigni.

Hesitating, stopped.

Bertha:

"Madame Coltet wants to overthrow the government."

She shrugged her shoulders.

"She thinks she's Joan of Arc."

"But there really was one once, a Joan of Arc," said Gramigni.

"If you're going to reason like that," said Bertha. "No kidding, do you take that stuff seriously?"

Gramigni blushing started to scratch at a spot on the tablecloth with his fingernail.

"Pierre I can understand," said Bertha, "what else could he do."

"Pierre's a serious fellow," said Clemence.

Bertha didn't push the matter; they must be keeping something from her.

"And the Cramms," asked Gramigni, stopping in his domestic task, "they don't see them anymore?"

"No they still don't."

She's sure now that they must be keeping something from her.

"Couldn't you play us a little more music," said Bertha.

Gramigni radioted enthusiasm, until the neighbors banged on the ceiling.

CVIII

When Gramigni arrived, most of the members were already there. He sat down between the butcher Rouillard and Pierre, Baron Hachamoth's chauffeur. The meeting was being held above a café in the Avenue de Neuilly; the waiter was going around taking orders and handing out black coffee and beer. M. Coltet had democratically put himself between the butcher Laffure and Benoît, valet to the Count de Z... of the Avenue Maurice-Barrès. At nine by the Observatory clock, he made some noises to indicate that the meeting had begun. People were smoking so fast and furiously that they had to half-open the windows. M. Coltet reminded the audience of the reason for this meeting: the formation of the Neuilly-Southwest local of the N W C. He explained to them that the NWC would establish in France a true democracy while at the same time ridding the country of Communists, Socialists, Radical-Socialists, international banking, Freemasons and narrow-minded conservatives. The renewal of France was possible only through the abolition of classes and not through the supremacy of one over the other (the proletariat for some, the bourgeoisie for others). This abolition was possible only through a political takeover by the NWC and this takeover was possible only through action not limited to ordinary electoral politics. As everyone approved of this declaration, all there was left to do was take in members, collect money and choose officers. M. Gramigni was elected head of the local, Pandroche-Dudreuil, in advertising, second-in-command and Major Vésicle du Fernacle, Ret., treasurer, an office he already held in the five other existing locals. Then they set the date for the next meeting and took leave of one another in an atmosphere of cordial exaltation.

Coltet climbed into his two-seater and took Pierre in the rumble seat. Vésicle du Fernacle and Pandroche-Dudreuil called a taxi.

"You saw, didn't you," said the former, "he's already acting like a demagogue. He takes a servant home but dumps us royally so to speak."

"The aim of our movement is not, after all, to permit servants to go riding about in cars," joked Pandroche-Dudreuil.

Agnes was waiting for Coltet.

"How did it go?"

"Oh very well. Very well. The local's been formed: naturally. Sixteen members. Gramigni head. Pandroche second."

"Isn't he already head of the Passy-Centre local?"

"That doesn't matter for now. It's like with the major. I had him elected treasurer again."

"I don't trust them. Could you show me the membership list?"

He took it out of his beautiful zippered pigskin briefcase.

"This isn't exactly a working-class group of recruits," remarked Agnes.

"What do you mean, not working-class? One grocer, two butchers, five domestics, two bank clerks, three office workers."

"There's not one laborer."

"You couldn't really expect that. In that neighborhood we'd have to invent him."

"And yet we had agreed to direct our efforts toward the working class."

"Wait, wait: we mustn't rush things. We have to put together locals where there are interested people, before launching into adventures."

"Adventures! My plan of action is not an adventure."

"No, of course not. I just meant that a certain haste…"

"Well, you followed advice completely different from mine. I wanted to start in Saint-Denis and Belleville."

"You don't think that was a little—utopian?"

"How about trying to cross the Seine? We could put together a local in Courbevoie. That's right near here."

"You think so? I'll suggest it to the central committee."

"And the paper, how's that going?"

"Badly. There's so much competition."

"Of course. We haven't really distinguished ourselves from the others yet. Sooner or later we'll have to get rid of Pandroche-Dudreuil. He's a mercenary anyway."

"What do you mean?"

"That he's a reactionary. He misunderstands the meaning of our action, as do others for that matter, but with him it's deliberate. He knowingly and unimaginatively deforms my ideas, our ideas: because he needs money."

"I've been meaning to tell you too Agnes: there's something that's hurting us: we're not anti-Semitic enough; it's a little awkward telling you that. People think it's because of the baron who gives us funds."

"Who thinks that? The major? Pandroche? No, we're not going to be anti-Semitic: it's a reactionary attitude."

Coltet went into the next room to dress.

"You're not coming down?" asked Denis. "Bridge."

"No," answered Agnes. "I'm going to keep reading."

"What are you reading now?"

"*What Is to Be Done?* by Lenin."

Sil.

"That must be interesting," said Denis.

Sil.

"Yes. Tell me Denis, don't you think the NWC might interest Ast?"

Coltet reappeared suddenly, half redressed.

"You're crazy."

"I beg your pardon?"

"You have strange ideas."

She started to laugh, very sure of herself, feeling very strong.

"You have no objection to my seeing Ast and talking to him about the NWC?"

"I don't know. I don't know what he'll think of it. I don't know what Naomi'll think of it."

"Why shouldn't I talk to him? We're still friends."

"That's what they say. Do what you want, you're free."

Like a coward, he went to finish clothing himself in his room.

Sil.

"Denis?"

"Agnes?"

"I'm going to see Ast tomorrow."

"Let me know how it goes."

Sil.

Coltet came back clothed as it is proper to clothe oneself to play bridge.

"Won't you come down? They were waiting for you."

"No. Please make my excuses."

(Joking) "I'll tell them you're reading Lenin."

"Why not?"

"No, no, I wouldn't want to scandalize them. Good night."

"Have a nice time."

CIX

There was a moving van in front of the apartment building; chairs were waiting on the sidewalk, and baskets with dishes. Strong men were transporting furniture. Agnes thought: it would be curious. She took the elevator: it really was Ast who was moving out. She'd talk to him anyway.

The door was open. After letting a bed go by, she went in. In a room Ast was working hard at closing a suitcase. He didn't seem surprised.

"Are you here to see Naomi?"

"No, you."

"I'll be with you in a minute."

A little piece of shirt was escaping from the luggage closed with such difficulty. Ast pointed to a box; sat down on another.

"I have the impression we're no longer close," said Agnes.

"It seems that way to me too," said Ast. "It's up to you."

"I came to talk to you about more important things."

"Did you notice? I'm in the process of moving."

"Have you seen Arnolphe lately?"

"I hope that's not the important things. Poor Arnolphe."

"He's a member of the central committee of the NWC," said Agnes.

"Really? What's that? The important things?"

"Exactly."

Ast was watching the activity of the movers out of the corner of his eye. You could hear Naomi's voice in a neighboring room giving them some last-minute instructions. Ast listened, nodding his head approvingly, then his attention returned to his sister-in-law.

"So?"

"Haven't you heard that we were in the process of forming a new political organization?"

Ast got offuv his box.

"I thought it was about important things."

They came to take away the boxes. Agnes also had to get up.

"I thought your attitude toward us had changed," he added. "I thought maybe you were becoming more reasonable."

"We've called our organization the N W C, that is the Nation Without Classes: it's our program in a nutshell."

"So now you're a Communist," said Astolphe absentmindedly.

A mover stopped to listen to the conversation.

"Not on your life," exclaimed Agnes. "Quite the contrary. The Communists believe that the dictatorship of one class—the proletariat—will lead to the disappearance of the other classes, we on the other hand want the simultaneous abolition of all classes and national unification."

Another mover stopped to listen to the conversation.

"Because," added Agnes, "this simultaneous abolition of classes is possible only in a national framework and we want it from a national standpoint."

A third mover stopped to listen to the conversation.

"France," continued Agnes, "will become a great nation again only when she is one and when she is no longer divided by class struggles."

All the movers were now listening to the conversation.

"If that's what you think," said Ast.

To the movers:

"We're far from done."

"OK, OK," is what the movers said.

"Wait," said Agnes filled with emotion and excitement at speaking before a working- class audience.

She opened her bag and took out little leaflets (the program of the N W C) which she distributed to them. They took them politely and moved away horrified:

"She's a fashist," is what they said to each other in disgust.

"Her paper's not even fit for wiping your ass: it'd give you boils on your butt."

Meanwhile, carried away by her debut in propaganda and by this first contact with the working class, Agnes was going on with her speech.

"… and our action will not be limited to the electoral plane."

"Ast," called Naomi, "what are you doing?"

"Excuse me Agnes," said Ast. "I have to go. By the way why are you talking to me about this N W C?"

"I was hoping you'd join us," said Agnes.

"Surprising idea," murmured Ast. "All that business really doesn't concern me," he added in a neutral tone.

"You're not interested in the destiny of France?"

"Ast," called Naomi, "will you come help me?"

Agnes gestured impatiently. Ast took her hand.

"We'll talk about it again some other time," he said, adding prudently: "maybe. Goodbye, Agnes."

He left her. She left. The movers watched her.

"What were you doing so long in the other room?" asked Naomi.

"Agnes was here."

"She's interested in our move?"

"You'll never guess why she came."

"Is she gone?"

"Yes. I think."

"She didn't want to see me?"

"She didn't say so."

"You could have suggested it."

"Her visit had nothing to do with what happened between us. Apparently at least. She suggested I join some kind of political party she's doing propaganda for, even among the movers. It's called the NWC, the nation without classes; it's really not important. That's all she talked about. I told her we'd talk about it again later: naturally I haven't the slightest intention of doing so."

Naomi sat down on a box since it was the only thing in the apartment you could still sit on.

"She's got some nerve," said Naomi sadly. "After acting the way she acted, after talking the way she talked, then to come and bother us here. We won't let her have our new address, all right?"

"Certainly not."

The movers took away the last box. Ast and Naomi inspected the bare rooms one last time. They went down. The loading of the van was nearly completed. They urged the concierge to give no one their new address.

They left.

CX

Demoralized for a few days by his first visit, Toto-the-Pallor-of-Living eventually overcame his melancholy mood and returned to roam in the vicinity of the Rue de Longchamp. This time Gramigni was minding the store by himself. Clemence was nowhere to be seen: the-Pallor-of-Living was most delighted about this, for after all he scarcely knew her while he'd had more than one drink with the grocer. So he went in.

Gramigni didn't recognize him at first; then apologized and shook his hand. After all, he was glad to see him, because of the memories of La Ciotat; he asked him for news from home; the other fellow didn't have any, but invented some that was probable; that his father was still running the Café du Port, for example.

Then they talked radio. Young Bossu described machines like those he'd dreamed of building. He impressed Gramigni.

At that point Clemence arrived; she sent them off to talk in the neighboring bar, so she could do her accounts in peace. She was sure Onorato wouldn't let himself be talked into another radio; she'd given him instructions; she'd known it would happen: that the other fellow'd be back.

Each in front of his glass, they got around to the past, and for Toto to what was over and done with.

"The Hachamoths, the Chambernacs, they do live around here, don't they?" asked young Bossu.

"Over there," said Gramigni, "Rue de Longchamp. They're not like they used to be anymore."

"Ruined, huh?"

"They've just got two cars left: one for the baron who has his chauffeur, Pierre, you didn't know him, and the other one, that M. Coltet drives himself. And Mme. Hachamoth or Mme. Coltet when they go out they take the bus. They'd even take the subway if there was one. I guess there's going to be one some day. That would be good, it would help business around here, which isn't all that great."

"Mme. Coltet, she's the tall blonde, right?"

"That's right. And the little one's married too."

"The tall one her name was Agnes and the little one Naomi, I remember all right, I still remember how I could work myself up just thinking about them."

Gramigni gave him a shocked look. He went on with his exposition:

"She married her uncle, Naomi I mean. She married M. Astolphe de Cramm, you remember, the big blond guy, the snob, the one that had such a not ordinary car?"

"Do I remember him," said the Pallor-of-Living, "even that once he had an accident."

"I'm telling you this between the two of us, but it made loads of trouble, that marriage, especially because of Mme. Coltet. She said you don't marry your uncle, not even with a dispensation from the pope and the president, unless it was the bishop and the prefect, anyway you bother important people. She said it was incest: that's what it's called. But she didn't say that in public: just in the family. We heard it from Bertha. Remember Bertha? Yes of course you must remember."

"Sure I remember Bertha," said Robert who'd forgotten the couple of clouts.

"She did everything she could so it wouldn't work, Mme. Coltet the marriage. She invented loads of things to make trouble between her sister and the guy. But they must have really loved each other because it didn't faze them, not at all. Afterwards we didn't see them anymore in the neighborhood. A funny business. Keep it to yourself, we heard it from Bertha."

The Pallor-of-Living was listening with an attentive and saddish look as if he understood something about all this. In fact, he didn't dig it at all, according to an expression he'd gotten used to using in spite of the disuse into which it had already fallen at that time.

"Well well," he said pensively.

CXI

Nel mezzo del cammin di nostra vita.

CXII

There was at the far end of the garden a cabin where his predecessor used to abandon all unusable, nicked, busted objects. They'd thrown out the bulk of it as soon as they'd arrived, but there were still a few forgotten little things waiting for the broom.

Ast begins with the corner where an old shoe box lies collapsed, and here comes the box sliding forward, followed by a few flakes of gray snow. Behind it a little wave of dust forms, progressing methodically from right to left then from left to right and so on until it joins the box. And so the middle of the room is reached. Then Ast interrupts his work and looks at the result with satisfaction. One quarter of the floor is now clean and toward the center a fluffy little mound leans against a side of the main pile. All of that must be abandoned and the work taken up in another corner where lie an old bicycle bell, two bottles with red labels, three very sooty matches, evidence of some nocturnal visit, and a toothpick, convictive proof of some diurnal visit after the noon meal. The broom takes this collection in hand and the objects roll like a cast die; the two bottles gallop and, at their first and only attempt, reach the door against which they stop. The bell follows far behind tintinnabulating faintly and lamentably, asthmatically so to speak, with a feeble, metallic panting, a sort of ferrous, stannous, plumbiferous emphysema, a faraway memory of excursions and rides, a rusting. Very far behind the bell the matches walk with gouty steps soon to be joined by the first waves of dust. But the toothpick won't budge. It refuses to budge. It rolls but takes refuge in a crevice from which it is certain that it cannot be dislodged.

So the operator must show some finesse. The broom will no longer work longitudinally in long hyper- or parabolic, parallel movements, rather similar to the pendular gestures of the sower. From the moment a subject demonstrates a will contrary to that of the sweeper by taking cover in some crack, the implement must be used in a direction perpendicular to the preceding one, consequently laterally; next, be maneuvered in sharp little flicks, not necessarily nervous, but rather in discontinuous pulses. The subject moves along the fault until an obstacle interrupts its flight when it is forced to spring from its lair. A rapid flick of the broom, this time longitudinal, carries it off along with the dusty little wave extracted from the trench; and it all goes to join the main body of the waiting troops.

Between the two cleaned quarters remained a long dune going from the starting wall to the point of convergence. Ast therefore resumed the operation a third time in order to eliminate the line of demarcation; the heap grew accordingly. Then Ast operated on a single front, making simultaneously for the two corners and pushing the central mass toward the door; starting from one wall he sighted an angle and so walking parallel to the exit reached the other wall, there gave an extra sweep and set off again boustrophedonically. It was a matter of putting together an expulsionary mass at some distance from the exit, a distance such that one could open the door to go get the shovel and bucket without dispersing the dust again. The box, skillfully nudged, occupied the chosen spot; now all that remained was to go around reaching into the two corners and shoving toward it the two bottles stuck against the sill, and thus describe an ellipsis one of whose foci was occupied by the expulsionary mass while the other remained empty, rather like the solar system if at least one accepts the official results of cosmographic science.

So having described this ellipsis, Ast could finally survey with satisfaction the beautiful sweeping job he had just carried through to a successful conclusion, methodically, without haste but with steadiness, like a plowman. So he opened the door and the realization that his eye had been accurate added to his joy: nothing was dispersed. He came back with the shovel and the bucket. The operation continued without notable difficulty: the only one being the little margin of dust that never lets itself be drawn into the shovel by the broom. One manages to thin it without ever making it disappear entirely; when one realizes that to try to diminish it even further would be to set oneself an illusory task devoid of all practical significance, the simplest thing is to disperse the residue to the four corners of the room.

Which is what Ast did.

He took the broom in one hand, the bucket and shovel in the other. He was leaving. He surveyed the premises one last time. Over there, planted in the floor like a cossack's dagger in the floorboards of a night club, was the toothpick. It was not that it hoped to escape its destiny, nor from excessive lack of good will; but it had caught its paw in a crevice, as in a trap. Without disgust, Ast came and pulled it out with two fingers to throw it away with the rest.

He put his tools down outside and closed the door behind him.

CXIII

A large, cut-throat crowd was waiting for the BE at the corner of the Rue Tronchet. Two full buses passed; Mme. Hachamoth, whose number allowed her only a thread of hope, unobtrusively picked up from the sidewalk that of a gentleman who, tired of waiting, had just thrown himself into a taxi.

"My God," she muttered, "thank you for making me find this good number."

Indeed, a few moments later, the only one chosen, she was getting into a Madeleine-Avenue de Madrid. After chewing out a pudgy passenger who was taking up an entire seat all by himself, she buried him under her packages. A second discussion locked her in battle with the conductor who claimed not to have change for one hundred francs.

The man opposite her stongly approved of the vigorous way she'd put down the ticket taker and concluded his praise with a harsh critique of labor unions. Mme. Hachamoth answered with an allusion to the way in which France was Radical-Socialistically governed—if one could call that govern! Indeed, rejoined the other, could one call that govern? And yet France was certainly in need of governing.

He was talking very loudly so people would hear him, so people would listen to him.

Mme. Hachamoth was smiling to herself at the thought that her son-in-law was going to change all that. Little Denis Coltet, who would have foreseen that one day he would found a political party destined perhaps, no doubt, most certainly, to seize power here like the National Socialists over there? A little Mussolini, her son-in-law was a little Mussolini—that was really strange. So God had wanted her to become the mother-in-law of a dictator. After murmuring a prayer of thanks, she again began to pay attention to the gentleman's speech. He assured her of an imminent change in the political situation of the nation. She answered that it would be none too soon. They chattered on like this to the end of the line and finally the gentleman concluded by asking whether he could see her again.

Mme. Hachamoth immediately made a date, quite determined—honorable and faithful as she was—not to keep it, but well aware that it's the best way to get rid of a lecher.

That evening she had as guests Pandroche-Dudreuil and Major Vésicle du Fernacle, Ret. Daniel first announced he'd eat out, then resigned himself. They started by talking about unimportant things; books, films, plays. They chatted. Names, titles brought up haphazardly made three little rounds then went away. They chatted. They handed out glory, notoriety, genius to so-and-so and what's-his-name like fictitious grain to phantom chickens. They chatted. Not Daniel.

Pandroche had retained from the mediocrity of his origins the habit of not becoming witty until he'd imbibed a few glasses of wine. His verve was born at the very moment when the common stock of literature, theater and cinema was drying up. So in his wake they plunged into politics. Not Daniel.

For Pandroche politics consisted more or less exclusively of a detailed and almost always alleged knowledge of the private lives of his adversaries. He was a specialist in defamation. He knew that X… had, like all students, stolen books from booksellers in the Latin Quarter. He knew that Y.. had been caught by a constable screwing a girl in the woods. He knew that Z… had a brother who had himself whipped in a brothel in the Rue des Martyrs. Relentless repetition of these stories fleshed out the substance of his articles. As a result of his brief association with the anarchists he smelled the police everywhere and his nose was so good that even with his nostrils full of the aroma of countless Hamburgers, he was still able to ferret out Jews.

He was not unaware of the fact that Agnes' grandmother was German, nor her step-father: Jewish. The baron, fully conscious of the total Semiticity of his ancestry, never saw Pandroche open his yap without a little shudder; the illustrious lampoonist it is true had tact and saved his antisemitism for other venues. But he always committed at least three blunders per meal; and when the wines were really fine: five.

So he began to tell his string of little infamies to the great satisfaction of the major, the lesser of Mme. Hachamoth, the polite of Coltet. The baron, who highly approved of squashing anticapitalists, dreaded his guest's racist belches. Agnes, a little uncomfortable, would have liked to see the conversation's moral tone rise a notch; she wanted to shoot her enemies, not dishonor them. As for Daniel, he was totally disgusted. What difference could it possibly make to him that this particular left-wing deputy was the bosom buddy of that particular shady financier? What was the meaning of this right and this left relative to a rostrum? He knew only the right and the left of God, and he saw Pandroche there on that left, burning with love for the things of this world, gobbling and guzzling, defender of the greed of others.

After a particularly degrading story, even more so for the one who was telling it than for the one who was supposedly its "hero," Agnes asked if one couldn't struggle against institutions without defaming individuals. Pandroche snickered; he'd had enough too many to dare be insolent to ladies; one struggled *with* institutions, but *against* individuals. Agnes then insinuated that if he gave a different tone to his polemics in the paper it would distinguish him to his advantage, and the NWC.

"Nobody's every complained about the tone of my articles," answered Pandroche highly offended.

Coltet, who dreaded him, at once plaited him a little garland of praises. Agnes so as not to displease him was silent. Pandroche continued to shine in the glow of the cigars. Then they had a game of bridge, to sober him up.

CXIV

When he had left, and Vésicle du Fernacle, Daniel took Agnes aside and said to her:

"A fine bunch of friends you have."

"They're not my friends," said Agnes.

She looked at him surprised. He wasn't in the habit of talking this way; first, as a general rule, he didn't talk at all; then if he did talk, it was always pleasantly, and just for the sake of saying something. He actually did this so well, that people always thought of him, even those close to him, "he's a nice fellow," and not "he's an enigma." Agnes looked at him surprised.

"I don't give a damn about politics," said Daniel, "not yours or anybody else's."

He'd obviously been drinking, nearly as much as the illustrious lampoonist.

"There are things—'things'!—that are far more important."

No, he didn't seem drunk. His rage came from within.

"Vulgar bastards, that's the only supporters you can find."

Why did he attribute to her the maternity of the NWC? She hadn't confided in him. It was understood at home that Denis was the originator of the movement.

"That's all I wanted to tell you."

After this speech he went away without waiting for her to answer.

She went into Denis' room. He was taking off his pants.

"Daniel thinks they're bastards," said Agnes. "And I agree."

Denis interrupted his maneuver abruptly and nearly fell.

"Excuse me? Daniel? Who are bastards?"

"Daniel told me that just now; he thinks Pandroche and the major are bastards."

"Really? What's come over him? I don't understand."

"What do you think of Daniel?"

Denis rebuttoned his fly and began to want to think; but flabbergasted couldn't manage it.

"I really don't understand what this is all about. I don't see what Daniel has to do with Pandroche, or what he's got against him."

"Never mind Pandroche. Tell me, Daniel was really very much in favor of Naomi's marriage, wasn't he? I'm sure now that he was for it. People have kept so many things about that from me. Tell me what you know."

"That's ancient history," sighed Coltet.

"Yes, ancient history, history less than a year old."

She wanted to cry.

"Why, why did Daniel talk to me like that?"

Then, she started to cry.

Denis was consoling her.

She interrupted him:

"Did you decide anything about the Courbevoie local?"

He promised to think about it seriously.

When they made love, they took a great many precautions because Agnes felt that maternity was incompatible with the historic task she had assigned herself.

CXV

The-Pallor-of-Living, encouraged by Gramigni's reception, ventured for a third time into Neuilly. He entered the shop, this time with assurance, and found the grocer with an arm in a sling and his head wreathed in bandages.

"An accident?" asked Toto.

Clemence raised her arms and let them fall back onto her stomach.

"I fell off a ladder," said Gramigni.

He looked glum.

"Well," said Toto, "you did quite a job on yourself."

Clemence sighed.

Toto scratched his head at a loss for words.

Someone came in.

"Say," exclaimed Bertha, "it's Monsieur Robert. How are you? Do you recognize me?"

Toto was always pleased to see faces from before the age of Injustice; faces and bodies, because he reappreciated Bertha right away: really stacked.

Bertha had turned to Gramigni.

"So you've got your little secrets. It's not nice not telling me you were, just like that, the president"

President! is what young Bossu said to himself pricking up his ears.

"of the Neuilly Southwest section of the N W C. That's all. And on top of that you went and got yourself beaten up in Courbevoie. It looks like they worked you over. Pierre told me all about it. He's another secretive one: he could have told me before that you were in Mme. Coltet's gang."

Young Bossu was listening for all he was worth but didn't understand a thing and was glad of it. It's always good to know secrets. Now he'd get Gramigni to talk.

"Why do you call it 'Mme. Coltet's gang,'" said Gramigni sourly. "And why shout it from the rooftops."

"Tell me how it happened," said Bertha impervious to the reproaches.

She's nice, is what the Pallor-of-Living said to himself looking her over from head to foot, and she's got cute little boobs and must have some money stashed away.

"Hurry up, Gramigni," urged Bertha seeing the grocer's discomfort, "I don't have all day."

"It happened when we were coming out," said Gramigni with difficulty. "Everything was fine till then; it happened when we were coming out. They went and stole bricks from a construction site nearby and when they were done throwing their bricks, they ran away. That's all."

"That's politics for you," said Bertha innocently. "What do you think Clemence?"

"I hope they get even," said Clemence.

"I hope so too," said Bertha. "I have to run. Goodbye everybody."

The Pallor-of-Living watched her move away. Her buns were as nice as her boobs. That made him dream for a moment.

He came back to reality and said to Gramigni:

"So just like that, you're the president."

"I guess I'll have to tell you about it now. For that matter it's no big secret. It's politics. It's a party that was founded by M. Coltet. You remember him?"

"Of course. And what's it all about?"

Gramigni gave a little cough.

"It's called the NWC."

"What does that mean NWC?"

A customer came in.

"I'll tell you about it tonight. Why don't you come for dinner."

That dinner really made him happy, Toto-the-Pallor-of-Living.

CXVI

While waiting for dinner, Toto-the-Pallor-of-Living went for a little stroll in the Bois de Boulogne to admire autumn's splendors. A few minutes after he'd left, there came into Gramigni's store: Agnes.

She'd decided to do the rounds of her wounded: Gramigni first, then an employee of a commercial firm who lived on the Rue du Pont, that is to say: two; the others: just scratched, she wouldn't visit them.

Gramigni flushed with pleasure when he saw her come in and wriggled with delight at her compliments; it's like as if he got the Military Cross. Clemence smiled politely, flattered as well of course. But she was thinking:

"After all she's only my niece; I may be a bastard, but I'm still her aunt."

She tried hard never to think about her family relationship with the Chambernacs. She'd sworn to remain silent. She didn't want to come out of her bastardy. All the same, she was her niece, this girl that acted so smart, that she'd served for years, that she'd known as a kid, that she'd seen grow up. And this Agnes wasn't supposed to suspect anything about her grandfather's misbehavior. Aside from that, he was a decent guy, the baron, paying the two hundred thousand francs without a word of complaint while he himself was tumbling down from his high position. If he'd wanted to, he could have gotten around it. He was really a decent guy, that Jew.

After crowning with metaphorical laurels a Gramigni purring with vanity and vainglory, Agnes continued on her way. The commercial employee, a man named Rabounauld (Lucien), lived at 111 Rue du Pont, in a little apartment with his mother. You had to go up four floors without an elevator to get there. The stairwell smelled of cat piss and the scratched walls were pathetically showing their plaster.

"What can I do for you mademoiselle?" asked a dignified little old lady who in the movie studios of Joinville-le-Pont would have been transformed into a marquise.

"I should like to see Comrade Rabounauld," said Agnes.

The old little old lady looked at the beautiful young milady.

"He's in bed you know. He had an accident."

"What do the doctors say?"

"The doctors? The doctor. The doctor said that Lucien, my son, would have to stay in bed for two three weeks."

"I am Mme. Coltet," said Agnes. "I should like to see Comrade Rabounauld."

The little old old lady looked at her with respect and had her come in. He lived in a shabby apartment, Comrade Rabounauld, an apartment consisting of a tiny vestibule adorned with a ridiculous clock, a dining room with a sewing machine, a bedroom where his mother probably moldered away—perhaps poverty forced them to sleep in the same room—and his own bedroom where he was lying and assimilating the brickbat that had damaged his tibia, a bedroom that looked down onto the courtyard from rooftop height. All the same you could see the sky and some chimneys.

"I am Mme. Coltet," said Agnes holding out her hand.

Very impressed, the man named Roubinauld shook it, ran his hand blushing over his unshaven chin and asked the visitor to sit down on a leather chair polished by long use but of decent appearance.

"It's not too serious?"

"No. I have to stay in bed for three weeks. It's nothing important."

"I've come to bring you my husband's congratulations."

This room didn't smell very good.

"I was only doing my duty," said Comrade Roubinauld.

"Those brutes," said Agnes.

"We'll get them," said Comrade Roubinauld who seemed to have at his immediate disposal a considerable stock of historic phrases.

There was definitely a very bad odor hanging almost tangible in this bedroom. Agnes took from her purse an envelope that she put on the night stand. Comrade Roubinauld wanted to refuse. She explained: the party had a relief fund. Comrade Roubinauld said thank you. The little little old lady too.

Agnes dabbed at her nose with her handkerchief while going down the stairs.

CXVII

Baron Hachamoth was starting to find that it was ending up costing him a lot of money, this nation without classes.

CXVIII

For several days now Daniel had been feeling the air close in around him, wrinkle, crumple. And that night when in bed he was about to fall asleep, inside his chest, he felt the space closing in, crumpling, wrinkling, contracting like an old parchment. He straightened and sat up in bed and wondered whether after some ten years he was going to start having asthma attacks again. He lay back down; but his breathing was getting slower, more difficult, ready to come

.

to a standstill. He straightened again and sat up, hunch-backed, automatically assuming the asthmatic's position, that of Peruvian mummies those you put in jars, that of the embryo.

Perhaps it wouldn't come. His breathing seemed to be getting more regular. He stretched out; but soon he had to resume his fetal position. He waited. He studied the rhythm of his inhalations and exhalations. The Larousse dictionary says, and it was one of the entries he knew by heart along with the account of Damiens' execution:

> "In all countries, among all peoples, there has been an attempt to fit the punishment to the crime or the offence committed. Since the human body is very sensitive to pain, the utmost has been done to vary infinitely the methods of torment which could be inflicted upon it. And as invention, in this matter, is limited only by imagination and as imagination relies on physiological and psychological observation, there has resulted an appalling efflorescence of *tortures*, in which the peoples of the Orient have particularly distinguished themselves."

Daniel got up to take some aspirin: two or three tablets. Perhaps this mild treatment would be adequate. He was

·

still hoping the menace was illusory. He went into the bath-room and swallowed his three tablets. He came back into his room, and wandered about uncertainly.

Since childhood, this had been his principal subject of reflection, his only object. He'd read the philosophers, but their silence regarding the matter had disappointed him. Because for him, pain in its radical, elemental form—the form which is the essence of torture—was the stumbling block and the death of all philosophies. A tortured man over-turns all systems and destroys all ideologies. The evil that is pain can surpass all measure and nothing can compensate for it. Time destroys happiness, but sufferings never fade. They remain, they are acquired, forever, and cannot perish.

He eventually lay down again, stretched out on his back. Then he remembered his first attack, in La Ciotat. He hadn't known what was happening to him. Afterwards, it had gone on for years, in spite of the medications; then, in the army, strangely, it had suddenly stopped. Everything is relative in this world, except pain. Happiness leaves no trace, it van-ishes with the past; but suffering remains. Dismemberment is an absolute. All is fleeting but the evil that is pain grows endlessly. Nothing redeems the death pangs of all the tor-tured men.

Withdrawn into himself, he felt the suffocation coming. When he used to go fishing in La Ciotat, he'd always watch in horror as the fish flipflopped, mouth wide open, bleeding from the hook torn out, trying to grab hold of a breathable space in this great mass of air that was choking him. From the eel skinned alive to the crucified owl, evil certainly had cause for rejoicing. For it is suffering that is evil, and not crime. But if crime delights in suffering, then it is an evil. Daniel had made an exhaustive study of this casuistry.

True evil is that which comes from man; not that which comes from nature. The long agony of the cancer patient, the stabbing pains of tabes dorsalis, were nothing in the absolute since the will of man is not involved. A man dying of thirst in the desert did not move Daniel; he felt no pity for him. But the man sentenced by some court or the good pleasure of a tyrant to die of thirst in a dungeon disclosed a philosophical impasse.

It was a genuine attack. Sweating and panting, he struggled for his gulp of air. From time to time, he succeeded in expectorating granular, blackish spit, not at all like when one has a cold. Congested, migrainous, his heart beating full to bursting, he was waiting for the attack to peak and come to an end. There was so little breath left in him that he might have thought he was going to die. But he knew he would come back to life.

No one could justify the existence of the evil that is pain. This man who screams in the hands of the executioner, his suffering will last and perpetuate itself and, detaching itself from him, will survive him to the end of time and beyond, increasing the mass of horror which has constituted itself since the beginning of the world—opposite God. Pain was so strong, its power so fabulous that it tore away from God broad patches of being. A spot of blood fallen into the domain of existence was gradually, slowly, surely spreading like oil. And this blood was not that of Abel, but that of the first victim of torture. As Christians always see the five wounds of Christ bleeding, Daniel saw flowing from the depth of the ages a scarlet river carrying along pus and minced flesh. And which did not come from God. But who had scribbled on the blueprint of creation with this foul ink? Who had scored it thus?

And now the attack was over. Little by little he stretched out, with breath that could from now on flow freely. He still spluttered, from time to time; and sweat was freezing on his body. But stretched out motionless, he perceived his happiness. He smiled, in the night. And dawn came.

The screaming sphere of evil continued to shake with its convulsions the troubled sphere of good. Will the just rejoice over the howls of the damned? Evil for Daniel was not sin, but these torments inflicted on the face of the world, on the surface of perpetuity. For many years now he'd no longer been Catholic although he occasionally went to mass, to make Mme. Hachamoth happy. But he loathed the mawkish liberals who conjured away Hell. Yes the sufferings of the damned would have no end.

> When he was a Catholic:
> Why don't the demons disobey God by rewarding the sinners? Instead of punishing them? Like He?

But he also loathed those human philosophies that seemed ignorant of the fact that there had been, were and would be men who would perish in torments. They were mute on this subject: stakes, gallows and crosses reduced their chattering to silence. Martyrs found their reward in heaven and the damned their punishment in hell, but on the surface of the earth there remained the viscous shade of tortures.

Daniel searched in vain for the thrust that might break up this abject phantom.

He searched. He searched.

When dawn had come he fell asleep.

CXIX

Since he'd been clinging to the clogs of the grocer from the Rue de Longchamp in Neuilly, Toto the-Pallor-of-Living was experiencing a singular sensation: he was soaring. He didn't think the injustice of the world was in any way diminished by the fact that he was having dinner regularly twice a week with the Gramignis and that's why he was experiencing this singular impression. In other respects his life was becoming more difficult; one of his women had dumped him; he suspected the other of wanting to do likewise, and he couldn't muster the courage to harness up and start over with a new mount. He felt heartened only on Sundays at around six seven o'clock when he would dust off his shoes with his handkerchief and scratch the dirt from under his fingernails with his little knife before leaving for the West heading for the Neuilly bridge.

When he got off the AT bus, he'd start with a little break in a bar. Then around eight, eight thirty he'd make his entrance into the grocery store. They'd drink a pastis in remembrance of La Ciotat, while waiting for the last customers, in the back room. After that at around quarter to nine, Gramigni would pull down his shutters and lock up. You ate well at Gramigni's and it warmed your insides to find something like a family.

He was still supposed to be selling—and making—radios. But he thought less and less about this facade, forgetting his role when he talked; with the result that he decided that one day he'd end up selling his workshop and his salesroom.

Politics was what interested him the most now, or at least the N W C. With Gramigni after dinner they jawed away to beat the band. They worked themselves up over the minister and Toto thought a nation without classes was great as long as you could make a lot of money. This business was maybe going to play a dirty trick on Injustice. And then he'd always been a Nationalist and he'd never been able to stand Communists, Socialists and other lazy bums.

Gramigni was proud as could be of the success of his propaganda. He was sure that quite soon young Bossu would be joining the party: as it happened there was no local over in the République area. Young Bossu would found one.

But young Bossu had something at the back of his mind.

"So," is what he said to the grocer, "you showed up in Courbevoie just like that, with your hands in your pockets? Unarmed? Without checking the place out? It's lucky you had the police on your side! And then who did you have there? Now I don't want you to get mad. But damn it all, just commercial employees, flunkeys, big lummoxes. I don't mean you Gramigni but you've got to admit you're not used to fighting, you don't know how to go about it, do you? It's just not your line. Every time you go do something like that, you're going to get yourself licked good I'm telling you."

"You're just a defeatist," said Clemence.

"I just see things the way they are," said Robert.

There was some truth in what he was saying. Gramigni

didn't much care for fighting. A decent shopkeeper doesn't like to scrap with hooligans. Now that he'd gotten himself mixed up in this business, he couldn't chicken out. What would Mlle. Agnes say? But all the same there was some truth in what he was saying, young Bossu.

"As far as fighting goes," said Gramigni, "we'll get the hang of it."

"You're certainly not coming home every Saturday with bandages around your head," said Clemence.

"I," said Robert who was rediscovering his I, "know what I'd do if I was you."

"Well what would you do," said Gramigni.

"Well here's what I'd do," said Robert.

He paused most effectively. They were going to hear what they were going to hear.

"If I was you," he resumed, "here's what I'd do. Right now there are heaps of guys on the streets that don't know what to do with themselves, the unemployed is what they call them. I'd choose a few that are real gorillas and I'd give them a hundred sous every time there was a meeting. And nobody'd give you any more trouble. That's what I'd do."

Gramigni tried to take in this plan.

"It's clear as day," resumed Toto. "The cops, when it comes down to it you can't really count on them. If you had twenty or thirty guys that are good at getting things their way, that would give you what you might call a private police force. And I'll take care of finding them for you the twenty or thirty guys."

Gramigni could hardly believe his ears.

Toto-The-Pallor-of-Living sits down at the table with the fuzz—two of them—and tells them:

"I talked to the grocer and I explained the thing to him. He didn't get it for a long time, but I finally got him to say: yes, it's a curious and interesting idea. So he put on his best clothes and he went to see Mme. Coltet, because like I told you already she's the one that does everything and her husband he's just window dressing, because a woman at the head of a political movement wouldn't look serious. So then Gramigni put on his best clothes and got up like for a wedding he went to see Mme. Coltet and explained the thing to her. Gramigni told me later that she told him it was a great idea and that she was very happy about it. And then she told him just like that that she wanted to see me and as quick as possible seeing it was urgent. So when I went to see him the next day he told me she wanted to see me and so that's how finally I went to see her. A nice house. Rue de Longchamp. High society. Servants. I know all of them now. Pierre the chauffeur, Bertha a pretty little kid she's Mme. Coltet's chambermaid, Julie III she's Mme. Hachamoth's chambermaid, Marie II the cook, M. and Mme. O."

"That's not a hard name to remember." (Laughter.)

"They're the concierge and the gardener. Them I don't know. They never go out. So anyway, they take me to Mme. Coltet. A little room with books and party posters pinned to the wall. Mme. Coltet said hello in a real friendly way, she remembered me from when I was working for her grandfather, the Claye that threw himself out of a plane while he was throwing me out on the streets, I'm the one that's saying that of course not her. Then she sat down in a big arm-chair and I explained the thing to her and got a good look at her legs. Could I ever have it off with that beautiful ma-dame. For that matter it'll happen some day. I get the women I want and just because this one washes her ass every day that won't keep me from fucking her back and front."

"OK, OK, don't get all worked up," said one of them.

"You can tell us your dirty stories some other time," said the other. (Laughter.)

The Pallor-of-Living resumed irritated:

"Well anyway I explained the thing to her. She liked it. Then we discussed the price. Finally we agreed that I'd bring her twenty guys every Saturday and Sunday at ten francs a meeting. And I'd get five hundred francs a month."

"That's what you say," said one of them.

"I swear. And I'm telling you it's all arranged. We start next Saturday. Meeting in Asnières."

"Is that all?" said the other.

"Don't you think it's enough?"

He added:

"We're just talking after all."

"Natch," said one of them.

"One more thing."

"Ah," said the other.

"She told me just like that that since I was like you might say the chief of her secret police she wanted me to do her a little favor and find her a fellow to find out where he lived since he moved from his former lodgings without leaving a forward-ing address. I'll avail myself, gentlemen, of your kind services."

"Well well she already trusts you completely huh," said one of them.

"He's already in her good books," said the other.

"Natch," said the-Pallor-of-Living.

CXXI

A taxi took her to Boulevard Lefebvre, a bit further than the Parc des Expositions. She told the driver to wait for her and got out. Opposite, she saw a little house surrounded on all sides by walls and separated by an empty lot from sheds on which it said: "A. Claye, Rags and Old Paper." A long, thin, metal chimney like those of laundries was smoking.

Agnes rang, a maid (a cleaning woman rather, supposed the visitor) came to open the gate and asked her what did she want. But Agnes in the garden caught sight of Naomi. She walked right in. Naomi watched her come and kind of felt like crying.

Behind Agnes the cleaning woman trotted along.

"Naomi," said Agnes. "Naomi."

The cleaning woman halted. Arms dangling at her sides, not knowing what to do, she waited.

Naomi wasn't answering.

"I'd like to talk to you," said Agnes.

At the far end of the garden, there was a sort of structure, like a workshop; outside, barrels and bags; a workman who seemed to be doing something. Agnes was astonished, and looked about her with undisguised curiosity.

Naomi irritated made a sign to follow her. The cleaning woman thus abandoned walked back to the above-mentioned person to tell him all about it: that a lady had come in shoving her actually almost, without saying who she was, and that Madame didn't look very happy to see her and that she the visitor was calling her Madame by her first name. All that didn't seem very interesting to Cical who went on with his work, impassively.

"What do you want," asked Naomi, "what did you come here for?"

"Nothing," said Agnes sweetly. "I wanted to see you."

"Why? What for? Do you want to ask me to join the NWC?"

Agnes started laughing.

"No. Don't be afraid. I simply felt like seeing you."

"Well I don't. You didn't ask how I felt. Now that you've seen me again, you can leave."

"Ah!" went Agnes in gentle reproach. "Listen Naomi, since you're taking it this way, listen to me: if I've done things, that you didn't like, please forgive me."

"Naturally," said Naomi. "I forgive you. So now that you're forgiven, you can leave. I would never have thought you'd go so far as to spy. How do you know we live here? Actually I don't care. So there: we're no longer on bad terms: goodbye."

Agnes didn't answer, examining, admiring perhaps, the shape of her shoe. She was groping for sentimental phrases, of which there weren't many in her repertory. She finally said:

"You're my little sister. Life can't separate us this way."

It was Naomi's turn to start laughing:

"What on earth has come over you!"

And now Agnes was wondering what she really had come for. She didn't feel the least bit like making up with her little sister. Was she behaving this way out of simple curiosity? What did it matter to her that Astolphe had become a ragman? She'd known already after all; Robert Bossu had told her. Had it really seemed so extraordinary that she'd wanted to check it out for herself? She considered herself far above such insignificant concerns. So she said nothing.

Outside, at the far end of the garden, Cical was hammering. The cleaning woman passed by beneath the window, an uncertain little humming announcing her presence. Then Cical started some other work, quieter. From time to time a car purred by on the boulevard.

Then in this silence, Naomi heard herself say:

"I'm going to have a baby,"

and realized immediately that Agnes, who had made a point of rushing over drawn by her instinct, ought not to have known about that.

Her strength ebbing away, she could do no more than marvel that the woman who inspired the NWC could give her such advice.

CXXII

The attacks had multiplied and came every other night now, which made for a day darkened by emphysema. Daniel had stopped smoking although he knew that this habit neither accelerated nor intensified his asthma. A doctor was having him take ephedrine and this substance distanced him from the world. When, thus drugged, his breathing still stertorous, he roamed the streets where the winter wind raced, he perceived a singular phantasmagoria of quivering forms and lights, an entire life henceforth unfamiliar.

He wasn't working any more, having gotten himself certified sick. Mme. Hachamoth was worried and the baron suggested he see some famous professor; but Daniel made do during the strongest attacks with injections of sedol and morphine.

He had before him long empty days which he alternately spent in his room and: aimlessly. He was detaching himself more and more from this existence that had been his: the factory, Paris, his family.

One day in a café where, his lungs whistling, he was having a drink, a soldier of the Salvation Army sold him a Bible for ten francs.

He read, there and in other versions:

> … so the LORD will rejoice over you to destroy you, and to bring you to nought…
>
> (Deuteronomy XXVIII, 63)
>
> Whithersoever they went out, the hand of the LORD was against them for evil…
>
> (Judges II, 15)
>
> Then God sent an evil spirit between Abimelech and the men of Shechem…
>
> (Judges IX, 23)
>
> But the spirit of the LORD departed from Saul, and an evil spirit from the LORD troubled him.
>
> (I Samuel XVI, 14)

And it came to pass on the morrow, that the evil spirit from God came upon Saul...

(I Samuel XVIII, 10; cf. XIX, 9)

And again the anger of the LORD was kindled against Israel, and he moved David against them to say, Go, number Israel and Judah... And David's heart smote him after that he had numbered the people. And David said unto the LORD , I have sinned greatly in that I have done...

(II Samuel XXIV, 1 and 10)

Cf:

And Satan stood up against Israel, and provoked David to number Israel. And David said to Joab and to the rulers of the people, Go, number Israel... And God was displeased with this thing; therefore he smote Israel.

(I Chronicles XXI, 1, 2 and 7)

Again there was a day when the sons of God came to present themselves before the LORD, and Satan came also among them to present himself before the LORD… And the LORD said unto Satan, Behold, he is in thine hand; but save his life.

(Job II, 1 and 6)

What? shall we receive good at the hand of God, and shall we not receive evil?

(Job II, 10)

I form the light, and create darkness: I make peace, and create evil: I the LORD do all these things.

(Isaiah XLV, 7)

Shall there be evil in a city, and the LORD hath not done it?

(Amos III, 6)

… and I will set mine eyes upon them for evil, and not for good.

(Amos IX, 4)

Wherefore God also gave them up to uncleanness…

(Romans I, 24)

For this cause God gave them up unto vile affections…

(Romans I, 26)

God gave them over to a depraved mind, to do shame-

ful things. He has filled them
with every kind of injustice.
(Romans I, 28 and 29)

And Daniel was filled with astonishment.

CXXIII

Baron Hachamoth celebrated Christmas like a Christian,
that is, on that day, he ruined his stomach for a few weeks;
and, on the first of the year, he had to content himself with
slices of ham and boiled potatoes. There was nonetheless a
first-rate meal on New Year's Day, Mme. Hachamoth wanted
it so, quite intimate just family. But then Ast and Naomi
weren't there.

Daniel exhausted by a violent attack was sharing the diet
of his step-father. Preoccupied, Agnes was eating oranges;
but her mother and Coltet were devouring the duck.

"My God," exclaimed Mme. Hachamoth, tearing apart a
wing, "make this year '34 not be as bad as this meal seems
to forebode. My God, if only misfortune doesn't strike. I
can feel it coming."

"My stomach isn't any worse than in other years," said
the baron.

"And Daniel?" answered Sophie. "With his asthma. It's
incomprehensible. You'd completely gotten over it and now
it's starting up again. Why?"

"God's will," said Daniel calmly.

Mme. Hachamoth uttered a piercing and disillusioned
Ah while shrugging her shoulders, all this looking as if it
meant: Does one know? Then:

"Denis and I are the only true Catholics left in the family. Him: he's Jewish, you: you're unbelievers. You especially, one could even say you're an atheist."

"I am," said Agnes.

Licking her lips, Mme. Hachamoth sighed.

"My God," she muttered, "if only all this doesn't bring us misfortune."

Coltet said:

"Why don't we talk about something besides misfortune. Talking about misfortune attracts it."

Daniel said:

"They're not Catholic, they're superstitious."

Coltet, with whom this didn't register, said:

"I drink to the NWC."

"The NWC is goddam done for," said Agnes.

"What did you say?" asked Mme. Hachamoth.

"I didn't say the NWC is done for," said Agnes, "I said it's goddam done for."

"Don't be so pessimistic," said Coltet, "my dear."

"What makes you think that?" asked the baron with interest.

If the NWC was goddam done for, he'd save quite a bit of money. He had to see what the situation was.

"The Stavisky Affair is going to bring us lots of members," said Coltet.

"Don't you believe it," said Agnes. "On the contrary our people are deserting us."

"But why?" asked Hachamoth.

"Because we're revolutionaries. And the movement that's taking shape is a conservative movement."

"If we manage some day to get rid of the Chamber," said Coltet, "that'll be something anyway."

"Pooh, they're completely incapable of it all those veterans without principles, all those Louis-Philippe royalists, all those reporters in the pay of big banks and fat cat industrialists."

When Agnes talked politics, it was never very comprehensible, thought the Hachamoths. Coltet did his best, to understand.

"Take Pandroche," continued Agnes, "you saw how he dropped us. It didn't take him long to see how the wind was blowing. Now he's slinging mud at me in anonymous gossip columns. I'm considering having Robert Bossu smash his face in."

"I could go challenge him to a duel," said Coltet.

"And the major? Flown the coop. All those people are only interested in defending their own little privileges. They didn't understand the first thing about my program. And all the current unrest is making the reactionaries crawl out of their holes, and alienating those who might be enthusiastic about a France that is one, without classes, dominated neither by the bourgeoisie nor by the proletariat."

She concluded:

"In the end I'll be alone. But when the bourgeois reactionaries will have demonstrated their powerlessness, when Muscovite tyranny threatens, then people will turn to me."

"My God," cried Mme. Hachamoth, "what a daughter you have given me!"

Denis, who'd never thought of himself as particularly great, felt himself becoming very small, he who found, without daring to say so, the right-wing *Jeunesses Patriotes* very much to his liking.

Baron Hachamoth

And Deborah, a prophetess, the wife of Lapidoth, she judged Israel at that time. And she dwelt under the palm tree of Deborah between Ramah and Bethel in mount Ephraim: and the children of Israel came up to her for judgment.

(Judges IV, 4–5)

said:

"So Agnes, you really think that you hold the fate of our country in your hands?"

"I'm driven to that conclusion. Everyone is floundering in error."

"The rivers of Hell have overflowed their banks," said Daniel, "and behold their waters are reaching the summits of the highest mountains."

They turned toward him with a certain surprise.

But no one commented on his words. The chocolate and cream dessert that Bertha III was serving permitted this silence.

CXXIV

It started to rain unexpectedly, violently.

"Here comes the rain," said the proprietor.

People agreed.

And thereupon there suddenly entered a fairly elderly gentleman, carelessly dressed and stippled with a few drops of water. He took out from under his overcoat something about 21 centimeters wide and 27 centimeters long, the commercial format. Then he sat down, carefully putting his burden down next to him.

The people present examined him for a few short moments; then each one returned to his deranged occupations: cards, newspapers, daydreams, crossword puzzles.

"What'll it be?" asked the proprietor.

It was a small bar, there was no waiter.

"I'd be happy to have a cup of hot milk with a little glass of rum in it," said the gentleman. "Excellent beverage for warding off the flu."

"A hot milk with a little glass of rum in it," said the proprietor.

While waiting for the excellent beverage for warding off the flu, the fairly elderly gentleman had moved his package and crossed his arms over it, as if to brood it. His neighbor, abandoning the search for a seven-letter word that, etc., looked at him out of the corner of his eye and, in the corner of the eye of the fairly elderly gentleman, he saw wild glints that flickered and went out like will-o'-the-wisps on a pond.

The proprietor brought the cup of hot milk, with a little glass of rum that he poured into it all at once. Outside it continued to rain violently.

"It's better than rain anyway," said the proprietor.

And he went back behind the bar.

The fairly elderly gentleman drank the excellent beverage for warding off the flu in little sips. A convulsive movement shook him every time he took the roof off his mouth.

"Lousy weather," his neighbor said to him.

The fairly elderly gentleman appeared to hesitate before

deciding to have a chat. But the desire to talk about his misfortunes got the better of his mistrust. Consequently, when they had exhausted the topics of meteorology and epidemiology, he began to recount various incidents of his own life. And first of all that he was on his way to the home of relatives living on the Rue de Longchamp and that his journey had been interrupted by this unexpected rainfall.

The person he was speaking to expressed interest in the identity of said relatives, justifying his curiosity by a thorough knowledge of the neighborhood and by the interest he took in all incidents, accidents, events, modifications and changes which might affect the stability of its condition, the neighborhood's.

With a minimum of craftiness this person he was speaking to thus soon learned that this fairly elderly gentleman who feared rains and flus had been going, before showerfall, to see Mme. Hachamoth, his sister-in-law; that his name was Chambernac; that he was a principal emeritus; that he was coming to live in Paris; that his widowerhood affected him deeply; that he had written an extraordinary work contained in this package; that he wanted for himself peace and tranquillity and for this work glory; that strange incidents had cut into the course of his life.

Now the attentive listener was able to pinpoint quite well in the vagueness of his memory the individual who was thus describing to him the most important aspects of his existence. He could see him again sitting on the terrace of the café and talking to his father; it was during the war, it was about politics and foreign affairs; the little boy was running between the tables. Quite a few indistinct customers had come to sit on this terrace, but this one immediately stood out from the others, because of membership in a certain family.

"Say it's stopped raining," remarked the proprietor.

This observation, perfectly true, brought about the rapid departure of Chambernac, who went off holding pressed to his heart the manuscript of the *Encyclopedia*.

Robert Bossu, most pensive, got back to his crossword puzzle.

CXXV

Chambernac was fleeing.

CXXVI

One eve when it was eve
one eve would you believe
one eve when it was night

someone knocked on the door
someone knocked more and more
someone banged thall his might

Purpulan dozed away
Purpulan blinked away
Reading in the dim light

Reading some old memoirs
va madman tthot he was
a new messiah quite

Got up from where he read
got up from his warm bed
got up nturned on the light

Went over to the door
listened to knocking more
at the door with such might

He asked in a loud voice
He asked for yad no choice
Who's turned up here tonight?

A voice said it's a pal
a voice said might as well
open the door all right

Purpulan worried so
Purpulan had to know
Who thDEVIL's here tonight?

A devil I am not
a fable's not my lot
the stranger did recite

I am a man not tall
I am a man quite small
I am a man of blight

I'm called Bébé Toutout
My name's Bébé Toutout
It's clear as day all right

Purpulan all ashamed
to see his teacher famed
behind the door blushed bright

What a fine how d'you do
cried out Bébé Toutout
don't make me wait outside

Then t'other took the key
he scratched his nose slowly
opened the door a mite

BOOK SEVEN

"I," said Chambernac, "therefore then began to compile the fourth part: history bounded by the coronation of Napoleon I and the abdication of Napoleon III; on the one hand, I thus avoided tackling the problem—a delicate one—of the diabolical origin of the French Revolution as it was formulated by Jacques Baudot and the Abbés Fiard and Wendel-Wurtz; and on the other, I avoided speaking of authors who could actually still be living or living on in thin-skinned descendants. You see how prudently I proceeded. Finally this period: 1804–1870 seemed to me to constitute an epoch and fill the exact course of two generations since two times thirty-three is sixty-six and 1804 + 66 = 1870.

"My first chapter was devoted to AN ADVERSARY OF NAPOLEON, Claude Villiaume, born in Charmes in 1780. Soldier, then 'attaché at staff headquarters in the capacity of secretary,' then defense attorney before courts-martial, a bill of 1803 'regulating the judiciary' deprived him of his 'position.' He went to Paris and 'at the Invalides construction site' approached the First Consul who sent him to his aide-de-camp, General Savary; the latter 'believed he discerned in him signs of mental disorder' and had him arrested. He was found to be in possession of two pistols. Locked up successively at Bicêtre, le Temple and Charenton, he escapes after thirty-two months of 'captivity.' He comes to Paris, moves about the city freely for eight months, is again arrested, sent to 'exile' in Troyes, agrees in 1807 to sign a 'letter of apology,' returns to Paris where he opens a marriage bureau—the first, which made something of a splash. In 1814, during the campaign of France, he conceives the plan to 'seize Buonaparte.' His plan doesn't come off, but following a fuss about an unpaid cab and a fistfight with the cabman, he's again interned, then taken to a private mental institution where 'they wanted, through the processes of ventriloquy, phantasmagoria and magnetism to bring confusion into [his] imagination and make [him] dream horrors which never existed.' They showed him 'a mother who reproached [him] with the death of her son, a wife with that of her husband, a husband with that of his wife,' etc.

"He escapes from this institution and in March 1815, he makes contact with Saint-Clair, the murderer of the Beautiful-Dutchwoman (Balzac's Sarah Gobseck, as you all know) and with the Marquis de Maubreuil, one of his former 'clients' (he'd wanted to marry him to Robert-Lenoir's daughter) who, the preceding year, charged by Talleyrand, hm? with the assassination of Napoleon, had merely carried off the Queen of Westphalia's baggage. They bought pistols. In Villiaume's opinion, Maubreuil was at this time insane; as for him, he had only one intention: to kill Napoleon. He next goes to Ghent, then he's present at the Battle of Waterloo.

"In 1817, he's again at Charenton; released, he returns the following year. The last trace I was able to find of this individual, is a *Guide Of Persons Who Wish To Find A Job, Go Into Partnership, Get Married, Etc.*, published in Paris in 1824; in 1821 he'd published a *Calendar* of the same sort.

"To draw up his biography, I'm using:

"*M. Villiaume Painted By Himself And Misrepresented By Others, Or His Bureau And His Marriages*, 1812.

"*Extract From The Portfolio of M. Villiaume*, 1813.

"*My Detentions As Prisoner Of The State Under The Government Of Buonaparte*, July 1814.

"*M. Villiaume Dozing At Charenton, Followed By The Awakening Of M. Villiaume And His Return Into The World*, 1818.

"'My life,' he wrote, 'was truly extraordinary.' Indeed, he claims to have been a close friend of General Moreau, which explains the hatred with which Napoleon is supposed to have pursued him; to have saved Maubeuge in company with General Latour; in company with General Lecourbe, to have given chase to Souvaroff 'on the mounts of Helvetia;' to be able to go from Paris to Troyes in forty-eight hours; to have swum across the Seine in the dead of winter fully dressed; to have gone so far as to drink in a single day four bottles of 'this deadly and lethal liquid,' brandy; finally, to have played an important role in the two Restorations.

"That's really a most curious incident.

"But what is accurate in his account of Maubreuil's (second) conspiracy? It's curious to note that 'historians' like F. Masson (in *The Maubreuil Affair*) and E. Daudet (in *Conspirators and Actresses*) adopted it without hesitation. Now the lampoons put out by Maubreuil or inspired by him never mention Villiaume's name. I should have continued my research in the Archives Nationales, which I did later for a similar case, that of Buchoz-Hilton. For one can suppose two things: either, everything is imaginary and Villiaume dreams in 1815 of copying the Maubreuil of 1814 and identifies with him; or else he was a more or less unaware agent of the Count of Artois. And this would be an early example of the use of semi-lunatics by the police."

CXXVIII

"A persecuted man, son of a persecuted man, thought by his father to have been perverted by his persecutors, then taking up again on his own account the paternal claims; such is the subject of my second chapter: A LEGACY OF THE REVOLUTION.

"Le Turc senior, 'distinguished engineer,' embassy attaché in London, traced the origin of his misfortunes back to 1767; it's around this time, so it seems, that he destroyed a lace-making machine the secret of whose manufacture he'd brought back from England and which he didn't want to let fall into the hands of one of his three principal enemies, the mathematician Vandermonde, the two others being the Minister of the Navy Fleurieu and the illustrious geometer Monge, 'the most cowardly and savage of [his] persecutors.' He accused them of being responsible for the French Revolution and at any rate for the decline of the national navy, because the money they spent to maintain the agents of their 'dark designs,' of whom there were 'more than two hundred, of all ages, of all sexes, of all conditions,' could have been used, says Le Turc 'to establish a large fleet with all its rigging.' The persecution reached its height in 1793; evicted from premises he was occupying at the Quinze-Vingts hospice, he demanded 800,000 francs in damages and interest, which he was never granted. He then became convinced that his son had become 'the instrument of the passions of his enemies.' '[My father], says Le Turc junior in *Destiniana*, demanded that I communicate to him all the facts which had come to my knowledge relative to the persecution of which he was the victim. But far from being able to satisfy him in this respect, I was not even able to guess what might have led him to believe that I knew anything but what he had told me himself.... We separated equally dissatisfied with one another.'

"H. J. Le Turc, the son, had an incredibly eventful life. When he was still quite young, he served on a corvette as 'writer for the provisions clerk,' then on a gunboat 'as helmsman.' In 1801, we see him as 'housemaster' in England. He changes employment twenty-two times. 'It was,' said he, 'a remedy against reflection and melancholy.' He begins to complain of the 'surveillance' to which the other housemasters subject him. The latter want to get him away from London. He sends memoranda relative to his 'case' to the members of the cabinet, but they don't want to undertake the investigation he's asking for. In 1806 he enlists in the British navy, then, immediately thereafter, asks to be sent to a hulk, a prison ship, as a French prisoner. He is sent there; he escapes. He nevertheless continues to live in England. From time to time, he's imprisoned. Finally, he's deported. He disembarks in Rotterdam in 1812; he remains there for three months. Napoleon then makes 'proposals' to him: 'he wanted,' he says, 'me to recast and complete my work... to have it distributed in England without going there myself. A thousand reasons prevented me from considering these offers as being to my advantage.' After a great many difficulties, he obtains a passport for Lille; the prefect 'received him very well' and, according to him, 'offered him an annuity of one hundred thousand pounds on conditions nevertheless which were unacceptable to him.' So he goes to Munich; a few days later the French take him prisoner, and we consequently find him in the Strasbourg prison in 1814. He recovers his freedom at the time of the Restoration. He subsequently spends his life coming and going between London and Paris, publishing memoirs in French as well in English. These memoirs describe the persecutions to which he's exposed and they're a carbon copy of those his father endured. He also adopts his demands and until around 1850 submits petitions concerning the lodgings at the Quinze-Vingts. But, strangely enough, he himself is most indulgent toward his adversaries in spite of the fact that they reduce him to poverty, force him to go to one doctor rather than another, want to force him to marry, prevent him from reading and when he's having coffee send him 'individuals who bother him considerably.'

"'… As they imagined without the slightest foundation,' he writes, 'that I must necessarily like all the general and individual things which would have suited them reasonably well; when I returned from England in 1816, they made me marriage proposals, undoubtedly believing that if in the future I led a more peaceable life, I would leave them in peace themselves; but also, I must honestly admit, in order to compensate me in part for the reverses I had suffered…. I shall omit here many of the spiteful things which were done to me; experiments of all sorts that they took the liberty of conducting in the hope of making some new discovery regarding the manner in which I am morally and physically constituted. There has never been a person on earth who has been the object of as active and as meticulous a surveillance. Those with whom I have to do are not however lacking in tact, but their curiosity is much the greater.'

"He tried to ask them the reason for their actions, but they were incapable of giving the slightest explanation: 'My adversaries' —excuse my accent," said Chambernac as he went on in English, "'continually find out new reasons for keeping me in misery, and as I always prove that their reasons are bad, they sometimes answer: very few men care for what is done to their fellow creatures, however unjust and cruel. We can therefore do what we please, and there is not even any necessity for giving any reasons... My adversaries have not yet been able to invent one good reason for their conduct towards me.'

"The persecutor, an engineer and an inventor, became persecuted; the son, persecuted, became, if not an engineer, at least an inventor, and here are several of his discoveries:

"bomb a city by means of parachutes carrying explosives;

"aerate the Chamber of Deputies with 'sail wheels' and refresh it by installing 'spurting fountains';

"have specialists read the speeches of the deputies who do not have 'a voice with enough resonance';

"fight unemployment (1833) by decreasing the working hours and the wages of the workers;

"replace bridges with tunnels;

"capture fortresses by surrounding them with a wall and 'by threatening to fill the interior surface with water';

"improve 'the manner in which the characters are distributed into their compartments.' ('I suppose...,' he says, 'that each character has a different specific gravity... throwing all of them together into a vessel containing a liquid as light as the lightest metal, I would for example, have all the A's.' He adds: 'I soon saw that this method was not workable and I no longer spent time on it.')

"Later, toward 1855–57, he's then some seventy-five eighty years old, he's preoccupied with the infinite, comets, the duration of the world. He still complains of the 'perfidious' matrimonial plans of his adversaries, plans that he was already denouncing forty years earlier.

"In conclusion, I point out that of the nineteen of my authors whose dates of birth and death I was able to determine, eight lived more than eighty years, only one fewer than sixty-five (sixty).

"I didn't linger over the details of Le Turc junior's 'inventions.' Inventions are a subject I've deliberately neglected, as well as perpetual motion. But two names encountered in the course of my research occur to me: Boisseau and Lassie. In his *Archimedes' Fulcrum Discovered. Experiment To Slow Down and Accelerate At Will The Daily Movement Of The Earth*, 1847, Boisseau proposes this experiment: one hundred million men and more than ten million domestic animals begin to walk toward the East; 'one will see,' he says, 'how much later the daystar will appear on the horizon and the proof or absence thereof that the earth responds to the slightest amount of force.' In his *Complete Solution Of Aerial Navigation*, 1856, Lassie imagines a flying machine formed by an aluminum cylinder 300 meters long 'ending in two hemispheres and covered in its length by an immense spiral... screwing itself into the air.' The 300 crewmen placed into a 'tunnel' inside the cylinder turn the spiral by walking; between the tunnel and the envelope, there is 'pure compressed hydrogen gas separated at intervals by partitions.'

"You see the progression from childishness to simple gratuitousness."

CXXIX

"My third chapter," continued Chambernac, "is entitled 'MESSIANISM' AT THE BEGINNING OF THE XIXTH CENTURY. I've brought together various authors who at that time thought themselves messiahs. Such as Paul Lacoste, who was born in Jouan, a township of Bélaye (Lot), on October 26th 1775 and died in Paris on August 16th 1852. His work consists of 22 little brochures published between 1826 and 1849.

"Lacoste, who, while thinking himself immortal, sold his property in return for a life annuity, found it natural that his position as messiah go hand in hand with a vast fortune; of which he had been robbed. He expected the French government to give him a pension of twelve million. The British government had as a matter of fact given him some islands, but he hadn't been able to take possession of them. And one day as they were dining together in a restaurant of the Rue de l'Odéon in Paris, the pope had recognized him as the first and true pope.

"Lacoste lived in Bélaye. Not far from there, in Montcuq, lived his cousin, a man named Soubira, who also thought himself something of a messiah although in a less peremptory way. Jacob-Abraham Soubira, who was born in this village in 1768 and died there on December 15th 1842, is the author of 65 little brochures published between 1812 and 1841. Like his cousin, he was, Greil tells us, very 'careful about his financial interests' and extremely close with his money. A notary by profession, he would sell his works, most often simple flyers, on public squares. His signature was followed by various epithets: Poet of Lot, Poet of Israel (he claimed to be of Jewish origin), Emigré in 1791 (it was true), Correspondent of the Apocalyptic Society of the Lower Pyrenees, Delegate of the Messiah. He was also a prophet, naturally, and I'm going to read you one of his prophecies entitled 666 because the sum of each line is equal to that number according to a numerical alphabet he invented and from which he excludes the letter J since it is the initial of Judas. This letter is replaced by the syllable GE and Geudas is pronounced like wager."

CXXX

"'1—The 19th century will run up storms!
Its worldly zephyr
Will modify its norms
And uproot the vizier.

2—The 19th century will bring down paganism,
Will kill the Alcoran,
Will pummel vandalism
And cut back the Vatican!

3—This century will clean up Europe,
In order to check its ambition,
And thank God for the horoscope
That's supposed to sweep up Albion!

4—This century will transfix Asia,
Will cancel the stylet,
Will take hypocrisy prisoner,
And reform Mahomet!

5—This century will rouse Africa,
Will poke and prod the crook,
Defame his things political,
And will discalce the frock!

6—This century will fix the N. World,
And will regenerate Panama,
To rule its waters thus unfurled,
And to depose its lama!

7—This 19th century will finally magnify the Bible,
And roast the Geudas
Who stabs the peaceable
And parches these climates!

8—In short, the naive prognostication
Of the appearance of Gog
And the Messiah's regeneration,
Will soon crush Magog!

9—In spite of the terrible Alcides,
Dobrowsky (1)
Skilled at all things noisy,
In *do, re, mi fa sol la ti,*
Will watch as his aegis recedes!

(1) 'There is currently being published in Astrakhan a journal of Asian music, by the music teacher Dobrowsky.'"

CXXXI

"What," said Chambernac, "is remarkable in this prophecy, is that it is a true prophecy, in spite of certain obscurities. Indeed, the first quatrain announces the decay of the Ottoman Empire; the second, the conquest of Algeria (vandalism being the land of the Vandals) and the end of the temporal power of the popes; the third the decline of the British Empire; the fourth Mustafa Kemal (the second line applies specifically to the reform of writing); the fifth, colonialism, the Wilson Affair, the resignation of Jules Grévy and the anticlerical policies of Combes; the sixth, the development of the United States and cutting through the isthmus of Panama; the seventh the Bible Society and missions.

"Although Soubira was quite polite to his cousin, the latter couldn't stand the presence of a competitor in his vicinity; so he soon began to tell people that God had punished his relative for not having recognized him as the true messiah. This punishment, of a rather exceptional nature, was not reserved for Soubira alone. All who had stolen his goods and his revenue, all who did not adopt the universal religion he was teaching, all who 'did not abjure the religions still professed,' and notably all who continued to adore the Blessed Sacrament, which was in his eyes idolatry, were also struck in the same way: they were castrated. As to the women, they lost their 'nature.' Soubira, according to Lacoste, had even shown to the electoral assembly of Montcuq, 'his cock and testicles' preserved 'in a vase with brandy.' Among those who had been 'denatured' were also the Saint-Simonians, the Bishop of Bordeaux, the Bishop of Cahors, all the Cahorsian seminarians and all the inhabitants of Bélaye.

"Lacoste believed himself to be immortal, for God 'had made him die, and at the same time rise again… he would no longer die… he would remain the same, without aging any more, at a determined age.' Now, his precise contemporary, since his writings were published between 1827 and 1851, Gabriel Galland, also thought he was a messiah and immortal: God had 'made known' to him 'that until the end of the world [he was to] remain visible on earth.' He was to die and like Jesus Christ rise again; like Jesus Christ, he was to sacrifice himself for humanity: that's why the guillotine was to be 'kept until the end of the world…for the one who will present himself as a sacrifice.' He called himself 'the son of man' and the 'immortal person.' In 1828, he'd wanted to have himself thrown in chains into the harbor of Marseille; three days later, he would have risen. This was to be the proof of his mission. He was not able to give it, and later, apologized for 'sometimes not keep[ing] his word;' 'it is not his fault, but really that of his enemies.'

"He claimed to be the angel Gabriel, or rather half the spirit of this angel; he never calls his parents anything but his 'foster parents.' The merchant Constant Cheneau, who wrote between 1840 and 1851 and who was more or less Swedenborgian, succeeded in convincing his father no longer to call him 'my son,' for he was not his father; 'man is not a creator, he does not have this power.' To him God had said: 'You are my Chaînon, my Link, your name is no longer Cheneau, but Chaînon; I charge you with an important mission; I will guide you if you do not close your heart.' At around the same time, between 1822 and 1853, another Swedenborgian who by the way did not remain completely unknown, the Abbé Oegger, wrote: 'I have been chosen to proclaim definitively on the earth the existence of [the] new terrestrial Jerusalem.' Judas, 'the ill-fated disciple,' had laid his hands on him. In his *Unexpected Relationships Established Between The Material World And The Spiritual World By The Discovery Of The Language Of Nature*, of 1834, he interprets dreams; and two most curious plates accompany this work, illustrating dreams. (I point out in passing that in the *Abridged History Of The Life Of Jean-François Marmiesse, Diocesan Priest of The Diocese of Cahors Written By Himself, Containing The Divine Revelations Which Were Given Him*, published in Paris in 1828, there is also a plate illustrating a dream. This abbé, who was born in Cahors in 1745 and died in 1830, also wrote: 'I shall prove that my mission is extraordinary.' He had had prophetic dreams. Among the remarkable details he tells about himself, he claims to have during an 'attack' devoured five raw chickens 'with feathers.')

"I conclude by quoting a few significant phrases from famous authors of that day, such as Saint-Simon ('Princes, listen to the voice of God who speaks by my mouth.' As the founder of a religion, he will have the right to preside over 'all the councils.' 'He will keep this right,' he has God say, 'all his life and, at his death, he will be buried in the tomb of Newton') and Auguste Comte ('I have publicly taken hold of the pontificate that had in the usual course of events fallen to me').

"All believed in their mission, but history alone is the judge. As for me, my mission is to bring out of oblivion these errant minds and to hold them up as examples for the times to come. There. That will be all for tonight."

CXXXII

For the sixth time Chambernac resumed his discourse:
"My fourth chapter is entitled THE ENEMIES OF LOUIS-PHILIPPE and the first of them is de Buchoz-Hilton whom I alluded to yesterday. But at the outset I should mention that several of our authors claimed to have predicted the revolution of 1830, notably Galland and the abbé Mayneau whom I'll speak about later. So. Buchoz-Hilton is known to us as much through his writings which extend from 1830 to 1855 (the Bibliothèque Nationale has only some of these) as through the observations of the psychiatrist A. Tardieu in his *Medico-Legal Study on Madness* (1872).

"Buchoz-Hilton appears suddenly in history in July of 1830 as Colonel of the Volunteers of the Charter, a rank to which he had appointed himself. Very little is known about his earlier life: he's said to have been born in 1788 and, according to Tardieu, is supposed to have been the object of lawsuits—repeatedly—for fraud, vagrancy, etc., as early as 1816. On the other hand, there are the *Observations On the Cadastre of France* by Buchoz-Hilton, first-class engineer-geometer, published in 1830; but is it truly the same person?

"In August 1830, the 1st Regiment of the Volunteers of the Charter was dissolved and the volunteers sent to Metz to form the nucleus of a new regiment, the 65th line regiment. Buchoz-Hilton, decolonelized, demanded the government give him 300,000 francs in damages and interest; his request was denied, he was even sentenced to one month's imprisonment for impersonating an officer, and he thus became a personal enemy of Louis-Philippe.

"So, 'capitalizing,' says Tardieu, 'on a grotesque caricature to which party rivalries had succeeded in giving a political meaning,' Buchoz-Hilton builds a vehicle in the form of a pear and starts to drive up and down the streets of Paris selling Soft-Pear polish, Soft-Pear walking sticks, Soft-Pear ink and finally even signs his satirical tracts Buchoz-Hilton a.k.a. Soft-Pear. He's arrested more than fifteen times and is finally sent to Nimes under surveillance. In 1840, he turns up in Bordeaux writing handbills advertising the Carter Circus. Then he comes back to Paris and opens a cabaret at the foot of the Buttes-Chaumont. He walks around the outside of his house with a bayonette stuck to the end of a stick, dresses dummies as soldiers and puts them in the windows and keeps goats in the house; 'rumor has it,' Tardieu tells us, 'that his behavior is strange beyond the wildest imagination.' He fastens bits of wood to a dead tree and attaches to them leaves of zinc that he's painted green; he tells anyone who will listen that the tree will bear pears.

"In 1844, he flees to England and there, incredible as this may sound, the *Court Gazette* of August 5 1849 attests to it, he obtained a judgement against Louis-Philippe from the Queen's Bench, a judgement entailing civil imprisonment for the royal debitor. But when Buchoz-Hilton wanted to have this sentence carried out, the English magistrates countered with a demurrer. He then returns to France, is arrested, interned and, it seems, fairly rapidly released. Later, he was to claim he drew a government pension between 1845 and 1848. From 1848 to 1850, he publishes rather irregularly a Franco-English newspaper, the *Lucifer*. He demands 150,000 francs when the civil list is abolished. At that time he's living in the Porte-Maillot district where he's opened a cabaret, headquarters of the Club To Wipe Out Revenuers, for the employees of the internal revenue service have replaced the ex-king. He hangs them in effigy and gives a bottle of red wine to anyone who buys his paper, which he sells to aristocrats for 1 franc 50 and to proletarians for seven sous. He publishes a *Taxer of Lawyers* in collaboration with a man named Courgibet (sic). After the establishment of the Empire, he calms down and the last trace I've been able to find of his existence is a *Methodical and Simple Treatise Accessible To All To Protect Against Poisoning By Brewers, Manufacturers Of Cider, etc.*, published at the time of the Exposition of 1855; at which time he was calling himself a 'representative of exhibitors of the Kingdom of Great Britain and of the United States of America.'

"When I came to Paris in July 1932, I went to the Archives Nationales and did some research on this individual. I discovered under the call number BB^{18} 1189 (A7 4347) a file created at the time of his imprisonment in La Force in

1830 which proves that Buchoz-Hilton was during the Restoration an agent provocateur among French refugees in Brussels. He involved or rather compromised them in a plot he concocted; but, in spite of the protection of the ambassador of France, he received the harshest sentence of all. He subsequently requested a 'job as spy,' but without success.

"I will leave you to draw any conclusions that might suggest themselves regarding this interference between the domains of the police and of mental pathology."

CXXXIII

Chambernac sighed:

"It's when I returned from this stay in Paris that I found my wife suffering from an inexplicable illness. You all know that she died shortly thereafter. But you don't know why. That's my own story."

He sighed. Then resumed:

CXXXIV

"On February 14, 1831 the palace of the Archbishop of Paris was plundered. This incident reminds me of the Abbé Paganel, not that he participated in it in any way, but because of the pretext he found in it. This abbé had become famous through his polemic against Lamennais, but as a result of eccentricities that Legrand du Saulle doesn't explain in his work on persecution mania (Paris, 1871), he was suspended in 1830.

"After the sacking of the archbishop's palace, it was noticed that a sum of one million three hundred thousand francs had disappeared. Mgr. de Quelen accused the rioters. The Abbé Paganel retorted: the thief was Mgr. de Quelen himself. The abbé was sentenced to eight months in prison.

"The rest of his life is of little interest to us: in 1850, during a session of the National Assembly, he insulted his old adversary Lamennais. Interned in Bicêtre, he was freed on several occasions, but returned each time; he died there in 1866 at the age of 66. The autopsy revealed that his brain weighed 1,306 grams, that it was quite healthy and that there was only one very localized area of softening, in the extraventricular nucleus of the left corpus striatum.

"This abbé is merely parenthetical since his adversary was only a substitute of the king. But now we have Lady Newborough, Baroness of Sternberg, who as of 1830 claims that Louis-Philippe is none other than the son of an Italian jailer named Chiappini. She herself was the true descendent of Philippe-Egalité. Her memoirs, entitled *Maria-Stella Or Criminal Exchange Of A Lady Of The Highest Rank For A Fellow Of The Lowest Condition* delighted all the polemicists who attach any importance whatsoever to questions of heredity; and Naundorfists as well as legitimists made a show of taking them seriously. More than ten pamphlets were inspired by them and *Maria-Stella* was reprinted several times, even as recently as 1913, and translated into German and Italian.

"Maria-Stella-Petronilla Chiappini was born in early April 1773 in Modigliana, a little town in the Grand Duchy of Tuscany. Her father, Laurenzo Chiappini, was a jailer. Maria-

Stella had a sad childhood: her mother beat her and her father didn't much care for her. She detested them and preferred 'important people.' 'I was very much hurt,' she says, 'when they forced me to consort with common people.' Her parents made an actress of her and married her off, at thirteen, to an old English lord who died in 1807. Three years later, Maria-Stella remarried a Russian baron. Her life is spent in continuous travels and it was in Sienna in 1821 that she learned of the death of her father who left her a letter in which he revealed to her the secret of her birth: 'The day on which you were born to a person whom I cannot name, and who has already passed into the life beyond, there was also born to me a boy. I was requested to make an exchange, and given my financial situation at that time, I consented to repeated, attractive propositions, and I then adopted you as my daughter, in the same way that my son was adopted by the other party.'

"From then on Maria-Stella set out in search of her true family. She thinks she discovers that her father's name was Louis de Joinville and consequently has her name legally rectified. But she cannot identfy this Joinville; she becomes the prey of swindlers who exploit her. Suddenly, she notices a resemblance between Louis-Philippe and her so-called father. She has found her genealogy: she is the daughter of Philippe-Egalité. Doesn't the county of Joinville belong to the Orléans? Didn't the Duke of Chartres pass through Reggio in 1773? It's true that at the time of her birth, the newspapers report the presence of the Duchess of Chartres in Paris; but, answers Maria-Stella, those are conventional accounts of official ceremonies and not the 'historical and faithful relation of an event.' She as easily refutes the various other objections she raises, notably the following: Maria-Stella was born in April and Louis-Philippe in October; why was not 'the birth of the supposed prince' made public 'immediately?' 'An invincible sense of decency' said she, 'of necessity kept them from doing, in the case of trickery, what they would have done without fail in the absence of any fraud.'

"It has in fact been proven that the Duke and Duchess of Chartres were actually in Paris in April of 1773 and that the birth of Louis-Philippe in October was not in the least mysterious. I refer as proof to a definitive article by the Viscount de Reiset in the *Weekly Review* of May 1909. Nonetheless, there is a nonetheless, it does seem that Maria-Stella was indeed not the daughter of Chiappini, but of an Italian count.

"Lady Newborough spent the end of her life in a ground-floor room of the Bath Hotel on the corner of the Rue de Rivoli and the Rue Cambon. She stuck to her windows satirical cartoons against the Orléans family and 'addressed to a host of people strange notes filled with coarse insults concerning Louis-Philippe which she signed de Joinville or even Marie-Etoile d'Orléans. 'Half-mad,' according to the testimony of Alexandre Dumas who saw her at that time, 'she lived more than five years without going out, fearing, so she asserted, that she would be arrested.' She died on December 28, 1843.

"My fifth chapter," continued Chambernac, "is entitled ON THE FRINGES OF SAINT-SIMONISM (1833). After the arrest of D'Enfantin and the end of the retreat in Ménilmontant, Lyon had become, since January 1833, the rallying center of the dispersed Saint-Simonians. There they were organizing the 'peaceable army of workers,' making friends with laborers, working in the shops, giving parties and dances, engaging in very active propaganda. But this agitation had in the end seemed futile to Barrault who was leading the movement in the absence of the Father. In Saint-Simonian circles they'd long been looking for the Mother, the Woman-Messiah without whom the movement lost all significance. Now Barrault had just had a revelation: 'I know where the Mother is! In the Orient!' He then founds the association of the Companions of Woman and at the end of March he leaves Lyon for Marseille where he was to embark for Constantinople.

"In April of the same year there appears in Lyons *Monfray To Those Who Wish To Hear Him*, a brochure followed by *Prophecies, Edicts, Proclamations And Speeches Of The King Of Human Intelligence*; *The King Of Intelligence To The French*; *To The Prostitute*; and *To The Carlists*. I'm going to read you one of the Edicts and one of the Proclamations."

CXXXV

"'EDICT

"'We, Monfray, by order of the spirits, provisional king of human intelligence, greetings, fraternity, friendship, love, for all men and women;

"'Considering that it is important that our royal occupation be regulated;

"'Considering that it is important as well to situate our royal residence, we have ordained and do ordain the following:

"'Our rising is scheduled to take place between 5:30 and 6 o'clock, we shall proceed to our daily occupations at 6:15 6:30, at no. 2 Rue Mercière, a shop specializing in fine fabrics woven with differently colored threads;

"'We shall breakfast at the foresaid shop between eight and nine.

"'Our hostelry is situated at no. , Rue de l'Arbre-Sec, at M. Rostaing's, the little private room to the left, when entering by the lane;

"'Dinner is scheduled from 3 to 3:45;

"'We shall leave our daily occupation between 8 and 8:30 in the evening.

"'As to our supper, we shall not have an appointed time, reserving unto ourselves a total independence from 8:30 to 10 o'clock in the evening.

"'We shall be visible at our royal residence from 10 to 11 o'clock in the evening.

"'Our royal residence is situated in Lyon, no. 34 Rue Neuve, wigmaker's lane, on the 2nd floor, at Mad. Vidal's; Except Sundays and holidays.

"'The spirit of order is charged with the execution of the present edict.'

"'PROCLAMATION.

"'From us, Monfray, king, provisional peaceable Napoleon of human intelligence;

"'Greetings, greetings, love, love, friendship, friendship, fraternity, fraternity, to all men, to all women, for all women, for all men.

. . . .

"'All decent people of all classes, of all professions from kings to proletarians, who do not yet recognize the great principle, evermore definitive, of the equality of man and woman will be considered as being not yet sufficiently worthy of our fraternal association; all those who do not want work according to their abilities and remuneration according to their works will be regarded as not yet being able to belong to the great family.

"'I am taking an hour of rest, I am going to go for a walk.

"'What do you know, it's raining, I have no umbrella. Here, let us continue:

"'If you want wonders, I am going to perform some: if you want miracles, they are going to flow from my pen; unbelieving little humans, if you deny the power of genius, I shall hurl my thunderbolts at you.

"'I want to shake you to your very core, what do you want of me?

"'If I want, I shall make you weep in tragedy, laugh in comedy, shudder in drama.

"'If I want, I shall create, I shall create, I say, within two years, a new stage, tragedy, a new opera, a new comedy, a new poetry, a new novel; if you want to speak of rhetoric, logic and morality, religion, politics, art, science, come and let us speak.

"'Do you want to speak of agriculture, of fields, forests, vineyards, wheat, fruit, history, theology, plants, geography, the growing of flowers, the art of the weaver, of weaving with differently colored threads, of printed calico, handkerchiefs, novelties, cloth, linen, *escamette*, and even of *garat*:

"'Do you want to speak of philosophy? come and let us speak.

"'If you want to see how I write, come see and see whether I make many deletions.

"'Come see whether I must make a great effort to find a thought.

"'Come see whether if I don't draw at an inexhaustible spring of living water.

"'Yes, I say unto you, I have an immense treasure, but I waited until I came of age, I waited, I say, until I was a man before making use of it, now I am twenty-one years and three months old, and three days ago I opened the door and am now drawing it out by handfuls.

"'Once again what do you want to make of me, do you want me to be mad, I shall be mad.

"'If you want me to be insane, dumb, ignorant, I shall be those things as well.

"'If you want me to become insipid, unbearable, hateful, I shall be those things as well.

"'If you want me to be wicked, a liar, a thief, lascivious, I shall never be those things.

"'Come to me, upon seeing me, you will love me, and I shall love you.

"'I want everyone to say: There is the man we need, the most profound, the most original, the most sensible, the most ingenious, the most amusing, the most mischievous, the best fellow, not proud, in sum the most extraordinary man who has ever appeared on earth.'"

CXXXVI

"In 1844 Monfray was 'illegally confined' for two months at the hospital of Antiquaille in Lyon; after which he wrote *A Rehabilitation* and, reusing an old title, *Monfray To Those Who Wish To Hear Him*. People want to cure against their will, he says, those 'whom society calls insane, and to do this they use tyranny, violent means.' 'I know,' he continues, 'that they will give me excellent reasons to justify these means; but they are in part founded on the law of the jungle. Perhaps I shall try to combat them; but today I must limit myself to saying that mental illnesses are phenomena, mysteries which human science has not yet unveiled; may we be permitted to penetrate them; but in studying them, we must respectfully contemplate these immense misfortunes which we cannot understand, and we ought never forget in their presence the stern word of the master of science, of the greatest of philosophers: "Whosoever shall say to his brother: you are mad, deserves to be condemned to the fire of hell" (Gospel of Saint Matthew, chap. V, verse 22).'

"In 1833 Monfray claimed to draw his inspiration from Saint-Simon and Father Enfantin, even proclaiming the latter to be the 'leader of living humanity'; but when, ten years later, a newspaper relating the acts which led to his internment called him a Saint-Simonian, Monfray replied: 'I am not a former Saint-Simonian, but I am what I believe I have always been, what I hope I still am, *a true Christian born of the old stock*.' He also called himself Servant of the Savage of the Forests and Knight of the Strong Woman ('This is what a woman insisted on calling me').

"These titles were not imaginary, I mean that a small

number of people acknowledged them, even that of peaceable Napoleon of human intelligence. The proof is in the letter that I'm going to read you and that I discovered in the Saint-Simonian archives of the Bibliothèque de l'Arsenal, a letter from a certain Dubeau to Father Enfantin, countersigned by Monfray. Later, in the last chapter, I'll tell you who the 'Strong Woman' was.

"A digression. I stated that, for me, isolation and obscurity characterized the 'literary lunatic'. A working hypothesis. A 'literary lunatic' finds no echo. Now, you've seen that Maria-Stella did find this echo, and Buchoz-Hilton, and even Villiaume; and here Monfray is no longer isolated but the representative of a group. It's a matter of method. We're no longer dealing with thoughts but with acts. Sceptical along with my century, I can assess thoughts only by the stir they create; as for acts, society cannot ignore them. Instead of zero, I had to take a minimum.

"Here then is this letter:

CXXXVII

"'Paris, the 2nd Sunday of the month of July, 1859.

"'Confidential epistle from Father Dubeau to Father Anfantin.

"'Although you know me neither by sight nor by name my heart tells me that I should call you *my father* even though you were to refuse me the sweet satisfaction of caling me your son.

"'Permit me my dear Father to begin my confidential epistle by giving myself a burlesque label.

"*I am a juggler by profession.*

"'I am going to explain to you how your son was call to adopt this vocation.

"'It was following a cruelly rude remark that the prosecutor addressed to you know who right in the middle of a session of the court of assizes.

"'*A man* a young man *cried out* since such men are accused of doing jugglery Im going to do it too.

"'That man Thats me.

"'from then on preoccupied with doing jugglery in a big way. ON A VAST SCALE. i looked for volunteers daredevils, Collaborators in Jugglery while travelling without being much wealthier than *a wandering Jew.*

"'I went to pay my respects to the city of troie birthplace of my childhood where I converted a few friends incapable of serving actively but good sedentary national guard.

"'I got to Lyon in the company of a Group of Companions of the woman (corps commander barrault) without never the less being incorporated into their legion I felt for myself a very different destination.

"'*let me make a long story short*

"'at the performance of the drama thirty years or the life of a gambler I met my two principle actors, to consecrate the memory of our unions we formed a society whose goal is Creation and the staging of a *unique drama.* it's ending will be the end of the *ancient* world. ITS LAST JUDGMENT it will be condemned under pain of death. to *methamorphose* it's self into a new world BY THE RESURRECTION OF THE BODY.

"'this drama which we have undertaken to stage, to the last act we will thus call it *thirty yeers or the life of jugglers.*

"'The *first scene* began on Epiphany Day, 1833 between 10 actors five of one sex five of the other, and I was the eleventh one who cut up the cake and it was a woman that chance made queen.

"'On April 4, 1833 we baptized each other by each other with the water of the rhone river.

"'and on April 5 our birth certificate was consummated a single man signed it as solely responsible for the act. It ended with the DECRUCIFYING of Christe. Thus will also end our world for the Christe that they are still keeping nailed on the cross is the KEYSTONE of the pharrisees social Edifice on the day when he will be unailed their whole Scaffolding of lies and Egoism will fall.

"'How will that be don. very simply. very easly they communicated to us the SECRET BUT IT DOES NOT BELONG TO US. il blongs to her or him to whom it will be given to use it. everyone to his own job.

"'Our birth certificate was addressed to you from Lyon it was placed the 2nd Sunday of July, 1833 into the hands of one of your sons of ménilmontant who saw to giving it to you. (you were in prison).

"'recently (20 years ago) we apearred to the parrisians under the costume of SAVAGES OF THE FORESTS we had indeed just carried out voyages to the hart of virgin forests. without harming their virginity we do not know if your sons notified you of our apearrance on parrisian soil if they didnt do so they failled to keep their promesses.

"'We also entrusted to them in 1845 a little story of the adventure of one of our poor *miners*, proscribed for we ar for the most part. PROSCRIBED MINERS, WHO ARE WORKING UNDERGROUND. unknown to the wise men who imagine that their Ediffice will be eternally unshake-able. the foresaid miner was condemned to stay in the hospital of antiquaille of lyon under the prejudice of INOF-FENSIVE MENTAL DERRANGEMENT.

"'A curious story when it will be ellaborated to you in all it's details. The reason for his COMMISSION was the planting of three wooden crosses in the name of the mother of the father of the son of the Holy Spirit. it was the prediction of the end of the ancient world By the reconstruction of the NEW JERUSALEM and of its new temples *under the presidence of a* PEACEABLE NAPOLEON… These most extraordinary things will then become most natural most simpal.

"(a few blank lines)

"'*and are you not the soul who has prepared predicted anounced the fullfillment of all the prophetic Hopes.* and the last lines of your response TO THE FIXED IM-MOBILLE FATHERS you quite rightly say

"'=I feel him in *me* when I dare to defend myself against you, he is my shield and my strength for I affirm to you and to all that *now his kingdom is of this world.*

"'you quite rightly say that the crucified body of the god-man is on battlefields. it is in loathesome hovels. It is in unspeakable workshops… *he who speaks thus is in truth the father of all the suferers of all the under dogs, he is our Father in god.*

"'As he is 26 years old, we come to bring you our statement of gratitude and of faithfull friendship.

"'We present our peaceable cry no more War. happy we will be. if we merit your approval. most private. public approval there's no need the hour is not yet come It will come when we will be permited to ask you if we have been faithfull to the mission that you gave us.

"'=go where god calls you make yourselves all things to all men=. That is what we have done that is what we must still do but to finish what we must still do we need your *bennediction*. Be blessed our Father your self in the name of the mother the father the son the Holy Spirit of god who has brought us all forth created in his image Dubeau Father son of his father

"'Certified accurate and attestation of the truth.

>Monfroy
>Street of the hedless woman
>8
>ile saint loui

CXXXVIII

"My sixth chapter," continued Chambernac whom fatigue did not seem to be getting the better of that evening and who was regaining strength as he went along, "is devoted to J. J. B. CHARBONNEL, a disciple of Coëssin and an industrialist. In partnership with his master, then with Scipio Pinel, son of the famous psychiatrist, he manufactured lamps with a rotating base and, under the scientific direction of Thenard, ink and polish (perhaps it was *his* polish that Buchoz-Hilton sold). This individual is, moreover, a junction since we shall find him again later collaborating with another figure in the footnotes of history, the Count Léon.

"I shall not tarnish with remarks the few extracts that I'm going to read you from the *History Of A Lunatic Who*

Cured Himself Twice In Spite Of The Doctors And A Third Time Without Them, Paris, 1837.

CXXXIX

"'One day (in 1832) it so happened that I wanted to understand myself: a new idea had seized my entire being, and as I found it very beautiful, I wanted to belong to it, and I trembled at the slightest motion lest it escape me; so I forgot everything that surrounded me, and buried myself as it were in myself.

"'At that very instant I was placed into the hands of alleged friends, incapable at that time of understanding anything about my condition; I quietly got into the cab which was waiting in the street at the door and two young men placed themselves, the one to my left, the other on the seat opposite, and the cab began to go its way…

"'The spirit had seized me, and contracting the fibres of my neck, he was imprinting onto my head and my thought the direction that I was to follow. Little by little I stretched out in the cab, and I stiffened myself, and with a well and duly given slap in the face, I forced out the last of my guards, when he wanted to pull me out forcibly…

"'My imagination was struck by the idea that they were taking me to the cemetery; it seemed to me that they'd opened my side, and that all my blood was soaking the earth across which we were moving; but a mysterious voice, speaking into my right ear, was telling me clearly and gently: Say nothing, let yourself be led.

"'…I seem(ed) to be entering into one of those horribly

mysterious lairs, where sacrilegious men make abominable pacts among themselves at the expense of other men.

"'Indeed, two of these men seized me, and, having put myself in their hands, they carried me through narrow corridors; doors opened and closed with a great noise of hinges, keys and bolts, and all the bustling, convulsive movements of these men, combined with their impassioned sighs, excited by the efforts they were making, gave me the sensation of an infernal prison…

"'It appears that I remained in this state (of torpor with regard to exterior objects only) for a week, and when I asked my guard, the one I'd slapped on the cheek, how long I'd been there, I couldn't believe his assertion; for inwardly I had lived a beautiful life, and the time had appeared to last only one night, or rather it seemed I'd lived forever.

"'…I was fed during this whole time a mysterious food that placed itself upon my lips and my tongue, as if it had come from the air; this food was like manna and like the purest fine wheaten flour; I desired no other, for this food returned every time I felt hungry.

"(Second 'excursion'—1834)

"'One day, therefore, when I had given myself up entirely to my faith, I again lost the taste or the sensation of things foreign to this faith, and I trembled, examining everything around me, not knowing what this could be…

"'While wandering through the streets where the spirit was telling me to go, I expressed the thoughts that were preoccupying me in gestures which were sometimes extraordinary, but not a single person whom I met dared to make fun of me, nor even to follow me, and point me out to others; for a gesture or a look had quickly impressed them.

"'While going past the Vendôme column, I began to laugh with pity at the stupidity of people who erect bronze statues to the great men they have killed; for they are indifferent, I said to myself, to such vain honors.

"'So, gesticulating very expressively, I entered the garden of the Tuileries, jumping as it were over the two sentinels, or rather slipping between the two with a dummy move to distract them. I strolled along in my own way, or rather I gamboled about for a moment as though in spite of myself; I went as far as the Clock Pavilion, discovering sadly that the door was closed; and after grasping the arm of one of the garden guards, and giving him a friendly tap on the right shoulder and on his chest covered by the cross, I shook his hand affectionately, and went away turning around at intervals, and looking in his direction with a menacing air that was not at all meant for him. I left the garden by the same gate I'd entered, and came quietly back home manifesting nonetheless, by the way I looked, the ideas which were occupying me.

"'But once again I had to come out of it; they sent for a cab, and I was ruthlessly thrown into it.

"'…The gate of the great garden was opened to me, and I strode all over it, raising my hands to the heavens, and singing the praises of the Most High with the word *alleluia*, of which I first pronounced each vowel separately; it seemed to me then that I was in a descending fire, and I saw clouds come together rapidly and form an elongated circle, and darken above and around my head, while the sky was serene almost everywhere else; the more active this fire became, the more I felt that I was walking in flames, and the more my inward joy increased and manifested itself in the strength and majesty of the song my mouth was uttering. My imagination was lovingly summoning the lion, the lioness, the tiger and the most ferocious animals whose strength I felt as it were within myself.

"'They let me calm down, and they led me to the little room that I'd occupied before; upon entering, I saw that it was full of black smoke; I made the sign of the cross above it, and this vapor instantly disappeared, and I felt good there.

"(Third excursion—1836)

"'The cab seemed like an enchanted chariot that was travelling all over the world, or else a skiff sailing on the sea. Every bump that made the carriage tilt was for me a mountain that one of its wheels was crossing, or else a wave that had just lifted the boat.

"'The dust that the cab was raising, chased by the wind, represented for me populations destroyed or near ruin, and I saw with secret horror in each atom of dust a man disappearing, carried off and dispersed by the wind.

"'A deep sadness thus gradually came over me, and when I got out in the courtyard of the home in Charenton, which I did not know, for that is where they were taking me, I saw everywhere a black vapor that filled the air and covered the entire house. Like the first time, I thought I'd arrived at the cemetery, and that they were going to bury me alive or put me to death there.

"'…I have ascertained… that, if science does not proceed in ways that are absolutely true, one must admit that its ways are right, and that they are generally directed with care, attention and humaneness by those in possession of this science. But what can all the treasures of science do with a lifeless body? Must the mind of the patient not also aid science?

"'So I saw that science was good in itself and I also owe it some gratitude.'"

CXL

"My seventh chapter," continued Chambernac without taking a breather, is devoted to THE LAW OF 1838 which governs in France the condition of the insane and the question of 'arbitrary illegal confinement'. In it I examine the cases of Jules Allix, Bouzeran (already mentioned), Gagne (I shall speak of him again), E. de Garay (M.K.D.M.—Here I've run into a mysterious bibliographical problem), E. Garsonnet, Gautrin (I'll speak of him again as well), Journet, the Count of Lawoestine, Roustan (I'll speak of him again), Hersilie Rouy (I'll speak of her again), Sandon and of a few anonymous authors. In an appendix, I say a few words about contested wills, about Simon Lenormand who wrote his memoirs on stamped paper and about sundry family troubles. This brings me to a digression on senility and the examples of Martin Merrier, widower, an illiterate man who became a poet at the age of 68, and Antoine Husson, an old fellow of 73, author of the *4th Part Of The Pharmacopoeia For My Personal Use*, seventy-five pages of details relative to his health: his stools, his wet dreams, etc. Thus driven to stick there whatever didn't fit anywhere else I added a second appendix on Nicolas Cirier on the pretext that his two principal works, *The Typographic Eye* and *The Apprentive*

ADMINISTRATION appeared respectively in 1839 and 1840. He was a foreman at the Government Printing Office who, having reason to complain about his superiors, resigned. These two works are 'pamphlets,' remarkable chiefly for their disorderly use of all the 'graphic arts' (chiro-, tachy-, typo-, litho-, auto-, chalco-, cassitero-, phello-, xylo-, polytypo-graphy, as he tells us himself), the multiplicity of sketches and stickers of all colors and the variety of characters used (Greek, Arabic, Chinese, etc.)—in short a delight for devotees.

"As for me, I'll say no more about it.

"That will be all for today.

"I'm going to bed.

"May I?"

CXLI

For the seventh time Chambernac resumed:

"SECRET POLICE AND INFORMERS, that's the title of my eighth chapter. We are now in 1846 and here we have in the same year *Theodore Or Fifty-Nine Years Of The Life Of A Level-Headed And Noble-Hearted Man* by Major, Army Corps of Engineers (Ret.) Theodore Choumara; and *The Secret Police, Machiavellian Studies*, little autograph loose sheets that Jean-Baptiste Gautrin 'general head of the *Do what you ought come what may* Society' continued to publish until 1851.

"According to the former, the secret police, 'returned to the control of the Jesuits' after the assassination of the Duke de Berry, are responsible for the death of all the liberal orators under the Restoration and for the 'suicide mania' preying on antiroyalist youth. According to the other, on the contrary, the Jesuitic police are in the service of France whereas the Judasic police are backing Louis-Philippe 'crowned Robert-Macaire.' After his commitment to a mental hospital, Gautrin writes: 'Finally His Majesty Louis-Philippe has collared me. We've got one another; it wasn't easy; he needed quite a bit of coaxing. Now it's a matter of finding out which of the two of us will beat the other. The contest will be fierce if God does not abandon me, which I hope.'

"After 48 and the fall of Louis-Philippe brought about by the Jesuitic police backed by the 'conjuration of decent people,' the Judasic police did not disappear, but transformed themselves into the 'ex-secret' society of the Rights of Man which wants 'a red republic' to make people 'regret the House of Orleans.' Choumara, who sometimes compared himself to Abel and sometimes to Job, sometimes to Socrates and sometimes to Jesus, sometimes to Samson and sometimes to Rousseau, sometimes to Pascal and sometimes to Ulysses, accused the secret police (Jesuitic in his opinion) of far more complicated and subtle misdeeds. They want to make him out to be a 'visionary' and 'it will take the entire Paris police force to achieve this tremendous result.' Flatfoots project beams of light into his eyes to make him think he's having dizzy spells; others dressed in his clothes engage in eccentric behavior in the streets and accomplices say: it's an officer in the Army Engineers who's crazy; others, examining the direction from which the wind is coming, place themselves in front of him and start to scratch their sores and their pustules, so as to 'send (their) dust onto (his) clothing and into (his) face'; others, when he is in a public establishment, throw onto him 'hair covered with little scales of ringworm'; others take over all the apartments surrounding his, 'establishing communication by means of trap doors, rotating fireplaces or mobile panels, raising sections of wall by means of counterpoints or making them turn on pivots, slide into recesses, raising and lowering parts of the floor by means of jacks and return screws, making floors entirely mobile by means of mechanisms similar to those of bascule bridges or seesaws, opening door panels by means of simple pressure on springs known to them alone and hidden by moldings'; others enter his room while he is sleeping and he awakens 'ill' 'in the situation of a virgin who would find herself pregnant without having had, to her knowledge, relations with a man. *Et nunc intelligite*'; others, during his walks, take advantage of his absence to change or damage his furniture and his books; and still others project onto him a 'very fine dust which seems to have the property of attracting flies, so that (he) find(s) (him)self preceded by *flies* and followed by *finks* who smilingly point (him) out to passersby.'

"A few years later, Francisque Tapon-Fougas, playwright and State Poet, was to accuse his persecutors of shooting at him, by means of a 'little oral instrument' a substance he likens to chili pepper extract and which 'produces in the small of your back the same effect as one thousand feet of flies, *mouches*, all tickling your spinal cord at the same time. That is probably,'—he adds—'what has given the name *mouchard*, informer, to those who use this glorious instrument of torture.'

"He too accuses the Jesuits: they debase to the 'standard of nothingness' the thinking of their adversaries and their preferred agent is carbon sulphide. They used 'atmospheric poisoning' on Victor Hugo, which is why he 'did not produce what the world had the right to expect of his immense leisure' (his exile—we're only at the end of the reign of Louis-Philippe, I'm getting ahead of myself). Furthermore, Victor Hugo is an enemy of Tapon-Fougas and portrayed him in *Les Misérables* as Thénardier of whom he says that he had the look of a weasel and the appearance of a man of letters and that 'he resembled the portraits of the Abbé Delille.' Tapon-Fougas, compatriot of Delille and man of letters, sees in his words 'allusions as out of place as they are hideous' to his person.

"'The quadruple alliance between the detectives of Semitism, the detectives of Jesuitism, the detectives of Freemasonry and the detectives of Hugolatry' has as its aim 'the implacable and unceasing destruction of the name and the moralizing work of the old State Poet, F. Tapon-Fougas,' work which to my knowledge comprises no fewer than forty-seven books published between 1850 and 1882, satires, poems (among which the *Antimisérables*) and above all comedies and reforming dramas describing the persecutions of which he is the object and ending in the fifth act with the rout of the torturers. The means employed in his case are moreover analogous to those used by Choumara's flatfoots, with however a marked preference for physico-chemical methods.

"Tapon-Fougas died in Roanne, over eighty-five years old, still believing himself to be persecuted. Choumara, who lived to be about eighty-four, appears on the contrary in his old age to have given up his persecutors and busied himself with astronomy, aerial navigation and foreign politics. As for Gautrin, at seventy-three, although he had forgotten the d'Orleans and 'their more or less secret agents,' he still called himself 'general head of the *Do what you ought come what may* Society'; he finished his existence raising rabbits and publishing anticlerical and pacifist brochures.

"But I can judge them only by their printed publications. I did not engage in detailed research or thorough investigations of each of my authors: I could have located their families, dug in the archives of the asylums. I had to limit myself. I'm offering only simple surveys. Thus I didn't speak of Gautrin's committal to a mental hospital, of the lawsuit for 100,000 francs in damages he brought against his father, etc. I'm just passing through. I'm merely turning my lantern onto the obscure deceased. I'm hauling them up to the light of day and we shall all present ourselves together, they and I, before the people here present and those to come.

CXLII

"My ninth chapter, THE MYSTERIES OF THE HISTORY OF FRANCE, is devoted to Hersilie Rouy. Her memoirs (*The Memoirs Of An Insane Person*) were published only after her death, in 1883, but it is now, I believe, that is toward the middle of the century, that it is best to situate the questions that preoccupy her.

"There are three sources of documentation for Hersilie Rouy.

"1. The foresaid memoirs, written with an apologetic aim to vindicate the claims of the author, and one can say: expurgated;

"2. The observations of psychiatrists, and above all the

article by Sérieux and Capgras, 'Novel And Life Of A False Princess,' heavily documented and using the archives of the asylum of Auxerre and the hospice of Orleans;

"3. The works of Le Normant des Varannes, director of this hospice. In 1866 he'd made the acquaintance of Hersilie Rouy confined in this establishment; convinced by her, he succeeded in having her discharged two years later. He continued to see her until her death and it is he who published her memoirs. Under the pseudonym of Edouard Burton, he wrote a novel *The Memoirs Of A Sheet Of Paper*, published the preceding year, whose heroine is Eucharis Champigny, that is Hersilie Rouy. The fact that she inspired this work in which her historical pretentions are detailed is proven by a passage from another production of Le Normant des Varannes, a *History Of Louis XVII*, of 1890, in which he defends the thesis of the survival of the dauphin. 'All the details,' he writes (concerning Petrucci and his secret society, you'll see later what that's all about), are the exact reproduction of what has been told us about them by the woman who was at the same time their affiliate and their victim,' that is Hersilie Rouy.

"Her father, I mean the father of Hersilie Rouy, was a very curious individual; a former grocer who became a mathematician and an astronomer, he was in addition bigamous. In 1788, he had married a Mademoiselle Stevens by whom he had a son, Daniel. But a short time later, he abandoned her and, in 1813, married a Mademoiselle Chevalier. Three girls and two boys were born of this marriage which everyone naturally thought was perfectly legal. Hersilie was the eldest of these five children. She received a good education, became a schoolteacher, then a piano teacher.

"In 1845, when her younger sister married her nephew, that is the son of Daniel, the latter, on this occasion, had the legal status of the children of the second marriage rectified—illegitimate—and they had to bear the name of their mother, Chevalier. A short time later, one of her brothers, Charles, went into a mental hospital. Finally, her father 'got' a persecution mania and died senile at the age of 78, in 1848.

"Six years later, Hersilie Rouy was committed. It seems that the neighbors' complaints were what made the police intervene; in any case, her half-brother played an important part in her 'kidnapping.' As Sérieux and Capgras very rightly point out, certain legal prescriptions were not observed; on the other hand, Hersilie was committed as was right, under the name of her mother, Chevalier. She was to draw multiple conclusions from these two circumstances: first of all, she had good reasons to protest against her 'arbitrary illegal confinement'; and then, she concluded that there existed a society which modified, as it pleased, the legal status of whomever it wished.

"In her memoirs, Hersilie naturally defends herself against the charge that she was 'mad.' If she claimed to be the daughter of the Duchess de Berry, it was to capture people's imaginations. She produces documents proving that she is not the daughter of Charles Rouy; they are in her handwriting: it's because the originals are lost. And for that matter, she declares that she will not assume 'in any way responsibility for their contents.' Among her papers there was found a love letter to the Antichrist; answer: 'among the innumerable quantity of extravagant letters I've been accused of writing, this is the only one people ever show me.'

345 ◂

"But she wrote things like the following to a government minister: '(A person, 'whom I discovered later to be the Baroness del Lago,') told me (in 1849) that I had as godfather a Pierre, son of Pierre, who, while keeping this appellation constant, took several different surnames;

"'That the surname most generally adopted by him was that of *Joseph-Pierre Petrucci*, which did not keep him, as can be seen in our certificates, from taking others (Petracchi, Petroman, Petrowich) but always keeping Pierre to form a family name from it, or repeating twice the name Pierre;

"'That, as goddaughter of Pierre, I was involved in an enormous inheritance matter; that no one could inherit unless all the conditions of the will were fulfilled, which was most unfortunate for me.

"'She revealed to me that it was she who, under the name of Hersilie Rouy, had given concerts and played in several places, in order to add to my reputation and draw me from obscurity, which could prove fatal to me in that people would forget me and which would enable them to make me disappear for good.'

"In 1872, she writes to the Vicount d'Aboville, deputy of Loiret who had become interested in her cause: 'Before my kidnapping, toward the middle of August, a *stranger* came to warn me that they were going to make me out to be mad, change my name, say that I was dead, dispossess me so as to make my return into society impossible, search through and seize my correspondence, because they believed me to be in possession of secrets and papers concerning my godfather, Pierre, son of Pierre, who was the head of a powerful society, whose ramifications extended to the far corners of the globe.' She adds that they make a point of calling her mother *Marie*-Henriette instead of Jeanne-Henriette and that (one of her brothers) 'is in Valparaiso with a Marie Chevalier who passes herself off as his mother and (who) speaks of a daughter *who has died* whom she's supposed to have had by the Emperor Dom Pedro Ist, with the result that the name *Pierre* is again and always linked with that of Marie.'

"During the fourteen years that her confinement lasted, she drove the psychiatrists who fell into her hands to despair. 'This megalomaniac,' writes one of them rather comically, 'is above all known to the doctors who have treated her by the tribulations of all sorts that she has caused for them, by the disruption that she brought into all the departments that took her in, by the persistance and tenacity of her ravings.'

"Discharged, Hersilie succeeds in obtaining from the Empress Eugenie 500 francs in aid. Using as support the fact (accurate) that her brother Daniel and Doctor Baron de Kinkelin did not observe the prescriptions of the law of 1838 when they committed her, she pursues her claims. In 1874 the Republic accords her a pension of 125 francs per month, raised to 150 in 1877 and to 300 the following year plus an indemnity of 12,000 francs. Hersilie is not satisfied; she multiplies her letters to deputies, magistrates, journalists. *Le Rappel*, in 1880 publishes an article in her favor. She is hoping to obtain new advantages when she dies in 1881 in Orleans of pulmonary congestion, at the age of sixty-four.

"The 'case' of Le Normant des Varannes appears even more interesting to me than that of Hersilie Rouy. 'One can see,' write Sérieux and Capgras, '...to what extent administrators and magistrates can let themselves be impressed by the intellectual keenness of these 'reasoning madmen,' by the accuracy of their writings and the cleverness of their reticences; they even manage to justify an ambitious delirium that is strange, but is based exclusively on interpretations.'

"Not only does Le Normant des Varannes adopt the 'theories' of Hersilie (whom he believes to be the daughter of the Duchess de Berry), but he goes on to support them with all the authority of his erudition: he thus discovers that, under the Consulate, a certain Pierre Petracchi claiming to be Pierre son of Pierre and of Russian or Polish origin, was deported as suspect. 'Is it her godfather?' he asks himself.

"Le Normant des Varannes was also a proponent of the survival of Louis XVII. And in connection with this I must say that that subject is too well known for me to dwell on it. Nevertheless I cannot remain silent about an individual like Gruau de la Barre, former notary, author of *Intrigues Unveiled*, a comprehensive survey of false-dauphinism and who after claiming that Hervagault, Mathurin Bruneau and the Baron Richemont, three false-dauphins who appeared successively, were one and the same person, finally claimed that he himself was Louis XVII. Le Normant des Varannes adopts these identifications (except the last) in his *History Of Louis XVII*; he attaches great importance as well to the prophecies of Nostradamus, to the strange apparition of Thomas-Ignace Martin de Gallardon, to the assassination of Fualdès and to a great many other mysterious incidents or seemingly so, his principal source naturally being the memoirs of the Baron de Richemont (who, according to Le Normant des Varannes was still living in 1889), the above-mentioned book by Gruau de la Barre—and the confidences of Hersilie Chevalier."

CXLIII

"You think there's no truth in any of that?" interrupted Coltet.

"I," said Chambernac, "am going to tell you one thing, or rather two, or rather three. First of all there is no doubt a *secret* history; one can assume that; but then it's not *this one*, that of the claimants and the interpretants. It remains hidden to them as well as to you, to the 'daughter' of Philippe-Egalité as much as to the 'daughter' of the Duchess de Berry, and to Gruau de la Barre as to Le Normant des Varannes.

"I'll resume. Here we are then in 1850 (as Sérieux and Capgras have shown, Hersilie Rouy's 'psychosis' is conditioned by the legendary 'atmosphere' of 1848—remember that it was at that time that spiritualism (which Hersilie seems to have practiced) appeared, here we are then in 1850, right in the middle of the xixth century and two thirds through my history; I'm going to take a break and talk to you about someone who in my *Encyclopedia* represents hygiene and exercise and is here only to create an interlude because his *Revolution In Walking* was published that year; I'll continue with the title, *Or Five Hundred Natural And Infallible Means To Find what is comfortable in the different ways of Walking: Wearing Down one's Shoe as one wants; Not Getting it out of Shape, avoiding Corns on one's feet; Not Tiring while Walking, as well as while Working; Walking with assurance on slippery paths; Not Getting Muddy,*

or if one Gets Muddy in a forced Walk, Getting the Mud off
when it's dry in a pleasant way without making dust and
without damaging the Fabric; Straightening Through Walk-
ing the gait of Those who Limp, Including Games And Hy-
gienic Exercises for frail people of all ages: Preserving Sight
And Giving It The Strength To Withstand The Brilliance Of
The Sun Without Tiring It; Finally Contributing powerfully
to one's health, moderately to one's happiness and somewhat
to one's beauty, Simply By One's Own Movement.

"I'll content myself with reading you two passages, sim-
ply to take a break.

CXLIV

"Perfecting the hat.

"'If to protect oneself against rain one had only to bring
certain movements into accord with one another, we'd be
delighted; but since one cannot reach this goal without a
device, we count on the zeal of our inventors to make us
one, one might say this one: one would take a round of oil-
skin taffeta at least as much as from one shoulder to the
other in diameter, and whose rim would be held up by a
little stiffener that would be arranged in such a way that in
pushing it the two ends could run the one over the other to
tighten up the taffeta, as one would do it by means of a
runner to reduce its dimension, so that this little device could
go into the hat and serve as a lining.

"'Now the means of fastening this sort of umbrella to the
hat is very simple; one would make a second runner accord-
ing to the same principle, which would form a small round

inside the big round, but large enough to serve as an exterior lining to the crown of the hat, and one would only have to tighten this little runner to keep this device on the hat, then do the same with the large runner to align it with the small one. One could strengthen this device with little screws, which one would only have to turn to make them stick into the hat.

"To complete this little double-duty device, we would turn it inside out to put it inside the hat, and the points would take the place of the stitches that hatters ordinarily make to fasten the lining to the inside of the hat.

"'Now, so as not to be exposed to seeing this new umbrella carried off by a gust of wind, it would be very easy to make a sort of invisible chin strap, by means of a black lace fastened to the inside of the hat, and that one would bring down behind the ears to fasten it under the chin.

"'This newly invented umbrella, also capable of serving as parasol during our walks in the country, could moreover because of its shape replace a basket in case we should have to carry something light, such as flowers or light fruits.

WALKING BACKWARDS.

"'The idea of walking backwards might appear strange to the French character, and of no importance whatsoever. Nevertheless, if one thinks back to the times of our greatest military glory, one will see that some of the generals of our Empire immortalized themselves by executing skilful retreats. One can see the importance one should give to the exercise of walking backwards, when one considers that in case of retreat, the more one can face the enemy while walking, the sooner one will be ready to seize the moment of attack.

"'Regardless of the usefulness of improving walking backwards for times of war, which for the good of humanity ought not to come again, would it not also be most useful in times of peace? Indeed, have we not seen officers of the national guard, unskilled in military maneuvers, who, at a turn in the street, walking backwards to give the order for this turn to their troops, bumped their heels into the sidewalk, and after making vain efforts to remain upright, inevitably lost their equilibrium.'"

CXLV

"My," continued Chambernac, "tenth chapter is entitled THE SECOND OF DECEMBER. And here is Gautrin meeting the Prince-President Louis-Napoleon Bonaparte at the traffic circle on the Champs-Elysées one September day in 1850 and commenting on the matter thus: 'This was moreover a rather singular encounter that took place, at such a precise spot, of two men both of whom are in various ways reproached with being pretenders; the one escaped from the prison fortress of Ham, slowly descending, in great array, the grand avenue, the other escaped from the insane asylum of Charenton, slowly climbing on foot and in rags, along the sidewalks, toward the Arch of Triumph.' On the morrow of December 2 of '51, he wrote: 'After all, you and I, we aspire at this hour to monarchic power in France; you in order to have the happiness of being master and by ambition, I in order to wipe out the system of banditry of which

I am victim and by devotion; I clearly, squarely, openly, you deceitfully, traitorously, surrepticiously… However that may be, my little prince, you would do well to clear out as quickly as possible; you know, for that matter, how it's done, and it is as I see it, the best way to avoid the cage, the axe or the rope.'

"One month after Gautrin, Joseph Jocteur, 'philosopher and prophet,' was, in turn, meeting Napoleon 1st.

CXLVI

"'… It was behind the fort on behalf God on the covered way; he was alone and I alone. When we were face to face with each other, that gave me a great feeling in me and made me change color.—To come across this great man there as close to me as that! We were so close that we could have held out our hands to each other if we had wanted to without moving from our places.

. . . .

"'… I recognized him all right according to the nature of what I had seen beforehand in my deep sleep.—He still had a full face—the same when I saw him and also greatly ruddy.—Yes, I got a good look at the chin of this man which was flat in the middle and turned up afterwards, which made the tip of his chin look pointed. That's what I was looking at the closest along with the point of his nose that seemed pointed.—I thought that his legs were a little big and thick on his back; that looked to be a little stooped.—When I was straight across from him, I looked at him hard and he noticed it. He went faster but completely and properly. He was walking much faster, then he turned toward me again to see if I was watching him walking so fast… Yes, according to the nature of God and also according to your star, I can say myself that I really saw you close to me and that I recognized you even.

. . . .

"'The Star of Napoleon the great man made its 3rd trip having come to pass round the back of the capital of France in the sky toward the end of the spring of 1851. Everything that the stars do the day before and even all the meanings that appear in the sky in several ways, that announces to you, Peoples, that you never expect that, and that you are not surprised at it and surprised will not be at what happens the day before in the sky, and then at the events that happen afterwards.—It is for real that we will have him the great man full of health and divinity.—The man they say died on Saint Helena will again command all of entire Europe before he dies, and will master it on the plain of Saint-Fond near Lyon. In this awful fight the youngest of the kings will defend himself the most and afterwards the People will be happy.—For example, the great man he must laugh often in himself about what is happening today. Also, L. Bonaparte bearing great secrets in himself.—When he dies the great man he will die in the middle of his whole army full-size justified. And L. Bonaparte our president will die on French territory, and his star is contained by a circle of little stars. I know it naturally. With his star and also the circle that surrounds it, one can know when one works to cause his downfall. I am not telling you in the place where it is, for fear that he will be displeased with it, our president, because myself, I wouldn't like that to be done to me, because already his Uncle, when I saw him, I did not show him to the people for fear of bothering him too seriously.— The laws of the Emperor Napoleon will last 500 years, and of Louis-Philippe there are some of his works that will last 200 years.—There are only 2 little white stars left in the sky for the Bourbons, that you can hardly see and they're on the other side of the path of Saint-Jacques. There is no more strength in the sky for the Bourbons.

. . . .

"'Before very long a new invention will come, 4 strong wheels. It will have, according to the 4 stars that are for announcing it, and also a great movement it will have, that will come and go often according to the 5th star, which is a bit removed from the 4 that is for announcing it.—This great movement will give much strength to the invention, and then steam will be abandoned in general, because it will be found to be too costly. It will no longer be useful and this new invention will have immense strength. It will replace steam everywhere and it will give power to large workshops. It will not need either fire, or coal, or water. It will have 2 fine boilers the same as I saw in nature. The man who will make this invention will die in one winter and he will not have a son living. Not many years will pass and you will see it work, for you are on the watches in part of all that.— There are four stars in the sky that were for announcing steam, 2 together and the 2 others on each side and near the capital of England in the sky little white stars.—Commerce will go badly as long as the great man has not come back, which produces poverty in the People. He had taken France low and low he will take it again, and in France peace will put there and abundance will bring back there, and the eagle his ears will prick up and forward he will march, and before he comes back, the great man! in the sky the eagle will reappear.—In the family of the great man 2 great warriors there will be, counting the 1st.—They will be fairly old the 2 of them.'"

CXLVII

"That's how this loose sheet ends, the only known—to me—work of Joseph Jocteur, prophet and philosopher.

"Napoleon returns, but with the number III. The coup d'etat of December 2nd is approved enthusiastically by J. J. B. Charbonnel, co-director of the *Journal Of Men Free In Jesus Christ* along with Count Léon, a bastard of Napoleon. Demonville, the astronomer I spoke of in the second part, claimed to have called down upon the Prince-President the 'imperial omnipotence.' Paulin Gagne, who later invented philanthropophagy, sings:

> On the Second day of December,
> By a saving burst of the sun,
> Napoleon, crushing the Chamber,
> Founds the empire—happiness won.

"The official candidates express themselves similarly: Bontoux in Pontoise speaks of 'the providential act of the second of December' and Belmontet in Tarn-et-Garonne calls the 'mission' of Napoleon III 'regenerating'; and people like V. Hennequin, a Fourierist who's generally classified among the 'literary lunatics' but who is not in my *Encyclo-*

pedia, write to the new emperor: 'I have been commanded to tell you personally that you have a providential mission'; Madrolle, a disciple of Vintras, 'claims to have predicted this political change' and Wronsky sees in the second of December an 'act of high morality' thanks to which there will be 'instituted in Europe (a) new political state,' Messianity. Finally that's when Fortuné Roustan appears, a 'collector on leave of the Department of Registration and Property, moral accomplice of the insurrection of the Var.' In order to please 'a beautiful young child named Victorine,' in September 1852, he goes around Paris reading a prophetic poem, 'To The Prince Louis-Napoleon Bonaparte. All Of France, The Rural Areas Above All Ask For the Empire,' which he had written 'with the speed of lightening and in the grip of a sort of nervous attack,' and indulges in several other displays of this sort—which leads him to Charenton, then to Bicêtre; for a few weeks.

"A detailed account of this incident can be found in a brochure of 1853 entitled: *A Noble Inspiration Of Victorine Or My Problems With The Police Of Paris Concerning The Proclamation Of The Empire Which I Made Publicly*. The following year, in *Victorine, Most Truthful Story Of A Pretty Girl Of The Breda Neighborhood*, he was to tell things in a very different way, will claim to have wanted to appear 'original' only in order to compel success and regain the 'favors' of Victorine, a person 'as self-interested as she is interesting'; the 'eccentricity' of his writings was 'inserted deliberately and was never genuine.'

"Anyway I'll have to come back to this author.

"If you don't mind we'll stop here for this evening."

BOOK EIGHT

CXLVIII

"Does he have much longer to go," said Hachamoth, "I wonder. He's been imposing this reading on us for a week now. We can't get out of it naturally. All the same, I hope he doesn't have much longer to go now."

"He's mad," said Mme. Hachamoth.

"I don't know," said Hachamoth. "It's very curious: all these madmen."

"My God," exclaimed Mme. Hachamoth, "I take back what I just said. Do you remember that quotation from the Gospel? That he read us? 'Whosoever shall say to his brother: you are mad, deserves the fire of hell.' I never said he was mad."

"Let's say he's a bit odd," said Hachamoth. "But what are we going to do with him?"

"I don't know," said Mme. Hachamoth. "He's quite all right here for the moment."

"Whatever could have happened to him?"

"God knows. But I'll eventually get him to tell me."

"This reading, just now, it's strange. In any case it takes our minds off things."

"I prefer that to hearing about politics. My God make me hear the least possible about politics. What's happening with the NWC?"

"In practice it no longer exists. All its members have joined other groups, all, well, there are a few left. But I don't understand why Agnes is digging her heels in. It's

361

money down the drain, the subsidies I give her, and her ideas are absurd."

"She's my daughter," said Mme. Hachamoth.

"Excuse me, my dear. But what does 'a nation without classes' mean? I'm well aware that she wanted to fight the Communists and Socialists, all the same their ideas appeal to her, I find that dangerous. And then you can't mix contradictory things. At least that's what I think. However, I'm gratified to see that Agnes is beginning to get quite discouraged."

Mme. Hachamoth sighed:

"All the same it would have been so nice to see my daughter save France."

CXLIX

Denis sat down next to Agnes, took her in his arms and kissed her. She looked at him and immediately understood that he'd betrayed her.

"These readings are starting to get awfully boring," said Coltet. "And I'm somewhat worried about the state of your uncle's mental health."

"I couldn't care less."

"You don't think he's a little—funny, your uncle?"

"Why should that concern me?"

"My dear Agnes."

He took her in his arms again and kissed her.

"When are you going to hand in your resignation?"

"What resignation?"

"From the NWC."

"I, don't, understand."

"You don't want to admit it!"

"Ah. You guessed? I was just going to tell you."

"You don't have to. I don't much care to know what reactionary gang you've gone and gotten mixed up with. I just wanted to point out one thing: don't you find that, THAT, incompatible with your position as head of the NWC?"

Coltet got up:

"It's a bit ridiculous."

"What's a bit A BIT ridiculous?"

"This position as head of the NWC. You know as well as I do that the NWC no longer exists. And it's not the NWC that'll get rid of the swindlers and freemasons for us."

"The NWC still exists. I still exist, ME, I still exist. You, you don't exist any more. Not for the the NWC and not for me."

"Let's stop this joking, this game."

He wanted to take her in his arms. (Probably to kiss her: see above).

Agnes drew away from him.

CL

While war veterans were light-heartedly holding the streets of Paris and frequenting the corridors of City Hall and the young royalist Camelots du roi were jubilantly pulling up the metal gratings around the trees, Agnes advanced anguished through these streets where her endeavor and her doctrines were so utterly misunderstood. She knew full well now that the NWC had lived, and had died. Its members

carried off by the petit-bourgeois swell of down with the rob-
bers were having the time of their lives in the ranks of re-
spectably reactionary associations. Agnes realized bitterly that
the people of France were damned hopeless when it came
to fascism, her kind anyway; and, when all was said and done,
she felt drawn only to this left-wing government that the
extreme left was indeed calling fascist. And what disgusted
Agnes the most was to hear the slogans of the right-wing
manics enthusiastically repeated by the Communists: they
must therefore be bad.

After going back up the Champs-Elysées animated by a
joyously and capitalistically patriotic spirit, then the Avenue
de Wagram where the hookers and semi such were deplor-
ing the recent events interfering with their business, Agnes
went into a café of the Avenue des Ternes where Robert
Bossu was waiting for her.

She wanted to give him the job of calling together the
debris of the N W C. She did not yet know just why; probably
to confirm them in their hopes and to reveal herself to them
as, probably, "providential." Agnes couldn't help thinking with
growing unease of all those poor ignored, misjudged, mocked,
forgotten, disdained, alienated, rejected, abandoned, un-
heard, refused, excluded, unknown, deceased people who
thought they had some historic mission to fulfil on this earth
and succeeded only in furnishing the subject matter for the
wild imaginings of Uncle Chambernac. And yet the illustri-
ous, the known, the admired, the famous, the perpetuated,
the glorified, the assimilated, the integrated, the followed,
the heard, the admitted, the included, the known, the ap-
peared,—the recognized, they too believed in their mission.

She too believed in her mission. And yet she no longer believed in her mission. She too believed in her mission.

Robert Bossu was waiting for her, most impressed. And while waiting for her he'd stirred the thing around under his hat so much that his head was all topsy-turvy. Just seeing this so beautiful girl, this so pretty woman, this so elegant perfumed lady made him dizzy. Things started going round and round like in a ride at Luna-Park. Behind the front wall of his skull he saw in succession at full speed all the imagery of his memory just like saved drowning victims tell you. Agnes was talking to him, was explaining to him what she expected of him: a recall of the routed. He heard her, he heard her, but that didn't keep a big top from humming away inside him, a big top that was a lot like a thing they'd told him in public school was called the conscience.

Behind his attentive to orders facade, he was now bemoaning his ratting rottenness, spying on a woman he would like to have made it with, a woman he always imagined having when he was fucking somebody else. It wasn't his fault after all, it was Injustice that made you such a bastard, it was life with a small l that got you to do such lousy things.

All the same he remembered that he wasn't a guy just like everybody else, he was quite sure of that, he was capable of doing things that others don't do, he didn't become an engineer, no, he didn't become the lover of Agnes de Chambernac no, he didn't become the lover of Mme. Coltet no, this was all he'd succeeded in doing in his existence hounded by Injustice: tell the police little stories about the most beautiful chick he'd ever met, all the same he wasn't a guy like everybody else.

Sssooo he told her little stories about himself the skunk and about the police. Then, with a purified conscience, Toto-the-Pallor-of-Living beat a retreat.

CLI

The recent incidents had greatly excited the Parisian population, and the Neivillian every bit as much, but on the Rue de Longchamp in the house of the Hachamoths three people lost interest in them effortlessly: Agnes first of all, Daniel, Chambernac finally who that evening, it was a fifth of the month, imposed his discourse for the eighth and last time:

"Chapter XI: THE ANTICHRISTS OF 1856. According to Abbé Toussaint-Jacques Mayneau in his *Triumph Of The Truth*, these were: the medium Hume, a famous conjurer of the day named Bosco ('This great magician Bosco,' he writes, 'by the vast expanse of his phenomenal mind, has carried to the highest repetend the diabolical pomp with which a man possessed by Lucifer, can momentarily blind the genius of the scholars and sages of various enlightened nations') and the bear of the Jardin des Plantes zoo who with his two cubs formed 'as it were the figure of the triple dragon, or of the three beasts' and performed 'astonishing magical tricks.'

"The following year saw the appearance 'in the ligneous theater of Béziers' of 'the academy of the forty brute learned antichrists,' who were none other than ten monkeys and thirty dogs acting in little plays. 'Thus these animals act marvelously without knowing what they are doing, by the power of the black magic of the magicians, whose enormous vices get on well with the ferocious beasts and the evil spirits that lie in their entrails.'

"But the very year in which these antichrists manifested themselves was also that of their 'collapse.' Hume was chased from Rome, the bear Martin died and, thanks to the prayers of Abbé Mayneau, the ceiling of the theater of Béziers collapsed onto the head of Bosco who however was only very slightly injured. In 1857, still thanks to these prayers, the 'forty learned antichrists' put on a pathetic show and acrobats find themselves 'prevented' from executing their flying trapeze exercises. Finally, in 1858, the antichrist Buddha is vanquished (war of China) as well as the antichrist of oidium.

"And all these 'monsters' were vanquished by him, Abbé Mayneau, vicar general of Palmyra, of Babylon and of Columbia, him 'the solitary scholar of good Latin faith,' 'the most illustrious victor of the most formidable revolutionary antichrists.' 'Would it be possible,' he writes, 'that Béziers, the smallest city of God, in its obscurity, among so many famous warrior cities of the Christian universe, could have struck in the twilight of the week of milliary years, the great decisive blow against the throne of the infernal serpent, and that it could have entirely crushed its head while still letting its broad, long tail move, so that the universe might there see its virus dying?' He also pulverized the antichrist Galileo: 'When my bronze pen, cold-tempered, published its discovery, proving mathematically the daily and annual revolution of the sun and the impossibility of the revolution of the earth around the motionless sun; not a one of the famous astronomers of the capital dared come with his quiver to shoot at it his rich and all powerful arrows. This was on March 25, 1847 in Paris, in person, not incognito, but publicly, in the great theater of the empire of letters.'

"Abbé Mayneau had also defeated 'in several literary combats the audacious renegade Oéger,' he had foreseen the Revolution of 1830, he had miraculously escaped some twenty perils of death which he enumerates in his *Biography Of Abbé Mayneau*. His life was 'shot through with eminently collapsing catastrophes from his cradle to this day,' and nonetheless he always enjoyed 'prodigious health.'

"The style of this clergyman who proposed 'swearing modern-style': 'false gods damn it, billions of false gods damn it,' merits one or two examples:

"'… the engineers of the criminal matters saw in a most succinct distance, their victory assured and their triumph complete; they installed their Lucrecian artillery in the fortresses of the freemasons, they opened fire on all the lily branches, they loosed the tigers of the plebeian crowd: the mass of Barbary besieged its sovereign palace, it (the tax department) could, with the explosion of a single bomb, overthrow these black forests of leopards; but it did not want to shed the blood of any of these monsters, it stopped the burning fuses on the cannons of its army which were going to open fire with its triumphant indignation.'

"'These monsters (the unbelievers) ravaged the ramparts of common sense, they bulldozed the boulevards of good sense, they mined the fortresses of reason, they popped them with the powder of epidemic crossroads mud, they bore the flag of hydrophobia, covered with the purple mantle of brutal instinct, which delights only in the most atrocious carnages.'

"Chapter XII: PHILANTHROPOPHAGISTS, MORAL

MAMELUKES AND LOCK KEEPING BROTHERS. 1865–1868 is from our point of view a period of abundance and if I may say so of prosperity and exaltation. It was, in fact, during those years that Paulin Gagne invented philanthropophagy, that Fortuné Roustan, mentioned earlier, took the title of Moral Mameluke of Napoleon III and published his prophecies 'whose complete fulfilment will be,' said he, 'the proof of (the) divinity (of Jesus Christ),' and that Abbé Xavier Cotton first came to public attention through his letter to Princess Clotilde.

"Paulin Gagne (1808–1876) and Fortuné Roustan (1821 - ca 1901) are two of our most prolific authors; my bibliography of Gagne includes 36 items, among them *The Unityide Or The Woman Messiah, Universal Poem In Twelve Cantos And Sixty Acts* (a volume of 726 pages); *The Martyrdom Of The Kings, Regi-Tragedy*, 300 pages; *The Anarchiad Of Decentralization, Flagellating Archi-Drama In Five Flashes*; *The Archmonarchide Or Gagne The First, Arch-Monarch Of France And Of The World*, etc. I'm acquainted with 49 works by Roustan, in general small pamphlets; the only important ones are *Of Urgent Reforms To Be Made In The Administration Of The Department Of Registration And Property*, 1857, which earned him three months in prison and a 500-franc fine and *The Subtleties Of The Parisian Book Trade*, 1864–1865, in which he tells of his difficulties with the Black Band and what sort of lawsuit he lost. He had set up shop as a bookseller in Versailles. It is then, in 1865, after his conversion to Catholicism, that he takes the title of begger in black habit and of Moral Mameluke of Napoleon III. He prophesies: 'By the month of July one thousand eight hundred sixty-six, *very probably,* and, *in any case and with certainty, before the end of the current year,* the beggar in black habit will receive, *at his request*, and from the hand of His Imperial Majesty, the decoration of the Legion of Honor... New Saint Vincent de Paul and modern Jew Mordecai, the beggar in black habit *will remain poor* and thus preserve a free and independent position. Admitted nonetheless more than once to the councils of the Emperor and his ministers, he will be considered the intelligent head of all honorable beggars... Catholicism is entering a new phase. *Temporal power was and will again be taken from the pope...* In a future that is not very far off the seat of Catholicism will be transferred to Paris... *in the course of the present year one thousand eight hundred sixty-six*, I shall bless, *in my capacity as prophet and envoy of God*, the Imperial Prince *and his posterity...*' Finally he foresees for 1876, a war between France and Spain on the one hand and Russia and England on the other. He will be killed in the melee after assuring victory by a 'stroke of audacity and genius.'

"I shall tell you in the next chapter what became of Roustan during the Franco-Prussian War. The rest of his life falls outside this History. In short: in 1877, he foresees that Napoleon will 'soon' come 'to power, but by regular and legal means' and he writes: 'My political prophecies have always come true.' He prophesies the impending canonization of Joan of Arc, the *sine die* postponement of the Exposition of 1878, an imminent war between Russia, France and Austria on the one hand and Turkey, Germany and England on the other, etc. He then remains silent for fourteen years (the war did not take place, as for the exposition, it did take place, Napoleon IV was killed in 1879, etc.).

"Fortuné Roustan ended his life in an asylum. He was a 'most intelligent old fellow with an astonishingly active mind.' He wrote poems under the inspiration of Joan of Arc and Our Lady of La Salette and saw in the fact that he became a poet at the age of eighty proof of the divine origin of his inspiration. In actual fact, his first work had been a poem and he never ceased writing them. You see how sad was this life of a prophet who was always wrong and sometimes lied.

"In 1868, Paulin Gagne, the 'advocate of lunatics,' invented philanthropophagy, 'the only new fact under the sun,' 'the love of man for man given as food;' in the 'voluntary sacrifice of men and women giving themselves fraternally and religiously as nourishment to the victims of the hunger that is devouring the world,' Gagne discovers the definitive solution of the 'social problem': 'archphilanthropophagy, which will overthrow barbarism and all crimes, can alone say the sacred *never* to universal famine which, if no one sacrifices himself, will devour us on the great vessel of the earth deprived of provisions.'

"On the Place de la Concorde four crosses will be set up. There will be a charge for admission into the sacrificarium, except for the ground floor which will be free: 'one can definitely predict that all Paris will be there.' The arms and legs of the 'christ saviors of humanity' will be tied with 'golden rings,' 'their heads will be slipped into diamond-studded bands or circular razors according to their wishes; the sacrificers positioned behind the crosses will arm themselves with the tourniquets to be used to tighten the bands and the sharp blades, and, at the moment when the bells of the sacrifice were made to peal and when all the spectators fell to their knees, the execution would take place in an eternal minute, which would fill the heavens and the earth with love, glory and blessings.' Then the victims would be 'solemnly transported into archamphitheaters, prepared in various ways and put on plates decorated with laurel leaves and everlasting flowers. The corpses of those who have died of hunger or illness would be eaten, if there is no danger, in order to reduce the number of voluntary victims.' 'Those who might not wish to die will have the option of simply having their legs and their least useful arm cut off.'

"'As for me,' says Gagne, 'I'd rather become the sacred nourishment of my fellow creatures, who will venerate me, than to be the stupid, ignoble food of worms.' 'I ask as a sweet reward to have myself crucified and philanthropophagized.' He would also like M. Jules Favre to 'sacrifice himself with a sacred dagger on the altar-platform in order to send his *luminous body* to Algeria which would bless him.' He himself, the 'victor of the battle of the Obelisk,' is ready to send one of his legs to Algeria, another to America, an arm to Ireland, the trunk of (his) body to the entire world!'

"He also discovered diabolophagy. I shall rapidly pass over this question.

"Abbé Joseph-Jacques-Xavier Cotton belongs to the history of the Third Republic since it was then that he became Fulmen-Cotton, the shadow acting under Sadi Carnot, the chemist of Language, the installer of the Sortege and the organizer of the Lemanat. In 1865–66 he was still only 'the eminent thinker, poet, painter, priest, the first Definer and official Vulgarizer of the Primordial Idea of the Word made flesh.'

"He had been committed in 1858 for having gone and danced, dressed in his priestly vestments, on the tomb of his father in order to pay him public homage and also due to 'far more dangerous actions' which the psychiatrist who is here our source judges impossible 'to record.' At the asylum of Montdevergues, Abbé Cotton proved to be the doctors' 'bane.' Indeed, he took an interest in his neighbors, questioned them and made remarks which confirmed them in their delusions. 'To a patient who feared he would be poisoned, he said: the doctor gives you pills, don't swallow them; they contain an enormous dose of poison that will kill you in just a few days. If these Gentlemen don't always get rid of the unfortunate people who are suffering here, it's because they make their death pangs last longer in order to get larger salaries.'

"In the night from the fourth to the fifth of March, 1860, Abbé Cotton escaped, displaying 'an astonishing courage and coolness.' During the years that followed he lived in religious houses devoting himself chiefly to painting. In 1865, he publishes his letter to Princess Clotilde which ends as follows: 'The Servant of the Servant of the Servants of God... *Jesus the Word* made flesh... considers it a duty, an honor and a pleasure to furnish, either verbally or in writing, all the desirable clarifications on the *primordial Idea of Christianity*... both to the men of desires and good will who believe themselves called to become the friends of the bridegroom in the Institute of the Lock-Keeping Brothers, and to the daughters of Eve, gifted with the heart... of Mary Magdalene who burn to be ever so slightly... the friends of the bride in the congregation of the good women gardners of the divine gardner. (It is not necessary to write immediately... and to find the clarifier of the great matter go to 9 Rue Férou, 9, from 6 p.m. to 6 a.m., rather than from 6 am

to 6 PM…like Nicodemus… finding the night better-suited…
for fervent discussions…'

"'And the author of this incredible pamphlet is a priest,'
exclaimed a journalist of the time, 'a parish priest! and he
isn't in Charenton!!!'

"On January 29, 1866, following menacing letters ad-
dressed to the man he called 'the upstart of the cloth': Mgr
Darboy, he went into Bicêtre where he was to stay more
than four years. 'I have become *wise* and *great* among the
lunatics and the ordinary people at Bicêtre,' he wrote to his
mother. Finally he escaped. According to an extremely sus-
pect source, he is supposed to have participated in the Com-
mune of Saint-Etienne: I have not been able to verify this
fact. In 1871 he is a candidate in the legislative elections,
going from one end of Provence to the other 'bareheaded, a
crown of thorns on his forehead, with a long iron chain
around his waist, a cross over his shoulder and dressed in a
red robe.' He received 35 votes in Vaucluse. And leaves my
History.

"One can find abundant details on the last period of his
life in the *History Of Bicêtre* by Paul Bru, 1890; in *System-
atic Delusions* by Marie, 1892; in *Language Disorders
Among The Insane* by Seglas, 1892;, in *Decadent Poetry In
The Presence Of Psychiatric Science*, by Laurent, 1897; in
Writings and Drawings In Nervous And Mental Illness by
Rogues de Fursac, 1905 (under the name Maurice N…); in
Mysticism And Madness, by Marie, 1907; in *Art Among
Lunatics*, by Réja, 1908; in *Art And Lunacy*, by Vinchon,
1924. He is, along with Berbiguier, the 'literary lunatic'
whom psychiatrists have written about the most.

"Around 1900, when he is nearly seventy-five years old,

we find Abbé Cotton once again committed or rather as he expresses it 'become a living Stiff destined soon to be buried without honor, in the common grave of their Rubbish Field, in a state of human debris as loathesome as it is formless, worked on by the medical students of some school or other.'

"And the thirteenth and last chapter of the fourth part of *The Encyclopedia Of The Inexact Sciences*, by Henry de Chambernac, former principal of the high school in Mourmèche: WAR. And, since war does not have natural causes, Gagne, epically, comes up with the Warriad which incites

with furor, everywhere

The French to a craving for a war they can share.
"He continues:

Everywhere the deaf pavingstones hear in a din:
'To Berlin! To Berlin!! To Berlin!!! To Berlin!!!!'
"Adolphe Bertron, a retired merchant, 'conceived in the city of Angers on June 9, 1803, the day of the Christian Corpus-Cristi' and 'born in La Flèche in the old castle of this city on the Loir River on March 5, 1804,' telegraphs to Queen Victoria: 'Godvictoria!... Your Mission... To Tell... French... Prussians... you will not fight... Time of Wars Finished Choose... Prussia... France... Each one two Arbiters to harmonize all... Godwoman Victoria Will Preside!! For Humanity instruct yourself, keep yourself informed by telegram or letters.' (My little silences show that the ellipses are the author's.) On August 1st he publishes a letter from Fanny Junique of Lyon, whose signature he declares to be 'genuine and sincere, to William III king of Prussia': 'An abdication on your part, let us be frank, Sire, would be al-

most superhuman!.. would be truly sublime!… Would it not be forever… the substitution of good for evil?… of peace for war?' This letter closes as follows: 'in any case, Sire, a prompt answer from your Majesty, would be useful and agreeable to us being of the highest interest for the present moment. In the hope of your immediate support, you can count, Sire, on our eternal gratitude.'

"On August 12, from up in the galleries of the Legislative Body, Roustan demands the death of Marshall Leboeuf, of Bismarck, of de Moltke, etc., and, on the same day, in Lyon, Bertron addressing 'all of humanity' claims to recognize one God only: Woman, 'sole natural and true creator of the Human Race.' '…For the triumph of this Religion, the only true, the only worthy, we must at once and for always: Demonarchize the Universe… Demaster the terrestrial Globe… Deboss the entire World…For the result to be complete and sublime And for it to be, above all, durable: THERE MUST BE ONE SINGLE AND SOLE FATHER-LAND… THE UNIVERSE… One universal human language… And above all and in a word,—*All things free of charge*; which is summarized thus: To Each his Free Budget, assured a year in advance, from birth to death… this is the platform of : Adolphe Bertron, the Human Candidate.'

"Roustan demonstrates in the streets of Versailles, crying out: 'Down with the laws of public safety.' He was later to assert that in so doing he had implied these words: 'and with him who has abused them'; in this way he claimed he had prophesied the fall of Napoleon III. Arrested, he is acquitted on August 28th.

"On the 30th, the patients confined at Bicêtre are evacuated and Abbé Cotton takes advantage of this to escape.

"On September 2nd, Napoleoon III surrenders in Sedan, but does not for all that lose his messianic character in the eyes of Gagne:

> As with sovereign ardor himself he sacrificed,
> Napoleon the First was Saint Helena's christ;
> Perhaps people will say that, in his sad elan,
> Napoleon the third was Christ-man of Sedan!!

"On the 16th, Roustan harangues the crowd, on the Boulevard of Montparnasse, waving a flag in Joan of Arc's colors. He is arrested and committed to Sainte-Anne hospital the very day of the beginning of the siege of Paris. He is examined by Legrand du Saulle 'the great criminal, the secret accomplice of all the turpitudes of the Empire, the insanist doctor who passed off as mad and interned as such, the energetic republicans who gave umbrage to the ex-emperor Napoleon of infamous memory.' For at this time Roustan claims that he has 'never disavowed (his) republican principles.'

"Released after twenty-four days of confinement, he issues a writ for 10,000 francs in damages against Legrand du Saulle and Dagonnet, another psychiatrist: two more lawsuits that he was to lose. He spends a great deal of time at political clubs where he unfurls his Joan of Arc standard, but he is met everywhere with 'boos, catcalls, ironic applause, impiety, pride, immorality and physical and intellectual licentiousness.'

"With different opinions, Bertron never met with a better reception. On January 1, 1871, the first day of 'the new era of the human family,' he has printed, in Chambéry, the first issue of a periodical entitled *The Social Philosophical Humanitarian Human Candidate*. Until his death in 1886, at the age of eighty-two, he remained the 'human candidate' and appears here as an example of a numerous species; in 1885 he was still asking to be elected President of the Republic, assuring that he was 'apt and capable, by his mature experience, of *rapidly* making of the human race a single nation and of the terrestrial globe a single fatherland.'

"Meanwhile, beginning in 1870, Amélie Seulart had declared that she 'was officially taking up residence in the hospice of the Salpêtrière, the refuge of insane women while the armies of kings defile the soil of the motherland.' Amélie Seulart, who claimed to be Joan of Arc reincarnated, 'the new inspired woman of *Vos-Couleurs*' (Vaucouleurs), Your-Colors, whose 'name means *Ame-élue*, Soul-elected to teach the world the Sole-Art of making peace' (as Christopher Columbus means 'Christ of the *colombes*, or doves'), Amélie Seulart was the Strong Woman whose knight Monfray claimed to be, and the force behind the little group whose existence is suggested to us by Dubeau's letter to Father Enfantin. Founded on April 5, 1833, this group became in 1859, the *Work of the Planter-Farmers of the Peaceable Olive Tree*. From 1859 to 1872, they published seventeen pamphlets, most of them entitled *No More Wars, No More Idolatry!!!* and countersigned by Monfray; the other planters named are a certain Julie Desrennes and Richemond, an ex-infantry sergeant. As for Dubeau, he had been a 'junior employee in embassy offices abroad.' After 1872 I have been unable to discover a trace of the *Planter-Farmers of the Peaceable Olive Tree*. They were, as you can see, unimportant people and, as Dubeau wrote in his letter, probably scapegoats, of whom at least two were sent not to prison, but to the asylum and who wanted society to

CLII

"'sacrifice a few scraps of its immense resources to make of the exceptional world of the insane the happy kingdom of lunatics.'

CLIII

"Finished," said Chambernac.

Baron Hachamoth said:

"It's very interesting,"

and Mme. Hachamoth added:

"Very interesting,"

and Coltet said:

"Really very interesting."

Finally it was finished.

Coltet continued:

"Where are you going to publish this?"

"There's no lack of publishers in Paris," said Chambernac.

He was smilingly straightening the sheets of his manuscript with little taps.

Daniel got up to go to bed. He felt his asthma attack coming on. He remained a few more minutes, out of fear.

"Naturally I haven't read you the bibliography or the index," said Chambernac; "which exist naturally; nor the list of the authors whose possibly interesting works I've been unable to find."

He added:

"And I apologize for errors and omissions."

"I bet there aren't many of those," said Sophie amiably, emptying her glass of brandy.

She added:

"All those lunatics are galloping about in my head. There are too many, and all kinds of them."

Madness too comes from God. God is hidden there too. Daniel went up to his room to take a tablet of ephedrine, first a quarter, and two minutes later another quarter, and the attack was coming coming, and five minutes later the last half, and he licked from the hollow of his hand the white powder produced by breaking the tablet.

"Daniel is going to be sick again tonight," said Mme. Hachamoth, "it's such a shame it's such a shame,"

and she began to think of all the worries her children were giving her, her daughter Naomi married to a ragman since it was true that Ast was devoting himself to this singular trade and to curious activities, her daughter Agnes whom she saw there before her eyes all doleful and as if in mourning, and her son Daniel with his asthma. She would go sometime, very soon, to see Ast's absurd activity for herself, she'd just decided. How did Agnes know that? An endoublyoucist had told her, that was it. And that was another worry, that Agnes had never wanted to see her sister again and that she'd acted like that when she got married and in that way Naomi and Ast had so to say disappeared, had disappeared: they didn't even write; a brother she'd so loved and a daughter she'd so cherished, Mme. Hachamoth had lost them. Were they crazy? spiteful? They were defending their love, Naomi had written her, because Naomi had, after all, written once in awhile. And was that then their new life, rags and old paper?

Coltet and the baron started to talk politics, they were very interested in the latest events; not Chambernac.

Agnes let Denis talk now. Her historic mission was finished. What could she still hope for? After so many betrayals. And this other thing too, this reading, of te fabula narratur. She had understood, no more Joan of Arc than Amélie Seulart.

The next day after hesitating for a long time she went out to see the riot. And while walking along the streets, she changed her mind; one should never despair of one's cause. The NWC would continue.

But Agnes was killed around nine p.m.

They gave her a beautiful funeral, with flags, delegations; and Robert Bossu followed in the crowd.

Mme. Hachamoth was able to see Ast and Naomi again. It was high time.

CLIV

They crossed the boulevard scored by the trajectories of cars and sat down on a little mound, all that remained of the fortifications. Solvay rolled a cigarette and Coigule took a pack of Gauloises out of his pocket. They started to smoke in silence, digesting the corner bistro's boiled beef. Nice weather was returning, day by day, slowly, processionally.

Sunshine.

As for Cical, he brought his lunch; he made himself comfortable near the laboratory, on a cask: that was how he, who'd been there the longest, did things. Toine brought him a cup of coffee: a favor. Then he too had a smoke.

Coigule, the newest of the three, said to his fellow-worker:

"The way the boss is going about things he must be losing money."

"Probly," said Solvay. "He's searching. Searching always costs money. All inventors are like that, they lose money."

"But he's not an inventor," said Coigule. "He doesn't seem to know what he wants. Just what does he want?"

"He's searching," said Solvay.

"I wonder how it was he got started," said Coigule.

"I know how," said Solvay.

"Well tell me," said Coigule.

"Like I 'splained to you already, he's the son of the Claye that fell from an airplane, so he was broke. Relatively naturally. Me or you, we'duv been happy with what he had. But he thought it was time to get to work. Guys like that just work when they're down to bedrock. I don't have to tell you it was a brand-new experience for him. He just studied chemistry a little when he was young, but since then he's been twiddling his thumbs. That's hard to imagine people that don't do a damn thing all their lives. Aside from all that before he was a sponger and now he's an employer which is better huh, we can discuss that some other time."

"There's nothing to discuss."

"So then when he moved into this villa that you see there he didn't know exactly what he was going to do. He started to fix up the shed in the back that's now the laboratory to do experiments to see but that wasn't it yet it was just to make the switch you know from idleness to work. So his idea was to buy old paper and sort it to look for rare things, unusual ones that are valuable and that people throw away without paying attention. I don't think he ever found anything interesting but that way he became a dealer in rags and old paper, a small dealer. Then afterwards he thought of making paper himself like they used to in vats and like you're making now with me and him and us we're gonna end up making paper so tough it'll stand up to the mold of centuries not newsprint not toilet paper not paper like you see now that books are printed on now no what he wants to produce is paper that'll last for seventy-seven generations."

"Why seventy-seven?"

"Only you see it's not a going concern yet. He's searching. Sometimes he turns to one thing, sometimes to another. Sometimes it's making paper, sometimes the rag trade, sometimes chemistry."

"So he's still an amateur."

"A researcher is more like it. And there really is something positive in his work. And then for awhile now he hasn't been himself something's wrong."

"What?"

"I dunno. It's none of my business."

"The old guy coming?"

"No. It started before. I told you I dunno."

They threw their butts into the distance.

"That's what I mind the most," said Coigule, "not smoking."

"You get used to it," said Solvay. "Is it that time?"

"Let's go."

They crossed the boulevard.

"You see," said Solvay, "before, that piece of land there didn't belong to the boss. It's only been part of the property for a month."

Rissoir and Butry rode up on their bikes. They were the ones who handled the rags and old paper, sorted and smashed, classified and selected. And Butry drove the pickup.

From the corner, standing at the edge of the sidewalk, a guy was watching them. His motionlessness betrayed his hesitation and his morticious expression the deepest defeats. Slowly he came toward them.

And from the other side of the street, another individual was also watching, not hesitating but spying. He was getting ready to cross when he noticed that someone had gotten in ahead of him. He stopped.

The indecisive individual continuing his forward motion slowly got to where Solvay was, and said to him:

"Would there be work for me here?"

Solvay looked him over critically.

"Don't think so," he said.

"Who does the hiring?"

"The owner."

"Could I see him?"

"Not here."

"What time will he be here?

"Not before three."

"I'll be back."

"If you've got time to waste."

"A guy can always try."

"Well try then."

"I know what I'm doing."

"Good for you."

The door closed again.

The spy most interested crossed the boulevard came up to the other fellow and said:

"They hiring?"

"No."

"For that matter there's no sign."

"No."

"You thought they were hiring?"

"None of your business."

"I was looking for work too."

"Forget it here."

"Are you forgetting it here?"

"No. But I've got reasons."

"They don't apply to me?"

"No. It's personal reasons."

"Might I ask, if I'm not prying."

"There's no secret."

"So you've got reasons not to forget it."

"Yes. I know the owners."

"You worked for them before."

"No. I know them personally."

"You don't say."

"I do know them, the owners."

"So."

"So you see, they've got to hire me."

"I see. Why don't we go have a quick one."

"All right. I have to wait till three."

"Should we go here?"

"Yes. You see, they've got to hire me."

"A Beaujolais for me."

"Same here."

"What if they can't?"

"They'll find a way."

"And you think they wouldn't have something for me too?"

"I can ask them."

"You'd be a real buddy."

"I'm not promising anything but I'll put in a word for you."

"That's good of you."

"What do you do? I'm an electrician and know radio. If there wasn't the depression I'd be an inventor by now."

"Between you and me, that's not very useful in the old paper business what you do."

"But I'm telling you I know the owners. You'll see. All I have to do is see them."

"You're lucky."

"Me lucky? Not on your life. Rotten luck. I've always had rotten luck."

"Sorry about that."

"Let's not talk about it."

"Let's discuss something else."

"So what do you do?"

"I know all about old paper. That's my specialty."

"Really?"

"I'm telling you. I've been in old paper for years."

"Then it'll be easy if they want another person."

"Actually it would be even easier for me than for you."

"How's that?"

"Seeing it's my line of work. It's not yours."

"So?"

"If we both show up together they'll give me preference seeing it's my line of work."

"Yes, but I got here first and I know the owners."

"That's what I was saying. It's not fair. It's not your line of work."

"That's no concern of mine."

"Why don't you look for work in radio? instead of taking other people's jobs in their line of work?"

"That's no concern of yours."

"I'm not trying to get into electricity, so why would you take a job in old paper?"

"I've got my reasons. I can't explain."

"Admit it's not fair."

"Fair or not fair I was the first to get here and I know the owners."

"Yes but you see my rotten luck. If they hire you you take my job and it's my line of work."

"I'm not saying no. But I'll put in a word for you."

"You swear?"

"I promise."

"I'll have another."

"Same here."

"Because if they hired you and I don't have anything that wouldn't be fair."

"You'll see I'll get you hired."

"Because I have a feeling if they hired you and not me it would bring you bad luck."

"Why do you say that?"

"Because it's a feeling I have, it would bring you bad luck, yes: I'd be afraid."

"Afraid: afraid of what?"

"Everything. If they hired you and not me."

"But I'll get you hired. I know the owners."

"Yes, but I'm in that line of work."

"So what are you getting at?"

"I'll go first, they'll hire me because it's my line of work and then I'll say I've got a pal that says you know him you ought to hire him and then they'll hire you. That way we'll both be hired, while if they hired you and not me it wouldn't be lucky for you."

"You think so."

"Naturally. It's like I'm telling you."

"Then maybe you'd better get going."

"I'm off."

"You won't forget me."

"You can count on me."

"Good luck."

"And if they hire you you'll remember that it's thanks to me."

"Of course."

"By the way, what's your name?"

"Robert Bossu."

"And where do you know the owners from?"

"For starters I worked for old Claye the one that made radio sets."

"And then?"

"Then that's all. That is, when I was a kid I lived in La Ciotat where Claye had a house and then M. Chambernac and then Baron Hachamoth. And even when they had that house rebuilt I'm the one that did the wiring you see they must know me. Robert Bossu's my name."

"Say you know the fellow named Chambernac?"

"Chambernac got killed in the war. He was Mme. Hachamoth's husband."

"No not him his brother. An old guy. Principal. Former principal now."

"I saw him when I was a kid in La Ciotat and I ran into him not very long ago. He was living at Baron Hachamoth's."

"You don't know where he's living now."

"How would I know."

"I'm going to tell you. He's living at Claye's, the one they used to call Cramm."

"That's strange. Say. By the way. How do you know all that."

"Never mind. Stay here. I'll be back in fifteen minutes."

Bossu stunned and disconcerted is left resting his elbows on the bar of the bar.

Half an hour later the other fellow comes back.

"So."

"So that's it."

"They're hiring me?"

"Not yet."

"How do you mean?"

"Come back here to the bistro tomorrow and we'll talk."

"So they're not hiring me?"

"You were even lucky to meet me. Otherwise it was hopeless."

"And now?"

"There's a little bit. Thanks to me. There's hope."

"You told them I knew them."

"That wouldn't have been smart. It would've screwed everything up."

"You think so."

"I'm sure of it."

"So there's really some hope?"

"Since I'm telling you. Come back here tomorrow and we'll talk."

"Thanks. You're a real buddy."

"You're welcome. It's nothing."

"How about you?"
"They're hiring me."
"Since it's your line of work."

CLV

The moving van disappeared around the corner. Gramigni went back into his shop, took his hat and overcoat and by the successive means of the CL and the AM he reached the Brancion gate.

Going down Boulevard Lefebvre, he arrived at the building site of a church under construction and sat down on a nearby bench facing the still unformed stones. But a name was already becoming associated with this location.

CLVI

Saint Anthony of Padua
since this is your church
I came another time to say thank you
One left then the other one died
they killed her
then the house emptied
the old loony disappeared
M. Daniel went away
and so did M. Coltet
the baron and his lady Mme. Hachamoth moved away
the house is for sale or for rent
the NWC was dissolved

young Bossu never came back
But I'm staying
in my grocery store on Rue de Longchamp
far from the young ladies
one left then the other one died
they killed her
Saint Anthony of Padua
my fellow Paduan
I came another time to say thank you
you did not abandon me
you did not leave me alone
you gave me Clemence to live with me and remind me
of the young ladies
one left then the other one died
they killed her
But I'll live on Rue de Longchamp
with my faithful wife Clemence
thanks to you you the great Saint
of this neighborhood near Plaisance
Saint Anthony of Padua
I owe you one hundred more sous

CLVII

Astolphe hadn't recognized Purpulan and Purpulan wasn't
in any hurry to grab Chambernac. He was waiting for some
spectacular incident to do that. As for Bossu, outclassed, he
took long breaks in bistros or else strolled along what re-
mained of the fortifications watching buildings go up. He
was interested in masonry. One day he caught sight of

Gramigni wandering in the vicinity; uneasy he hid in a doublyoucee. Was the NWC on his tail?

But during the days that followed Gramigni did not reappear; as things were going smoothly, Bossu lost his fear. He was too comfortable in this sort of life to be frightened to the point of worrying. Of course Videl had taken his job but he had nothing to complain about. The other fellow was paying for his food drink and even the movies, generously. All in all he Bossu had gotten the better deal. The other fellow was slaving away and supporting him; he was living in the sunshine, and not in old rags.

Moreover he didn't need to work for Claye to take part in the life of the firm. Not only did he have lunch every noon now with Coigule and Solvay, and Videl whose guest he was, but in addition every day he saw one or the other of the inhabitants of the villa of Boulevard Lefebvre pass by his observation post: sometimes Naomi who certainly didn't recognize young Bossu in this diminished individual sucking on a cigarette butt in a sunny corner; sometimes Astolphe; finally sometimes Chambernac who couldn't have identified the vague customer of a little cafe in Neuilly, even less the little boy who used to run around the tables at that cafe alongside the harbor during that last year of the war.

By hearsay or by direct perception, Bossu thus once again felt linked to his august patrons and beyond them to his hometown. He forgot now that for several months he had shamefully spied on Agnes; or rather he was convincing himself more and more that by his splendid and noble confession, he had in some way shattered Injustice; and that he was now able to see its happy results. He no longer thought of becoming an engineer nor of passing himself off as one;

he had rid himself of all those fancies; just as he no longer thought nor hoped he'd sleep with Mme. Claye; he no longer got himself into a state over all that. He'd simply come so they'd give him some sort of work; now a stranger hands him a line and gets himself hired in his place; and he has nothing to complain about. That certainly proved one thing: that Injustice was no longer tormenting him.

And when one day Videl came to tell him that he'd gotten him hired by Claye he found that that too proved that Injustice was no longer tormenting him since he was obviously meant to be hired since he knew Mme. Claye and relatives of Mme. Claye. This job was his by right, it was only just that they hire him. Bossu accepted every change of condition with an idea like this one, that this was precisely what he wanted. He floated on the surface of events, lighter than a banana peel.

CLVIII

Agnes' death had touched Daniel only slightly; he desired solitude; he left. Mourning her daughter Mme. Hachamoth practically ignored him. Daniel found his solitude in a second-rate hotel in central Paris. There he accomplished his asthma attacks in a little room at the foot of which busses slid noisily by. He was determined to stay there as long as his bit of money lasted, one-thousand-franc bills. Wandering on the boulevards, sitting on the terraces of crowded cafes, waiting motionless for the lights to turn green, suffocating he continued to seek God.

He had ceased thinking that He could be the author of

Evil or rather he had ceased thinking that his good and his evil must necessarily be His. With great pains he tried to assure himself and to affirm to himself that what seemed good to him and what seemed bad to him might not have this value for Him at all. Going back to his first concerns, he had to admit that tortures and torments even the most inexplicable ones imposed themselves without explanation and without excuse. God did not need an excuse: He wanted.

Daniel sometimes started to laugh thinking of the punyish conception that people could have of the Omnipotence of God. They limited it in accordance with their pleasure, in accordance with their weaknesses, in accordance with their wishes; they adapted it as they saw fit, as if one could con God.

Individuals who got dizzy when they climbed a ladder discussed this Omnipotence without emotion. They chatted about it without terror. They'd fabricated a marshmallow goodlord that you could lick without getting a sore tongue. They'd made of him a nice fella half-way between President Lebrun and Santa Claus, a nice little old man who didn't want any more than people granted him and who was agreeable to any arrangement.

Sometimes Daniel was outraged at this idol and sometimes he foundered in dread before this God whom he'd made to loom up out of mediocrity. Sometimes he was outraged. He shuddered with shame when he saw how casually the midges messed with the Almighty. He blushed to hear them speak in His place, for all the world like ventriloquists agitating marionettes before a demanding audience, an audience demanding that you didn't scare them to death, an audience that's quite willing to shiver at a blood and thunder melodrama but refuses to tremble before the terrible prime mover of the world's blood and thunder. And sometimes Daniel foundered in dread.

Then he understood his vanity: first of all to think that he was alone in having an accurate conception of God, and next that he was capable of forming an accurate conception. The idea of this double self-importance made him laugh for a long time one day when he was walking along the Boulevard de la Madeleine; and people feeling pity turned to look at him. He didn't feel any less pity for himself. He was very humble now as he had always been. He recognized himself in his smallness and was amused that his tininess had inflated itself with several ounces of nothingness. He stumbled before the abyss of divinity, more vast than His rigor. Overwhelmed he piled up the negations of his knowledge and stammered before God like a simpleton and like a child.

While Daniel was struggling in his weakness, his money had run out. He had to vacate the hotel leaving his suitcases as hostages, a particularly cruel renunciation for they contained all his pharmaceutical equipment, his drugs, his vials, his syringes. Daniel rescued a tube of ephedrine which he put into his vest pocket, then he went away.

CLIX

"I've quite gotten over it: psychiatry, that is," said Chambernac sipping coffee that he was making more and more syrupy every day, "it doesn't explain a thing, and besides it's pretentious. I've also read books on psychoanalysis, you know what that is?"

"Of course," answered Astolphe who prided himself on having been one of the first to speak of Freud in distinguished circles.

"That explains things," resumed Chambernac, "but as far as psychopathy, as they call it, is concerned, they admit that it's still a bit beyond them. They straighten what's gone awry, they don't reassemble what's broken. You follow me?"

"Of course," said Astolphe.

"I," said Chambernace, "see things differently. I don't want to do either psychoanalysis or psychiatry. But I've examined all the lunatics, mine not others, and here's what I've observed: madness is the self-deification of an individual entity in which no collective entity will recognize itself."

"Ah," said Astolphe.

Chambernac salvaged the browned sugar that decorated the bottom of his cup.

"When I say madness," he resumed, "I mean 'their' madness."

Chambernac folded his napkin.

"I must go," he said. "I have an appointment with a publisher at three o'clock."

"You have time," said Naomi.

"I'm going to walk," said Chambernac, "it'll get me out for awhile."

"Are you optimistic this time?"

"Yes. I think it'll work out. Of course my *Encyclopedia* is bound to find a publisher somewhere. If not it just wouldn't make sense. You know I've already had five rejections. Incredible."

"Good luck," said Naomi.

"Good luck," said Ast.

When Chambernac had left, Ast poured himself a glass of red wine; he'd developed a taste for wine which he now preferred to coqtèles; it was something, for that matter, of which he was rather proud.

"Do you think Uncle Henry will manage to find a publisher?" asked Naomi.

Ast made a face to indicate he had no idea.

"I have no idea," he added.

He got up.

"I'm going to get to work."

On the steps, he stopped; he looked at the shed that he used as a laboratory and the shed he used as a factory and the shed used for sorting and the shed used as a shed. He looked at the memory of his trials and his research. He looked at the image of these seven men who were working for him.

He looked at his financial situation.

It was bitter.

"What are you thinking about," asked Naomi.

"I don't feel like working today."

"What's the matter?"

Ast sat down on a step and Naomi sat down next to him. In a corner of the yard, Cical was smoking an old pipe while reading a paper.

"I don't know what I want," said Ast. "As Cical says, there's no rhyme or reason to what I'm doing. Incoherence. Sometimes one thing sometimes another. And here I am with seven workers; or laborers. They have to be paid. And I'm losing money."

"Just the other day, you were explaining to me so clearly how you'd organized everything."

"Yes. But it was a fantasy."

He was silent.

"I'll drop old rags," he murmured.

He was silent.

"Can you make good paper out of bad? No. Cardboard is all you can make."

He was silent.

"Of course you don't write on cardboard. It's not like Holland paper. But what dishonor is there to that? in spite of the hierarchy. We must save matter."

He got up.

"I'm going to get to work."

He kissed Naomi.

"You still love me," asked Naomi.

Astolphe answered that he did.

He went back to where Cical was.

"What's new in the paper, Cical?"

"Bah the Prince affair. A lot of nonsense."

Ast went into the laboratory and glanced at his glass-blowing bric-a-brac. He absentmindedly examined a sheet of vegetal parchment, vaguely shook a test tube in which Schweitzer's solution was dissolving something, cellulose probably.

He came back out.

"I have an errand to run," he said to Cical.

And he gave his instructions.

He went up Boulevard Lefebvre to the Versailles gate and took the AG. He didn't know where he was going. Four tkts. allowed him to reach the end of the line, which is the Stock Exchange.

People were shouting in front of the building.

Ast ran into Pouldu, whom he did not like. A conversation started.

"How's the paper business," asked Pouldu.

Ast didn't know what the people he formerly socialized with thought of him; no doubt they made fun of his fall into ragdom; and probably they didn't really take seriously his more artisanal than industrial and less chemical than dilettantish endeavors. Thus he was astonished to find in Pouldu an understanding and sympathetic listener; and attributed to him the latter quality all the more so because he'd been expecting less.

"At first I didn't have any definite intentions," said Ast inclined to confide readily in an almost stranger. "I was hiding from everyone and wanted to start a new life; but you see I didn't know how. I'd never worked. I first started as an amateur. I had fun installing a sort of laboratory but that didn't get me anywhere. Next I had an idea, a more substantial one. I've always had a taste, this will probably seem strange to you, a more or less disguised taste for trash and rubbish. This must seem strange to you in someone like me; I eventually realized it, what can I do about it? and I'll spare you all the forms this singular tendency of mine has managed to take on."

"It would interest me though," said Pouldu indiscreetly.

"No no," said Ast who saw clearly the limits of the area he was conceding to the person he was speaking to. "Well be that as it may I finally set myself up as a dealer in old paper, not only to gather and sort it before reselling it, but also in order to sort with a view to saving interesting items, in short to direct a part of the old paper toward recasting as it were and the other toward conservation. Unfortunately I didn't find anything interesting to start out with, and I got tired of it. That's when I undertook to make paper myself and I started to buy rags. But that's really a luxury. Excuse me I have to go an appointment see you soon good-bye."

He walked away leaving Pouldu in the greatest uncertainty as to the commercial and industrial capabilities of the person he'd been speaking to. Ast found himself back on the boulevards grumbling about his incoherence; and weighty with worry. He went down toward the Madeleine church looking at women.

CLX

Purpulan came out of the metro station just as Astolphe was about to go down.

"Hullo Videl what are you doing here?"

"I have no excuse," said Purpulan.

Ast looked at him with curiosity. He tried to adopt a boss's attitude but was sidetracked by another aspect of the matter.

"It's strange it seems to me I've seen you somewhere before."

"That's a line men use on a certain kind of woman," said Purpulan.

He gave Ast an insolent look. Ast blushed.

"I wanted to talk to you anyway," said Purpulan.

"Had we arranged to meet?"

Ast was trying to recover his former casualness.

"I knew I'd run into you around here," said Purpulan.

"Really."

It would have been reasonable to tell him "Get the hell out," but Ast didn't want to be that sort of person.

"We could go discuss things in a nearby bistro."

"By all means," said Ast.

He now recognized the individual but without yet being able to identify him beyond the Videl who handled old paper.

They sat down on the terrace of a cafe nicely embellished with first-class prostitutes crossing their legs in the June sun.

"We have already met somewhere," said Purpulan. "You're right."

"I can't seem to remember where."

"It was in September, 1929."

"Really."

"Your niece was with you, not this one, the other one: the one of February 6th."

"You're well informed."

"As well as I can be. So, your niece was with you and I read you some passages of the *Ratio Of The Diameter To The Circumference*, by a certain Lacomme, and you went away without my succeeding in interesting you."

He considered it pointless to describe to him his subsequent reactions.

"Ah Purpulan. You're Purpulan. And M. Chambernac, does he know you're here? By the way hasn't he seen you?"

"There will be no meeting as long as I don't want one."

"Really."

"I imagine M. Chambernac must have spoken to you about me."

"Very little."

"He couldn't have spoken well of me."

"Nor badly. He tends to avoid talking about you. Which is even rather intriguing."

"Isn't it though?"

"Yes."

"So he didn't speak to you about me."

"No."

"That's what I thought."

"But I have the impression he'd find it rather unpleasant to see you again."

"I know. He's running away from me."

"Why's that?"

"I frighten him."

Which made Ast laugh.

"Why wouldn't I frighten people?"

"I'm sorry," said Ast. "I didn't mean to offend you."

"That's all right. That's all right."

"But if he's running away, um: it looks as if you're pursuing him."

"Precisely."

"And why?"

"We have to have things out."

Purpulan made a sweeping tragic gesture.

"M. Chambernac is slandering me."

"I assure you he hardly talks about you, and never goes into detail."

"Yes but he thinks ill of me."

"Why did you apply for work with me under a false name?"

"No more false than the other. My name is not in your vocabulary."

Now Ast thought he understood: Chambernac's secretary must be mad. He looked at him with curiosity: a fairly handsome tall blond young man, with an intent gaze (intent on the legs of the girl at the next table) and fetid breath. What was he going to do with him?

"Why take a false name," resumed Astolphe. "Why hide?" Perhaps he was being too rough.

"I'd like M. Chambernac not to think ill of me any more."

"What ill can he be thinking of you?"

"That I want to ruin him."

"Really. He thinks that about you? Ruin him. How on earth?"

"There are all sorts of ways. I mean: he attributes to me all sorts of ways. Some very elementary: for instance poisoning his wife."

"Actually my sister has always thought that her death wasn't natural."

"There. You see."

"But what else?"

"All sorts of things I'm telling you. He takes me for a demon. Me? Me! Me a demon: and all I am is a poor devil."

"In short according to you, M. Chambernac accuses you of persecuting him."

"Something like that."

"You worked with him I think long enough to know what that means."

"I'm listening."

"According to you M. Chambernac is mad. Persecutor and persecuted."

"I don't believe a word of it. M. Chambernac is a great mind. There has simply been a slight misunderstanding between us and I only wanted to ask you, that's why I particularly wanted to talk to you in private, I only wanted to ask you to try to straighten things out."

Ast looked at him again: no, he didn't appear to be mad. Mad, mad, mad, what did that mean. Following Purpulan's gaze, he happened upon a rather pretty leg showing off a silk stocking."

"Pretty girl," said Purpulan.

Ast looked at her. She smiled at him. A whore.

"Well what do you want me to do?"

"You can gradually get him used to the idea of seeing me again, and tell him what a good and decent fellow I am."

"I haven't the slightest proof of it," said Ast.

"Monsieur, I assure you: there's not one word of truth in all that M. Chambernac thinks."

"That's what you say."

"Monsieur I swear it."

Ast remained undecided.

"But then what on earth were you up to in this neighborhood?"

"I had an errand to run on Rue Tronchet. Solvay sent me."

He showed him a note. It was true.

"Then why tell me you had no excuse."

"You see, Monsieur Claye, it's a failing of mine. Now you can understand how people can end up misjudging me. It's little things; but people eventually think I'm a bad person."

Ast asked:

"So you were M. Chambernac's secretary for four years?"

"That's right. And I might say that I was a great help to him with his *Encyclopedia*."

"And how did it all end?"

"I told you: M. Chambernac imagined lots of things about me, wrong things, completely wrong, I swear, Monsieur Claye."

"What happened?"

"One day M. Chambernac disappeared, suddenly. At that time we were living together in a little villa over near Asnières. I reported it to the police, yes monsieur. I was worried you see. But then I had to get out of there, because of the bills. He'd left me without money, that wasn't very nice of him. Then, I started looking for him, I ran in all directions, but never would I have thought he'd come to take refuge with his sister-in-law and then with you. He didn't like you very much."

"Ah."

"I was about to call at Rue de Longchamp when he disappeared again. He probably happened to catch sight of me."

"So all the things you told me the day I hired you were just lies."

"Yes, monsieur. But I couldn't have done anything else."

"You're sure?"

Purpulan didn't answer.

"All right. Go run your errand. I'll talk to you tomorrow."

"It would be so nice of you if you'd please straighten things out between M. Chambernac and me. I'm sure that if I were still his secretary the *Encyclopedia* would already have found a publisher."

"That'll do. I'll see. No leave that."

Purpulan put his wallet back into his pocket and walked away with a spring in his step. Ast put a hundred sous into his saucer.

His neighbor asked for a light. He lit her cigarette with his lighter; then left.

CLXI

Chambernac was returning with another rejection. He sat down in front of the window of his room and looked dully at the young leaves of a tree. He was holding his manuscript on his lap, the unique *Encyclopedia* destined to remain unknown. He drummed his fingers on its cover, his eyes fixed absentmindedly on the vegetation and his heart sick. He had to admit to himself that since he'd gotten rid of Purpulan through flight, everything was going just as badly.

There was a knock. He said to come in.

"I'm not bothering you," said Ast. "What news?"

"Bad. Well: I'll just have to try yet another publisher."

"C'est dommage. I would have expected them to snap up your book."

"Frankly, I'll be honest with you: I can't get over it. I must be dealing with madmen."

Ast laughed politely; then:

"Pardon me, I'd like to ask you an indiscreet question."

Chambernac rubbed his lined jaw with a white hand.

"I may very well not answer."

"Are there that many secrets in your life then."

"Yes."

"It was about your secretary."

"I don't have one."

"You did have one."

"What do you want to know?"

"Everything."

"Why? Have you seen him? Has he found me? Not surprising. I could have found a better hiding place. He's found me? I'm not afraid of him any more. What did he tell you? Did he talk to you? Has he already gotten you to do something stupid?"

"To talk to you about him."

"There: you see. Be careful: he's a subtle, despicable being: a piece of filth from the muck heap."

"The devil," exclaimed Claye.

"You said it."

"What did I say?"

"What he is."

"A devil?"

"You said it."

"In what way?"

"In the only way. The true and unique way."

"Pardon me if I smile."

"Smile smile. Where is he? Where is he?"

"I'd like to hear a bit more about this remarkable individual."

"Whatever for? I don't feel like telling you the story of my life. I'll just say this: he served me for four years then afterwards he poisoned my wife, he plunged me into debauchery, despair and wretchedness."

"Really."

"He's a homosexual, you know."

"And during the four years he served you, you had no reason to complain of him?"

"He was my slave."

"Your slave?"

"Yes. He'd signed a pact with me."

Astolphe couldn't think of anything to say.

"Where is he?" Chambernac asked softly. "Where is he?"

Ast hesitated. What to do with Chambernac. What to do with Purpulan.

"Where is he," asked Chambernac, "I'm not afraid of him any more. And I'd like to talk to him."

His mildness frightened Claye.

"Tell me where he is," insisted Chambernac without losing patience. "We'll talk."

"Well he's working here. He doesn't look as wicked as you say."

"You're young, Astolphe, you're not yet familiar with the disguises of evil and the demons' carnival. So he's one of your workers?"

"Yes."

"And how long has he been spying on me?"

"About three weeks. Let's see: he'd been here exactly two weeks when he asked me to hire a friend of his who as it happens at one time worked for my father."

"He has a friend with him?"

"Yes. A fellow named Bossu."

"Robert Bossu?"

"You know him? Ah! you remember him? The son of the owner of the Café du Port in La Ciotat?"

"My son you mean."

"After that the three of them left together."

"Do you think Chambernac is Bossu's father?"

"Why not? He could have slept with Mme. Bossu. I really can't remember her at all."

"Neither can I. What a business."

"I haven't the slightest idea what's going to happen now."

"Where did they go?"

"I suppose they're going to have dinner together. Naturally Chambernac hasn't said anything to Bossu yet."

"So all his life long he took no interest in his son?"

"That's what it looks like. There are people like that: they don't like their bastards."

"You know, there's something I've always thought: it's that Clemence was grandfather's daughter."

"Possible. What a world of bastardy. Anyway there was nothing to boast about."

"Poor Clemence. She made a good honest marriage. Tell me. Talk to me some more about Uncle Henry."

"If he fell into the hands of a psychiatrist he'd commit him."

"He might not consider him dangerous."

"Taking a flesh and blood individual for a devil is very much frowned upon."

"And what do you think of this Videl-Purpulan?"

"If nothing else he's a little s.o.b."

"Maybe it wasn't a good idea to let Uncle Henry leave with him."

"I never thought about it. He seemed so sure of himself."

"I only hope things don't turn nasty. Poor Uncle Henry. With his book he can't find a publisher for on top of everything else."

"Well now he has a son."

"Yes."

"He's found a son."

"There's maybe no more truth in that than in the demono, the diabolo…"

"the demoniality"

"the demoniality of Purpulan?"

"Maybe. In any case this business doesn't make me particularly happy. As if my personal worries weren't enough."

"Egotist."

"Yes. That's true."

"You don't love me any more."

"Why do you say that. We were talking about your uncle I think."

"No about you. You don't love me any more."

"Yes I do."

"No. If you loved me you'd prove it."

"And I'm not proving it?"

"No. And you know very well what I mean."

"But you know I. You know very well I don't. You're not going to hold it against me?"

"Oh, no. I still love you."

"Why are you talking about all this now?"

"Because of the way you said to me just now: now he has a son."

"And how did I say that?"

"Tragically."

"That's true."

"If you don't love me any more it's my fault."

"But I do still love you you know that you know I still love you."

"Agnes came here and it was all over."

"Never mind Agnes."

"No. I should have talked to you months ago. Months ago."

"Months. Months already."

"I was crazy enough to listen to Agnes. And now you see you've drawn away from me and you draw away further every day. And you don't dare tell me I disgust you because of what I did. And Agnes is the one who advised me and she's the one who took me to that doctor and she's the one I listened to, stupidly, stupidly, I couldn't resist her and you you agreed and you see how she's gotten back at us, how she's gotten back at us."

CLXIII

Between Purpulan and Chambernac Bossu felt a bit uncomfortable. They went to have dinner at a little restaurant; Purpulan had suggested it, Chambernac approved. During the meal, those two talked about the *Encyclopedia* as if nothing had happened. The ex-principal told of his disappointments with the publishers; the ex-secretary sympathized with him in his failures. The conversation even turned purely technical: Purpulan asked Chambernac whether he'd been able to lay his hands on *The Origin Of Electricocontepimania* by Hayot; Chambernac did not have it; or whether he'd found the lost works of Ernest de Garay: he did not have them.

Bossu didn't much understand what was going on between this M. Chambernac whom he'd met on Rue de Longchamp in Neuilly and this Videl they were now calling Purpulan and whom he'd met on a May afternoon on Boulevard Lefebvre. He listened, finding them excessively learned, which on the part of the former did not appear at all surprising but which on the part of the other astounded him considerably.

In any case they dined well and drank copiously.

Afterwards Purpulan felt like going to the movies. It was his idea. Bossu didn't say no. Chambernac's affability willingly agreed. It paid for the movies, the newsreel and the two feature-length films, one French and one dubbed. Afterwards Chambernac insisted on a quiet bistro.

He said:

"Purpulan do you remember what I told you one evening?"

"You've told me a great many things, Monsieur Chambernac."

"Don't you remember, it was the evening we celebrated your first anniversary, I mean your first year as secretary, we had champagne, don't you remember?"

"Vaguely," Monsieur Chambernac, "very vaguely."

"Don't you remember that I shared a secret with you? I told you don't you remember? I told you I had a son, an illegitimate son, a son born of adultery?"

Maybe it's me, thought Bossu who hadn't stopped nursing a novelistic imagination.

"I'd forgotten," said Purpulan. "I was too sloshed or else I thought you were handing me a line."

"Well here," said Chambernac with a huge smile, "is this son."

And he pointed to Bossu.

Neither Purpulan nor Bossu had a single moment of doubt. The one said to himself: shit to think I hadn't scented that, what a damn fool I am, but what's he driving at; and the other: so then I have noble blood in my veins, I knew it all the time, I'm not like everybody else.

Overcome by this additional emotion, he began to weep and cried out:

"Father!"

Chambernac held him off with a noble gesture.

"Don't forget, my son, that since you were born I've never paid any attention to you. I have no paternal streak whatsoever."

Bossu disconcerted sat down again. Purpulan found he wasn't wasting any time.

"My son," resumed Chambernac, "you don't know who I am. I am going to tell you."

He gave a little cough.

"I am the author of the *Encyclopedia Of The Inexact Sciences.*"

He gave another cough.

"For long years my mind has wandered along strange paths."

He looked around him. The neighboring tables were unoccupied.

"I've devoted myself to the exclusive study of lunatics and demons."

Bossu in his anxiety rested the weight of his body now upon his right buttock now upon his left. He would gladly have talked genealogy and family traditions. Let's see: so he was now the half-nephew of Mme. Hachamoth and the semi-cousin of Naomi Claye. Oh joy! Oh joy! He was finding a family, the very one he wished for. He'd like to have wept, danced, yelled, jumped over the tables, eaten his cap. Instead, his father—he had two fathers now, which was not too many for a guy like him—his father was uttering enigmatic and agonizing words.

"Is he your friend?" Chambernac asked him abruptly pointing to Purpulan.

"Yes. No."

"What do you mean I'm not your friend," exclaimed Purpulan. "M. Chambernac, he sponged off me for more than two weeks."

"How long have you known him?"

"About a month. We met by accident in front of M. Claye's house. We were looking for work. Videl, Purpulan I mean, got himself hired, he managed it but I had to wait."

"What are you insinuating," asked Purpulan.

"I got there first," said Bossu.

"If it weren't for me they wouldn't have hired you," said Purpulan.

"I see," said Chambernac.

The other two were silent.

Chambernac passed his pale hand over his lined jaw. He took a hundred sous from his pocket and called the waiter.

"What do you say to a little stroll," he suggested.

He took each of them by an arm and they went down the Rue de Tolbiac toward the Seine, at first in silence.

"You see, my son," said Chambernac finally, "I've had a strange sort of life and it's not over yet."

He turned toward Purpulan:

"Isn't that right, Purpulan?"

"Probably."

He turned toward Bossu:

"One day, my son, I'll tell you the story of my life. If I told you now, it would be like pouring molten lead into your ears."

Bossu smiled without enthusiasm. There was again a long silence. Purpulan was thinking as hard as he could to discover a way to gain control of the situation after so many disturbing incidents. Bossu was still thinking about his genealogy. Both were worrying about Chambernac's behavior.

"And you my son," resumed the latter, "what have you done in your life, made of your life?"

"I haven't had any luck," said Bossu.

"Who's ever had any?" said Chambernac.

"Really," objected Bossu.

"No," said Chambernac.

Bossu thought his father was overdoing it.

They passed under the railroad bridge then arrived along the Seine. Chambernac suggested they go sit on the bank.

Funny idea, thought Bossu.

It was mild and night. The Seine was flowing slowly like black batter.

"Well, Purpulan," said Chambernac, "you're not very talkative this evening. You couldn't be surprised to see me."

"Of course not."

"Well? Are you cooking something up? Poor Purpulan, you're a bit disconcerted."

"Oh no, not at all."

"You're boasting Purpulan. By the way, that pact of ours, you cheated when you signed it, eh, and I didn't notice."

"We're not going to talk about that now, are we?"

"When I think that you poisoned Agatha."

"Whom you were cheating on. There's the proof."

He indicated Bossu.

"You wretched sprite who are you to lecture me. When I think of the life you made me lead in the villa in Asnières. When I think that you ruined me, that you soiled me, that you tore from me the very roots of hope. And when I think that all of that was nothing but a shadow and that you did not win."

Bossu was listening listening and would really like to have understood. What a night, he was saying to himself, what a night: find a father and discover a murderer. How right he'd been to always think he wasn't just an ordinary guy.

Chambernac turned abruptly toward him.

"You see this young man, my son," he said pointing to Purpulan, "he's disinterested. He makes a damn lot of trouble for everybody and doesn't get a thing for it. He derives no profit from his wickedness. He's more perverse than a man and why? Because it's his nature? Because it's his nature?"

Bossu found Purpulan an awful nuisance; he had by the way thought so from the first day, he remembered it well. This Videl, if it wasn't for him, he could have talked about the Family with his dad…

"You see him eh," resumed Chambernac, "you see him? Well he's not of our kind: he's a demon, a real one."

The Seine continued its voyage in the night and on its miry film the Moon's mercury rolled in little droplets.

Bossu shivered.

And Purpulan said:

"Equidem sum qui semper fui."

Chambernac shrugged his shoulders.

"Imbecile," he muttered.

He got up. He seized Purpulan by the collar of his jacket and dragged him to the edge of the bank. With his foot he gave him a shove. Purpulan toppled over and went plop as he fell flat into the water.

Bossu rushed up to see, in spite of the big tears of sweat that were running from his forehead to moisten his mouth.

Purpulan had managed to grasp hold of an iron ring, but he was beginning to melt with a little crackling sound, the same sound that french fried potatoes make when you plunge them into boiling oil; but he was melting like sugar. He was even melting rather rapidly. Already the stumps of his legs were stretching out like marshmallow. Then soon it was his trunk's turn to disappear.

Chambernac leaning forward supervised this dissolution.

Purpulan was looking at him, eyes staring, mouth closed, expressionless. When there was nothing left but the top part of his body, he let go and, deliquescent carrion, let himself be swept away by the current. Already the stumps of his arms were stretching out like marshmallow. Then soon it was his head's turn to disappear.

Chambernac was walking along the bank, was following the debris.

Purpulan had now completely melted; all that remained of his earthly appearance were his hair his teeth and his eyes scattered upon the surface of the river. His hair was the next thing to dissolve, then his teeth. The two eyeballs floated a few strokes further. Then it was over.

CLXIV

Robert Bossu who for a time was called Toto-the-Pallor-of-Living was running along the embankments, running at full tilt, running at top speed. Occasionally he stopped, struck his forehead with his closed fist and whimpwailed:

"Oh dear! oh dear!"

Then he started to run again.

CLXV

Chambernac had climbed back onto the embankment; a heavy tiredness was congealing his muscles; he wanted to sit down on a bench but before he could reach it he fainted.

A poor wretch wandering in the night came up to him, dragged him and hoisted him onto the bench. Chambernac came round on his own slowly; he passed his white hand over his lined jaw; he turned his head to look at the man.

"Why it's you," he said without surprise.

He added:

"Where is Bossu?"

"I don't know. You were alone, lying on the ground."

"He was probably frightened. What a pathetic offspring."

He smiled. Then letting his chin fall to the knot of his tie he murmured:

"I'm exhausted."

"What do you want me to do for you?"

"You might take me back to Boulevard Lefebvre to Naomi's. To Claye's."

"That's far. Will you be able to walk all that way?"

"Let's take a taxi."

"I don't have any money."

"Astolphe will pay for it."

There were no taxis in that neighborhood at that hour. They had to walk; but after a hundred meters Chambernac was obliged to sit down again, Daniel at his side. With his head in his hands he started to reflect: he looked at scenes of his childhood, at episodes characteristic of his life, and finally at what had just happened. Then he rejoiced in his heart and congratulated himself on the suppression of Purpulan. He sat up straight and his face brightened like a Chinese lantern lit by a candle and he rubbed his hands together.

Not displeased with himself and resolved to forget Bossu, Chambernac turned to his nephew and asked him what he was doing in these parts looking the way he did.

"I was wandering, it's my life," answered Daniel. "Just now. I detached myself. A period of transition."

Chambernac didn't insist on a commentary. He got up.

"Let's go. I'm feeling better."

"Stay here," said Daniel. "I'm going to go to the Orleans Station and I'll come back to get you."

"I'll wait," said Chambernac.

At the Orleans Station, several drivers refused to take Daniel. Finally one of them trusted him.

Chambernac had stretched out on his bench and was dozing peacefully. Daniel had him get into the taxi and at around three o'clock they arrived at Boulevard Lefebvre.

CLXVI

Quite naturally Daniel took the place of Purpulan and of Bossu because between the two of them they hadn't exactly been knocking themselves out and Daniel had always been a conscientious worker. He was coming out of beggary, as he had foreseen, to pursue in manual labor a meditation which had nothing to do with the romanticising of large cities and did not share in their confusion. He aspired to no originality; not even that of illness, one of the most common.

In the meantime Astolphe was bringing matter out of its fallen state.

CLXVII

During the months that followed, Chambernac abandoned all hope of publishing the *Encyclopedia*, reluctant moreover to do it at his own expense or rather at that of Astolphe or the baron or any other person likely to lend him several tens of thousands of francs, for by putting into circulation a book which met only with indifference he thus risked joining in his turn the category of "literary lunatics." So the thick manuscript now reposed in a drawer in his room; as for him, lodged on Boulevard Lefebvre, he was making himself as they say useful and waiting peaceably to die, being as unobtrusive about it as he thought himself able.

From time to time he and Daniel began a dialogue but

soon retired into silence. They witnessed with sympathy but disinterest the growth and modifications of the Claye enterprises and collaborated loyally but with detachment in the working of the firm, each according to his abilities.

Toward the end of the year they had to deplore the decease of the baron, vanquished by his hepatic and gastric viscera. Mme. Hachamoth retired to a convent leaving her fortune to her brother with the exception however of what they demanded of her in order to live a life of poverty. So the Sophial gold came to germinate for matter. How simple it was.

Chambernac was fading ever so slowly in this ascension, the candle in the Chinese lantern. He was happy. Sometimes he went down to the Versailles Gate and sat on the terrace of a cafe across from the Parc des Expositions and watched the crowd coming out of the metro and the people bustling about and when it was cold he sat in the window and that way he could watch the people come out of the metro and the crowd bustling about.

On such a day in March or thereabouts he had another encounter. A fellow next to him, a guy of about thirty wearing specs, addressed him. By dint of hanging out in publishing houses, Chambernac had become a familiar figure to people in the business.

"Monsieur Chambernac?" asked his neighbor.

"Yes, that's my name."

"We've met several times," said the stranger; "in the offices of the NRF, at Paulhan's and in the offices of Denoël."

"I think I remember," said Chambernac indifferently.

"Pardon my indiscretion," said the anonym: "your great work on the literary lunatics hasn't come out?"

"No monsieur. None of the publishers wanted it. I may add that they were right."

"Why's that?"

"Useless."

"Pardon?"

"I said it's a useless book. In any case I'm not interested in it anymore."

"No?"

"No. I have other things on my mind. My manuscript is in a drawer and it will stay there until I die and even beyond. You're not interested in it, are you?"

"Um. I'd be curious to see it."

"Really? I don't know who you are but you're going to see what I'm like. If you find it at all interesting, I'll give it to you. You can do with it as you please. I've completely lost interest in it."

The man he was talking to was quite surprised. The next day at the appointed time Chambernac did indeed bring the pile of paper which constituted the *Encyclopedia Of The Inexact Sciences*.

"There you are," said Chambernac. "Keep all that and sort it out however you can. It's a gift. But I'm warning you it's a gift of little value."

Some days later they saw one another again.

"Well?" asked Chambernac smiling.

The other fellow said to him:

"Would you have any objection to my attributing your work to a character in a novel I'm writing?"

"Not at all," said Chambernac laughing. "I find the idea comical. Do you write novels?"

"Naturally your name would be on the cover along with mine."

"Unnecessary," exclaimed Chambernac. "I don't care about that. Don't do anything of the sort. I have no vanity."

"But…"

"No. No. Attribute my work to one of your characters if that makes sense to you. As for me I'm all too happy to be rid of the hefty tome. And it really makes little difference to me whether my name survives or not. I repeat: I have no vanity left. Make these old papers over into a new book if you have to; and if you can. As for me I'm quite satisfied without them: I'll be able to die in peace. You'll be doing me a favor."

Chambernac resumed:

"And this character, what's he like?"

"He's the principal of a little provincial high school. He's married, has no children. One day a demon gets into his bathroom."

"Wait a minute. Why don't I tell you the story of my life. Wait a minute. I don't consider it extraordinary but it could give a touch of realism to your book."

"I don't know how to thank you."

"But it's nothing I assure you my dear monsieur, Monsieur what's the name?"

"Queneau."

"It's nothing, my dear Monsieur Queneau. I assure you: it's nothing."

CLXVIII

Daniel was waiting for Astolphe downstairs. The latter finally came down. It was past one.

"They asked me to come back later," said Astolphe, "in half an hour. I'm going to go have lunch next door."

He swallowed a sandwich in silence, and his beer on top of it.

"You'll see," said Astolphe, you'll see, we'll do fine work, respectable durable work. We'll go back to old traditions."

He left Daniel who returned to work on Boulevard Lefebvre, and came back to the hospital. They led him into a room where an infant lying next to Naomi was crying lustily.

Astolphe thought he looked like a nice fellow.

Bleeding in a basin lay delivery.

1930–1938

POST-SCRIPTUM

The texts quoted by Chambernac in his *Encyclopedia* are *naturally* authentic.

Appendix

I give only the first clause of lengthy titles and have modernized capitalization. Works preceded by an ° are those which I have not had the opportunity to consult.

I. Works quoted in *Les Enfants du Limon*

B., Auguste (lyonnais anonyme). *Découverte de la véritable organisation matérielle de l'univers*. Lyon: libraires, 1855.

Berbiguier, Alexis-Vincent-Charles, de Terre-Neuve du Thym. *Les Farfadets*. 3 vols. Paris: l'auteur, 1821.

Bertron, Adolphe. (Recueil de pieces autographiées, concernant la guerre de 1870. Signées: Adolphe Bertron, candidat humain). Lyon, 1870.

Boisseau, J.-M. *Point d'appui d'Archimède trouvé*. Paris: impr. Dugessois, 1847.

Bousquet, Augustin. *Le Nom du livre intitulé le mystère de l'être*. Béziers: libraires, 1879.

Bouzeran, Joseph. *L'Unité linguistique raisonnée*. Agen: impr. Prosper Noubel, 1847.

Buchoz-Hilton, Louis. *Introduction aux procès de Buchoz-Hilton*. Bordeaux: impr. A. Castillon, n.d.

————. *Traité méthodique simple et à la portée de tous pour être à l'abri des empoisonnements par le fait des brasseurs*. Paris: impr. Aubusson & Kugelmann, 1855.

Charbonnel, Joseph-Jean-Baptiste. *Histoire d'un fou qui s'est guéri deux fois malgré les médecins et une troisième fois sans eux*. Paris: impr. Le Clère, 1837.

Cheneau, Constant. *Troisième et Dernière Alliance de Dieu avec sa créature révélée à son serviteur Cheneau ou Chaînon*. Paris: impr. Paul Dupont, 1842.

Choumara, Théodore. *Le Fou du roi*. Paris: impr. Bourgogne et Martinet, 1841.

————. *Un Ingénieur militaire et la police parisienne*. Paris: impr. Bourgogne et Martinet, 1840.

————. *Théodore, ou cinquante-neuf ans de la vie d'un homme de tête et de coeur*. Paris: impr. Bourgogne et Martinet, 1845.

Cirier, Nicolas. *L'Apprentif* ꓤOꓒⱯꓤꓕSINIꟽꓷⱯ. Paris: l'auteur, 1840.

Cotton, abbé Joseph-Jacques-Xavier. *Première Lettre de l'abbé Xavier Cotton (de Bedouin) au sujet de l'idée primordiale du christianisme [...] à Son Altesse Impériale Madame la princesse Clotilde*. Paris: impr. Walder, 1865.

Delhommeau aîné. *La Boule mystérieuse ou géométrique à deux mille cinq cents facettes et quatre points de vue différents*. Béziers: impr. A. Granié, 1868.

Demonville, Antoine-Louis Guénard. *Le Vrai Système du monde*. Paris: l'auteur, 1852.

Drojat, Sébastien-François. *La Maîtresse-Clef de la tour de Babel*. Paris: Benjamin Duprat, 1857.

Gagne, Paulin. *La Guerriade, déesse de la guerre*. Paris: libraires, 1873.

————. *L'Histoire des miracles par M. Gagne, avocat des fous*. Paris: l'auteur, 1860.

————. *L'Unité. Journal Universel et Pantoglotte de l'Avenir*. no. 5 (fév. 1868); no. 7 (avr. 1869); no. 8 (mai 1868); no. 10 (juillet 1868).

————. *Voyage de S.A.I. Napoléon. Ses Discours à Lyon et à Bordeaux. Itinéraire et entrée à Paris*. Paris: Ledoyen, 1852.

Gautrin, Jean-Baptiste. *Fais ce que dois, advienne que pourra! La paix! La paix!* Nogent-sur- Seine: impr. A. Lemaître, 1884.

————. *La Police secrète, études machiavéliques*. Paris: impr. Boulland, 1846.

Gruau de la Barre. *Intrigues dévoilées*. 4 vols. Rotterdam: H. Nijgh, 1846–1848.

Hussenot, Louis-Cincinnatus-Séverin-Léon. *Chardons nancéins*. Nancy: impr. Dard, 1835–1836.

Husson, Antoine. *4ème Partie du codex à mon usage*. Nice: impr. A. Gilletta, n.d.

Jocteur, Joseph. (Visions et prophéties de Joseph Jocteur, prophète et philosophe). Lyon: lith. Buisson, 1850.

Karcher, L. *La Quadrature du cercle*. Paris: Firmin-Didot, 1867.

Lacomme, Joseph. *Rapport du diamètre à la circonférence*. Paris: impr. Mme.Lacombe, 1856.

Lacoste, Paul. *Les Plus Importants Mémoires adressés aux rois de France, Louis XVIII et Charles X*. Paris: impr. Anthelme Boucher, 1826.

Lassie, J. *Solution complète de la navigation aérienne*. Impr. Goujon, 1856.

Le Barbier, Pierre-Louis. *Avis au commerce, aux armateurs et capitaines, au genre humain*. Rouen: Marie, 1827.

————. *Dominatmosphérie. Instruction pour les propriétaires et cultivteurs*. Rouen: impr. Marie, 1822.

————. *Dominatmosphérie, la Nature ouvrant ses trésors à l'observateur... Instruction pour les marins*. Rouen: impr. Marie, 1817.

Le Quen D'Entremeuse. *Sirius, aperçus nouveaux sur l'origine de l'idolâtrie*. Paris: Didron, 1852.

Le Turc, H. J. *Destiniana*. 1814.

Livre de raison ou l'Institution Primitive. Marseille: Camoin, 1855.

Lucas, Jean-Pierre-Aimé. *Traité d'application des traces géométriques aux lignes et surfaces du premier degré*. Paris: J. Franck, 1844.

Lutterbach, P. dit F. *Révolution dans la marche*. Paris: impr. Prève, 1850.

Maigron, Jules. *Les Sics illustrés*. Montpellier: l'auteur, 1866.

Mandy. *Le Naturisme*. Lyon: Porte, 1865.

Marmiesse, Jean-François. *Histoire abrégée de la vie de Jean-François Marmiesse*. Paris: l'auteur, 1828.

Matalène, abbé P. *Anti-Copernic, astrométrie nouvelle*. Paris: Mansut, 1842.

Mayneau, abbé Toussaint-Jacques. *Triomphe de la vérité*. Béziers: C. Bertrand, 1859.

Monfray, Jean-Benoît. *Monfray à ceux qui veulent l'entendre*. Lyon: Marle Aîné, 1844.

———. *Prophéties, ordonnances, proclamations et discours du roi de l'intelligence humaine*. Lyon, 1833.

———. *Une Réhabilitation ou justification d'un prisonnier libéré de l'hospice de l'Antiquaille (Lyon)*. Lyon, 1844.

Newborough, lady, baronne de Sternberg (Maria-Stella-Petronilla Chiappini). *Maria-Stella*. Paris: libraires, 1830.

O'Donnelly, abbé Térence-Joseph. *Extrait de la traduction authentique des hiéroglyphes de l'obélisque de Louqsor à Paris*. Paris: Schlesinger, 1851.

———. *Extrait du mémoire présenté à Monseigneur l'évêque de Versailles à l'occasion de la découverte de la prononciation et signification originale de l'hébreu et autres langues primitives*. Versailles: impr. Klefer, 1849.

———. *Les Vraies Mathématiques aux prises avec la pierre philosophale*. Bruxelles: l'auteur, 1854.

Oegger, l'abbé. *Rapports inattendus établis entre le monde matériel et le monde spirituel*. Paris: Heideloff et Campé, 1834.

Renault (ou Regnault de) Bécourt. *La Création du monde ou système d'organisation primitive*. 2nd ed. Givet: impr. Gamaches-Barbaise, 1816.

Roustan, Fortuné. *L'Anti-Labiénus. Plus de lois de sureté générale*. 2nd ed. Bruxelles: 1865.

———. *De la Sequestration arbitraire dans les maisons de santé*. Paris: libraires, 1870.

———. *Dieu, Jeanne d'Arc et Napoléon IV*. Versailles: Roustan; Paris: Dentu, 1876.

———. *Du Droit de réponse en matière politique aux articles calomnieux et diffamatoires des journaux sous le régime radical de M. Jules Simon-Suisse*. Paris et Versailles: libraires, 1877.

———. *Une Noble Inspiration de Victorine*. Paris: Blondeau, 1853.

———. *Pièces détachées et concourant à un même but*. Paris: Noblet, 1866.

———. *La Prochaine Revanche de 1870*. Paris et Versailles: libraires, 1877.

———. *Les Subtilités de la librairie parisienne*. Paris: F. Roustan, 1864–65.

———. *Victorine, histoire très véridique d'une jolie fille du quartier Bréda*. Paris: l'auteur, 1854.

Roux, Pierre. *Traité de la science de Dieu*. Paris: Victor Masson, 1857.

Rouy, Hersilie. *Mémoires d'une aliénée publiées par E. Le Normant des Varannes*. Paris: Ollendorf, 1883.

Saint-Mars, Desdouitz de. *Essai d'un dictionnaire d'étymologies gauloises*. Rouen: impr. F. Mari, 1785.

Sarrazin, N. J. *Nouvelle Trigonométrie raisonnée, théorique et pratique*. Metz: Pierret, 1818.

———. *Opuscule sur les matières les plus importantes en mathématiques*. Pont-à-Mousson, 1814.

Soubira, Jacob-Abraham. *666*. Cahors: impr. Combarieu, 1824.

°Tapon-Fougas, Francisque. *Antimisérables*. After searching in vain for the source material on Tapon-Fougas, I had the opportunity to read some of Queneau's manuscript notes. Those on the *Antimisérables* and the two works below apparently contain the material in quotation marks in Chambernac's section on Tapon-Fougas.

°———. *Poèmes moralisateurs*. Roanne, 1882.

°———. *Sur la Mort d'Eugène Sue*. Bruxelles, 1875.

Vernet, Antoine. *Contemplation universelle, manuel des voyages autour de l'univers*. Valence: impr. Mme. Chaléat, 1853.

Villiaume, Claude. *Mes Détentions comme prisonnier d'état sous le gouvernement de Buonaparte*. Paris: l'auteur, 1814.

———. *M. Villiaume sommeillant à Charenton*. Paris: impr. Mad. Ve. Cussac, 1818.

II. Secondary sources quoted or used as background in
Les Enfants du Limon

Andrieu, Jules. *Excentriques et grotesques littéraires de l'Agenais*. Paris: Alphonse Picard, 1895. Background on Bouzeran.

Bru, Paul. *Histoire de Bicêtre*. Paris: Progrès médical, 1890. Cotton.

Brunet, Pierre-Gustave. *Les Fous littéraires. Essai bibliographique sur la littérature excentrique, les illuminés, visionnaires, etc. par Philomneste Junior*. Bruxelles: Gay et Doucé, 1880.

°Campagne. *Traité de la manie raisonnante*. Paris: 1869. In his manuscript notes Queneau says he used this work for Cotton.

Champfleury, Jules-François-Félix. *Les Excentriques*. Paris: Michel Lévy frères, 1856. Berbiguier.

Delepierre, Octave. *Histoire littéraire des fous*. London: Trübner, 1860.

Greil, Louis. *Etudes biographiques. Les Fous littéraires du Quercy*. Cahors: J. Girma, 1886. Chambernac uses this extensively for background on Lacoste, Marmiesse, Soubira.

Hécart, Gabriel-Antoine-J. *Stultitiana*. 1823.

Jacob, Alexandre-André (pseud. Erdan). *La France mystique*. Paris: Coulon-Pineau, 1855. Berbiguier and Cheneau.

Larchey, Lorédan. *Gens singuliers*. Paris: F. Henry, 1867. Berbiguier, Bertron and Lutterbach.

Laurent, Emile. *Poésie décadente devant la science psychiatrique*. Paris: A. Maloine, 1897. Cotton.

Legrand du Saulle, dr. *Le Délire des persécutions*. Paris: Henri Plon, 1871. Berbiguier, Paganel, Roustan.

Lenormant des Varannes (pseud. Burton, Edouard). *Mémoires d'une feuille de papier*. Paris: Ollendorf, 1882. Rouy.

Leuret, François. *Fragments psychologiques sur la folie*. Paris: Crochard, 1834.

Marie, Armand, dr. *Etude sur quelques symptomes des délires systématiques*. Paris: Octave Doin, 1892. Cotton.

———. *Mysticisme et folie: étude de psychologie normale et pathologique comparée.* Paris: Girard et Brière, 1907, Cotton.

°Nodier, Charles. *De Quelques Livres excentriques.* Paris, 1835.

Réja, Marcel. *L'Art chez les fous: le dessin, la prose, la poésie.* Paris: Mercure de France, 1907. Roustan.

Rogues de Fursac, J., dr. *Les Ecrits et les dessins dans les maladies nerveuses mentales.* Paris: Masson, 1905. Cotton.

Séglas, Jules. *Troubles du langage chez les aliénés.* Paris: J. Rueff, 1892. Cotton.

Tardieu, A. *Etude médico-légale sur la folie.* 1872. Buchoz-Hilton and Gautrin.

Tcherkapov, Auguust Ivanovitch. *Les Fous littéraires. Rectifications et additions à l'essai bibliographique sur la littérature excentrique, les illuminés, visionnaires, etc. de Philomneste Junior.* Moscou: W.G. Gautier, 1883.

Vinchon, Jean. *L'Art et la folie.* Paris: Stock, 1924. Cotton.

III. Other Works Mentioned in *Les Enfants du limon*

°Bertron, Adolphe. *Le Candidat Humain. Journal Social Philosophique Humanitaire.* Five issues in 1871.

Buchoz-Hilton. *Observations sur le cadastre de la France.* Paris: l'auteur, 1830.

°Charbonnel, Joseph-Jean-Baptiste. Ed. *Journal des Hommes libres en Jésus-Christ,* 1851.

Cirier, Nicolas. *L'Oeil typographique.* Paris: Firmin-Didot, 1839.

°Condorcet, Antoine-Nicolas de. "Lettre à l'Assemblée Nationale du 28 janvier 1791." In *Oeuvres.* Vol. I. Paris, 1847–1849: 525.

°Gagne, Paulin. *L'Anarchiade de la décentralisation, archi-drame flagellateur en cinq éclats.* 1865.

———. *L'Archimonarquéide ou Gagne premier archi-monarque de la France et du monde.* Paris: l'auteur, 1876.

°———. *Le Calvaire des rois, régi-tragédie.* Paris: F. Henry & l'auteur, 1863.

°———. *L'Unitéide ou la femme messie.* Tous les libraires de France et de l'Etranger, 1857.

°Haton de la Goupillière. In *Revue des Travaux Scientifiques pour l'Année 1884:* 221–224.

°*Histoire de l'Académie Royale des Sciences.* Paris, 1775.

°Hobson, E. W. *"Squaring the Circle," a History of the Problem.* Cambridge, 1913.

°Hussenot, Louis-Cincinnatus-Séverin-Léon. *Provinciales. Système de la traduction inouïe sans points ni virgules.* Nancy: impr. Raybois, n.d.

°Klein, Félix, *Leçons sur certaines questions de géométrie élémentaire.* Paris, 1896.

°Le Normant des Varannes (pseud. Burton, Edouard). *Histoire de Louis XVII.* Orléans: H. Herluison, 1890.

Lucas, Jean-Pierre-Aimé. *Qu'est-ce que l'Institut?* Paris: A. Franck, 1845.

Maigron, Jules (pseud. Nelson). *Motivisme universel, découverte de la révolution solaire.* Paris: impr. Bachelier, 1838.

°Maillet, ed. *Introduction à la théorie des nombres transcendants et des propriétés arithmétiques des fonctions.* Paris, 1906.

°Maupin, G. *Opinions et curiosités touchant la mathématique.* Paris, 1898, 1902.

°Mayneau, Toussaint-Jacques, abbé. *Biographie de l'abbé Mayneau.* Béziers, 1860.

°Monfray, Jean-Benoît. *A La Prostituée.* Lyon: impr. Perret, n.d..

°———. *Aux Carlistes.* Lyon: impr. Perret, n.d.

°———. *Le Roi de l'intelligence aux Français.* Lyon: impr. Perret, n.d.

°———. *Plus de Guerres, plus d'idolâtrie.* 1859–1872.

°Montucla, J. E. *Histoire des recherches sur la quadrature du cercle* Paris, 1754; Paris: Lacroix, 1831.

°Morgan, A. de. *A Budget of Paradoxes.* London, 1872.

°Renaud (or Regnault de) Bécourt. *Tombeau de toutes les philosophies.* Briey: impr. Bancias, 1834.

°Rouse-Ball. *Récréations mathématiques*. 2nd. ed. Vol. II. Paris, 1908.

°Roustan, Fortuné. *Au Prince Louis-Napoléon Bonaparte. Prophétie*.

°————. *Des Réformes urgentes à opérer dans l'administration de l'enregistrement et des domaines*. Paris: impr. A. Blondeau, 1857.

°Roux, Pierre. *L'Hygiène pure et nouvelle*. Paris: Lagrange et Garnier, 1850.

°Schubert, Hermann. "Die Quadratur des Zirkels in Berufenen und Unberufenen Köpfen." *Sammlung Gemeinverständlicher Wissenschaftlicher Vorträge*. ns, 3rd ser. 67. Hamburg, 1889.

°Sérieux et Capgras. "Roman et vie d'une fausse princesse."

Villiaume, Claude. *M. Villiaume peint par lui-même et travesti par d'autres*. Paris: impr. Nicolas Vaucluse, 1812.

————. *Extrait du portefeuille de M. Villiaume*. Paris: l'auteur, 1813.

Raymond Queneau

Long considered a writer's writer, French novelist and poet
Raymond Queneau (1903–1976) has gradually come to be
recognized as one of the major voices in twentieth-century
literature. His publications include fourteen novels, fifteen
volumes of poetry, and four collections of essays. Although
they are known above all for brilliant wordplay, stylistic in-
novation, and the incorporation of spoken French and pho-
netic spelling into works of literature, Queneau's novels are
also rich in historical and philosophical allusions while pre-
senting a lively picture of French society in the first half of
our century. Among his better known works are *Exercices
de style* (1947; *Exercises in Style*, 1958); *Le Chiendent* (1933;
The Bark Tree, 1968), *Un Rude Hiver* (1939; *A Hard Win-
ter*, 1948); *Pierrot mon ami* (1942; *Pierrot*, 1950); *Le
Dimanche de la vie* (1951; *The Sunday of Life*, 1976), and
his best-selling *Zazie dans le métro* (1959; *Zazie*, 1960).
Queneau worked for the French publisher Gallimard for
nearly forty years, first as an English reader, then as a mem-
ber of the powerful editorial committee and finally as edi-
tor of the *Encyclopédie de la Pléiade*. Queneau was also one
of the founding members of OuLiPo group that includes
authors such as Italo Calvino, Georges Perec, and Harry
Mathews.

SELECTED SUN & MOON CLASSICS

LAURA (RIDING) JACKSON [USA]
Lives of Wives 71 (1-55713-182-1, $12.95)

LEN JENKIN [USA]
Dark Ride and Other Plays 22 (1-55713-073-6, $13.95)
Careless Love 54 (1-55713-168-6, $9.95)

WILHELM JENSEN [Germany]
Gradiva 38 (1-55713-139-2, $13.95)

JOHN JESURUN [USA]
Everything that Rises Must Converge 116 (1-55713-053-1, $11.95)

JEFFREY M. JONES [USA]
J. P. Morgan Saves the Nation 157 (1-55713-256-9, $9.95)
Love Trouble 78 (1-55713-198-8, $9.95)

STEVE KATZ [USA]
43 Fictions 18 (1-55713-069-8, $12.95)

THOMAS LA FARGE [USA]
Terror of Earth 136 (1-55713-261-5, $11.95)

VALERY LARBAUD [France]
Childish Things 19 (1-55713-119-8, $13.95)

OSMAN LINS [Brazil]
Nine, Novena 104 (1-55713-229-1, $12.95)

JACKSON MAC LOW [USA]
Barnesbook 127 (1-55713-235-6, $9.95)
From Pearl Harbor Day to FDR's Birthday 126
(0-940650-19-3, $10.95)
Pieces O' Six 17 (1-55713-060-4, $11.95)

CLARENCE MAJOR [USA]
Painted Turtle: Woman with Guitar (1-55713-085-x, $11.95)

THOMAS MANN [Germany]
Six Early Stories 109 (1-55713-298-4, $22.95)

F. T. MARINETTI [Italy]
Let's Murder the Moonshine: Selected Writings 12
(1-55713-101-5, $13.95)
The Untameables 28 (1-55713-044-7, $10.95)

HARRY MATHEWS [USA]
Selected Declarations of Dependence 128 (1-55713-234-8, $10.95)

*

Individuals order from:
Sun & Moon Press
6026 Wilshire Boulevard
Los Angeles, California 90036
213-857-1115

Libraries and Bookstores in the United States and Canada
should order from:
Consortium Book Sales & Distribution
1045 Westgate Drive, Suite 90
Saint Paul, Minnesota 55114-1065
800-283-3572
FAX 612-221-0124